"Are you family?" the nurse inquired.

"Friend," Fran said. "Friend of the wife. She called and . . . asked me to meet her here."

The nurse pointed down a narrow corridor with rooms on either side. She stopped when she heard Julia's voice, entered the room. Julia was talking with a man in green scrubs. Dry-eyed and composed, she made the introductions.

"I'm sorry," the doctor said to Fran. "I've just finished explaining to Mrs. Markem how the weight cut off the air supply and precipitated the death."

"*Excuse* me?" Fran said, shocked. "What are you saying?"

"Tyler's dead," Julia said bluntly. "There was an accident in the gym. Tyler was bench-pressing and the weights fell on him, across his neck." Julia put her own hand to the front of her throat, her long, slender fingers resting lightly across her windpipe. There was something—a certain detachment, an edge—in the way Julia revealed this information.

"Oh, God!" Fran began to cry. "Oh, oh my God!" How many times in the past few weeks had she herself said "I'd like to kill that bastard"? But now . . . *dead?*

Tyler was dead. Truly and forever dead. And Julia was as calm as a madonna . . .

Love
LIES

FERN KUPFER

ZEBRA BOOKS
KENSINGTON PUBLISHING CORP.

ZEBRA BOOKS are published by

Kensington Publishing Corp.
850 Third Avenue
New York, NY 10022

First Zebra Books Printing: September, 1995

Printed in the United States of America

Acknowledgments

My thanks go to Iowa State University for granting me release time to finish this book; to Chuck Adams, whom I trust with my words, and Molly Friedrich, whom I trust with my career; to the weight-lifters at Ames Physical Fitness Center, to the Ames Police Department and graphologist Eileen Bowers, for sharing their expertise; to wise reader and good friend, Jane Smiley, for asking "What if"; to my friends and family and to the women of Friday Club who were all there for me during a difficult time.

To my husband Joseph Geha

Just Love

No Lies

Prologue

Fran Meltzer looked in the mirror on the bedroom door and decided that black wasn't her color. Not anymore. Now strands of gray were beginning to thread themselves into her thick dark hair, and what used to be an attractive olive complexion looked sallow and sickly in certain light.

She had just slipped on a two-piece black jersey bought years ago when the Modern Language Association was meeting in Chicago; she had been invited then to read from her book, *The Laughing Woman: Feminism and the Ironic Vision in Contemporary Literature*. For an academic work, it had sold very well. Not that she was Allan Bloom or anything, but the book was on the required reading list for almost every English department that had a course in comedy. On a shelf in her bedroom were copies of the book translated into French, German, and Japanese. The Japanese version had the best cover. Pure white with a colorful orange and red splash, in the center of which was a smiling woman's face. The woman looked cunning and devious.

Fran's picture on the back flap of *The Laughing Woman* was an appealing complement. The picture, taken by her second husband exactly a year before they divorced, was of a pretty, dark-haired woman full of integrity and seriousness of purpose.

Last year, Fran was made full professor at Stimpson, one of the most prestigious liberal arts colleges in the Midwest, though, if the truth be known, the students had gotten progressively dimmer in the time she had been there. Also richer. A year at Stimpson cost as much as it would to feed an entire village in the Third World.

Fran was forty-two years old and one of only two women full professors at the college. The other, Dr. Katherine Nottingham Taylor, an ancient woman with a stride like a high school marching band, was a veritable institution in the psychology department. There was talk that she would be retiring soon, and already there were plans to name a building after her.

Fran was happy in her career, although sometimes, seeing Dr. Taylor make her way alone across the Stimpson campus, Fran felt a small, involuntary shudder.

Today the sunshine came streaming in through the pink mini-blinds in the bedroom, and motes of dust danced in the light. Fran looked in the mirror again and sighed. Forty-two years old and today she looked it. Despite her professional success, life had not been a laugh a minute. She'd been married and divorced twice, had three miscarriages, and now owed several thousand dollars on her credit cards. Two years ago both her parents were killed in a car accident during a vacation in Mexico. She was, more than many people, a survivor. She was also bright and fast with the lip in an irreverent, wisecracking sort of way, but she was also totally honest and very perceptive, just the sort of person you'd want to have on a jury if you were called to trial.

"Damn," she said aloud, stripping off the skirt and kicking it across the messy room. Sighing, she stood back, hands on hips, in front of the mirror, looking at herself in a black bra, black slip, and off-black panty hose: a short but substantial woman with masses of dark curls, a strong nose, and what her sister Roz called "Jewish thighs."

Which seemed to have spread since the purchase of the black

skirt. Now, seeing the skirt in a heap at the foot of her bed,
Fran remembered it on the floor of a room in the Chicago's
Palmer House Hotel some years ago, a lover waiting for her
in the kingsize bed, gazing admiringly at her softly rounded
body. They had just drunk too much, smoked too many cigarettes, and shared one carefully rolled joint Fran had tucked
away in her makeup case for such an occasion, then made wild,
wet love for most of the night. The lover had coarse black hair
all over his body except for one perfectly baby-smooth circle
of skin right above his belly button, which she had delighted
in kissing.

Fran looked through her closet for something else dark,
appropriate for the occasion, lamenting that what had been sexy
at one time now made her look like a middle-aged widow from
an Italian movie. Most of what was in her closet these days
was red, purple, fuchsia. But could she wear any of that to a
funeral? She went across the room and picked up the black
jersey. Maybe it would be all right with a colorful scarf. Next
year the MLA was returning to Chicago, but this time, of course,
there would be no more cigarettes, marijuana, or sex with
handsome strangers. Fran sighed. Call her a traditionalist, but
she missed the good old days.

She looked at her watch, realizing she was running late as
usual. The funeral was that afternoon at two, but she had promised to come early to be with her best friend, Julia Markem,
for moral support. "Damn," she said, breaking a nail as she
reached to pick up the phone on the first ring.

"It's me," said a small, whispery voice in her ear. "Franny,
I think I need some more Valium."

"Julia? Where are you?"

"I'm here already. I'm helping them put together the music.
My parents are coming later with the girls. Do you think you
could bring the Valium with you? I only have one left from
what you gave me before. I feel as if I might scream during
the service."

Now it's happening, Fran thought. Julia is finally getting upset. For the first few days after Tyler's death, Julia was peculiarly calm, giving the details about the accident in a detached, almost clinical way. Fran had thought perhaps her friend was in shock. "No problem. I'll bring more," she said now. "I'm leaving as soon as I put my dress back on."

"Back on?"

"That black jersey with the raglan sleeves. It makes me look like a sausage, but I don't have anything else black."

"I'm not wearing black," Julia said. "It's June."

"You don't have any summer black?"

"It doesn't matter, Franny."

"I could wear dark purple. That's as sedate as I go," Fran said, looking into her cavernous closet.

"Fran, I don't care what you wear, just get here with the Valium." Julia began to cry. "Oh, dear, this whole thing is a nightmare. Tell me that this isn't happening."

"It *is* happening, but you'll be all right," Fran said soothingly. Usually it was placid Julia who was the comforting one, calming an upset friend or a fretting child. Up until a month ago, Julia's life—a husband, two wonderful daughters, a good job—was decidedly unremarkable. And now, all this. Fran added, "Do your parents know?"

"About Tyler?"

"Yes, did you tell them yet?"

"I didn't." There was a long, ragged sigh on the other end of the phone. "I don't know. It happened so quickly, Tyler gone and suddenly they're flying here to a funeral. I didn't have the heart to tell them anything more. They're broken up, my mother especially."

Fran wondered what "broken up" meant for Julia's parents. They were from Maine and as far as Fran could tell registered about .02 on the emotional Richter scale. Fran's own parents had been a different story. They had flown out from New York each time Fran had a miscarriage, her mother wailing and beating her chest as if she herself had lost an only child, her father threatening the doctors and cursing God.

"Are you going to tell them at all?" Fran asked. "They're going to be here for a few days, aren't they?"

"I'll see. Frankly, I don't know the point of it, though. What could telling them about Tyler do but hurt them? Look, someone's coming in with more flowers. Let me go over and put them someplace. The whole room is filling up with flowers. People keep sending them. I wish they wouldn't. It's awful."

"Like a funeral," Fran said shortly. "Look, I'll be over in about twenty minutes. Hang on."

A funeral. Tyler Markem's funeral. Fran recalled seeing Tyler that last time, laid out in a regular hospital bed, loosely covered by a sheet, just as if he were a patient taking a nap; a lock of blond hair curling boyishly out from his forehead; and Julia looking blankly at his peaceful face, his muscular chest, and down at the body under the sheet. Fran had felt angry: all he had done to Julia—to come to this!

Now, in a sudden moment of decision, Fran went over to the closet and pulled out an electric blue jumpsuit of washed silk. With it, she put on large silver hoop earrings and a silver bracelet that snaked its way up her arm. She took the clip from her hair and shook the black curls loose over her shoulders. "Go fuck yourself, Tyler," she said into the mirror.

She was opening the garage to get the car when she saw them getting out of the police car: one, in uniform, young and blond, with the full face and thick neck of a high school football hero; the other, dark-haired, midforties, also tall, but stoop-shouldered in a world-weary sort of way. The older one was wearing a light gray suit and those spooky reflective sunglasses.

Fran's heart began to beat wildly. Immediately she thought of the hundreds of dollars' worth of parking tickets accumulated from her visits to family in New York. She hated to fly. The idea of it panicked her. Sometimes, she had to. But when she had the time, she preferred to drive the nine hundred miles from Grandview to New York.

The parking tickets were all in the glove compartment of her car. Last month a collection agency had called, a woman's voice, viperous and threatening. "I don't intend to pay," Fran said simply, hanging up the phone.

New York got more and more ridiculous. Unsafe. Dirty. No place at all to park. Somehow over the years, Fran had rationalized that parking illegally was her due, and that not paying the parking tickets was a personal political protest against the spiraling unhabitability of her birth city.

So, they finally caught up with me, she thought, watching the police as they walked across her driveway. The gig was up. A bit abashed—she was, after all, a full professor, respected in this town—she smiled perkily as the two men approached.

"Francine Meltzer?" The older man straightened up, removing his glasses to reveal soft brown eyes that seemed unexpectedly kind. Immediately Fran felt yes, she could surrender herself to this man, pay the tickets, come clean.

"Yes?"

"You are Francine Meltzer?" the man said.

"I am." Fran looked him right in the eye.

"Detective Frank Rhodes." The man held up something in the palm of his hand, which Fran presumed to be some sort of identification. She pretended to read it. The uniformed officer, who stood slightly behind Frank Rhodes, was not introduced. "Could we please ask you a few questions, Ms. Meltzer?" Detective Rhodes asked. He was casual, nonthreatening. He'd put his hands in his pockets and was chewing gum.

"You could," Fran said. She waited, wondering if protocol meant she was supposed to invite them in. Her living room was a mess, strewn with books, papers, shoes. "Would you like to come inside?" She gestured lamely at the door.

"Thank you, but that won't be necessary, ma'am."

Ma'am? Fran fought the urge to make a joke, but somehow that kind of banter seemed inappropriate.

Officer Rhodes began, "I know you'll be going to Professor Markem's funeral this afternoon." He looked solemn and paused as if to pay respect. "I won't keep you but a few minutes."

Fran waited. Was she being watched, under some kind of surveillance? How far back did those parking tickets go, anyway? She should have paid them, of course. Or not have taken the car into the city in the first place. Isn't that what her sister Roz always said: "Leave the car here in Plainview. What the hell do you need to schlep it into the city for?"

"Am I correct in saying that you were an associate and close friend of Julia and Tyler Markem?" Detective Rhodes asked.

Fran nodded, puzzled. What did Julia and Tyler have to do with her parking tickets? Perhaps the police needed character witnesses. Really, those unpaid tickets were the only black marks against her record as an otherwise upright citizen. That and perhaps the general state of disarray of her house.

"Would you happen to know, Ms. Meltzer, if the Markems were experiencing any sort of marital problems prior to Professor Markem's death?"

"Excuse me?" Fran took a step backward and looked up at Rhodes. He was quite tall, a few inches over six feet. It was not as if she hadn't heard what he said, it was just that she had no idea why he was saying it. Why was he talking about Tyler and Julia?

"Marital problems," Frank Rhodes repeated. "Problems in the marriage."

"Why are you asking me this?" Fran said, regaining some of her composure. Dawning upon her slowly, "a ribbon at a time," as Emily Dickinson used to say, was the realization that this visit was not about parking tickets.

"I'm sorry, but we can't really discuss the details of the case at this time," Rhodes said.

"You want me to talk to you about Julia and Tyler's marriage?"

"That's what we'd like, Ms. Meltzer."

"I don't know." Fran looked past the two policemen. Her next-door neighbor, Kathy Sanders, was just coming up the block pulling her two toddlers in a red wagon. "Mommy, look, the police!" one of them called, thrilled, as Kathy tried not to stare too hard at Fran, who lifted her hand and gave a half-hearted wave. "There *was* trouble in their marriage," she began.

"Yes, I would say that." Frank Rhodes waited, nodding slightly. The other policeman, still as he was, might as well have been a statue. "Well, I mean, everyone has trouble in their marriage at some time or another, don't you think?" Neither of the men responded. "But Tyler and Julia had some difficulties as of late. I mean, before he died. They were going through a rather difficult time." Fran paused to take a breath. *Difficulties as of late?* Why was she talking like this?

"I'd like you to come down to the station sometime after the funeral, Ms. Meltzer," Rhodes said. "I'll be down there this evening until seven. I'd really appreciate it." He held out a hand to shake, sealing her agreement and indicating that the current interview was now over. Frank Rhodes's hand was solid and warm.

"Could I ask what this is about?" Fran asked. "I mean, why are the police investigating this? What happened to Tyler was . . . I mean, it was an accident, wasn't it? You don't think there's anything that—" She stopped abruptly.

"I'm afraid we're not at liberty to say at this time," Frank Rhodes said. "See you this evening, then."

"Good-bye," the young officer said, turning on his heel, as he followed Frank Rhodes back to the car.

Betrayal: May

1

In the mornings, less than a month before Tyler Markem died, his wife, Julia, would awake with her fists so tightly clenched that she thought her nails were beginning to curl, like fangs. There was the brief thought that the past few days had been a bad dream, that the twenty-year marriage she had believed good and strong was still intact. But then grief washed over her like a wave. It started in the pit of her belly, moving up until her breasts ached and she felt the pain etching new lines in her face.

I want my life back the way it was, she said.

She had said that earlier to the therapist, then realized immediately that wasn't what she really meant. She wanted her life back the way she *thought* it was. What Julia had seen, what she had chosen to see, was not the reality of Tyler's and her life together. She was reminded of an optical illusion, when you gasp because in the blink of an eye, the beautiful princess turns into a hag.

It was Tyler who had been cheating, but it was she, Julia, who was living with lies and illusions. This is something your best friends won't tell you (even if they know); it's something you won't even admit to yourself. If you have a good therapist, you start reinterpreting your personal history, a process infinitely more painful than root canal.

The first time she met Julia, the therapist said: "You seem like a bright, intuitive woman. And you are saying that you didn't know what was going on?" The therapist, Colleen O'Rourke, was a prim, petite woman with black Shirley Temple curls and a tiny pug nose. Her doll-like appearance was deceptive. After a few sessions, Julia realized that Colleen always went right for the emotional jugular.

"I didn't know," Julia had protested weakly.

There was a tree full of grackles outside the office window that day, frantic in their twittering. Colleen sat silently and appeared encouraging.

"I didn't know," Julia said again, her voice sounding hollow in a room with too little furniture. She looked at Colleen, who looked back at her until Julia felt her pale skin flushing rose pink. *Did* she know what was going on? Did she have a glimmer of a secret life—only a portion of which was revealed in a teary confession the week before in his office—of the man who had been her husband for twenty years? Who was Tyler, after all, this man she had lived with for half her life, a man whose looks and sounds and smells were as utterly familiar to her as her own? How could she not have known? Julia shook her head, feeling the blush recede. "I don't know what to say."

Colleen waited patiently, sitting up straight in her chair, her legs crossed demurely at the ankle. The silence, in contrast to the cawing of the birds outside, made Julia's chest feel heavy.

The two women were facing each other, seated in identical blue canvas chairs, in a modern office with lots of plants and splashy watercolors of ocean and sky. Julia felt as if they were producers, talking about making a movie. She had never been to a therapist before and didn't know the proper way to act.

Wanting to be engaging and lucid, instead she sat for a long time and simply looked miserable.

"What are you thinking?" Colleen asked.

"I'm thinking how much this is costing," Julia said.

"Sixty dollars an hour," Colleen said. "Most of it is covered by insurance."

There was a really terrific insurance policy at the college where Tyler and Julia both taught. It had a five-hundred-dollar deductible for the whole family so that even if you had open heart surgery and a kidney transplant and twin babies who needed intensive care, you still had to pay only five hundred dollars for the year. And yet Julia still felt guilty about sitting here at sixty dollars an hour. It was her New England background. Her mother cut her own hair and washed aluminum foil.

"I wish I knew what to say." Julia looked at Colleen for guidance.

"What do you want to say?" Colleen asked softly. In the first few sessions she was gentle, kind. Fran Meltzer, an old hand at this, said it was a therapist trick to make sure that you came back to see them again.

"Are you able to work?" Colleen asked a little later.

"Well, I'm lucky, I guess. I had a leave this semester to do some research, so I don't really have to go in to teach at all. And I just finished an article. It's on some of Shakespeare's lesser-known plays and . . ." Julia stopped herself, smiling, she realized, for the first time that day. She had always loved doing research in the ivy-covered library on the older part of campus. Her mother was the librarian in the paper-mill town in Maine where she had grown up, and Julia had worked as a shelver all through high school, so she always felt right at home among rows and rows of books.

They were lucky, she and Tyler, Julia had always said—both to have tenured jobs teaching college. Weren't there hundreds of professional couples who could not live together because there were not two jobs to be had? Or one person who had to give up a career? (Like Damian, who had followed Fran to Grandview and found nothing to do but drink.) Lucky, was what Julia occasionally told her husband when he complained about living in a midwestern city, flat and boring as an iron skillet. Grandview—a college town where there was nothing either grand nor scenic as far as the eye could see.

And wasn't Tyler doubly lucky, too, that in this age of specialization he could teach both philosophy *and* poetry? Tyler had actually started off as a poet, but halfway through graduate school in creative writing, he switched and got his Ph.D. in philosophy. Here at Stimpson he could teach an introduction to poetry course and once every couple of years, when Stimpson's alcoholic resident poet, George Lawson, was drying out in some clinic, Tyler took over the poetry seminar, his real love. Regularly Tyler also taught a philosophy seminar in *his* specialty, ethics—the irony of which had become especially apparent to Julia only the week before.

"Ethics!" she had screamed. "You hypocrite! How could you teach ethics and live such an unethical life?"

Tyler's response had been that one didn't have to be an exemplar to be a good ethics professor.

"But you are a liar and a cheat!"

"Shhh. Do you want the girls to hear you?" Tyler whispered hoarsely.

The children, Beth and Caty, were upstairs in their rooms doing homework, though one of them was sure to be talking on the phone; strains of rock music drifted down the stairs.

"Tyler," Julia said more calmly, "they're going to have to know. Our lives have all just fallen apart." Beth and Caty, both in the throes of tempestuous teenhood, didn't need their lives to fall apart. Julia was certain of that. Though, feeling sorry for herself at forty-two, she supposed that nobody was ever at a right age for a life to fall apart.

"I'm sorry," Tyler said, bowing his head. He was standing under the chandelier in the dining room, and the light made his hair look golden. That's how he had seemed to Julia the summer they had first met when both were both graduate students—he was so tanned and blond: golden boy. "Julia, you know I never meant to hurt you," he said. "I should have come to you before and told you how unhappy I was. I never meant for you to find out this way."

"I hate you for this," Julia hissed at him through clenched teeth. "I wish you were dead!"

"Do you want to make it next Tuesday at this time?" Colleen asked, opening her leather appointment book. She didn't have a secretary or a receptionist. Julia liked that. It was oddly reassuring, coming in to see Colleen, who organized her own time. It was also, Julia thought, having believed herself to be stable and well-adjusted, embarrassing to be seeing a therapist.

"I have an answering service if you have to change the appointment," Colleen added. "Just call and leave a message."

Julia nodded, slipping the card into the pocket of her raincoat. In the silky lining, she felt the stubs of two movie tickets. Only two weeks ago, she and Tyler had gone to the movies and then out for ice cream. Julia had her usual, strawberry with chocolate chips. Tyler had coffee with hot fudge.

That night they had made love. Julia remembered because both girls got up at different times to go to the bathroom, and she had stopped, catching her breath, hearing footsteps in the hall. Now she tried to recall the lovemaking. It was the regulation children-still-up, married kind of sex, cozy and comfortable. Afterwards, she had fallen asleep on Tyler's chest, then turned to spoon against the curve of his back until her hip grew numb before she went back to her own side of the bed.

She *thought* that's how it had been, although now she was so unmoored that was hard to trust her memory of anything at all.

"Actually, any day is good for me now," Julia told Colleen. Over the open appointment schedule, Colleen looked sympathetic. "Are you not sleeping well?" she asked. There were circles under Julia's puffy eyes.

"I saw my doctor this afternoon. She gave me something. Dalmane, I think."

Colleen nodded. "Be careful with that," she warned.

"Thank you," Julia said, opening the door to her waiting room. "I'll see you next Tuesday." She hurried out, past a pale girl who looked like a teenage runaway.

2

Julia insisted that she had not known. She thought she was telling the absolute truth. "I didn't know," she told Colleen and Fran Meltzer, and right on the spot she could have passed any polygraph test because it was not a lie at all, not in any part of her conscious mind. But there was something she just hadn't paid attention to. Like the white noise of a highway passing beneath a window. Like the uneasy, lingering memory of a bad dream. He'd be late, and she waited for the phone to ring, his voice, with the excuse so ready on his tongue without even a moment's pause, that—why would she question? She was in a good marriage, after all. She and Tyler talked. They had time alone. Good sex. No money problems. She had read the women's magazines enough to know the qualities necessary to make a good marriage.

But there was a look in his eyes sometimes, drifting away to a place where she wasn't welcome, a place where she could not reach out to soothe his loneliness. He needed, she used to tell Fran, time to be alone; she acknowledged that he had always had a private, solitary self—perhaps coming from his sensitive

poet's soul and the troubled home in which he grew up as the
only, doted-upon son of an alcoholic woman divorced while
he was still a baby. Tyler had never known his father, and his
mother died right after he graduated from college. So he was
used to being alone.

Julia gave him the space he needed. Time to write his poems
and work out at the gym. Time to be alone. He seemed to need
it more than other people.

What had happened? One weekend she and Tyler were planning a trip to Chicago for their twenty-year anniversary. The
next weekend he was talking about getting his own apartment.
Even ordinary, mundane lives such as theirs could be flabber-
gasting in their unpredictability.

Actually, Julia had met her even before Tyler did. They had
sat next to each other in the same row at the Booth Jenson
Memorial Lecture that Tyler gave last fall. (Booth Jenson was
a philosophy professor who had left a lot of money to the
department when he died a few years ago at the ripe old age of
ninety-seven. Academics seemed to have incredible longevity.)
Tyler gave a talk about the meaning of a liberal arts education. This might sound like dry stuff but not when Tyler put it
all together. Tyler played Mozart, read Yeats, had flashing slides
of Michelangelo's *Pietà,* Dali's *Crucifixion of Christ*—and all
the while Tyler talked, strutted, danced back and forth with
such energy that the room came alive. Oh, he was a spell-
binder. A truly charismatic speaker. Although it was difficult
for Julia not to see him differently now. Hard not to view
Tyler as some sort of slick snake-oil salesman, some smarmy
evangelical.

But Tyler's audiences were always rapt. Whenever he gave
a public lecture, students came afterward in droves to sign up
for his philosophy classes. The reason Julia remembered sitting
next to *her* that evening was that the girl was more rapt than

most. Her mouth was open wide, and every so often she gave a sharp little intake of breath, almost like a sob. Perhaps were it not for the erratic breathing, Julia would not have remembered her when, months later, she saw the pictures there in Tyler's desk. Even then, Julia looked at the photographs and felt peculiar; who the girl was hadn't quite clicked in. It was like seeing all those frames in Kmart with the photos of other people, blemishless strangers without a past.

The girl had the blond, bland prettiness of so many Stimpson students, midwestern girls all glossed and moussed, girls with names like Kimberly, Lisa, Jennifer. Girls with neat, round handwriting ("el ed handwriting," Fran Meltzer called it) who always handed their papers in on time. Although these girls hardly ever had anything original to say, they were enthusiastic and bright-eyed, and usually managed to get B's.

Kimberly. Lisa. Jennifer. After a semester or two they all blended together into a kind of generic young girl whose name Julia could never recall.

After dinner one night Tyler had told Julia that a student had come into his office intent on becoming a philosophy major, that after listening to his lecture she said she felt "ready to explode."

"What was she going to explode from?" Julia had asked in a somewhat offhand manner. At the time she was at the sink trying to get a mangled paring knife out of the disposal and concentrating on not severing a finger.

"She's just discovering what it's all about, Julia," Tyler had said disdainfully. "Truth. Beauty. All the things we're supposed to be teaching them."

"Uh-huh," Julia answered, grasping the jagged edge of the knife. Perhaps if she had looked up to see Tyler's face at that moment, she would have realized how the girl's ardor was reflected in his eyes.

* * *

The day that Julia found out began with her sitting at the kitchen table, finishing a list of things she wanted to buy for the garden. It was Friday afternoon and one of those glorious spring days when everything growing green and pink has suddenly burst open and the sky, the trees, and even the air dazzle with light. A sunny picture window in the newly remodeled kitchen let her watch the birds build nests in the ash tree beside the garage.

The semester was ending, and Tyler would soon stop teaching. In June he would do his own work—he had been writing poetry again—then in July they would go to Maine to be with Julia's parents at the lake. Her sister, Margaret, still lived in Maine, and her family had built their own cabin on the lake. Tyler came grudgingly to this family reunion, but Julia looked forward to it. Her parents were getting on in years, and she saw the time spent with them as precious and fleeting.

Julia had noticed that Tyler seemed distracted as of late. But then, he was, after a long fallow period, once again "in inspiration," a phrase he used to describe a time of intense creativity when the poems would just seem to come to him. He had been "in inspiration" the entire spring, writing madly. But a vacation at the lake would be good for him, Julia thought.

"What you want, baby boy? What you want, you sweet pie, you pumpkin face?" Next to the table the family dog, Princeton, whined and trembled, waiting for a scrap from Julia's plate. Princeton was an elegant name for a downtrodden-looking mongrel whom Beth had saved from the pound. The dog had arrived, full-grown and housebroken, already named. Beth said that it was bad enough to be given away, awaiting execution in a cage; to give him a whole new name would just be too much trauma for one dog to take. The dog, therefore, remained Princeton.

It didn't matter. Nobody ever called him Princeton. Something in the servile sweetness of the animal turned the entire family sappy in his presence, and they all cooed to him, talking the most insipid baby talk. Fran Meltzer, who was not a great animal lover, could hardly stand it. When she visited, she always requested that Princeton be put down in the basement.

"Here you go, cutie boy, num num num num." Julia held up a bit of toast while Princeton trembled and salivated lavishly. No one was supposed to feed Princeton from the table, but Julia and the girls sometimes did. Princeton knew it was useless to sit expectantly by anyone's chair if Tyler was in the kitchen.

Julia finished her list for the garden: a pot of geraniums for the front stoop, impatiens and zinnias on the south side of the house. And tomato plants, of course, in back of the garage. She thought of calling Tyler and looked at her watch. It was almost one. Tyler would be back from his workout at the gym. Maybe he had not gotten back to serious writing yet and would be willing to take a break and go with her to the greenhouse. Then she thought of just driving over to campus to surprise him. He would be more likely to go if she was there in person to encourage him.

Stimpson College had the distinction of being one of the few schools in the country that scheduled no classes on Fridays, a policy begun in the early seventies as an energy-saving measure and continued because of student demand (though there were always suggestions that applicants chose to attend Stimpson over other colleges because of the three-day weekend). The general staff worked ten-hour days and had Fridays off; some of the faculty devoted the day to their own research.

But this Friday was too beautiful for anyone to stay cooped up in an office, even to write poetry, Julia thought. Approaching campus, she drove by the sorority houses, past the girls in bikinis all slathered in oils and lying out on the lawns—their books, mere props alongside their blankets. Music blasted from speakers turned out from one of the windows, and a few boys in cutoffs, bandannas around their heads, sailed a Frisbee overhead. A circle of tulips in the campus colors of purple and gold stood in front of the brick entrance to the administrative building.

The campus police wouldn't be around to ticket on Fridays, so Julia parked in a spot marked "Medical Reserve," closest to Grayson Hall, home of both the English and philosophy departments at Stimpson. Grayson was the oldest building on campus and the least charming, having the ambience of a county jail. None of the windows opened—having been puttied shut, also in the energy-conscious seventies—and the building was shaped like a box, with no distinguishable entrance. Writing poetry in such a building dismayed Tyler, although he always seemed to spend an inordinate amount of time there.

From the car, Julia looked up at Tyler's office window on the second floor; she imagined him rubbing his forehead as he worked over a line of poetry. His writing had been going so well, he had been saying. No, he didn't want to show it to her just yet. It was new stuff, kind of experimental. He was excited, but just not all that sure yet. She was glad he was writing again.

Inside Grayson the halls were dim, and she blinked, trying to focus as she went up the back stairway. The building had a closed-up, schoolish smell, the way school used to smell in Maine—paper and wood and pots of thick white paste. Outside Tyler's office, she could hear him clacking away on his old Smith Corona. Tyler had a romantic's disdain for the computer, and Julia had been singularly unsuccessful in getting him to even try it. She stood in front of the door, hesitating to knock. Tyler hated to be interrupted while in inspiration. When the girls were little, they learned never to speak to him if he was writing.

Julia paused for a moment listening to his typewriter, feeling uneasy somehow, as if she were spying. Probably they were the only people in the building. All the office doors were closed, each with its milky, opaque glass. On Tyler's door was a poster of Hegel, Heidegger, Nietzsche, and Kant, all carrying briefcases and wearing dressed-for-success suits and yuppie haircuts.

"Tyler?" Tentatively she knocked and opened the door at the same time.

"Julia! What are you doing here?" Startled, Tyler pushed back from his desk, rising so quickly that he knocked over his chair. The clatter was startling in the stillness of Grayson Hall.

"I'm sorry," Julia said automatically. She felt her pulse quicken. Something seemed strange in the way he greeted her. There was an almost palpable sense of tension in the room.

Probably she would not have paid any attention to the long white envelope sitting alone on his desk had he not looked so very abashed at seeing her. So *caught.* She looked questioningly into his eyes, the eyes that Fran Meltzer always described as "fanatically blue." Immediately he sat on top of the desk, covering the envelope. "I was just finishing up. I've been working on this one poem and working on it and suddenly everything just all came together . . ." He went on in this vein, fairly babbling, while Julia stood there, waiting for him to finish. He had plopped himself toward the middle of the desk so that his legs dangled off the floor. It was a ridiculous position.

"Tyler, what are you sitting on?" Julia said. She could hardly speak. Immediately, something started building in her, rising up like bile in her throat. ("I didn't know," she said to Colleen later that week. But the white noise of the highway must have been getting louder as she stood there facing him.)

"What do you mean?" Tyler clenched both sides of the desk so hard his knuckles whitened.

"What are you sitting on?" She pointed to the desk.

Tyler looked down as if surprised to find himself seated there. "What?"

She could hear herself breathing. "Under you. What is in the envelope you're trying to hide?" Tyler lifted himself up and started to say something, but before he could answer, Julia reached under him and pulled out the envelope. Tyler moved toward her, but she was quick and took it over to the window.

The envelope, which had already been opened, was addressed to Tyler in bright purple ink. The script was neat and girlish.

Tyler stood by his desk, looking stricken, as Julia removed the contents. Inside was a greeting card. On the cover was a cute but angry bear cub with a balloon bubble: "I've Had It With You!" Inside was the bear cub, smiling, surrounded by hearts: "And Loved Every Minute of It!" Added in the same purple ink was a note: "My darling Tyler. Thank you for letting me love you." It was signed with a large, loopy "L."

Julia felt as if she were watching a movie and the film suddenly broke in midreel, the picture abruptly pulled away and jolted violently out of sync. Everything stopped. The lights went on. She blinked, surprised at the new reality. "Thank you for letting me love you?" Julia read out loud. It may have come out sarcastically, but sarcastic was the last thing she felt. "Who is this from, Tyler?"

Tyler stood, head bowed, looking, Julia thought, like Princeton when he had an accident on the rug.

"What's going on?" Julia asked. She could feel her blood, which seemed to be pulsing upward, pounding through her head.

"Julia, I'm sorry. I never meant to hurt you . . ." Tyler was actually sobbing.

Instinctively her arms rose to comfort him in embrace, but she stopped herself and instead watched him cry. He was crying. Wasn't *she* the one who was supposed to be crying? "Who is she?" she asked softly.

"It doesn't matter," Tyler said, sniffling now. He reached for a tissue from the box on the windowsill and blew.

"It doesn't *matter?*"

Tyler shook his head. Julia looked at his face and her stomach did a flip. Tyler wore on his face the expression of a teenager in pain, caught in confusion and longing. She had not seen this expression on the faces of either of the girls yet, but she remembered it well herself. It was the face of someone whose desire and need blot out all reasonable thought, the face of someone sick at heart, of someone *lovesick.* "Oh my God. Tyler," she asked in a whisper, "do you love her?"

Tyler nodded, staring down at his shoes, his face wet with tears. He looked miserable. "Yes," he whispered back, his voice barely audible.

"Yes?"

The word was like an electric shock, coming so quickly that even before her skin felt it, the pain was internalized. She felt the shock reach through her, down through her bones. "Who is she?" Julia asked again. "What's her name?"

"Julia, please. Oh, Julia," Tyler sighed, shaking his head back and forth.

For a moment she thought that the other woman's name was Julia. And it struck her, even at that awful moment, the irony and convenience of having your wife and girlfriend both with the same name. Then she realized that that wasn't it at all. That Tyler still hadn't answered. "Who is she, Tyler?"

"Julia, please stop. I'm not ready for this yet." Tyler looked put upon, as if she were nagging him to put up the storm windows while he was busy with another, more important, project. "It doesn't matter. Can't you see it doesn't matter who she is?" Tyler began to cry again and started across the room toward her. This time she pulled away, repelled. "Oh, Julia," he said. "I've been so unhappy."

"You've been so unhappy?" she repeated.

"Julia, I've been unhappy for years."

"You've been unhappy *for years?*" she repeated after him like a parrot.

"And I was a coward, I guess. Not to come and tell you."

"Who is she?" Julia asked again.

"It doesn't matter."

"Tyler," she said. "Of course it matters. We've been married almost twenty years and now you tell me that you're in love with someone else. Yes, it matters." She found herself becoming increasingly irritated by his attitude.

"Listen to me, Julia," Tyler said, turning suddenly hostile. "You don't seem to understand. The problems in our marriage are separate from who she is."

"What are the problems in our marriage?"

"You should know," Tyler said tightly.

This isn't happening, she was thinking. Right here, right now, this isn't really happening. Last week they had watched David Letterman in bed together, sharing a beer and eating fat pretzels dipped in mustard. When she had gotten up to go to the bathroom, Tyler wrote down half the comic's routine so Julia wouldn't miss anything. It was a woman talking about criminals being punished: "Why do you think they call it 'penal law?'" was the punchline. Tyler knew she would think this was funny.

"Who is she, Tyler? You have to tell me." She was practically begging.

"Julia, I don't *have* to tell you anything. That's one of the problems in our marriage. Your need to have such control." Tyler came over to her and abruptly took the card out of her hands. "Who she is doesn't matter," he said clearly. "And it doesn't really have to do with *her*. Are you listening to what I'm saying, Julia? I've been unhappy for a long time." Julia nodded, mute now.

"She was not the first," Tyler said. There was something in his voice now that was spiteful and mean. She knew this tone, had heard it sometimes when they argued, and it never failed to make the backs of her legs tingle. There were other women as well, he went on. Other women . . .? His words started coming out in a rush, a confessional torrent. Julia had the feeling that it didn't have to be *her* standing there in front of him, that anyone would do to hear all this and relieve Tyler of his terrible secret burden.

"This is sick," Julia said, instinctively moving backward toward the door.

"It's *not* sick," Tyler said, his mouth curled contemptuously. "You just can't stand to hear the truth, can you?"

She raised a hand in front of her face as if to ward off a blow. Her head was already spinning. Tyler stopped talking and she stood there a moment to look at him. Suddenly his handsome face began to look ugly to her, all puffy and jowly so that she imagined him like Dorian Gray and saw his flesh turn all rubbery before melting into something hideous.

"But I just didn't expect to actually fall in love," Tyler said, softer now, again stepping toward her.

Julia pulled back toward the door. "I'm going home," she said. Shaken, she felt her way out of Grayson Hall like a blind person.

3

She got as far as the lawn sculpture, a large piece of bent metal resembling an upside-down pig trough, and then sat down on the nearest bench. What she really wanted, though she hadn't smoked in almost ten years, was a cigarette. There was such a craving to draw the smoke, thick and delicious, into her lungs, to calm and slow her racing heart. Ten years without a single cigarette, and this was what she thought about—the roots of old addictions go so very deep indeed.

"Julia, I don't think I love you anymore." She replayed those words over and over again, and it hurt like worrying a bad tooth. She knew it was a cliche to say that something is so unbelievable. Her students said that all the time. "Oh, it was *soo* unbelievable!" But what she had just heard she was not able to believe.

There had been other women as well, Tyler had said in that guilty burst of self-disclosure. It was as if some dam had opened and she was not Julia, wife, lover, companion, but some anonymous Mother Confessor. Despite the warm sun she shivered, revolted by Tyler's weepy weakness.

Other women, he said. What other women? The year before, Tyler had been elected a Montague Lecturer, taking time off from teaching to tour around the Midwest. Two days in Lawrence, Kansas. Three days in Columbia, Missouri. But those were really the only times he was gone from home, she reasoned. Still, a university teaching job is better than most others for scheduling affairs. You show up for class, but otherwise there's so much freedom to do what you want. Time out for an affair and you could always say you were in the library studying nineteenth-century journals. Or at the office writing poetry. Or lifting weights in the gym.

Once she had read a short story about a woman who received a phone call from the police in another town. Her husband had been arrested for exposing himself in a parking lot. Driving to bail him out, the woman kept saying to herself, "This can't be true, this can't be true," as if repeating it over and over again like a mantra would indeed make it so. And yet, there was a hidden place deep within her that questioned: did she know? Something about that story had fascinated Julia, for it stayed with her over the years.

"This isn't happening," she thought, trying to reconstruct the sense of unreality she experienced talking with Tyler in his office. How the floor tilted strangely. How it sounded as if trains were passing through her head.

Shakily, she got up from the bench and went over to the car. It seemed unnatural that everything was working correctly. That she walked, upright, one foot in front of the other. That she could put the key in the ignition and the car started just as always.

She stopped at the stop sign, then the red light, then shifted to fourth gear, driving down the boulevard that separated the college from the main part of town. Without thinking, she made her way to Fran Meltzer's house and pulled up in the familiar driveway. Fran's dark brown bungalow with the wooden steps set between two enormous pine trees always reminded Julia of a girl scout cabin in the woods. She stopped on the porch for a moment and saw Fran through the window, seated at the dining room table, her reading glasses down on her nose, a pen in her hand. As if sensing someone was watching her, Fran looked up, letting loose a delighted smile of surprise.

"These papers," Fran said, opening the door. She gestured toward the table piled high with papers and books. "Do you believe I'm just starting and I got them two weeks ago? I promised them back on Monday."

"Tyler is having an affair," Julia said weakly, taking a breath so she could get it all out. "I don't know who she is, but he says he loves her and he doesn't think he loves me anymore. . . ."

"Baby," Fran cried, opening her arms before Julia broke down and cried onto the shoulder of Fran's white terrycloth robe.

Francine Meltzer was Julia's best friend in town, had been ever since they first laid eyes on each other that afternoon more than fourteen years ago. It was a hot day at the end of August, and Julia was moving into the office next door to Fran's. The pipes in the building were sweating some malodorous, rusty liquid all over the floors. Their wing of offices had a particularly hideous speckled floor, which was warped and mildewed from the leaky pipes.

As Julia passed the open door that day, Fran introduced herself and offered a cup of tea. Then Fran began to describe the dream she had the night before. She was grading papers in the office late at night, when a janitor who looked like Elvis Presley came to the door with a rattle of keys and before she knew it, they were both stripped naked, making love on the floor. "Afterwards, he asked me if I came," Fran said, plunking two lumps of sugar into some very weak tea. "And I said, 'Are you kidding? Did you get a look at this linoleum?'"

In the next hour, they talked about their work, their families, their lives. Julia asked about finding good day care for her two little girls. Fran revealed that as soon as her new husband, Damian, quit his job in Chicago to join her, she was going to get pregnant. They found out that they were the same age, born a week apart in September, and promised to throw a bash together for their thirtieth.

"Oh, the illustrious Tyler Markem," Fran had said, raising one eyebrow and sucking in her cheeks, when Julia told Fran who she was married to.

That spring, Tyler had had a book of poems, *Mirage,* published by a small press, and for some reason—no one seems to know the whys and wherefores of these things—it was reviewed along with a number of other poetry books in the *New York Times* just as he and Julia had accepted the jobs at Stimpson. The reviewer had called Tyler's poems "Just terrific! The best of a new generation." The praise had preceded them, so that by the time they arrived on campus, Tyler's reputation was made.

It was Fran who once observed that the praise sounded like a slogan for a soft drink. She teased him about it for a while: "Here's Terrific Tyler, The Best of a New Generation."

But then, years later, with no other books of poems published, Tyler wasn't part of a new generation anymore. He was over forty and settled into the kind of comfortable academic life that he had scorned as a young man. Now he had retirement accounts and a new station wagon. In the next few years he'd have to put two children through college.

They didn't get along, Fran and Tyler. Tyler said it wasn't that he didn't *enjoy* Fran sometimes, but she was just a little too "East Coast" for him. He said it wasn't that he wasn't really *fond* of Fran, but she was just a little too stridently feminist for him.

Fran said right out front that she didn't *like* Tyler. That she was sorry because she *loved* Julia, but if she and Julia were going to be friends, they would have to make some sort of peace with that.

And now, suddenly, Julia didn't think she liked Tyler either, and felt unable to defend him to Fran.

"Let's go find out who she is," Fran said, peeling off her robe and throwing it on the bed. French doors off the dining room opened to a bedroom strewn with clothes, books, odd glasses, and mugs. On top of a television set was a half-empty bottle of wine and a wicker basket of Wheat Thins.

"Find out?" Suddenly exhausted, Julia moved some of the clothing over on the bed, longing just to put her head under the pillow, to sleep and sleep.

"Who she is. The poopsie. The schtupee. The bimbette. I can't believe he wouldn't tell you. What a bastard! God, do you think she's a student?"

"No," Julia said quickly. "Tyler wouldn't do that."

"Don't be so sure. Some guys think it's one of the few perks of academia."

"Fran," Julia said. "The man *does* teach ethics."

"Julia." Fran shook her head. "Sometimes I find your naivete really touching."

"Still, I don't think so. A student?"

"You also didn't think that Samuel Poppycock was having an affair with a student. It wasn't until they were actually *living* together that you even admitted something was going on."

Samuel Hollyhock—Fran always called him Poppycock— was an English professor who left a wife of thirty-five years to live with one of his teaching assistants. All the while the rumors were circulating about the affair, Julia kept saying, no, not Sam, not Sam. Besides being old, he was singularly unattractive, bald as a bean with a large, globular forehead and an odd, Ichabod Crane gait. He seemed an unlikely candidate for an affair. Also, he taught a course in the Bible.

Yet there he was later that spring, walking across campus laughing with his girlfriend. He appeared blissfully happy.

Just a few days after that, Julia had met his wife, looking shaken and dazed, in Kmart. The previous time Julia had seen her was at a faculty party where she was proudly showing off pictures of their new grandchildren. "How are you, Helen?" Julia asked as they stood in the checkout line. She said she was all right, but it was clear to anyone who looked at Helen that she was not. She was buying stacks of new towels. Had Sam taken the towels when he moved out?

Now the thought of Sam gamboling along the campus with his new ladylove made Julia's teeth clench in anger. Sam with all the family towels in his new modern apartment. She wanted to bash him one, crack his bald head open like an egg on concrete. "How could we find out who she is?" Julia asked.

"His office. We'll go to his office. There's bound to be some incriminating evidence. The card was there, right? All right, her name wasn't on that, but there's likely to be something else. Love letters. Her phone number on a piece of paper."

"What if he's still there?" Julia asked.

Fran went over to the phone. "Give him a call and hang up. Ten to one, he left. Went to *her*. You think he's going to sit around and write a poem about it?"

Reluctantly Julia got up and dialed, one hand waiting to disconnect should she hear his voice. "He's not there," she said, after his answering machine picked up.

"I told you so," Fran said, rubbing her hands together. "All right, so let's get going. You ready for this?"

"I think so." Julia tried to perk up, buoy herself by the sense of adventure. "But how could we get in his office? It's locked."

"A master key for the building is in the main office in a filing cabinet," Fran said. "I know that because every time

George Lawson is in rehab, the secretaries ask me to go into his office and take him his books." Fran threw on an Indian print dress that had been wrinkled into a ball in the corner of the room and searched under the bed until she came out with a pair of sandals.

"You're in no condition to drive," Fran said, taking the car keys and then screeching out of the driveway as if they were in a police movie.

They drove back to campus, and Julia noticed that Tyler's car was no longer in the parking lot. "He must have gone home," she said to Fran.

"He went to *her,* to tell her that you know about her." Fran's dark eyes narrowed to angry slits. "I hate when men pull this kind of shit," Fran said.

"Women do it, too."

"Not with such frequency," Fran said sternly. "And not with such apparent entitlement." Fran's first husband, though living apart from his wife, was still married when Fran met him, a fact he chose not to share until he and Fran were sleeping together. Her second husband, Damian, was a kind, ineffectual soul who lay on the couch for the last year of their marriage, drinking himself into a stupor. Fran was somewhat bitter about men. As bitter, she said, as any semiconscious woman who lives long enough has a right to be. "That's why men always go after young women," Fran said once. "The young ones haven't caught on yet."

"There were other women, too. Did I tell you that? He seemed almost eager to confess." Julia paused, looking stricken. "Fran, you didn't know any of this, did you?" Driving back onto campus, they passed the dormitories and saw laughing girls with even tans.

Fran shook her head vigorously. "Nothing. I swear I would have told you, Julia." She parked the car and faced Julia. "I did hear some teaching assistants talking once. It was years ago, in the coffee room. They were saying how they all wished they had one of those long conferences in Tyler Markem's office because he was so good-looking. But maybe they were intimating that there was something going on."

"What did you say?" A family walked through the trail of trees that went across central campus. The man and woman were holding hands, and their two small daughters skipped ahead onto the grass. Suddenly Julia felt very tired and very middle-aged.

"I remember defending Tyler," Fran told her. "Saying that he was happily married. And you were my best friend, so *I knew.*"

"It was me you were defending, Fran," Julia said quietly.

They sat in the car and watched the family disappear into the trees. "Come on. Let's go in now," Fran finally said.

In the Nancy Drew mysteries Julia used to read as a child, Nancy was always clear-headed, her cool green eyes fixed somewhere on her goal. Not that she didn't ever feel afraid. She was scared sometimes. Her heart occasionally missed a few beats. But the goal was always firmly in her mind. Mysteries were puzzles to be solved, to figure out. George, her sidekick, was always game, reckless even, an androgynous free spirit who had good intentions. Together they'd go off in Nancy's blue roadster in search of answers. Where is the key to the widow Miller's safe deposit box? What is inside the green room in the cupola of that old house? And who is that strange bearded man who showed up at Mrs. Anders's funeral?

Plucky. That's what Nancy and George were. Plucky. But Julia didn't feel plucky when she and Fran approached Grayson Hall. Their footsteps echoed down the empty hallways. Everything was still in the main office, the machines all covered as if they'd been tucked in for the night. Fran went to the cabinet and reached behind a stack of manila folders. "Aha!" she said, coming away with the key. Julia followed her to Tyler's office

and paused before she turned the doorknob. ''You're sure you
want to do this now?'' Fran asked, as if it had all been Julia's
idea originally, as if Julia had pushed her into going along as
an accomplice.

''I want to know,'' Julia said, walking into the office and
switching on the overhead light. They blinked against the bright
fluorescence. ''Shut the door!'' Fran commanded. Julia obeyed,
standing against the door as she watched Fran open the top
drawer of Tyler's desk. ''Oh, God, Julia,'' she said with a groan.
''Look at this!''

4

As she stood with Fran in the doorway of Tyler's office, Julia realized that suddenly everything from now on was going to be changed, irrevocably altered. She watched, her heart pounding, as Fran's fingers nimbly went through papers in Tyler's top drawer.

The card was still on his desk. Julia picked it up, looked at it again and knew. The cute little bear. The bright purple ink. The overblown loops on her letters. "Thank you for letting me love you!" Julia read the words out loud. "Thank you for letting me love you." Of course she was young. Maybe she *was* a student.

Fran had taken something out of the desk and plopped down in the chair. "Holy shit. I can't believe this." She looked suddenly dopey, as if someone had just conked her on the head.

"What?" Julia asked.

"This." Fran carefully laid down four photographs as if it were a winning poker hand. Four pictures of the same very blond girl. Her eyes were big and round and blue. In one, her hair was short and spiky on the top. In the rest, her hair was

meticulously curled, framing a heart-shaped face. She was smiling in every picture, a toothy, yearbook smile.

Julia looked from picture to picture, trying to make some
connection. This girl and Tyler? Tyler and this girl? For a few
seconds, Julia thought that the girl must be a friend of Beth's.
In one of the photographs, she was peeking out from behind
a tree, looking coy. In another, she was standing in front of a
shiny red car, one hand placed over the hood, the other behind
her back in a mock cheese-cake pose.

"Lynette Rae Macalvie," Fran said, holding up the woodsy
shot.

"You *know* her?" Julia gasped.

Fran nodded, speechless.

"She's a student, isn't she?" Julia asked. She looked at the
pictures, studying each one. The smiling person there looked
bouncy and blond, pretty in a flat-faced, cheerful sort of way.
Julia couldn't stop staring at the pictures.

"She was in my world literature class last semester. She was
in the front row, seated between two girls named Stacy and
Tracy, also blondes. It took me all semester to tell them apart."

"She was in your *class?*"

Fran nodded. "Sure, Lynette Rae Macalvie," Fran mused.
"I think she got a B-minus."

Julia stared at the picture of the girl in front of the car. It
was the kind of picture that teenagers take sometimes, standing
proudly with their first cars. She was wearing white short-
shorts; her legs were thick and sturdy.

Julia held up another one of the closeups. "She looks familiar
to me, too," she said.

"You've probably seen her around campus. In this building,
even. I think she's a philosophy major," Fran told her.

On campus. Walking around Grayson Hall. Julia pictured
passing this girl on the steps. She knew she had seen her
somewhere, in one particular place, and for an extended period
of time. "She just seems . . ." Julia closed her eyes in thought

before it suddenly clicked. "Oh my God! It was the Booth Jenson lecture that Tyler gave last fall. Fran, I sat right next to her!" Julia remembered how, as Tyler spoke, the girl clasped her hands in front of her chest as if in prayer. "Fran, you had her in class?" Julia looked at the pictures again, stunned. "What was she like?"

"She's ... she's ..." Fran held out her open palms and shook her head, seemingly at a loss for words. "Julia, I don't know what to tell you. She's ... a *student!*"

"What's her name? Lynette May what??"

"Lynette Rae. Lynette Rae Macalvie."

"Lynette Rae Macalvie," Julia repeated. "Really—that's her *name?*"

"I know," Fran said. "It sounds like someone on 'Hee Haw.'" Fran looked back at the pictures, shaking her head. Then she looked at the card. "Oh, Julia, I don't know what to say. I mean, you know that Tyler and I clashed. But Julia, I don't know what he could possibly be thinking with this."

"He says he loves her," Julia said. "He told me how sweet she is. How everything seems easy with her." She picked up the pictures from the desk and stacked them together. "He said he thinks he wants to start his life all over again." Julia kept hearing again all the things he had told her only a few hours before. "I love her. . . . I don't know if I love you anymore. . . . I've been unhappy for a long time. . . . There were other women. . . ." It was as if there were grenades going off in her head.

"That's what he said? That he actually wants to start his life over again?" Fran's eyes were wild. "That makes me furious! Doesn't it make you furious?" Fran began to stomp around the office. For a moment Julia thought she was going to fling Tyler's books off the shelf in a clean sweep and rip them to pieces. Fran had once described a fight with Damian in which she had broken all the bottles of wine they had in the cellar over the roof of his Saab Turbo.

"I keep thinking it's a bad dream. That someone is going to wake me up from this," Julia said.

Fran sighed. "It's no dream, sweetie." She opened the drawer and found two more greeting cards, both with koala bears on them. On the bottom of one, in the same purple ink, was written, "Can't *wait* (underlined three times) until Sunday." The other card showed a bear wearing a pair of men's plaid underwear; she had written (same purple ink, her trademark): "And I love *you* in your boxer shorts!" Along the very bottom, she had added, "That's why they call me Luscious Lynette!"

"Luscious Lynette," Julia read aloud, feeling her stomach flip. Tyler was in love with someone who called herself Luscious Lynette.

Fran began emptying the entire contents of the drawer onto the desk. "What else is in here?" she asked, separating out the pile.

Julia put her arm out, stilling Fran's busy hands. "Fran, we have to be careful. We have to put all this stuff back just right, so he doesn't know I was in his desk." Julia looked nervous. Two spots of color appeared high on her cheeks.

Fran was scornful. "Why?"

"Because Tyler really values his privacy. He hates it if the girls and I get into his things."

"Are you kidding? You *are* kidding, aren't you?" Fran erupted again. "Your husband is schtupping a goddamned undergraduate whom he professes to *love* and wants to start his life over with. He won't tell you who she is and says it's *none* of your business. And you're afraid of not respecting his goddamned *privacy?* Where's the respect he had for you while he was carrying on this sleazy little affair?" Fran's dark eyes glowed hotly. "Don't you feel like just killing the son of a bitch?"

"I don't know what I feel. I'm in shock."

"I feel like killing him myself," Fran said grimly.

"Please," Julia said, holding her stomach.

"Are you all right, sweetie?"

Julia nodded.

"Well, let's just see what else is here, all right?" Fran spread everything out along the desk as if she were taking inventory. "Here we go," she said.

Julia the list maker tried to take everything in. There were:

- Two birthday cards: one humorous, one a long poem about special love
- A lace-trimmed Valentine's Day card with another poem
- A wooden music box that played "We've Only Just Begun"
- A long poem in rhymed couplets, whose first two lines were:

  I look at you and in your face I see
  Our love is but for all eternity
- An opened box of condoms
- A small stuffed bear holding a Stimpson banner with the school colors, purple and gold, and a note in purple ink: "Silly, but I couldn't resist. This cute li'l guy reminded me of you!"
- A pile of pornographic magazines with names like *Hot Puss, Boobs and Broads, Cycle Sluts*

"Fran, I think I've had enough." Shaken, Julia went over to the window and stared out at the tree-lined quadrangle.

Fran read the entire long love poem aloud, then brought an index finger to the back of her throat, pretending to retch. "And will you look at how much time she spent on this piece of crap?" Fran held up the poem, its painstaking calligraphy in purple ink on pink paper. Julia continued to gaze sadly out the window while Fran rummaged through the evidence. "When was Tyler's birthday?" she asked.

Julia turned. "March second, why?"

"Well, he's been seeing her since February at least," Fran said, holding the Valentine card.

Slowly Julia nodded, beginning to make some connections: Tyler taking all those naps and showers when he came home. Tyler going into the office at night because he was "in inspiration." Every Sunday afternoon he had gone to the office. The last few months he was working hard and talking about putting together another book of poetry.

She had been so pleased that he was writing again, she didn't mind eating alone sometimes with the girls and waiting up for him late at night. An artistic temperament did not conform to ordinary schedules. She accepted that, had even been proud of it.

He had called once, a few weeks before. It was after ten and she had been watching the news. "How's the writing going?" she had asked.

He said he was still in inspiration and didn't know when he would be home. "Is that all right with you, hon?" he asked, sounding actually lonesome.

"Of course," she had assured him.

Now she turned to Fran. "I'm so stupid. He was working so hard. I thought he was in inspiration."

Fran looked at the picture of Lynette Rae Macalvie in her tight white shorts. "The only thing he was *in*, sweetie," she told Julia, "was a B-minus blonde with a penchant for sentimental verse."

Outside, the leaves shimmered in the light and the fountain in the middle of campus spurted irregular tufts of foamy water toward the sky. "What are you going to do?" Fran asked, as they started to drive back to her house.

"I don't know." Julia looked sad but serene, staring out the car window like a sick person being taken out from a hospital for an afternoon ride. "I need some time to think," she added.

"Of course."

"Franny, I don't want you to tell anyone about this," Julia said.

"Who would I tell?"

"I mean no one. Not your sister. Not Friday club."

"I promise," Fran said, holding a hand over her heart. She looked at her watch. "Are you going this afternoon? It's at Drusilla's house."

Julia shook her head and began to cry. "I can't," she said. "I can't face anyone now. You make some excuse."

At a stop sign, Fran reached awkwardly over the gearshift to pat Julia's leg. "You need to wipe your nose," Fran said kindly. "There are tissues in the glove compartment."

Julia blew and then checked the mirror above the dash to see if she looked like a person who had just received some tragic, life-changing information: "I'm sorry, it's malignant. . . ." "Just one of those freak accidents. . . ." "Ma'am, there was nothing we could do to save your boy. . . ." "I don't think I love you anymore." Every day, people hear the most awful news and then they walk away, the same people with the same physical characteristics, still wearing the same clothes, still with the same hairstyles they had when they went out that morning, unsuspecting and trusting, to begin another day.

"Redheads always look terrible when we cry," Julia observed. Her eyes, pale with all the dark brown eyeliner and mascara washed away by tears, were puffy, and the freckles looked mottled against her wan skin. Her hand went to touch one of the gold drop earrings that Tyler had given her as an anniversary present a few years ago. They were Julia's everyday favorites. On the card, he had written an anniversary poem. It began, "We go back so far we've grown into each other like the roots of neighboring trees . . ."

Now she thought of his face, clearly in pain, as he had said, "Julia, I don't think I love you anymore," and involuntarily, a moan escaped from her lips.

5

"Franny! You're here!" Drusilla announced, coming to the door in an ankle-length white T-shirt painted with neon pink flamingos. Dru was a fiber artist who frequently wore her art. In the winter she was all woven scarves and ponchos and overcoats that looked like old quilts.

"That's a lovely piece." Fran pointed to a spiral of purple and electric blue hanging from the second floor of the stairwell.

"I just finished yesterday. It's a commission for the First Federal Bank." Dru wiped back tendrils of silver curls off her forehead. Dru had been gray at twenty-five. Now at fifty, she was an elegant, imposing woman always surrounded by swirls of color.

Maria and Jean came out from the kitchen, each with a bottle of beer in her hand. "Where's Julia?" Maria asked.

Friday club. The group was now in its twelfth year for Fran and Julia, though Jean and Dru and Maria had been meeting for Friday beer since their children, now grown, were toddlers. Then they had hired one babysitter to stay with all the children in one house while the three of them went to someone else's house to have a beer and adult conversation.

The rules and organization of Friday club were simple. Every Friday after four o'clock they met in each other's homes, someone saying, "My place next week," before they broke up by six. The hostess provided beer and wine and something like french bread (store-bought) and some cheese, or chips and dip. Simplicity itself. No hassle. No children. No men.

All the women (except Fran) had two children; all the women (except Julia) had been divorced at least once; all the women (except Drusilla) worked at Stimpson College. Jean was an editor at the college press. Maria taught French and Spanish and occasionally Portuguese and Russian; her accent fluctuated depending upon the semester.

"Beer or wine?" Dru offered.

Fran chose white wine and curled up on the sofa, as far away from Drusilla's cat as possible. "Julia's home. She didn't feel well," Fran told the group, feeling that, all things considered, it was not an out-and-out lie.

Then Maria took center stage, complaining about her younger daughter, who was dating a right-wing Republican. "I've always told her how she could go with anyone she wished, how tolerant I am," Maria said—she pronounced the word 'toll-er-ahnt'—"but now she has gone too far!"

Drusilla went into the kitchen to get more beer, so Fran answered the door when the bell rang. She thought for a moment that it would be Julia standing there: Julia in need of old friends' shoulders and a beer to cry into.

She was surprised to see Alice Blevins on the front steps. Alice was the assistant to the president of Stimpson college, loyally serving him for the last two decades. "Oh, hello, Fran," Alice said, smiling tentatively. "Is Drusilla in?"

"Hi, Alice. Sure," Fran said. "Come on in." She held the door open and gestured encouragingly. The laughter of the women in the living room as Dru came out of the kitchen with beer and a tray of cheeses made Fran embarrassed for Alice, who seemed unsure of her welcome.

"Oh, I thought you were going to call before you came to pick it up," Dru said bluntly.

"I'm sorry," Alice began. "I was just leaving work and decided . . ."

"Well, never mind," Dru interrupted. "I'll go get it. Come in. You know everybody, don't you? Come in and have a beer."

"No, no thank you, I don't want to interrupt," Alice said, standing stiffly in the hall. The women had stopped talking. Alice nodded. "Maria? Hello. Jean. How are you?"

There was a moment of awkward silence after they all exchanged greetings. "I'm picking up one of Drusilla's flamingo dresses," Alice explained, taking out her checkbook. There was a chorus of approval. "For my daughter—it's her birthday," Alice added. Everyone nodded. Alice herself, wearing a navy blue wraparound skirt and a plain white blouse pinned at the neck with a cameo, was not a likely candidate for a flamingo dress. She wrote the check hurriedly and apologized again for the interruption.

"I feel bad for her," Jean said after Alice left.

"Shhh," Fran signaled, a finger over her lips, pointing to the screen door, which was still open. The women looked out the window to see Alice getting into a shiny red sports car. *"That's* her car?" Fran asked.

"Maybe it's her daughter's," Dru said.

"We should have invited her to join us," Jean said.

"I did. I *said* come in and have a beer," Drusilla protested.

"But you didn't *mean* it," Jean said.

"Well, she didn't know I didn't mean it," Dru said.

"It's like high school all over again," Jean said. "I just felt that cruelty." She was sensitive to things like this, having grown up with a beautiful sister who had been her rival. Many Friday afternoons were spent analyzing Jean's particularly troubled teenage years.

"Jean, it's not like I made her wait on the porch," Drusilla said. "And anyway. She should have called."

At six o'clock, when everyone was getting up to go, Jean said, "My house next week," and Fran said she'd let Julia know, though she thought Julia would be going out of town that weekend. Dru told Fran to tell Julia that they all hoped she felt better, and Maria asked, wasn't it Julia's anniversary next weekend? She remembered Julia talking about going to Chicago. Just then Dru's husband, Charlie, came up the walk and asked advice about a border planting for the front walk. "Where's Julia?" he asked. "She's the gardener." Charlie walked over to some newly raked ground to the side of the porch. "Maybe I'll give her a call tonight." He kicked some loose stones with his foot.

"Don't call her tonight, she's sick," Fran said quickly. "I'll tell her to call to you." She started for her car, then turned. "I mean, I'll tell her to call you when she gets a chance." She saw them there on Drusilla's porch as she drove away, all of them looking just a bit puzzled at her speedy retreat.

Driving home, Fran caught her reflection in the rearview mirror, surprised to see how she was scowling; a straight, angry line had appeared between eyes that were narrowed into angry slits. "Damn him," she said aloud, angry at Tyler for making her lie to her friends.

A part of her was also upset with Julia, with how solicitous she was about Tyler and his precious privacy, even with the knowledge of what he had done. "Schmata," she said under her breath. "And a dope."

While it was true that she had done her share of stupid things concerning men, sometimes Fran could hardly tolerate the way Julia always deferred to Tyler, revered him, how she had this notion that he was some sort of genius who needed special treatment and saw herself as a supporting player ("the poet's wife") whose role it was to nurture, keep the peace, create the environment that would encourage his "inspiration."

Fran had read most of Tyler's poetry. She could recall not a single line.

Sometimes she thought she was jealous of Julia and Tyler, of their long history and nuclear coziness. And the children. Mostly the children. Fran used to count out the time: how long to meet someone, marry, decide to have a baby. (If she had ever tried again with Damian, she would have stopped teaching for the duration of the pregnancy, taken to her bed, anything to keep the fragile fetus from breaking away.) Now at forty-two, with no man in sight, she realistically accepted that having a child would never happen. The finality of this realization made her sad, but it also had a settling effect.

And if it doesn't happen, it doesn't happen. She heard her mother's voice. Generally, Sylvia Meltzer's philosophy of life leaned heavily toward the tautological. If you have to make it alone, you'll make it alone. You do what you have to do.

When Fran arrived home, she unhooked her bra, ran a bubble bath, and listened to the answering machine. There was George Lawson's blurry voice asking her to call back when she had a chance. "Right," she said aloud. "I really want to talk to you now, George."

There was something creepy about him, had been as long as she had known him. She just accepted who he was: sad, creepy George; she supposed she could even classify him as a friend.

When she had just come to Stimpson as a young assistant professor, still in her twenties, it was George Lawson who had taken her under his wing, had described the politics of the college. Even then, he was strange. He was married then, drinking intermittently. Fran had not known his wife very well, an agoraphobic who macraméed extensive wall hangings for the English department. No one knew exactly when George and his wife got divorced. It seemed to just happen one day. Supposedly, she went to live with a sister in Wisconsin. George never said a word about her leaving.

He went through a time when there were a lot of women—mostly waitresses or women he had picked up in bars—but for the last five years, he was increasingly remote. And drinking heavily. Fran had not known George to be with a woman, any woman, for some time now. It was as if the alcohol had somehow neutered him; the bottle sucked out all his juices, dried him up. Students complained of his forgetting to give back their papers, coming to class drunk. And then he went to that rehabilitation center in Minneapolis, paid for by the college—all three times. But money was tight lately, budgets were not what they were in the affluent eighties. The administration had become less tolerant. George was fifty-three years old, and it was not likely he could get another job in academia.

The last time George called he had been so drunk that Fran finally hung up on him. He seemed obsessed with talking about medical benefits, how he couldn't afford to lose them. Well, who could? she wanted to know. Just having two of her teeth crowned last year would have been a bundle without the dental insurance. No, that wasn't it. There was something else, George was saying. You can't really know what I'm going through, he was saying. You would be surprised.

How does anyone know what anyone else is going through? she thought now, settling herself into the bath. She had one of those rubber pillows and a tray on the side of the tub to hold magazines and drinks. On one bathroom wall was a greenhouse window, a quirky addition put in by the people who owned the house before her, now filled with clumps of plants all in various stages of decomposition.

She added more hot water, leaned back in the bath, and finished her glass of wine, relaxing as it spread a warm buzz through her body. "Boy-oh-boy-oh-boy-oh-boy," she said, blowing some of the bubbles off her knees. Surprise, surprise.

Fran remembered her mother, making dinner in the kitchen

in their apartment in New York so many years ago. She was saying to Fran's father, "Now nothing that anyone could do would surprise me anymore." Her father nodded silently and smoked a cigarette. "Sydney, I am shaken to the core," Sylvia Meltzer had said.

What had shaken Fran's mother to the core was the news about Mr. Dox, a popular teacher at the high school where they lived. As a history teacher Mr. Dox had a great deal of personal flair. Before every test, he gave out special study sheets called "Dox's Data" with timelines and maps and important facts.

He was married and had three children. Mrs. Dox, a big woman with a beautiful voice, had been Fran's girl scout leader years back. Fran remembered that their house always smelled spicy and fresh, and Mrs. Dox usually had some crafts project— embroidery or quilting—across the dining room table.

Then Mr. Dox was arrested. On the school trip to Washington, D.C., while Mr. Dox was the chaperone, he had been accused of luring a boy into his hotel room and making advances.

Fran's mother told this story to the family over dinner. She said that Henry Dox had *fondled* the boy in the hotel room. Fran remembered that because her sister, Roz, had asked why in the world would anyone be arrested just because he was fond of a boy in a hotel room?

Fran's mother explained the nature of Henry Dox's crime. "Those poor Dox children," said Fran's mother, clicking her tongue, a high flush in her cheeks from the heat of her cooking and the disquieting conversation. "And his poor, poor wife."

Fran was old enough then to be both thrilled with knowing something scandalous about a teacher and sympathetic to the family. Her father took a long drag of his cigarette. "I don't know," he said, addressing his wife. "A man's got to be driven by something pretty near out of control to shame his family so."

Now sitting in a hot bubble bath in her home in Grandview,

Illinois, Fran thought about George Lawson and Tyler Markem and Mr. Dox.

And Mrs. Dox, after all—her chubby, comforting arms, her lilting voice, pretty as a bird's song. Did Mrs. Dox know anything at all about her husband's longings and secret life? Were there questions? Inklings? Uneasy, nameless fears that crept into her dreams? Lying next to him in bed each night, did she suspect that something wasn't quite right? Had Mrs. Dox any knowledge of the little boys over the years that her husband had approached and touched, had been "fond of" in ways that he should not?

Now Fran rose from the bath, drying herself in a thick white towel. The whole bathroom was steamy and smelled mulchy and warm, like outdoors after a summer rain. And what does anyone really know after all? she thought. What does anyone really know after all?

6

Tyler was on the floor of the living room doing situps; a tape of Mozart horn concertos was coming from the speakers. "Were you at Friday club all this time?" he asked as Julia stood in the doorway.

It was close to six-thirty by then, and the smells of a neighbor's barbecue wafted through the screen door. Tyler looked concerned but continued doing the situps, his feet stabilized under the sofa and his muscled legs bent at the knee.

"I took a drive. To do some thinking," Julia said tightly. "Where are the girls?"

Tyler motioned upstairs with his head. He wore jogging clothes, and a yellow terrycloth sweatband was around his forehead. "They want to go out for pizza," Tyler said. Perspiration gleamed across his broad forehead.

"We need to talk," Julia said.

Tyler merely grunted.

"Do you have to do situps now?" Julia asked.

"I just have one more set to go." Tyler grimaced as he brought his chest toward his knees.

She didn't know what it was—the sight of him in his jogging outfit, the beautiful music, those last groans as he strained to complete the final set: Tyler taking *care* of himself—but she hated him at that moment. Really hated him. Wished-that-he-were-dead-on-the-floor-at-her-feet hated him.

So it just came. She didn't plan on telling him just then, but the words escaped from her lips. She quoted the poem, the couplet now engraved in her memory like a telephone number: " 'I look at you and in your face I see/ Our love is but for all eternity.' My God, Tyler. That is banal and pathetic," Julia said meanly. "How could you love someone who writes like that?"

In a flash, Tyler rose from the floor, blue veins of anger standing out along the side of his neck. "How did you know about that poem? Where did you get it?" He lunged toward Julia, but she scooted around to the far end of the dining room table and faced him.

"Don't you dare touch me!" she said clearly. They were both poised at either end of the table, breathing heavily, as if they were boxers resting between rounds. Upstairs, music from U2 could be heard over Mozart.

Tyler slapped the wall, looking menacingly at her. "God damn you, Julia! How did you get into my office?"

"A key," she said evenly. "I got the master key from the front office."

"You *broke* into my office?" Tyler was rigid with anger.

"I didn't exactly *break* into the office. I had a key—"

"Don't you *see* yourself?" Tyler interrupted. "Don't you see what you do?"

Now, facing the driving force of his disapproval, she felt herself begin to crumple. "How *could* you?" Tyler said, his jaw clenched. "How could you have broken into my office and gone through my desk without my permission?"

"Tyler," Julia answered, "how could I not? You wouldn't tell me who she was and I—" She attempted to explain when Tyler raised a hand to stop her.

"You invaded my privacy. I can't forgive you for doing that," Tyler said sternly.

"I'm sorry."

"Don't you see, Julia? That's one of the reasons why I feel I needed to escape from you. You're so controlling. You need to know everything."

Julia suddenly felt herself go from victim to villain. Tyler had perfected this technique during his philosophical training. When Tyler argued, he could say anything and make it so, his words twisting and turning like a mountain stream running over slippery rock, until she was sucked into the whirlpool, lost in an eddy of self-doubt.

There were other women, Tyler said again, but they never meant anything. "Don't you see? The marriage *must* have been in trouble, Julia. Or else why would I be doing that? I was unhappy and must have been looking for something. But that doesn't matter. That's over now. I'm not going to do that any longer. I didn't like being a cheat. I'm not going to be unfaithful again."

Julia was going to ask exactly who it was that he planned on remaining faithful *to*, but she was afraid of what she might hear. A pledge of eternal fidelity to Lynette Rae Macalvie was more than she was prepared to handle at the moment.

"You've changed," Tyler said. "You've lost that sweetness you used to have, Julia. That sweetness you had when we met."

"I was twenty-two years old when we met," she said.

Tyler shook his head, looking past her, longing for the girl she used to be.

"What do you suggest we do, Tyler?" she said miserably.

"We don't have to do anything yet, Julia. Can't we just play it out a little?"

"Play *what* out?"

"Does everything have to be always so planned and tidy for you all the time? I'm not saying this isn't a mess right now. So all right. This is a mess. God, can't you accept that for a while? This is our lives. Not a fucking academic article you're trying to finish up." Tyler stood against the wall breathing heavily. "Look, do you want to go out for pizza with the kids or not?"

"Pizza?"

"Yes, *pizza*," Tyler said slowly.

She thought: Something is wrong with this picture. The music. The situps. Tyler asking if she wanted to go out for pizza just as if it were an ordinary day. His exasperation that she was not able to treat it as if it were.

"Or maybe Chinese," Tyler said. "Do you want to try that new place in the mall?"

"Tyler, what are we going to do?" she asked again. She thought how much she had been looking forward to the summer. In the mornings, she would do research in the library while Tyler taught. Then, in late afternoon, she would garden, make pesto, wallpaper the new bathroom, read mystery novels in the backyard hammock. Beth had a job frying fish at McDonald's and was studying for the SAT's. Caty would go to the pool with her friends and was enrolled at a ballet camp for two weeks. At night they would have cold chicken picnics in the park and rent movies and play Scrabble on the porch and then at the end of July go to the lake in Maine. Julia sat down on the couch, hugging her sides. "Tyler, how can we not *do* anything? What about our *lives*?"

"Do you have to be so dramatic, Julia?"

She took a deep breath to steady herself. "Tyler, listen to me. You can't just keep living here. We can't just go on, just pretending nothing has happened and not say anything to the girls and—"

"Why not? For a while, why not?"

"What do you mean, 'Why not?' You're going to keep seeing this girl?"

"Yes. For now. Until I figure out what it is I want. Lynette is not a *girl*, by the way, a word I believe you and your friend

Fran Meltzer find politically incorrect. She's not nineteen, if that's what you're thinking. She was out of school for a while, working. She's not one of our typical empty-headed undergraduates. And this isn't a middle-age crazy. This just *happened*, all right. I didn't expect things to turn out this way. I don't know what's going to happen." Tyler sat back down on the floor and put his head to his knees. "This is exhausting me," he said.

"So you want to stay here with me and not tell the children while you figure out what to do with your life?"

"Yes, I think that's what I'd like."

It dawned on her that perhaps Tyler was crazy. She stared at him for a while, trying to bring his face into focus. "I don't think you can do that," she said tightly.

"Julia, I need some time to think this through. And, I'm sorry, but I'm not ready to give up seeing her."

"So you want to live with us and still see this girl."

"Lynette," Tyler said.

"And you expect me to not tell anyone. Not our family, not our friends. You want to keep this as a secret."

"For now," Tyler said. "Please. You're acting like this is the end of the world. In France, men have mistresses all the time. Women don't think of it as such a devastation." He attempted a smile.

"We live in Grandview, Illinois," Julia said.

"I *know* very well where we are, Julia," Tyler said sighing. He crossed his legs, examining a scab on his ankle. "Look, Julia, I'm asking you, begging you practically," he said finally, "just give me some time to think this through."

Julia shrugged. "I don't know, Tyler . . ."

"Please." He looked at her beseechingly. "Really, I especially don't want you to tell Fran. You always have to tell her everything, and I wish you wouldn't." Tyler shook his head. "I wish I could trust you not to always have to tell everything to Fran. Must you?'' Suddenly he looked as if the conversation were more than he could bear.

''Trust? You are using the word *trust?* You know,'' Julia said slowly, ''you are really *crazy.* You twist this around and make it sound as if *I'm* the one who's to blame here—''

Tyler got up off the floor. ''This isn't about blame, Julia. No one's to *blame.*''

''You've been cheating on me!'' Julia started yelling at him. ''You've been cheating on me with a student! There *is* blame here! You are a liar and a cheat!''

That's when Tyler started hushing her. ''You're very upset,'' he said. ''It won't be good for the girls to see you like this. You're filled with rage, but speaking against me is not the right thing to do. You'll only hurt them by that behavior, Julia,'' Tyler said.

''I'm going to hurt them by *my* behavior? Look how you turn everything around!'' Suddenly she felt as if she were going to throw up. ''I'm going to be sick,'' she said, turning toward the stairs.

''I'll take the girls out for pizza,'' Tyler said helpfully.

''Thank you,'' Julia said. She held on to the bannister on the way up the stairs and proceeded to throw up six times during the next hour.

Julia lay curled up in bed watching the sky turn dark and ominous when the phone rang. ''Thank God you answered! I didn't know if you'd be in the middle of something or what!'' It was Fran. ''I was going to hang up if it was *him.''* She said *him* in the same tone that one would use for the word *pus* or *cockroach.*

''Hi, Franny,'' Julia said weakly. ''I was going to call. I've been busy throwing up. How was Friday club?''

''Fine, I didn't say anything. Listen, what happened with you?''

"Tyler and I talked. He was furious that I went into his desk and found out who she was."

"Oh, and I bet he was thrilled about *me* seeing all that shit."

"I didn't tell him that you were with me."

"You didn't?"

"He'd just get angrier. He says that he's very confused. He doesn't want me to tell anyone. He wants to stay here and he doesn't want me to tell anyone. And he wants to continue to see her."

"No!"

"Tyler says we could just wait and see what happens. He says in France they do this all the time."

"Do what?"

"Have mistresses."

Fran snorted. "Yeah, and in France they also think that Jerry Lewis is funny and existentialism is deep."

"I don't know what to do."

"Julia—"

"What?"

"Look, I don't necessarily want your marriage to break up. You know I don't. I did it twice, and it's not something I'd ever wish on anyone else, especially not my best friend. But, honey, don't let him do this to you. Don't let him twist everything around so you're to blame, too—"

"Tyler says it's not about blame."

"Julia, you may not be the most perfect person in the world, the most perfect partner, but nothing *you* did deserves this, nothing deserves this betrayal or the way he's treating you now."

"Yes," Julia said weakly.

"He doesn't even sound particularly remorseful, even."

"Well, he *has* cried a lot . . ."

"Julia, don't let him make a schmata out of you."

"What's a schmata?" Julia asked. Fran was always using

Yiddish expressions. Julia, a transplanted New Englander now living in the Midwest, thought it was very exotic.

"A schmata is a rag. Something to wipe the floor with."

"Franny, I have to go. I think I'm going to throw up again."

"I love you, sweetie." Julia heard Fran's words just as she dropped the phone back into its cradle.

Leaning over the toilet bowl, Julia heard a crack of thunder. A warm wind blew the filmy bathroom curtains straight out. Caught between the bathroom window and the screen, a fat-bellied beetle buzzed for its life.

After two more empty heaves, Julia put cold water on her face and went back to bed. She waited until her stomach was settled, then took the two Valiums that Fran had given her. Soon she could sense the drug working its soporific way up her body; the whole of her spinal column felt as if it were a big Slinky toy. When she heard the sound of the garage door lifting, then the girls laughing in the hall, she was very nearly asleep.

She dreamed that she was going for a routine gynecological checkup only to find Tyler in the cubicle next to hers, standing there in a white coat in between the splayed legs of a teenage girl.

"Julia!" He looked up with false cheer. There were pails of blood and dismembered baby parts—a tiny limb, gnarly and pearly pale, like the gristle on a chewed chicken leg. Tyler held sharp, silver instruments that flashed blindingly under the harsh fluorescent lights.

"Tyler! How could you do this? *You* can't perform abortions!" she exclaimed. "You're not even a medical doctor!"

Shamed, the girl on the table covered her face with her hands.

"This is not your business," Tyler said severely, rubbing the surgical instruments together as if he were about to carve a roast.

"Is it the money? Is the money the reason why you're doing

this?" Julia screamed at him. She was naked in the corridor of the medical clinic, holding a sheet tightly around her.

"Go back into the examination room now, Julia." Tyler was icy. "You are making a fool of yourself."

At three in the morning she woke in a sweat, alone in the bed and trembling with loathing for a man who, only yesterday, she would have told anyone that she loved with all her heart.

7

Sleepless and dazed, Julia drifted through her days in a panic, anxious to *do* something. But what? Since the discovery, Tyler retreated, spending more time at the office, at the gym, drinking with George Lawson. And seeing Lynette Macalvie, who had a studio apartment in Campustown right above the Kinko's copy store. Tyler lived at home, sleeping in the back study behind their bedroom. When Caty did not have ballet and Beth was not working at McDonald's, the family ate together. The girls talked as usual, lively at dinner, while Julia and Tyler passed platters and made polite conversation, and Julia felt as though she were an actress in a family television show, her head always spinning, connections going off—oh, I was doing this, when *he* was doing that; I was over here, but *he* was over there. It was a reinterpretation of their personal history.

Sometimes she woke up in the night drenched in sweat, kneading herself into a frenzy as the suspicions rose up so ugly they swelled out of all normal proportion. One morning she dreamed that Tyler was next to her in bed, rubbing the back of her neck. He was saying, "God, I'm such a jerk. I'm really sorry about this, Julia." But he was acting casual, as if he were apologizing for breaking a wine-glass or forgetting to pick up something at the grocery store.

She awoke and sat up in bed. She looked at all the family pictures on the dresser, focusing on one of her and Tyler that she'd put in a silver frame. It showed them at her parents' lake in Maine, skipping stones; a breeze had caught her hair. She wore a white, gauzy dress that swirled around her legs. Tyler's eyes were as blue as the sky and his smile was dazzling. That was three summers ago. Was he as unhappy then as he said? ("I have been unhappy for years, Julia.")

Betrayed, embarrassed, hurt beyond all measure, she wanted to leave him, have *him* leave, but still she did nothing at all.

It was hot and muggy, even at seven, when she went out to run. Already a damp heat made it hard to breathe, so she took a shorter route than usual and ended by cutting across downtown. Running past the bakery, the shoe store, and a jeweler's that had a row of engagement rings sparkling in the window, Julia saw herself reflected in the glass: a grimacing, middle-aged woman, panting for breath.

The anger she felt toward Tyler at that moment was pointed and fierce. She would grow old, she thought. Alone. She could run and keep herself in shape, but she could not run from the inescapable truth of her predicament. Even if Tyler stayed, she could not trust him. If not Lynette, then it would be someone else.

In an hour she was making coffee, standing at the counter and reading the paper as she waited for the pot to drip full. On the front page was a picture of a teenager accused of leaving her newborn baby to die in a garbage dumpster. Julia read the whole story. The girl had delivered a healthy six-pound baby boy and no one, not even her parents, had known that she was pregnant. She was reported missing when her mother found blood all over the girl's room and called the police. How could a mother not know that her own daughter was pregnant? Julia thought. She sat down at the table and went through the rest of the paper. She knew it was odd, but the domestic horror story was the only thing she could focus on in the whole newspaper.

Last night Tyler had not come home at all, and she wondered if the girls were beginning to suspect anything. "Dad's been so busy," she said at breakfast, apropos of nothing. "End-of-the-semester crunch. He has all those papers before finals." Maybe the girls hadn't even noticed anything, she thought. Beth and Caty had just a few weeks of school left themselves and were busy with their own projects.

"I think he's in inspiration, too," Beth said casually, slicing a banana into her cereal. "He told me he almost has enough for another collection of poems. Oh Mom," she added, "before I forget: I need money for my yearbook. We have to pay by the end of the week."

Caty asked if she could wear her new tie-dye T-shirt before washing it. Beth said she didn't think it was fair that the seniors only had half-day school for the next two weeks. Caty said that she wouldn't be home for dinner because she was studying algebra with her friends at the library and then going out for pizza. Beth said that she wouldn't be home for dinner because she was taking someone else's shift at McDonald's so that she would be free this weekend to work on the decorations for the prom. They left in a flurry of kisses, the door slamming shut.

Julia sat back, a bit stunned at how easy it was to fool teenagers, who were so busy with the intricacies of their own lives that they were oblivious of what went on in anyone else's.

She and Fran were talking about anger. Julia thought that perhaps it was not in her nature to express anger, reserve being a big commodity in her family. Maybe she was afraid. Afraid that if she pushed Tyler out, the marriage would never be salvageable.

She was telling all this to Fran as they sat in a plastic booth in the pancake house off Highway 34. It was one of Fran's favorite places to eat. She liked the hash browns, the ambience, and the fact that the waitresses did not identify themselves by name.

In three weeks Julia had lost twelve pounds. Fran said she was jealous. Every time *she* went through a personal trauma she craved creamy white sauces, baked potatoes with lots of butter and sour cream, caramel custard, and anything Alfredo. Comfort foods were very fattening, she said.

"Your hair looks wonderful. You went to Mr. Phu?" Fran asked, cutting her skillet special; the runny yolk oozed over the mound of ham and hash browns, causing Julia to turn her head. Mirrors surrounded the booth, and Julia was surprised that today she didn't look as bad as she felt. This was, in part, because yesterday she had gotten a really terrific permanent. Mr. Phu was a Vietnamese hairdresser whom Fran had discovered in the JCPenney salon at the mall. "If anyone ever told me years ago that I would be getting my hair done in JCPenney. . . ." Fran sighed and shook her head. "I've been in the Midwest so long that it doesn't even seem unacceptable to me. The fact is," Fran went on, "Mr. Phu is really fabulous, isn't he? But on the quiet side."

Mr. Phu worked inscrutably in total silence. In fact, the two times Julia had seen him, she had yet to hear him utter a single word. Not even a single foreign word. She imagined that perhaps when he was a child in Vietnam, Mr. Phu saw something so terrible that he was traumatized forever into a life of silence.

"A great haircut," Fran said. "It looks soft and scrunched at the same time."

Julia was trying to choke down a half order of blueberry pancakes. Great hair or not, she still felt already battle-axed and gray. Betrayed. Abandoned. Sometimes in her night classes there were divorced women who had come back to school. They had a look about them. A little beaten around the edges. Nervous. Fine lines around their pursed mouths, so they appeared as if they'd been smoking two packs of cigarettes every day since they were twelve years old. Usually the women were bright but overanxious. When they responded in class, their answers spilled over into personal anecdotes inappropriate to the discussion, going on until Julia could see the other students giving each other smirky, sidelong glances. Sometimes Julia wanted to walk over to one of these women, to place a hand on her shoulder and calm her down. She wanted to say, "It's all right. You don't have to say *everything* all at once."

Now she wondered if she would become like these women, all wound up and frantic to tell her story.

And she was so suspicious all the time. Like the other day in the library, when Alice Blevins walked by and actually seemed to jump away, scurrying into the women's bathroom before Julia could even say hello. Could Tyler have had an affair with Alice Blevins, Julia thought? Alice Blevins, so earnest and plain, with her starched, crisp blouses and sensible shoes?

Yet Alice and Tyler had been friendly since they served together on the Board of Quartets, the college chamber music program. Julia knew that sometimes they had lunch together. Alice Blevins and Tyler, Julia thought, the print of the article she had been reading beginning to swim like tiny fish before her eyes. Could Alice Blevins have been one of Tyler's "other women"? The need to find out who the other women were obsessed her.

"I want to know who else Tyler was sleeping with," Julia said, pushing back the plate of pancakes.

Fran blotted her lips and looked thoughtful. She filled her cup with more coffee. "What about Carlotta Figueroa?" she asked finally.

As soon as Julia heard the name, a flush of perspiration broke out across her face.

Fran looked up, alert. "Sorry. She was the first that came to mind. What do you think?"

Some years before, Carlotta appeared at Stimpson as a visiting poet. Originally from Chile, she had been run out of her country when she was in her twenties because of her politics and her courage to speak out. At least that was *her* view. She was also the only woman who showed up to teach class during the midwestern winter wearing a dress that revealed cleavage.

"Remember she wrote that poem and dedicated it to Tyler at a reading? That sappy one, about moonlight reflecting on someone's wounded alabaster thighs?" Fran asked. "And that red velvet dress that went practically to her nipples?"

Carlotta was always saying "Latino" this and "Latina" that, as if she were in some kind of special sorority and everyone else was a hopeless, passionless Americano.

"Tyler loved her poetry," Julia said, sipping her coffee. "He said that her poetry best exemplified the South American sensibility of magic realism."

"I do miss those dinner parties," Fran admitted. "Her Cajun shrimp, especially. God, and that caramel flan she made with the Frangelico." Fran was practically smacking her lips. "So do you think that she and Tyler . . .?"

Julia recalled a dinner party at Carlotta's with Fran and Damian, and George Lawson with one of his long-suffering dates. And a couple of handsome Mexican students who gazed limpid-eyed at Carlotta across the table. Because of Damian and George Lawson there was a lot of drinking, loud talk, sexual innuendo. Julia remembered bringing some dishes into the kitchen as Carlotta was taking the flan out of the refrigerator. She turned and said, "You know, Julia, American women really don't know how to please their men." With a smug smile, she licked a dollop of custard from her finger.

Julia didn't know what to say. All night Carlotta had been flirting with Tyler and laughing, it seemed, at jokes which only the two of them thought were funny. Fran, coming through the swinging doors, answered, "Seems like an overvalued skill to me." She stood in front of Julia as if she were a school crossing guard protecting a young charge. "How lucky in love have you been, Carlotta?" Fran asked.

Carlotta had stared back boldly. "I have had many fascinating men in my time. But I will never marry. Do you know why?"

"Why?" Julia said over Fran's shoulder. Fran was a few inches shorter, and her curly hair tickled Julia's chin.

"Because," Carlotta replied, her black eyes flashing, "simply because no one man could ever satisfy all the different parts of me. Carlotta the woman. Carlotta the child—"

Fran nudged Julia, saying loud enough for Carlotta to hear, "Why is she speaking about herself in the third person?"

Carlotta was on a roll: "Carlotta the whore. Carlotta the revolutionary. Carlotta the poetess—"

"Poet*ess!*" Fran had said. "Poetess?"

"I am a poetess." Carlotta seemed dreamy. "And a romantic."

"She is a dip-shit," Fran had whispered in Julia's ear.

Now Julia pictured Tyler in bed with Carlotta, her dark hair spread like a fan across the pillow, Carlotta whispering a line from one of her magically realistic poems into Tyler's ear.

"Julia, are you all right?" Fran asked, reaching her hand across the table.

Julia straightened up and rolled her napkin into a ball. "I'm going to be fine." She picked up the check. "My treat," Julia said, leading the way past the truckers at the counter and the old farmers in seed corn caps in the booths along the wall.

"I'm worried about you," Fran said when they got out to their cars.

"You needn't be," Julia said quickly, kissing Fran good-bye.

Julia started the car with a roar, feeling suddenly a rush of anger so burning and raw that she peeled out of the parking lot like a teenager.

8

On a Saturday night around eight, just three weeks into the most peculiar living arrangement of her life, Julia was deciding whether or not to rent a movie when Tyler called from the office wanting to talk. "We hardly see each other anymore," he said, sounding soft and sad on the phone. "Living in the same house. It's ridiculous, Julia."

They had been keeping their distance from each other. He slept in the study, and by the time he got up the girls had left for school and Julia was off to the library. There were infrequent, quick dinners with the girls. Then Tyler went out—she didn't ask where. If he was home, then Julia would go to Fran's or would read in her room. She did as he wished. She did not tell anyone about her marital problems, except for Fran and her therapist. She gave him "space." Space in fact was what she pictured around him, floating him away from her, encapsulated in a big, empty bubble.

"What do you want to talk about?" she asked, her tone guarded. She had done little socially in the past three weeks, though her return to Friday club the day before went more easily than she thought it would. All her friends said how they missed seeing her for the last few weeks, and then everything seemed perfectly normal.

"I'd like to work out some sort of short-range plan, set some objectives," Tyler said.

"Tyler, why do you have to sound like an education teacher?" She knew she was turning him off. He hated when she was sarcastic like Fran. She couldn't help herself.

Tyler ignored the jab. "Are the girls there?"

"Caty's here. McBeth is at work."

"McBeth?"

"Never mind." It was Caty who coined the nickname when Beth began her job at McDonald's (poor Beth, who had burn marks up and down her arms from turning fish fillets). Caty would leave messages for Julia at the McLibrary to tell her she'd gone to the McMall with her McFriends.

"Well, we could meet someplace, then," Tyler said.

"All right, then." They talked for a while about where to go, then some more about the girls. He asked about her work.

"All right, Tyler," Julia finally said. "I'll see you soon."

"Twenty minutes," Tyler reminded her.

As soon as she hung up the phone, Julia spun around, went upstairs to wash, brush her teeth, put on makeup. "Why am I doing this?" she said aloud, as an unsteady hand applied eye makeup. Why was she getting ready as if Tyler were a date? They were going to meet at The Hull, a sports bar on the other side of town where Julia wouldn't know anyone.

She tried on a dress that Beth got for eight dollars at Pier One. It was a short black T-shirt dress, with a woven purple belt. She went into Caty's room. "What do you think? Too young?"

"Just a sec," Caty said into the phone. She was stretched out on her bed amidst a jumble of clothes and books and papers, polishing her toenails the color of cotton candy. The phone was always attached to one ear, her natural state, so Julia did not think to excuse herself. "Too young for what?" Caty looked approvingly at her mother. "You look great, Mom. My mom looks great," Caty repeated into the phone. "She's wearing my sister's black mini."

"It's not really a mini," Julia said, tugging the material down around her knees.

"Want to wear these?" Caty stretched, searching through a pile of jewelry on her side table and came up with a pair of silver earrings with black beads on the ends. "They look great with that dress. My mother looks totally hot tonight," Caty said into the phone.

"Who are you talking to?" Julia asked, putting on the earrings.

"Tammy and Bridget and Amber."

"At once?"

"Bridg is at Tammy's. We're conference calling." Into the phone, Caty said, "My mother still doesn't know how to use conference calling."

"Beth is at work," Julia said. "I'll be back in a couple of hours, I guess."

"Where are you going?"

"I'm meeting Daddy downtown for a drink," Julia said casually as she left the room.

"Meeting my *father* for a *drink*," she heard Caty say. "Weird."

What was weird was to be with someone she knew so intimately and see him apart from her, a stranger. That would happen sometimes when Julia would see Tyler on campus, walking across the quad; he'd be in a trench coat, swinging his briefcase, and for the moment she'd think, "What a handsome man," before she realized who he was, that he was Tyler, her husband. There was something momentarily exciting about seeing him that way—as a stranger.

Now it happened when she spotted him in the bar, only the strange part didn't turn into recognizable delight. Tyler's physical being was the same, but now she saw him differently, as in a movie when you realize that someone ordinary is really inhabited by an alien.

She was late by more than twenty minutes, having had some trouble finding the place. The Hull was one of those hole-in-the-wall bars that you have to know about to find; she had driven up and down the street before seeing the sign, a fancy scripted neon that was difficult to read. Tyler's car was already in the lot, and seeing it made her heart start to pound. She still had some of Fran's Valium but decided against taking it with a drink.

A row of men sat at the bar, all with their faces upturned, fixed on the television that loomed over the bar. They were watching a baseball game, and Tyler looked to be just another guy in the row, drinking beer, watching the game. Everyone at the bar seemed to be above average size. Thick-thighed, they claimed their stools, their broad backs forming an impenetrable line. Tyler was sitting between two huge men who looked like construction workers. He was wearing a navy T-shirt and shorts.

Feeling overdressed in Beth's black dress, Julia stared at the back of Tyler's head for a while. His hair was growing long. Blond curls were beginning to form around the collar of his shirt.

"Would you like to sit down?" She heard a voice at her elbow. Looking down, she realized she had been standing next to an occupied table, her hand resting on the back of someone's chair. A woman was there and two men. The man looking up at her was round-faced and pleasant. The three of them smiled expectantly. Each had a salt-rimmed glass, and in the middle of the table was a pitcher of something pink and frothy.

"Oh, no. Thank you." Julia took her hand from the man's chair and held it up in protest. "There's someone here. . . ." She pointed in the general direction of the bar.

"The story of my life!" the round-faced man said, and the woman broke into a peal of giggles, as if this was an extraordinarily funny comment.

"Julia, I'm over here." Tyler signaled from across the bar. "Can you get us a table in the back?" He gestured to a dark corner beyond the pinball machines, then up to the television. "It's bases loaded. I just want to see this pitch."

Julia went to the bar, ordered a bourbon and water, paid for it, and went to find a table. Walking past Tyler, she heard him remark to the man next to him something about the pitcher's arm, how it was all used up. The man nodded gravely and gulped what remained of his beer.

She sat at the table in the back, sipping her drink and trying to soften the way her mouth had involuntarily tightened, to ease her face into a soft mask of repose. By the time Tyler had turned from the game and come over to the table, she had almost finished the drink.

"Want another?" Tyler said before he even sat down.

"Sure. Bourbon and water."

"I know," Tyler said, smiling slightly. Bourbon and water was always her barroom drink. When he returned with the drink and a basket of buttered popcorn, she was feeling more relaxed. "Feels funny," he said, sliding into the seat across from her at a table so small that their knees bumped. "To meet like this in a bar. What did you tell the girls?"

"Only that I was going to meet you, that we were going to talk."

"You look nice," Tyler said, letting his gaze wander slowly over her.

"Thanks." Julia reached over and took a handful of popcorn and chewed mechanically, waiting for him to make the first move.

"We need to talk about what's going to happen. Some long-range plans," Tyler went on.

"I thought you wanted some time." She chewed the popcorn

slowly and took another sip of her drink. The guys at the bar cheered and Tyler turned for a moment to look. "You're the one who said we shouldn't rush into anything. Like separation or divorce," she added quietly.

"Right. That's right," he said, nodding vigorously. "But that's why we need help now. Before it gets *too* late. We need help in some of the decisions that we're going to be making."

"What decisions?" Julia asked. There was an undercurrent of manic energy in the way Tyler was acting, his jaw so firmly set that the muscles danced in his cheek. He scared her a little.

"I want us to go to a therapist, a counselor. Christ, a shrink, a minister, I don't care. *Someone*. We have to see someone to help work this out. To make this manageable, don't you agree? I feel so . . . unsettled. I haven't been sleeping well. I wake up in the night after a couple of hours. It's so painful." Tyler put his head in his hands for a few seconds.

"Yes, it is. It's very painful," Julia said stiffly.

"I'm a mess," Tyler said, his face suddenly tear-streaked. "Damn, Julia, I'm so sorry. I'm not an insensitive asshole. You know that, don't you? Don't you think I recognize what I put you through? I thought it would pass, this thing with Lynette, like the others. I thought it would be an infatuation, really. It wasn't passing, and then you had to go and find out. Rotten luck," Tyler said. His body seemed to shrink down, settling under a gray gloom. "I guess we do need some counseling."

Julia didn't exactly know what he was aiming at. She didn't know if he wanted them to go to counseling together to try to save the marriage, or go for counseling to work out an amicable separation.

He reached across the table and took her hand. His own was dry and hot, callused on the palm from all the weight lifting. Tyler looked so intensely into her eyes that she dropped her gaze down at the table. There were initials carved into the wood and an irregularly shaped heart.

"You were right, Julia," Tyler said. "I was sick. I did a lot of things to hurt you, but in the end I only hurt myself." When he looked up, his eyes glowed with tears.

For a second she wanted to hold him, to put her arms around him and smell the back of his neck, but the feeling passed quickly like the faintest breeze. "What do you mean you *were* sick?" she said.

"Well, recognizing something is wrong is the first step to getting healthy. That's obvious, Julia. I'm getting healthy now. I'm seeing a wonderful therapist. She's more than an hour away, almost into Springfield, but, believe me, it's well worth the drive. I like the drive, actually. It gives me a chance to listen to some tapes and contemplate some of what's been going in my life."

"Who recommended this therapist?"

Tyler grinned, then gave a hollow little laugh. "You're not going to believe it. I mean, I'm going to tell you because that's one of the things I'm working on, I'm not going to lie to you anymore. About anything. I made a promise to myself. No more lying." He looked up proudly, as if waiting for praise.

"That's good." She wanted to ask now about the other women. Who else had he ever slept with?

"Well, I know, this is just crazy." Tyler began to laugh again.

"Tyler, what's so funny?"

He leaned closer and she could smell the mix of beer and Zest soap. "Lynette's mother," he said, breaking into a grin.

"Lynette's mother?"

"Lynette's mother is a psychiatric nurse in Chicago. She gave Lynette the name of this therapist." Tyler looked pleased at this revelation and downed the rest of his beer. "I'm having a diet Coke. Can I get you anything?" he asked, getting up from the table.

"Lynette's *mother?*" Julia repeated. "Lynette's *mother* recommended a therapist for you?"

"Be right with you," Tyler said, walking jauntily up to the bar. Julia watched Tyler standing casually at the bar, watching the game. He said something to one of the men he had been sitting next to and they both laughed. Then he paid and came back to the table. "I've been drinking diet pop and the aftertaste doesn't get to me anymore," he said, taking a swig before he sat down.

"Excuse me," Julia said, trying to collect her thoughts. "You mean Lynette's *mother* knows that her daughter's lover is a middle-aged *married* man who was her *professor* and so she recommended a therapist for him."

Tyler gave a wan, slightly bored smile. "Not exactly."

"What exactly?"

"Hey, listen, Julia," Tyler said, his voice rising to an angry pitch. "I said I wasn't going to lie to you anymore. Okay, so I'm not. But that doesn't mean that you're entitled to know every goddamned little thing that goes on in my life. For your information, Lynette told her that this was for a good *friend* of hers—which by the way, *I am,"* Tyler said, scowling. "And she didn't make a big deal about it, all right? Jesus, you're so goddamned controlling!" Tyler pounded the table with his fist, and Julia saw the round-faced man look over at them.

"Please don't make a scene," she said softly.

"You're the one who's driving me to it. Always with your incessant questions, poking around in things that aren't your business. You never let up, do you? You're relentless!"

"I'm sorry," Julia said, cowed, feeling suddenly as if she could start crying and not be able to stop. "Oh, God." She closed her eyes for a second and took a couple of deep breaths.

"Look, Julia," Tyler said. "Honey." In a split second his voice was tender, seductive. "I want us to go together for counseling. If we're going to make it at all, we need to make that effort. We'll never have the marriage that we used to have. You know that. But maybe we can have a better, stronger one."

"So, we'll go together to this therapist that Lynette's mother recommended," Julia said miserably.

"Well, no. Not to her. I've talked about it with her, and I'd

like to take you to meet her, but she doesn't think it's such a
hot idea for us both to see her. She has my trust now and she's
my advocate. Bringing you into the picture would drastically
alter the interaction, would destroy the balance Velma and I
have created.''

''Velma?''

''She's from Chile. Actually, you want to hear something
funny?'' Tyler leaned forward, his face animated. ''Velma knew
Carlotta Figueroa. Remember Carlotta, the poet who was visiting here years ago?''

Julia nodded.

''Well, this is really a coincidence. Velma and Carlotta went
to the same high school. They graduated together in the same
high school class!''

''Amazing,'' Julia said. She looked at Tyler, boyish and
enthused, wondering how Carlotta Figueroa was brought up in
counseling. Did he reveal to Velma the therapist that her old
high school chum was also his former lover? Or was it just a
case of: ''Oh, you're from Chile . . . do you know . . .?''

''But you can understand Velma's point. How she doesn't
think it would be a good idea for both of us to see her together,''
Tyler said.

''Of course.'' Julia finished her drink, feeling more and more
awful. Carlotta Figueroa and Alice Blevins and Lynette and
her mother and all of Tyler's other women starting filling up
the room, elbowing her from either side of the table, sucking
up all the air in the room. ''So probably it wouldn't be a good
idea to see Colleen, my therapist, either,'' Julia said. ''I could
ask her to recommend someone, though.''

''Great, okay, let's do it,'' Tyler said, rubbing his hands
enthusiastically. ''You get the name, try to set something up.''
He reached across the table and squeezed her arm.

''What about Lynette?'' Julia said.

''What about her?''

"Well, I mean, you'll have to tell her that we're going for counseling, that you can't see her anymore."

Tyler chewed his lip thoughtfully but said nothing.

"You have to tell her," Julia said. Tyler looked up at the television again but did not answer. "Tyler?" Julia moved her head to get into his line of vision. "You have to tell her now. Before we start counseling."

"Julia, I can't do that now," Tyler said, obviously pained. "The whole reason she's staying in town this summer is because of me. She planned on being with me this summer."

"So?"

"Julia, please, I can't do this so abruptly. I don't want to hurt her like this—"

"Tyler." Now it was her own voice that made the round-faced man turn around. "What about hurting *me?*"

"Don't you think that I live with that every day, Julia? Don't you think that the knowledge of how I hurt you all makes me feel like shit?" Tyler said. They both sat for a while, silent. Julia played with a loose strand of wicker on the popcorn basket, which was empty now. Finally Tyler spoke, his voice heavy with a worn, sad patience. "I want to wait awhile before I say anything to Lynette. I'm not in good shape, Julia. You hate me. You don't want to be with me now. Lynette loves me and she's my life buoy now. I can't tell her yet."

Julia did not, could not speak.

"Tell you what. Let's give it the summer. If, by the end of the summer, we're really going somewhere with this counseling, and I feel we can really make it, why then I'll tell Lynette I'll never see her again, all right? I'll tell her I'll never, ever see her again, I promise. But Julia, you have to understand," Tyler added. He looked pleading, smiling his sad, sweet puppy-dog smile. "What if I tell Lynette that I'm not going to see her anymore and then it doesn't work out with you and me? What then? Julia, why then I'd be left with no one."

9

Julia drove through Campustown, looking for the Kinko's sign, next to which were the Greenbriar Apartments where Lynette Macalvie lived.

Confrontation was not usually Julia's style. But the conversation with Tyler at The Hull had set something off in her and she was feeling more like Fran—impetuous, spontaneous, a little bit crazy. Fran was always looming toward or coming to the end of some personal crisis, though most of it was not Fran's fault: the deaths of her parents; the tipped uterus that made it impossible to carry a baby to term; Damian. The small stuff—missed planes, lost car keys, overdrawn accounts—was perhaps her own making. "Only Fran," Tyler would say, whenever Fran called, upset and urgent—like the time she sent her whole Thanksgiving dinner party to the hospital with food poisoning because she defrosted the bird for two days on her kitchen counter.

Julia was not like that. Never had been. She was a cautious and responsible parent, careful and competent scholar. What would be words to describe her? Thoughtful. Reasonable. So why was she doing this now? At eight o'clock on a sunny Sunday morning at the end of May, after a run, a shower, with her hair clean and fluffed, Beth's black dress back on from the night before, Caty's same earrings ("Oh, my mother looks so hot!"), with Tyler asleep in the study (she could hear his even breathing through the door, though he had not come home with her from The Hull); why was she parking the car, going to the door of the Greenbriar Apartments and scanning the mailboxes for the name Lynette Rae Macalvie? To do what? To say what?

The Greenbriar looked shabby, student-worn, in need of patchwork and paint. In a large front hall were about a dozen bicycles locked to a steel bar; a few yellowing newspapers littered the stair. At this hour the building was quiet as a library. Julia started at one end of a bank of dented metal mailboxes whose names were mostly illegible, smudged with age, taped over, or blank.

Just then a boy in a faded muscle shirt bounded down the stairs carrying a basket of laundry. He paused, setting the basket down at the end of the hallway. "Shit," he said aloud, heading back up the stairs. Then, to Julia, "Forgot my soap."

She was still there, crouched at the lower mailboxes, when he came down again, carrying a very small box of laundry detergent. "Can I help you?" he asked politely. He was young, perhaps not even twenty years old. Soft, light hairs, like down, appeared on the side of his smooth cheek. Julia, picturing Tyler coming to this place, coming here to this apartment filled with young people like this eager, fresh-faced boy, felt herself blush. "I'm looking for Lynette Macalvie's apartment. She doesn't seem to . . ." Julia paused, pointing to the mailboxes. "She doesn't have her name here."

"What's the name again?" The boy stood next to her and squinted across the row of mailboxes.

"Lynette Rae Macalvie," Julia said, adding the middle name on Fran's class list.

The boy looked puzzled, shook his head. "What's she look

like?" Julia began to describe Lynette from the pictures in Tyler's desk. She got no further than "blond" when two girls came in looking like yesterday's party, sour and hung over. "Hey, you know Lynette somebody?" the boy in the muscle shirt asked.

"Macalvie," Julia added.

One girl shrugged and kept on walking. The other called over her shoulder, "She's on this floor." She pointed to a heavily dented door at the end of the hall. "The last apartment."

"Thank you," Julia said to the boy, who picked up his basket and trudged off. Through the door at the end of a long hall there were two apartments, 1-E and 1-F, right and left; neither door had a name on it, and Julia paused, wondering what to do next. The hall smelled like air freshener and old socks. She looked down at the black dress, brushing her chest and shoulders with her hand and, after a few moments, reached toward the left door and rang the bell; its *ding-dong* was surprisingly loud. She waited a respectable interval before adding a knock. Nothing. She was just about to turn and try the other door when she heard movement inside the apartment. "Just a minute," called out a sleepy female voice. Footsteps. The unbolting of locks. The door opened just a few inches, a round, blue eye appearing in the chained space between the door and the frame, a sleeve of something fuzzy and pink. "Yes?"

"Lynette? Are you Lynette Macalvie?" Julia was surprised at how friendly she sounded, as if she were tentatively identifying an old acquaintance.

"Yes?" The blue eye did not blink.

"I'm Julia Markem," Julia said, moving slightly toward the chained space. "I'd like to talk to you."

No answer while the door closed, unbolted, opened again. Standing before Julia was a young woman in a pink robe, her face still puffed with sleep, her blond hair matted limply against her head. "Come in," she said flatly, ushering Julia into a small living room furnished wall to wall with wicker: wicker couch, wicker chairs, wicker tables; wicker baskets of every imaginable size and shape covered an entire wall. A large wicker chair, hung by ropes, dominated the wall by the window. Lynette sat in that, curling her legs under her, and stared at Julia expectantly.

For a few moments Julia simply stared back, so overcome was she with the fact of her actual presence in this apartment, invading Tyler's secret place and secret life. Julia was taken aback, too, at the girl's total ordinariness, at the absolute improbability of *this* girl's being the object of Tyler's infatuation; this pink-robed girl the reason why Julia was now in therapy, why her family would be forever changed.

"I thought you'd want to see me eventually," Lynette said. "Tyler said you wouldn't want to, but I thought it would be a good idea for us to meet." She tucked the robe under her knees and folded her hands in her lap. The chair swung slightly. There was something matter-of-fact, even schoolmarmish about her. She *was* blond, a pale wheaty blond—yes, that was the first thing, maybe the only thing distinguishable about her. Her features were soft, undefined, and a little pad of fat was beginning around her chin. Her skin was milk white, but blotchy across her neck and chest.

Lynette saw Julia squinting at her as the light from the morning sun came through the window. "I'll pull the shade on that," she said helpfully, getting up from the chair and tightening the robe around her.

Whether from the morning run or nerves, or sitting amidst all that wicker, Julia's mouth was suddenly very dry. She wondered if Lynette would offer some refreshment or whether in this circumstance of an uninvited visit to the lover of one's husband, it was appropriate to ask for something to drink.

Lynette sat, self-possessed and calm. The only hints of stress were the red blotches that spread along her white, white neck and across one cheek. She looked intently at Julia, her fleshy chin held at a defiant angle. "Tyler and I love each other. We *really* do."

"Oh," Julia said.

"In many ways, you weren't there for him," Lynette went on. "Tyler is a talented, unusual person. I don't think you know that anymore. Or at least, you don't show that to him."

Despite the heat, Julia felt a sudden shiver. There was something more than brazen about Lynette, something—Julia couldn't quite put her finger on it—something chilling, almost predatory. Underneath the blond hair, the fuzzy robe, the soft white skin, there was something else: a focus, deliberate and cold. Julia imagined herself in Lynette's place: being a student, confronted by the wife of twenty years. In that position, Julia would have been ashamed, crying, apologetic. But there were no apologies on Lynette's part. Not even a hint of one.

"Well, I guess Tyler didn't tell you, then," Julia said evenly.

"Tell me what?" Lynette raised an eyebrow, looked skeptical.

"He was here last night, wasn't he? You did talk?" Julia asked.

Lynette set her jaw but said nothing.

"Oh, it really doesn't matter now, does it? I know he was here last night, Lynette. I'm just surprised that he didn't say anything to you." Julia shifted her position on the wicker couch. It was uncomfortable against her back, like leaning on sticks. Gazing down at the floral-patterned cushion, Julia wondered if Tyler and Lynette had ever made love on this uncomfortable couch.

"Tell me what?" Lynette asked again, wary.

"About the counseling."

"Oh, I *know* Tyler's been going to counseling," Lynette said smugly. "I got him the counselor's name."

"I don't mean the counselor your *mother* suggested," Julia said, watching Lynette's face.

"What are you talking about, then?" The rash on Lynette's neck reddened significantly.

"That Tyler wants me to go with him to see a marriage counselor this summer. He wants us to work together on the marriage." Julia paused. "That if he feels it's going to work, he's never going to see you again." She said the last statement with a certain emphasis.

Lynette focused a sharp, killing gaze across the room but remained placid. "I don't believe you," she whispered hoarsely. "You're lying."

"Lying," Julia said evenly, "is not what I've been about these past few months."

"Tyler loves me."

"I'm sure you think he does."

"He does."

"And he might even think he does, too."

"I don't believe you," Lynette said again, her mouth tight. It was a small, mean mouth on one so young and blond.

"Why don't you give him a call?" Julia suggested. "Go ahead. Call him at home. He's there. I just left him sleeping a little while ago."

"What if the children answer?" Lynette appeared troubled. A small, pink-tipped tongue rested thoughtfully on her upper lip. "Tyler told me never to call him at home."

"The girls are still sleeping, too. Besides, they'd never get up to answer our phone. They have a teen line."

"Oh."

"Call him. See what he has to say." Julia felt strangely exhilarated.

"I think I will!" Lynette said, as if the idea had suddenly come to her on her own. Uncurling herself from the chair, she moved quickly, a thick, pink blur, across the room to the kitchen. "Um, excuse me, Julia," Lynette said, popping her head back through the doorway. "What's your home number?"

At ten o'clock that same morning, Julia sat in Fran's kitchen drinking mango-pineapple juice made with Fran's new electric juicer. "I think you really should get one," Fran was saying.

"You're not eating right, you say it's hard for food to go down, and these little babies are great!" Fran patted a gleaming white machine which looked as if it belonged in a dentist's office.

"This is delicious," Julia admitted, pouring herself another glass. "Franny, really, I think this is a good ad. You should send it." Between them on Fran's cluttered kitchen table sat crumpled sheets of paper and one with a few paragraphs in Fran's handwriting.

"It took me a long time to write it. God, I worked longer on this fucking ad than I did my last article. I don't know, Julia." Fran shook her head, her black hair loose around her shoulders. "I mean, it's been a dry spell, that's for sure, but I'm just not sure about this. I do know that if I keep going this long without a man, George Lawson's going to start looking good to me." She, too, was in a robe this morning, a bright purple caftan with gold braiding. Julia thought Fran looked exotic, like an Egyptian princess.

"George would be thrilled," Julia said.

"Please, Julia. Even if he dried out, the thought is chilling." Fran leaned across the table conspiratorially. "I just heard the secretaries talking yesterday. He might lose his job, you know. They're doing an investigation in the dean's office, looking into all the time he's spent in rehab."

"I know. Tyler's on the review committee. He's quite uncomfortable about that."

"Because they're friends?"

"More because George knows that Tyler wants to teach the poetry seminars. I wouldn't say they're friends exactly." Although George and Tyler went out together sometimes, Julia sensed, in fact, that George had a deeply nourished resentment against Tyler. Jealousy, she had always thought.

"Tyler should resign from the committee," Fran said. "I mean, it isn't exactly kosher. George and Tyler do see each other socially."

"He may be off the committee, for all I know. I haven't spoken to Tyler recently about it."

"George won't quit drinking. He's going to drink himself into the ground." Fran stopped, catching Julia's eye. Both of them knew that the other was thinking of Damian, dead before he was forty-five of viral hepatitis. "Hey," Fran said, "do you know that that maniac Bill Chandler just wrote me?" Bill Chandler was a magazine writer turned survivalist whom Fran had met on a canoe trip. He was also an alcoholic. "Look at this." Fran retrieved a letter from under a pile of papers. "Even from the handwriting on the envelope, you can see how sick he still is."

"You can see how sick he is. I can't," Julia said. One of Fran's interests and talents was graphology. She had even taken a correspondence course. Often, at parties, people would ask her to analyze their handwriting.

"All those tightly closed *a*'s and *o*'s." Fran shivered. "This is the handwriting of a very fucked-up guy."

"Well, I like your ad," Julia said, tapping her finger on the lined paper. "I think it's very clever."

"Clever doesn't attract men, though," Fran said. "What they want is a twenty-five-year-old with big tits and long legs, who gives good head and doesn't talk back. Look at this." Fran held up a section of the newspaper which had three full pages of personal ads. "Listen to this one: 'Successful, fiftyish and fit CEO wants playful, statuesque woman, 20–34, with model good looks and a sense of humor to sail with him on a trip to the Bahamas, for companionship, long walks on the beach.'" Fran made a face. "A *twenty*-year-old! This guy, probably bald with a bellyful of gas and a face like an old sneaker, wants a *twenty*-year-old with model good looks to bang on the beach. She'll need more than a sense of humor for that!" Fran lifted her glass of mango-pineapple juice with great élan and took a healthy swig. "I don't know why I'm doing this anyway," she said, looking again at the ads.

"Yours is a good one," Julia said, encouraging. She cleared her throat and read aloud: " 'Lively and literate, semibeautiful professional woman, original nose. Wants well-adjusted man, 35–50, who can have a good laugh without bad-mouthing his ex-wife. No Republicans, please.'" Julia looked thoughtful. "Do you think you should keep the part about the Republicans? I mean, isn't that cutting your chances by more than half?"

Fran said that if Julia were single as long as she was and had dated as many creeps who voted for Reagan and Bush as she had, she wouldn't have to ask that question.

"Anyway, a Republican with a good sense of humor, some-one who could laugh at himself, he might even answer this ad." Fran looked over the paper, pencil against her cheek. "Maybe I should add, 'Alcoholics need not apply.' Shit, I know they will anyway. Alcoholics always find me. I must give off a scent or something." Fran pulled up the purple caftan and sniffed an arm. "Maybe I smell like Johnny Walker Black."

"I still can't believe you actually went over to see her," Fran said later. "That's real chutzpah, kid." She was dressed now, having thrown on cutoff jeans, a red T-shirt, and sandals; she was standing at the stove, stirring potatoes and onions and bits of honeyed ham.

Julia protested. Really, she didn't want anything. The juice was more than enough. But it was almost noon and the smells filling up the kitchen were making her hungry.

"How about some melted cheese over this?" Fran reached her hand into a pile of shredded cheddar.

Julia answered that she didn't know why she went to Lynette Macalvie's apartment. Curiosity, maybe? The desire for revenge?

" 'Revenge is sweet. Especially to women.' Who said that?" Fran asked.

"You just did."

"I think it was Byron." Fran turned off the stove, picked a piece of ham out of the pan and popped it into her mouth. "He sure died young." She took two plates from the cupboard and piled them with potatoes. "You do know that when Tyler finds out what you told her, he's going to be more than mildly pissed? Boy, what I wouldn't give to see his face when she tells him."

Fran put the ads aside, and they went back to talking about what had happened that morning. Julia had left nothing out: the boy doing his laundry, the wicker, the pink robe, Lynette's rash. Of course, Fran was disappointed when Julia revealed that Tyler had not answered the phone. "He might have been in the shower," Julia told her. "Or maybe he unplugged the phone in the study and was still sleeping."

"At any rate, she'll get in touch with him today for sure. He's going to know pretty soon."

"Thank you," Julia said as Fran put the plate before her. She brought a small forkful of food to her lips. "This is delicious, Franny."

"The secret is the chili peppers. Sliced thin and put in after the potatoes are done. Didn't I ever make these for you before?" Julia shook her head. "They were Damian's specialty. He added tabasco, too, but I think that's too much. Of course, that was Damian. If it's worth doing it's worth overdoing." Fran sighed, getting up to pour two coffees. She took hers light with lots of sugar. "Boy, I'd love to be there when Lynette tells him," she said again.

Now, several hours after the adrenaline rush that accompanied the meeting with Lynette, Julia was beginning to have some doubts. Or maybe it was fear. Always, she had been wary to risk Tyler's wrath. "I'm afraid something is going to happen," Julia said in a whisper.

"Something already *did* happen," Fran reminded her.

*　　*　　*

Later that afternoon Julia took Caty shopping for a bathing suit and sleep-walked through the mall, going into each dressing room, coming out again. "Mom, are you *listening* to me?" Caty asked at one point, exasperated. "How do you think this looks?" Caty was standing in front of a mirror in a white bikini with a fluffy seat that made Julia think of her as a fat-bottomed toddler, waddling down the pier at the lake in Maine.

At home, Beth had friends over. They had ordered in a pizza and were spread across the living room studying for finals. Music, of course, was blaring. Julia went over to turn it down. "I thought you'd like this, Mrs. Markem," one of the boys said. He had shoe-polish black hair, which was cut off in a wedge just below his ear. "It's the Black Crows. Very sixties."

"Daddy called," Beth said. She was lying flat on the couch dangling a slice of pizza over her head and catching the dripping cheese in her mouth. Just as Julia was about to warn her, a piece plopped across her chest. "Oops!" Beth said, lifting up the material of her shirt to suck it. "He's at George Lawson's," she continued. "He said something about George not being in very good shape and he might stay with him tonight."

"Well, when is George Lawson *ever* in very good shape?" Caty said, snorting. She had never forgiven George for throwing up in their downstairs bathroom after a party a few years back. It was she, coming down to breakfast the next morning, who discovered the mess.

"Caty!" Julia reprimanded.

"Well, you know it's true. Daddy said George might even be fired," Caty said, running up to her room to catch a ringing phone.

Tyler didn't come home for supper and didn't call again. Julia watched "Sixty Minutes," read the *New York Times Magazine*, and spoke to her sister, Margaret, in Maine. "Everything's fine," she said, feeling her stomach tighten at the deception.

She wondered if she had stayed home like Margaret and married a local boy, how her life would have turned out. Just a few years ago, Margaret and Sam had built their own cabin on the lake, an A-frame, the front all glass on two levels in a kind of chalet style. Margaret and Sam had designed it from a kit, adding their own personal touches: a walkway of potted geraniums, curlicued wooden balconies, Tudor window boxes. Tyler called the architecture "Yodel-ay-he-hoo contemporary."

Julia asked questions about Margaret's boys, the weather, local gossip.

"Is everything all right?" Margaret asked. "You sound funny."

Julia felt suddenly overpowered by lethargy. "I'm fine," she assured her sister. "Just tired, is all."

"Well, good night," Margaret said, signing off.

10

When Julia called the next afternoon, Fran was painting a chest of drawers she had found at a garage sale. Her sister's children were coming for a visit at the end of July, and she needed more storage space. "I tried you a couple of hours ago and left a message. Where were you?" Fran asked when she heard Julia's voice on the phone.

Julia sounded peculiarly distant. "It's Tyler," she said evenly.

Fran pursed her lips and waited for the new development, refraining from the sarcastic comeback: What was it he was suggesting today—that he and Julia and Lynette all go in for counseling together? Or that they all live together so he could take turns sleeping with them and reading them his poetry?

"Franny, could you meet me at the hospital? An ambulance just took Tyler to Emergency," Julia said.

"*What* did you say?" Fran asked, her voice rising, although she had heard Julia perfectly well. Her first thought was: heart attack. She had visions of Tyler hooked up to machines that beeped and blinked, keeping him and his fragile heart alive. That sort of thing was in the papers all the time. Athletes, running miles every day, biking to work, climbing mountains, and then *boom!* one day, everything explodes. The old ticker, despite the exercise and no cigarettes and low-fat everything, programmed by fate or genetics or congenital defect, gives way before you could even say "aerobic." Fran pictured it: Tyler, his wings clipped, an invalid; Tyler a stroke victim, learning how to walk again, to tie his shoes. Fran knew that Tyler, unaccustomed to being vulnerable, would make a truly terrible patient.

"Fran, are you still there?" Julia asked. There had been some sort of accident, she went on; she didn't know the details. There had been an accident in the gym. It was serious, judging from the doctor's tone. Would Fran come by the emergency entrance of the hospital to meet her?

"What kind of accident?" Fran insisted. "What happened?"

"I don't know," Julia said. "The doctor wouldn't tell me."

"What do you mean the doctor wouldn't tell you?" Fran asked, irritated by Julia's passivity. "He tells you there's an accident, wants you to drive over to the hospital like this is some sort of mystery. You could get killed driving across town all nervous and upset. Wait. Don't go anywhere. I'll come and pick you up."

"I'm all right, Fran. I can drive myself. I don't want to wait for you to come and get me," Julia said firmly.

"What could have happened?" Fran wanted to know.

"I'm going to the hospital," Julia answered.

"All right," Fran said. "I'll meet you there." She hung up, her fingers leaving little white dots of enamel on the phone, and took a couple of deep breaths. "Okay, okay," she said aloud, and started to rush wildly around the house searching for her shoes. She yanked two blouses from their hangers, putting on each before discovering one was missing a middle button, one had a stain on the collar. Why was it that she could never be dressed appropriately for an occasion so that when someone called she could just walk right out the door, simple

and clean; why was she always in overdrive, her energy ineffi-
ciently frantic? There were times she longed to be like Julia,
cool and gentile.

She put on black shorts and a purple T whose shoulder pads
needed to be cut out, having curled awkwardly after a washing.
Attempting to flatten them with the palm of one hand, she
poured a glass of orange juice with the other, spilling juice all
over the kitchen. She took one multivitamin, one Stresstabs
plus zinc before she headed out.

Sanford Greeley Hospital was across town, thirteen minutes
from Fran's house. The actual distance was shorter if she took
the Boulevard, but that route presented stop signs, and single
lanes with cars making left-hand turns. It was thirteen minutes
exactly taking old Highway 34, although the ride was one and
a half additional miles. Fran knew. How many times, through
how many failing pregnancies, had she and Damian made the
trip? Now it was past noon, and the two factories on the north
end of town were out for lunch. A steady stream cut into the
slow-moving traffic.

An accident in the gym. Fran's mind whirred. Every morning
Tyler worked out at eleven o'clock. Eleven o'clock, dependable
as the tides. Julia used to laugh. Lucky, neither of the girls was
born in the morning. They all learned, early on, to work around
Tyler's exercise schedule. Every morning at eleven (the gym
started getting crowded at noon) Tyler stretched, ran, lifted
weights, swam laps. It was a rigorous personalized program
perfected over the years, honed to produce the optimum result
for strength, endurance, flexibility. Strength, endurance, flexibility—Fran heard those words often over the years. Tyler was
evangelical when it came to exercise.

Once he had even talked to her about an exercise plan that
she could use: high-impact aerobics with muscle-strengthening
exercises, he had said, pointing to her tummy. Fuck you, she
wanted to say, but instead she had smiled and filled a loose-
leaf sheet of paper with his instructions.

Now when she pulled into the hospital parking lot, Fran felt a tightening inside her body similar to a contraction. The loss of her first baby, not the saddest for her but the most traumatic, had occurred here in the emergency lot in a burst of blood, spreading from the car seat to the pavement, running into her shoes, dripping down into the spokes of a wheelchair that someone had brought out and sat her in. She and Damian had been newly married. She was thirty years old and in love and thought then that her life was just beginning.

The doors to the emergency entrance opened with a *whoosh,* and she stepped inside to a peaceful lobby with scenic landscapes on the walls and piped-in music. They had redecorated since Fran had been here last. Gray-and-blue couches lined the waiting room, and everything was painted a cool, unpanicky blue-gray. There were a few people lolling about, reading magazines, and a woman holding a sleeping baby—no one seemed in the least state of emergency.

Fran went up to a blond nurse with owlish glasses. "Was Tyler Markem recently admitted?" Fran's voice seemed to echo in the hall. The piped-in music was playing a jazzed-up version of "Yesterday."

"Are you family?" the nurse inquired.

"Friend," Fran said. "Friend of the wife," she added as if she were going to be seated at a wedding. "I mean, his wife called and asked me to meet her here."

"I believe she's with the doctor," the nurse said kindly. "Would you like me to check for you? To see if you can go back to be with her?"

"Yes, please," Fran said, sensing that this level of politeness was really a cover for something terrible.

"You can have a seat if you like," the nurse said, walking down the hall. Fran looked over at those people sitting calmly on the blue couches and chose to remain standing, resting her elbows on the counter of the nurse's station. "All my troubles seemed so far away" was plucked out by a jazz piano with lots of syncopation. Fran's first husband, Paul Kravitz, was a jazz pianist. She had met him in a club on South Street during her first year at the University of Pennsylvania. Paul, who always reminded her of the taller Righteous Brother (and what ever happened to him, anyway?), was dark, brooding, silent—all of which she found tremendously sexy. He was married, then he was divorced, then he married Fran, then they were divorced—all of this happening in a space of two years. Eventually Fran thought of that time with Paul as less a marriage, more a long date. Even if she closed her eyes and concentrated, she could not now bring up a clear picture of Paul Kravitz in her mind's eye and saw instead a tall, dark-haired man singing "You've Lost That Loving Feeling."

"She will see you now," the blond nurse said, returning to the station; odd, Fran thought, saying "she will see you now," as if Julia, not Tyler, were the patient. "You can walk down this hall. They're in the second room on the left." The nurse pointed down a narrow corridor with rooms on either side. As Fran walked by, the nurse gave her a few consoling pats in a place where the pad had crinkled up under the T-shirt and fallen away from Fran's shoulder.

She walked quickly down the hall, looking straight ahead, and heard Julia's voice coming from the room, though Fran could not make out what she was saying. "Hi," Julia said when she saw Fran in the doorway. Julia was talking with a man dressed in green scrubs, a youngish man with a brown handlebar mustache flecked with orange. They were sitting together on a wooden bench, casually, as if they were feeding pigeons together in a park. Julia, dryeyed and composed, made introductions; Fran, who did not catch the doctor's name, extended her hand.

"I'm sorry," the doctor said to Fran. "I've just finished explaining to Mrs. Markem how the weight cut off the air supply and precipitated the death." When the doctor spoke, his mustache wiggled unevenly, dancing across his upper lip.

"*Excuse* me?" There was not another place to sit in the small room. Fran felt herself looming over the doctor, afraid she was going to fall into his lap. "What are you saying?"

"Tyler's dead," Julia said bluntly. "There was an accident in the gym. Tyler was bench-pressing and the weights fell on him, across his neck." Julia put her own hand to the front of her throat, her long, slender fingers resting lightly across her windpipe. There was something—a certain detachment, an edge—in the way Julia revealed this information that gave Fran pause.

"Oh God!" Fran unwittingly began to cry. "Oh, oh my God!" Tears, uninvited and unanticipated, began to stream down her cheeks, though there was a part of her that didn't even know why she was crying. How many times in the past few weeks had she herself said, "I'd like to kill that bastard!"? In how many fantasies was he summarily pummeled, punished, put away? But now, *dead?* All the energy and anger of the past few weeks dissipated with the awful finality of this news.

"I'm going to see him," Julia said, rising from the bench. "Would you come with me?" She took Fran's elbow as if to steady her. Julia's grip was sure and secure.

"Whatever you want," Fran said, wiping her cheek, embarrassed at her explosion while Julia maintained such composure. Julia reached next to an examination table and gave Fran a bunch of tissues. "I'll go," Fran said with as much strength as she could muster, knowing that she was supposed to be here as a support, but failing miserably.

This whole thing was throwing her for a loop. Tyler was dead. Truly and forever dead. Julia herself was calm as a madonna.

"Mr. Markem was moved to a room in the other wing," the doctor said. "I'll take you there."

They walked three abreast down the narrow hall, moving in silence. Mr. Markem indeed, Fran thought. *The body* of Mr. Markem. No more Tyler Markem. The illustrious Tyler Markem. She was not all that keen about seeing the body. Seeing the body with the life and personality and beingness of the person all sucked out so that what was left was only a representative container.

After her parents had been killed in the car accident, Fran and her sister had flown down to Mexico to identify the bodies. Her father, who had a very heavy beard, must not have shaved that morning; black-and-gray stubble flecked his cheeks. Had he convinced Sylvia (always particular about his being freshly shaven) that they were on vacation, after all, and why did he need to shave every day? Fran remembered seeing him on the slab: his jaw, bruised and blue, stuck out at an unnatural angle and his nose, smashed against the steering wheel, had been flattened so that he looked like a boxer who had just been knocked out.

Her mother, small and still, on a slab in the morgue. She was so white—as if her skin had been dusted with flour. Her hair was still perfect, a crown of black curls, the sides sprayed with something acrylic. Eyeshadow made two silver-blue moons under her brows. Fran couldn't help thinking, looking at her mother that one last time: Sylvia Meltzer in all her splendor.

"He's in here," the doctor with the orange mustache said, stopping in front of a room at the end of the hall. "If there's anything else you need," he said to Julia in a hushed voice. No, she didn't think so, Julia answered, thanking him, bidding him good-bye. Fran followed her into the room, where Tyler was laid out in a hospital bed. One hand was placed ceremoniously across his chest; the other lay restfully at his side. Fran waited, watching Julia for a sign, but Julia just stared coldly at Tyler. Then Julia pulled the sheet back, revealing Tyler's chest, the pectorals with the tight bulge that weight lifters have, the rounded curve of his muscled arms, the flat, taut abdomen. Fran pictured him alive, smiling, flexing in front of a mirror; Tyler, so proud of his broad, muscled chest with that silly weight-lifter vanity. Her eyes rested briefly on his neck, where the weights had fallen, where the bar had made a clear indentation into the skin. There were dozens of tiny red threads of broken capillaries along his cheeks and under his eyes, indicating the struggle. But his mouth, closed in repose, looked soft, the lower lip cushioned like a girl's. His eyelashes were long and fringy. Fran thought of the poem she had loved in high school, Housman's "To an Athlete Dying Young," and began to weep.

"It's very strange," Julia said after a while.

Fran looked up at her through a blur of tears. They were standing side by side, but Fran did not touch Julia, did not take her hand. "What is, sweetie?" Fran felt odd standing there by the bedside where he lay. Talking over Tyler's body this way seemed rude.

"It's just very strange. I look at him now, like this," Julia said flatly, "and I feel nothing."

Suspicion: June

11

Ordinarily Detective Frank Rhodes would not have suspected foul play in such a freakish and unfortunate accident. After all, Frank Rhodes was a man who knew about accidents and surprises: three years before, his own wife had been taken from him by such an unexpected twist of fate.

It was June then, too, thunderstorm season in the Midwest. Something was blowing up fierce that afternoon, and Carol had called him at the station to say that she was going to finish up some insurance work at the office before coming home. There was a lasagna to put in the oven. She had asked him to make a salad.

It was just the two of them then, the youngest child, Leenie, going off to college that year. At first Frank thought that he and Carol would be lonely, but it had turned out to be a wonderful time. Leisurely. Romantic, even. They went for breakfast sometimes, or after work met for pizza and talked about their day over a frosty pitcher of beer (he was still drinking then). They made love more often and went for late-night walks around the neighborhood. "You really get to know each other again," Frank told a couple of the young guys at the station.

There had been four children, born two years apart, the first one nine months after he and Carol were married. He loved the children, of course, but realized after they left how he and Carol had hardly had a minute to themselves.

He was cutting up radishes to put in the salad when he heard the crack. Carol did something fancy sometimes with radishes, making them look like roses about to bloom. He thought it was magic, the way everything she touched turned prettier in her hands. There had been hail an hour before and severe winds, but the storm had stopped by the time Carol came home.

He heard the car pull up in the driveway, the motor shut off, but then he did not hear the car door open. On public radio a man read books, and Carol sometimes sat in the car a few extra minutes to wait for him to get to the end of a chapter. Frank did not enjoy being read to like that over the radio. He grew impatient to get on with the story and did not much care for the exaggerated way the man on public radio acted out all the dialogue.

Suddenly there was an ear-splitting crack, so loud that it seemed as if the noise would shatter the kitchen counter where he stood. A crack and then a crash. Frank was wearing a striped apron and still held the knife when he raced outside to see that the walnut tree from their backyard had broken neatly in half, nearly obliterating Carol's red Ford Escort. He raced frantically around the car, calling to her, but he could not open the doors. By the time the rescue squad came, she was gone.

For at least a year he went to work feeling deadened inside; then he came home every night and drank until he passed out. He could not free himself from the bitter irony that *he* was the one who had the dangerous job; *he* was the one who had to go to work carrying a gun. And Carol—whom he always protected; whom he drove to work if it snowed; whom he

bought double-bolt locks for when he was working nights—
Carol was the one who died first. Carol, who had never done
anything more dangerous than stand in the kitchen on a step-
stool, was the one who had been killed, sitting in the driveway
of her very own house, listening to public radio.

The next fall, Leenie came home, transferring to Stimpson. She
said she was worried about him. "You drink too much, Daddy,"
she said one morning at breakfast. "You were passed out on the
couch and I couldn't get you up. You had wet your pants."

He looked across the table at the child who had always been
his favorite. Maybe because she was the youngest, the precious
last, who would forever in his mind be the baby. Not that
she liked that role much. She was small and spunky, newly
politicized from her women's studies classes at college. She
was taking a course with Professor Francine Meltzer: Race,
Class, and Gender. It really opened her eyes, she said.

"There's AA meetings at the Methodist church. I want you
to go," Leenie told him, her chin thrust in a stubborn set. She
stood by his chair, but even then, he did not have to look up
very far to meet her gaze. She was the smallest of the children,
the others, two boys and a girl, taking after his side of the
family, gangly, long-boned.

"All right," he said quietly, and he went that very night,
presented himself to a roomful of strangers. "My name is Frank
Rhodes," he said, "and I'm an alcoholic," aware how right it
felt, that most intimate introduction.

One of the things they tell you in AA is that you can't stop
drinking for someone else, but Frank Rhodes did not believe
this to be true. The image of Leenie seeing him passed out like
a common drunk, stinking of liquor and urine, shamed him so
that he made a vow in Carol's memory (she had reprimanded
him occasionally, when the drinking was in excess, but in those
days everything seemed all in good fun) that he would never
take another drink. Amazingly, he did not.

* * *

What was there to suggest that what happened to Tyler Markem in Stimpson College's gymnasium was anything but an accident, a careless and easily preventable accident? First, only the suspicions of G. P. Comstock, Stimpson's wrestling coach and Frank Rhodes's second cousin. G.P. and Frank used to belong to the volunteer fire department, when the town was still small enough to have a volunteer fire department; G.P. was also married to the daughter of Carol's boss at State Farm, and every year the three of them went on a ten-day fishing trip to Canada at the end of July.

A few days after the accident, G.P. came over to see Frank. A profile of Tyler Markem had run on the front page of the second section of the *Grandview Tribune* that evening, listing awards and accomplishments underneath a photograph of a handsome, strong-jawed man with a self-assured smile.

Now G.P. sat on Frank's front porch and scratched his head. Something was fishy, he said. Something wasn't quite right. At first, G.P. seemed most concerned about a lawsuit. Years before, a student at Stimpson had been paralyzed following a fall from a trampoline, and her parents had moved to sue the school, then settled out of court.

"I've been thinking about this since we found him," G.P. told Frank. "Thinking about how I felt strange, even then." G.P. sat in a redwood rocker, drinking a beer. It was a warm night and the mosquitoes were out in full force from all the rain they'd had in the spring. Frank lit a citronella candle, wondering as always whether they did any good; he brought G.P. another beer, himself a diet 7UP. He was proud of the fact that he could have beer in the house to offer his friends. Some of the people in AA could never do that.

"I didn't say anything to you yesterday, but I just had this *feeling* about the scene," G.P. was saying. "I mean, Markem was alone. *All* alone and bench-pressing more weight than I'd ever known him to do in his life. He usually did two-forty-five pounds, max. We were just talking about it the week before in the gym. And there he was, laid out with that bar across his throat, his eyes all bugged out. Jesus, Frank, there was over three hundred pounds there sitting on him. That poor kid that found him, a skinny guy, he couldn't get them off. Didn't matter. Markem was already dead."

Because it was right after finals and students were packing up to go home, the gym had been empty; one student who had been cleaning out his locker had found Tyler and managed to summon G.P., who called 911. When Frank had arrived, just minutes after the ambulance, Tyler Markem was already dead.

The police did the usual with someone found dead under suspicious circumstances: they dusted for prints, interviewed those who saw the deceased last. The procedure was routine because Markem was alone at the time of death. That was the only thing that made the death suspicious, as far as Frank Rhodes was concerned.

"Even two hundred forty-five pounds," Frank said now. "That's a lot to press for an average guy, isn't it?"

"Well, it's okay, I mean this guy's not your average wimp professor, he was real gung-ho for weight training. God, but three hundred pounds, right across his neck. I mean, the guy didn't have a chance," G.P. said.

Frank popped open his soda, listened to the crickets and the *swish-swish* of the cars on the highway a block away. They had been going to sell the house, he and Carol, after the new highway was put in. But then they decided that as long as the house was paid for, they could stay a while longer, save up for retirement, and get a really nice place somewhere in Arizona or California.

"It's just bothering me," G.P. said. Sitting back in the rocker the way he was, his feet hardly touched the floor. He was a short man, barrel chested, who looked just like what he was: a wrestling coach. A good one. That year, Stimpson had come in 10–2 and went to the state finals in their division. "This guy, Markem. He's a real experienced lifter. Comes into the gym every single day to work out. Swims, plays a little ball, lifts maybe four or five times a week. A regular routine. He's a careful guy." G.P. caught himself. "*Was* a careful guy. The thing is, I can't picture this guy Markem, an experienced lifter, doing heavy bench presses—*really* heavy bench presses—with nobody there to spot him."

"But that happens sometimes, doesn't it?" Frank asked. "I mean, it's usually the experienced swimmers who drown out in the ocean. They swim out too far, think they can handle anything."

"Yeah, but the way it fell, too," G.P. said, shaking his head. "I mean, even if he *did* lift all that, well, I could see him dropping it. You really can hurt yourself, tear a pec or something like that, but such a clean drop? The bar so nice and even across his jugular? I don't know, Frank. One of the first things I thought of when I saw the guy there like that, helpless, pinned under the bar: I thought, Jesus Christ, someone must have dropped it on him."

Frank Rhodes was interested in his cousin's comments, but not in the least convinced that Tyler Markem's death was something other than an accident. Accidents happened in Grandview. Premeditated killings of college professors did not. He knew this town, the lay of the land, the people, the patterns. Except for a few years in the service, he had lived in Grandview all of his life; his father had the shoe store downtown that sold saddle shoes and later Bass Weejuns and Birkenstocks to the college girls; his mother worked in food service at the Stimpson Student Union. Frank and his brother and sister had gone to the same high school that his own children later went to, that all the college professors' kids went to. And Frank's first arrest when he was twenty-three years old and a rookie cop was of a Stimpson student who, drunk or hungry for his mother's cooking or both, had broken the windows of Peterson's Bakery and stolen two apple cobblers.

Frank Rhodes had lived in this quiet college town all his life, had patrolled every back street and alley, had checked the locks on every store on the strip, had broken up fights outside of every bar. Sometimes there were fights between the students and the townies. Frank understood; they were separate, the townies and the college kids. You could tell the difference just taking a walk downtown. The college kids walked with more confidence, had teeth straightened by orthodontia, better haircuts.

But, all in all, people got on pretty well. For the most part, they kept a separate space: the college kids in the stores and eating establishments in Campustown, the townies, scoping the loop down Main. Frank's job was mostly taking drunks off the road; there were occasional break-ins, a couple of calls a month about flashers in the stacks of the library, the peepers over by the dorms who appeared with some regularity every spring. Given what was happening in cities all across America—drug wars and drive-by shootings and child rapes—Grandview was a pretty safe place to be.

And as for being a college professor, well, what could be a safer, easier job? A sugar tit. Working less than nine months out of the year, giving lectures, grading some papers. Some of Leenie's professors taught only three courses a semester. Three courses, that's all. In the actual classroom about nine hours a week, Frank figured out, less time than he sometimes put in for a shift. What the hell did those guys do with their time, he wondered.

Frank picked up a new book about the Mideast from the coffee table with anticipation. He had put it on reserve at the library and they had called him at work to say that it was in. Since Carol died, he didn't like to get into bed unless he was just about to fall asleep. Every night he got ready for bed, and read in a chair in the boys' old room until he could no longer keep his eyes open. Now, just as he was turning off the lights and locking up downstairs, the phone rang. Frank looked at his watch. One minute past ten. Past eleven, eastern time. Leenie calling as soon as the rates changed. She was in New York City, her first year of teaching in an alternative high school where all of her students, as far as Frank could determine, were having babies. Leenie was excited about living in New York, but hadn't wanted to leave Frank. He didn't want her to leave either—more because he believed New York was a dangerous place—but he didn't tell her. "Go," he had said, pushing her from the nest. "I want you to go, I'll be fine. Bobby's here. Patricia's just a few hours away." The other son, Mark, was stationed in Germany. Frank thought that maybe sometime in the fall, he would take a trip to see him.

"Oh great, Bobby," Leenie had said snidely.

"Ilene!" Frank hadn't wanted to get into it. Bobby, the eldest, was also the least mature, the most trouble: never able to keep a job, a girlfriend, even get the rent paid on time. Carol used to joke that as the first, he was the practice kid, so they did a lot of things wrong.

Frank had urged Leenie to go, to get on with her life. He didn't want her to feel guilty about not taking care of her old man. "Look," he told her, laughing, "you're cramping my social life here, kiddo."

That was not exactly true. There had been a few dates, most of them arranged by the wives of guys from work. Some of the women were nice enough, but he felt strange and clumsy in their company and by the end of the evening, he was counting the time when he could be back home with one of his books. He was an avid reader: mostly historical biographies and political analysis; in fiction he liked Elmore Leonard and John Macdonald or Le Carre. He stopped calling the women, and soon there was a long time, after Leenie left for New York, that he was alone.

Leenie always said the same thing when he picked up the phone: "Are you into your book yet, Daddy?" Lately it had been depressing him that he always was. For the past few months he had felt a restlessness, the need to change something about his life. Part of the change had to do with sex, wanting it again, needing it. Sorrow and alcohol had pushed these feelings down somewhere so deep that he hadn't felt the stirrings for a while after Carol died. Then this spring he emerged as if from a coma and felt as if all his senses had been sharpened.

"Are you into your book yet, Daddy?" Hearing her voice on the phone gave him a momentary pause. There was the same voice quality, the same timbre, the same light, lilting tease in her tone as Carol's. Everyone had always confused Leenie and Carol on the phone.

"As a matter of fact, I was just walking up the stairs. Sweetheart, how are you? Did the painters finally come?" For a long time, Leenie and her roommate, an Italian girl who was dancing with the New York Ballet, had been promised that their apartment was going to be painted.

"They were here last Wednesday. Did the whole apartment while we were at work. The whole thing. It's a shitty job, but at least it's clean. We had to wait a whole goddamned month." Since she had been living in New York, Leenie's language was peppered with profanity.

Frank agreed that clean was the primary goal. "Did they fix the ceiling?" he asked. He had seen the place, a tiny one-bedroom with soot-gray windows and hunks of falling plaster, when he drove with Leenie to New York the summer before.

They talked for a while about the apartment, about Leenie's students. Frank remembered their names. LaVonne was the one who was expecting twins, possibly even triplets. Mary was the one whose boyfriend had hit her on the head with a hammer, causing short-term memory loss.

Frank was proud that he knew the details of Leenie's life. For all the children's growing-up time, it was Carol who knew, who filled him in on what was going on with their friends, what was happening at school. At night, after they were in bed, she would tell him: Bobby was going to fail algebra again this semester; Patricia wanted a strapless dress for the prom; Mark had grown three inches in one year, the doctor said, and didn't need allergy shots anymore; she was thinking of signing Leenie up for gymnastics lessons, the teacher believed she was a natural. Next to his wife in bed, Frank would listen to a recitation of his children's achievements, defeats, needs, and desires, a part of him amazed and grateful at the competency with which Carol sorted it all out. Now with her gone, he realized it was necessary for him to listen harder, to pay attention.

When Leenie was finished talking and there was a lull, Frank told her about Tyler Markem, leaving out the part of G.P.'s visit and his suspicions. "Daddy, you're kidding! I can't believe that! Why didn't you tell me that first thing?"

Frank said he wasn't sure she even knew Tyler Markem, that he didn't know she'd be so interested.

She didn't know him personally, but she sure did know *of* him. "Oh my God, weights really fell on his neck? What a way to go!" Then, her voice taking back that teasing tone: "Daddy, are you sure with the reputation that Dr. Markem had, that it really was an accident?"

For a moment Frank lost his breath, as if someone had suddenly thumped him hard on the chest. "Leenie, what do you mean?"

"Oh, I'm just kidding, Daddy. He was just one of those kinds of guys."

"What kind?" Frank asked.

"Oh, I don't know . . . he was very handsome and boy, did he know it. People said he had affairs, that was the rumor going around. He was *supposed* to be a great teacher, but students either loved him or hated him. Also he had a temper. Remember Joyce Love, the girl I used to do my psych projects with? I brought her home a couple of times?"

"Uh-huh." Frank didn't recall, but he wanted Leenie to go on.

"Well, Joyce said in class one time a guy was reading the newspaper and Professor Markem told him to put it away and the guy didn't put the paper away fast enough to suit him and Professor Markem threw a chair at him."

"No kidding?"

"The student was really angry. I heard he and Professor Markem almost had a fistfight right there in the room. A *chair*, Daddy! I mean, no teacher throws a *chair* at someone in college."

"Not when the students are paying sixteen thousand a year they don't," Frank told her. Leenie had gone to Stimpson on a full scholarship when she transferred from State. The scholarship was because of her grandmother's food service job: one given out every year for families of service employees.

Leenie giggled. "So what do you think, Dad? Maybe Professor Markem was killed. Maybe he was offed by some student he threw a chair at or someone he was screwing."

"*Ilene*, please!" It still shocked him when she talked this way. "So when do you finish with school?" Frank asked, unsettled.

"Three more weeks. Then I just have a week break before summer session begins."

"Do you have to teach summer school?"

"Otherwise I can't afford to live here. How could I support all the roaches who are dependent on me?"

Frank winced, picturing his daughter in her bug-infested apartment. When he had stayed there that first night, he got up in the morning and actually *heard* them scurrying. "Why don't you ask the landlord to exterminate?"

"We did. They were supposed to come last month, with the painters. But I haven't seen so many roaches around lately. Maybe the paint fumes killed them."

"I love you, honey," Frank said when they were at the end of the conversation. He had taken to saying this lately to all the children. It was most difficult to say it to Bobby, but he did, at every parting.

"Or you know who else it could have been?" Leenie said, just as they were about to say good-bye.

"Who else who?" Frank asked, puzzled.

"Who else could have killed Tyler Markem," Leenie answered.

"Who?" Frank asked. There was a tightening in his stomach that he wished could have been relaxed by a stiff drink.

"His wife," Leenie said. "He had this really nice wife, she's a teacher there, too. She has beautiful red hair."

12

The day of Tyler Markem's funeral was a busy one for Frank Rhodes. He started off a little after six in the morning meeting G.P. Comstock at the Sage Memorial Gym. G.P. was sitting on the top of the steps yawning when Frank pulled into the parking lot. "Do we have to do this at the crack of dawn?" G.P. asked, as Frank walked across the dewy lawn.

"Pep up, G.P.," Frank said, slapping him on the back. "When you're an old guy like me who's been up pissing half the night, six o'clock doesn't seem all that early." G.P. was just a few years younger than Frank, but he seemed a different generation. Maybe because he still had young children, one not even in school yet, while all of Frank's were grown and gone. "Besides," he added, "better to do this when no one is here."

G.P. unlocked the heavy wooden door, which creaked when he opened it. Then he bowed from the waist, stepping aside so Frank could pass. "Enter, Inspector," G.P. said, assuming a Slavic accent.

"I'm just looking at this again because you asked me to,"

Frank said, though he was still thinking of the unsettling conversation with Leenie the night before.

They walked down a long hall filled with black-and-white photographs of Stimpson wrestlers taken over the decades. The boys pictured from the earliest years were unsmiling, thick and dull looking; the more contemporary athletes seeming to brighten up a bit.

G.P. too was a Stimpson boy. Full scholarship from Grandview High School because of his wrestling prowess. There was a picture of him, grinning, boyish and blond, dated 1969, the year he'd won the state championship. Frank noticed for the first time that G.P. had dimples.

The weight room was in the back of the gym, behind the basketball court. G.P. was wearing sneakers, but Frank's hard black shoes echoed across the floor. Frank stood in the doorway for a few moments, again surveying the scene. It was an ordinary college weight room, small and well used. There were mats and mirrors, some Nautilus equipment on one side, but the facility lacked the high-tech gleam found in the new private clubs.

It was not much of a crime scene. There had been no damage, no prints, no telltale anything at all. Three days had passed since the accident—no one was saying at this point it was anything but—and the room had been well used since then.

G.P. walked over to the gray mat where Tyler Markem had been found; weights of all sizes lay scattered around a bench with two Y-shaped rests bolted at either end. Frank grabbed one of the steel rests and tried to give it a shake. They were both solidly in place. "See, we tested those first thing," he said. He turned to G.P. "All right. Let's try this out for size."

"Is this what you want me to do?" G.P. lay down on the bench, his chest under a set of barbells.

Frank checked out the position. "Looks good. Now what do you think you can press?"

"Oh, two hundred should be all right. I could work up to two forty-five, if I was doing it regular and building up."

"And that's what Markem was doing, right? He was bigger than you, though," Frank said.

"Well, taller. Not any bigger. Not any more muscled, really." As he spoke, G.P. involuntarily began to flex. "He was a programmed lifter, though. Worked out with all the young guys. Was always giving everybody tips."

"Okay. Let me just set this up for you," Frank said, adding weights to either side of the bar. "That's two hundred. Let me see you do two hundred."

G.P. stretched, opened and closed his hands a few times, took a couple of deep breaths, positioned himself under the bar, and lifted. His face reddened and he let loose a noise, somewhere between a grunt and a moan; the explosion of sound followed by his panting breaths reminded Frank of Carol, pushing out her babies. "Okay now," Frank said when G.P. had the weights above his head, his forearms trembling under the strain, "let it down easy." G.P.'s arms came down, and the bar fit into the steel rest with a *clunk*. "Do it a couple more times, okay?"

"Yeah." G.P.'s cheeks ballooned from the effort. He did about five or six bench presses altogether before Frank stopped him. "All right, let me try something. I'm going to hand these to you." Frank noticed how vulnerable G.P. seemed beneath him, looking up at him expectantly. G.P. must have sensed it, too, because he smiled uneasily up at Frank: "No funny business, okay, Chief?"

The weights were heavier than Frank expected—no way *he* could get more than two hundred pounds up over his head— but handing the weights to G.P., that was another matter. There really was no strain just taking the weights off the rest and placing the bar in G.P.'s waiting hands. You didn't have to be a weight lifter to do that. Anyone, even someone out of shape, could do that. A woman could do that.

Frank waited until G.P. had hold of the bar, then he let go. G.P. grunted and strained, doing a few more presses. "Stop a minute," Frank commanded when G.P. had the weights above his head. "Keep it up there." G.P.'s face pulled back with a grimace, his teeth clenched. "Okay. Let me take it from you," Frank said, relieving G.P. of the weights and easing the bar down toward the rest. "Hmmm," he mused, while G.P. lay panting beneath him.

"What do you think?" G.P. said, sitting up, rubbing his biceps.

"Well, to just hand the weights to someone underneath you, someone who was waiting for them, well, you don't have to be all that strong," Frank said. "I could have done more weight if someone was helping me out, taking them."

"That's called a lift-off. You're just helping someone out to get him going," G.P. said. "See, that's what I can't understand with Markem. If he was trying to press more than usual, why would he try that at a time when he was all by himself with no one to help with a lift-off?"

"So you're thinking that he wasn't all by himself? I don't know, G.P.," Frank said, scratching his head. "That student, Lyle, who found him?"

"Lyle Dixon," G.P. said. "Not a regular around here."

"He must have come in right after Markem died. And he said no one was around. Didn't hear or see a thing. No one even in the locker room. I don't know," Frank said again. "Maybe I'll have another little talk with the kid."

G.P. rubbed his arms some more and groaned. "God, I haven't lifted in a long time. That damned near killed me."

"Killed Markem, that's for sure," Frank said.

By eight-thirty, Frank was at Grayson Hall, being handed a cup of coffee made by Charlotte Pintel, secretary to the philosophy department at Stimpson College. Charlotte had the gruff, abrasive manner of an army sergeant and a voice gravelly from years of cigarettes. "Sondra, take over the phones," she barked to a lank-haired girl in jeans and a halter top. "Work-study," she said to Frank, indicating the girl. Frank presumed that work-study was a category of secretarial help.

"Is there someone in charge?" Frank asked. "Someone running the department?"

"You're looking at her." Charlotte grinned, leading the way down the hall to a windowless room that served as a kind of warehouse piled high with books, files, pots of dead plants, old coffee makers. In the center of a wooden table was an ashtray filled with butts. "They don't let me smoke in the main office anymore, so this is where I have to take my breaks." Charlotte gestured around the room toward the stacks of books. "I could set myself on fire in here, for all they'd care." Then she shook her head apologetically. "I know, I know. It's really a good thing. Not to let us stink up other people's air. You smoke?" Charlotte coughed hoarsely.

"Used to." Frank took a seat at the table and unwrapped a fresh stick of gum. He had stopped a little more than a year ago after taking a course at the college where everyone stayed in a room and smoked themselves sick. Now the close, cluttered room reminded him of the stop-smoking class, and having a cigarette didn't appeal to him. But other times the craving was so strong that he felt himself virtually weak with longing. For him, giving up smoking had been ten times harder than giving up drinking. The other thing he missed was the company at the AA meetings, the friends he had gotten to know. There were no-smoking meetings on Sunday nights at the church, but Frank didn't find that group as convivial as the smokers and had gone only a few times.

"Well, I for one could not talk about the death of Professor Markem without a cigarette. Just the thought of it, the way he died and all. God, it makes me queasy down to my toes." Charlotte lit up a Camel and took a languorous drag. Fine lines appeared on her upper lip, which had a slight yellow tint. She was a petite woman with a small, pointed nose and a small pointed chin. "Why are the police getting involved with this?" she asked, her sharp eyes narrowing with suspicion.

"We believe what happened to Professor Markem was most likely an accident," Frank told her. "But because he was alone at the time of death, there is the obligation to check up on some things."

"I'll bet!" Charlotte took a thoughtful drag on her cigarette and tapped her fingers on the table. "You know, a lot of people did not like Professor Markem. Me included, if the truth be known."

"How come?" Frank asked.

"Oh, the way he behaved. His arrogance. I tell you, sir, I have worked for thirty-five years at this college in three different departments and for some *important* people. Do you remember Thomas Jamesokski?"

Frank said that he did not.

"That was when I was in biology about fifteen years ago. Dr. J—that's what we all called him—he invented a blood thinning machine. Had his picture in *Time* magazine. Don't you remember?"

Frank said that perhaps he did.

"Well, *there* was a man who was a *genius*. A *real* genius. And was he ever a gentleman! Kind. Soft-spoken. Not the least bit show-offy. Now Professor Markem was another story. Thirty-five years in this college and I have yet to meet a man who so thought he was God's gift to the universe. Do you know what he used to do?" Charlotte paused, leaning her pointy chin on one fist.

"What?"

"Well, in nice weather, you know like it was last week, Professor Markem would hold classes out there on the grass." Charlotte pointed to a wall as if there were a window there. "Well, he'd be out there and he'd take off his *shirt*. Sunbathing.

Just like one of the students! Well, you know he thought he looked good, all muscles and tan. Ridiculous, I'd say." Charlotte snorted. "Sunbathing on campus without a shirt! Do you think that's appropriate behavior for a professor?"

Frank said that probably it was not. "But what I'd like," Frank began, surmising that Charlotte's enthusiasm would be fueled by the prospect of being part of the investigation, "is your help."

"*My* help?" Charlotte reached for the ashtray and stamped her cigarette out with fervor. "Of course, Detective."

Charlotte Pintel was eager, but most of her information was strictly hypothesis. Yes, she thought Tyler Markem was cheating on his wife, but that was because he was "like that." Yes, she thought he had enemies, because "a man like that is sure to piss off normal people."

"Were there ever student complaints against Professor Markem? Students who felt they were treated unfairly?" Frank wanted to know. "I heard a story that Professor Markem threw a chair at a student once—"

"Brian Potts," Charlotte said, nodding. "Well, that wasn't the only incident. Professor Markem had quite a temper. If anyone was going to do the threatening, it was probably going to be him. Fancied himself rather a tough guy. You know, weight lifter and all." Charlotte snorted again.

"So a number of students felt intimidated by him?" Frank asked.

"Well, he did make a few students upset every semester, but the thing is, a lot of students really *adored* him. Followed him around like he was some sort of guru. There was always a fight to get into his classes. A few years ago he even won the Teacher of the Year award." Charlotte lifted her narrow shoulders in a shrug.

"These students complaints," Frank asked. "Is there some sort of documentation on them?"

Charlotte went to two file drawers and in about five seconds

produced a foot-high stack of folders. "Teaching evaluations.
We do them every semester. The most recent ones are on top."

"We'll be keeping this stuff for a while," Frank told her.

"My pleasure. Glad to clean up a little around here," Charlotte said. She got a box and helped him stack in the folders.
"Listen, Detective, do you really think that someone could
have *killed* Professor Markem?" she asked boldly, her eyes
bright.

Frank repeated that a routine investigation was always performed after a body was found under unusual circumstances.
Charlotte nodded, touching her tongue to a top row of small,
pointy teeth. "And you've been most helpful," Frank added.

Which was true. Charlotte Pintel had certainly kept her eyes
open. She knew Markem's whole routine: teaching, committee
meetings, writing time, workouts in the gym. She knew never
to schedule an eleven o'clock class for Professor Markem
because that was his gym time. That always had to take priority.
Charlotte knew the schedule of not only everyone in the philosophy department, but probably everyone in the building as well.
It was she who told Frank that George Lawson was most likely
one of the last people to see Tyler Markem alive. "Yes," she
said. "I know they walked over to the gym together that very
morning."

A few minutes later, Charlotte let Frank into Tyler's office,
turned on the overhead light, and stood in the doorway. "Thank
you," Frank said. "I'll lock it up on my way out."

"I could stay if you need me," Charlotte offered.

"I appreciate that," Frank told her. "It won't be necessary."
After she left, Frank closed the door. On Tyler's desk was a
picture of two teenagers, winsome, pretty girls, both freckled
and athletic-looking. They were sitting on the edge of a dock,
squinting into the sun. Frank opened the top drawer—just paper
clips and pens and regular office supplies. In the lower right

file drawer was the evidence that Julia had told him about when he talked with her the night before. It was all still there: the cards, the music box, the teddy bear, the condoms, the porno magazines. He held the drawer open, just looking before he touched anything. Then he took out a pair of rubber gloves and put everything in the cardboard box with the student evaluations.

He read a card from Lynette, postmarked almost a month before the death; he noted how "luv u's" were looped in purple ink all around the border. In the same drawer were more office supplies, folders, papers, forms, notes written in almost illegible script on pads and file cards.

In the bottom drawer there was a pair of gray socks, some mailing envelopes, a half-eaten can of salted peanuts, a shriveled apple and a weight-lifting magazine. Frank had himself a handful of peanuts and skimmed the magazine which had pictures of young men whose bodies were sculpted and copiously oiled.

Right before he was getting ready to leave, Charlotte again appeared in the doorway. "There are some other people you should speak to besides George. You want names?"

"Sure," Frank said.

"Well, there's Alice Blevins. She's the president's right-hand gal. Over in the administration building. And she and Tyler have always been chummy-chummy. I know her voice. She used to call him a lot." Frank wrote down the name. "Also Professor Meltzer. You should speak to her," she said.

"Meltzer," Frank repeated. The name had a familiar ring.

"Francine Meltzer. She's in the English department. She and Julia Markem are good friends. So you might want to talk with her. Only thing, I'll warn you. She's prejudiced, too."

"Prejudiced?"

"Yeah, against Professor Markem. She hated the bastard. Pardon my French."

"Thanks," Frank said, smiling. He thought that if Charlotte

Pintel was ever to work as a secretary for the Grandview Police
Department, he would probably let her smoke in the office.

Twenty minutes later he was back at the station, and after
telling his secretary that he did not want to be disturbed, he
poured a cup of coffee, placed an unopened pack of Big Red
cinnamon gum to the side of the desk, and began to sort out
his thoughts. On a yellow pad he wrote out a list of names:

Julia Markem
Lynette Macalvie
George Lawson
Francine Meltzer
Brian Potts
Lyle Dixon
Alice Blevins

A little before one o'clock, feeling antsy, Frank rounded up
Jonny Verlaine and asked him to go for a ride. "We're going
to see one of my daughter's professors from the college," he
told Jonny, who was no dummy but hardly ever talked. They
drove up a tree-lined street in companionable silence until they
came to a brown-shingled house set behind two pine trees. A
woman walking to the garage stopped in her tracks when she
saw the police car pull into the drive.

"Francine Meltzer?" Frank began, taking off his sunglasses.
He didn't know what he expected, but she wasn't it. Wild
black hair, full lips, hips, breasts, all of her in this shiny, silky,
shimmery blue that reminded him of oceans around tropical
islands, places he had never seen but could imagine. She pulled
back for a moment, appeared nervous. "Yes?" Her voice was
husky.

He kept her for only a few moments, apologizing for
appearing like this, right before a funeral. She told him that
she would be going over to Julia Markem's home after the
service but, yes, she would be able to come down to the station

afterward to answer some questions. Would six o'clock be all right?

In the car, Frank chewed gum, thought about women professors like Julia Markem and Francine Meltzer, and came to the conclusion that perhaps he had missed something by not going to college.

"Pretty woman," Jonny Verlaine said as Frank pulled up to the station.

13

Fran watched them walk away: Rhodes ambling toward the car with a long, loping gait, and the young, silent partner. For a moment Rhodes looked at her over the roof of the car and stood very still. He had a nice face. Clean and open with a solid chin, and a certain sensuousness about the mouth. There was definitely something sexy about him, she thought. Sexy in a middle-American, Henry Fonda kind of way.

They didn't drive right off. She saw Frank Rhodes reach toward the dash, then take out a stick of gum, unwrap it, deposit the already chewed piece in the paper, and pop the new one into his mouth.

Ex-smoker, she noted, watching as he started the car. She would have made a good detective herself, she thought, having that canny sense about people. About her students—the very first day of class—who the smart ones were; usually who the phonies and the brown-nosers were, too.

But why, then, had she never suspected Tyler? Had known nothing about his secret life?

She stood waiting until the police car was out of sight, as if they had been weekend guests she was seeing off; then she went back into the house, popped one of the Valiums that she had promised to Julia, and ran cold water along the insides of her wrists.

The cold water was a trick of her mother's. She used to stand Fran on a kitchen stool and run cold water: "This will calm you right down," she would say in a sing-song voice when the little girl was too choked with tears to talk. "Relax, sweetheart, relax."

As an adult, Fran soon realized that this tranquilizing method did not work quite as well as Valium, but, in her mother's memory, she would run the water sometimes—before getting on a plane or giving a paper at a conference.

"What's going on here?" Fran said aloud, looking out the window above her kitchen sink. The peonies, late this year, shone newly pink and fresh. "What the hell is going on?"

This, too, was a legacy from her mother: talking to herself. Sylvia Meltzer, busy about the house, making up a shopping list, would always talk out loud: "Okay, for dinner then, the lamb chops. What else? Tomatoes, I got tomatoes. Melons. Melons. Melons. Grapefruit. Oy, and the dry cleaning. Three o'clock? Gotta go. Okay. Okay."

Fran and her sister would watch their mother, all dolled up for Waldbaum's with her makeup, her shiny black hair in a bun of ringlets, her jewelry, chain bracelets and bangles jingling. "There she goes," Fran used to say to her sister: "Sylvia Meltzer in all her splendor."

Feeling a pierce of pain from the cold water, Fran turned off the faucet, dried herself with a dish towel, and checked her lipstick in the reflection of the toaster. Then she thought of Frank Rhodes and the slow, sure way he walked down the driveway to the car. She felt her nipples begin to tingle.

"Stop that!" she said, softer this time. What had happened was terrible. Tyler was dead. Possibly murdered. (Murdered?) Worse, Julia, who had a motive if ever there was one, might be considered a suspect. So how could she, Fran, Julia's very best friend, possibly be standing there on the day of Tyler's funeral, looking out her kitchen window, and thinking carnal thoughts about some middle-aged small-town cop with Nazi sunglasses?

The lobby of Dayton's Funeral Home was filling up by the time Fran got there. Soft strains of something understated, Haydn perhaps, came from speakers along the back of the room. People filed by in silence.

Fran scanned the crowd, which had already begun to assemble according to caste. Family, college administration, philosophy and English faculty were closest to the front. Fran spotted Friday club somewhere in the tasteful middle, although Drusilla had on an outrageous tie-dyed outfit that billowed like a tent. Stimpson students, out of deference or force of habit, seated themselves in the back rows. Scattered throughout was a smattering of neighbors; some girls of high school age, probably Beth and Caty's friends, whispering nervously behind their hands; other clots of faculty people; husbands and wives. George Lawson, looking sickly and miserable, suddenly came up next to Fran. She was just about to say "Hello, George," when he averted his eyes and shakily headed past her for one of the aisle seats.

She spotted Julia, demure in a navy blue linen dress with white collar and cuffs, standing at the front of the room talking with a very short woman in a gray suit whom Fran recognized as the town's new Unitarian minister. Over to the side were Julia's parents, her sister, Margaret, and Caty and Beth, both somber and still. Caty's hair was pulled back tightly with a white headband, which made her small face appear exposed, fragile. Both the girls were red-eyed from crying. Fran tried to see Julia's face, but she had bent her head to talk to the minister, who was shorter than Fran even, probably under five feet. In the pocket of her jumpsuit, Fran's hand circled the vial of Valium.

"A tragic accident. That beautiful, beautiful family." Standing beside Fran was Harvey Boxtel, an ex-rabbinical scholar now composition theorist in Stimpson's English department. Harvey, a sweet-tempered man with a physique like the Pillsbury Doughboy, was married to Shoshanna Kovner-Boxtel, a dour Israeli who taught kindergarten in one of Grandview's elementary schools.

"I can not believe such a thing happens," Shoshanna said, looking sterner than usual. She was draped all in black, black shoes, hose, a black dress with a cowl neckline. Standing next to Shoshanna, Fran felt like a floozy in her blue silk jumpsuit.

"The children, ach," Harvey said. Tears flooded his eyes as he looked at Beth and Caty. The Kovner-Boxtels had two daughters themselves, just a little younger than the Markem girls.

"Excuse me, please," Fran said, sounding thick-tongued. It was understandable; she was too broken up even to speak. Everyone knew what good friends she was with the Markems. Harvey gave her a few consoling pats on the back before she fled up to the front of the room toward Julia.

"I'm sorry," she whispered into Julia's shoulder as they embraced. There were additional components to Fran's sorry. What she was sorry for was coming late with the Valium. She was also sorry for having talked with the police about the state of her best friend's marriage.

"It's all right," Julia whispered back into Fran's hair, as if sensing the complexity of the apology.

"Here." Fran pressed the vial of pills into Julia's hand. "I also took one. I'm dopey as can be." They walked together out to a water fountain, Fran feeling as if she were wading through mud. "How's it going?" She guided Julia by the elbow. Even drugged, Fran felt she was more in touch than her friend. Julia had a strange, hollow look to her, and she moved mechanically, like one of the Stepford wives. "Did you take something already?" Fran whispered. She saw the pitying glances of everyone around them as they passed.

"Something?" Julia asked.

"Like a tranquilizer."

"Yes," Julia began slowly. "Nadine gave me something she had." Nadine was the diminutive Unitarian minister.

Great, Fran thought. A minister with a drug supply. "Well, you certainly don't need any more, then."

"No," said Julia vaguely.

"Are you all right?" Fran held tight to Julia's arm, afraid that with a loosened grip, Julia would float away.

"The police came over last night. They were asking me questions about my relationship with Tyler," Julia said a little too loudly.

"Shhh," Fran cautioned. "What did you tell them?"

Just then Chalmer Von Eaton, the president of Stimpson College, strolled by, looking as if he were about to attend baccalaureate. He was followed by the women from the administration building, who probably had come over from work together. They walked behind him in pairs, except for Alice Blevins, his right-hand gal, who at this time was not by his side but standing apart, her eyes cast down as she walked by.

"Let's just get a drink of water, then," Fran suggested.

"Good idea!" Julia turned to Fran, smiling broadly.

"Stop," hissed Fran into her friend's ear. What she meant was for Julia to stop smiling, but Julia ground to a halt before they reached the fountain, standing with catatonic stiffness and blocking the entrance for those entering the hall. People walking in excused themselves, looked awkwardly at Julia, and nodded in compassionate bereavement to Fran, the best friend, who seemed to be holding Julia up. Fran set her face with a seriousness that easily matched that of Shoshanna Kovner-Boxtel. "Stop smiling," Fran said again.

"Am I smiling?" Julia asked, her hand quickly covering her mouth.

"It doesn't matter," Fran said, suddenly realizing that anyone looking at Julia would be sympathetic. The widow was obviously in shock. Anything short of raucous laughter would be considered appropriate.

Katherine Nottingham Taylor marched toward them, looking like Goodwill on a bad day. "My dearest Julia," she said, touching Julia's shoulder as she went by. "I am so sorry." Dr. Taylor was wearing a blouse and skirt of assorted dark plaids, a man's fedora, and brown high-topped shoes.

"Thank you," Julia said, beginning another smile.

"Excuse us," Fran said, moving Julia over in a corner behind a potted plant. "The police were at my house right before I came here."

"I thought they would come see you," Julia said. "I didn't have a chance to call." As if to test for dust, Julia ran a finger across a large leaf of a fiddle-leaf fig.

"Julia, what did they ask you?"

Julia shrugged. "I don't really understand what's happening. They asked questions about our marriage. How Tyler and I got along. They asked questions about Tyler's life insurance policies. I shouldn't even say 'they.' One of them, Rhodes, he was the person doing all the talking."

"I know," Fran said.

"What did he ask you?"

"They were only there a few minutes. I'm supposed to go down to the station after the funeral." Fran paused. Across the room was a portrait of the founder of Dayton's Funeral Home. HOMER DAYTON, said a brass plate. For a second, Fran thought she saw the eyes move behind the picture. She leaned toward Julia, lowering her voice even more. "What should I tell them?"

"What do you mean?" Julia looked puzzled.

"The police. How much do you think I should tell them?"

"How much about *what?*"

"You know. About you, Tyler, going to his office, Lynette . . . the whole thing."

Julia blinked in surprise. "Franny, tell them the truth. Anything they ask, just tell them the truth. I told them that Tyler and I were probably going to get divorced. I also told them that I would like it if the children didn't have to find out about Lynette. There's no reason to tarnish their father's memory and hurt them any more. I don't even understand why the police are interested in this." Julia sighed. "They're doing all this just because someone was concerned about how the equipment was set up in the weight room. It's a safety check, more than anything else, don't you think?"

"I don't know." Fran gave Julia's arm a little squeeze. Underneath the silk jumpsuit she was beginning to feel her underarms get wet.

"Franny, you don't think . . ." Julia's voice trailed off and she shook her head. "You know, when the detective was asking all those questions, he seemed so apologetic." Her green eyes had cleared considerably and were now wide with injured innocence. "I don't have anything to hide!" Julia said. "It's too ridiculous."

"What is?"

"You don't think that they think that Tyler was . . ." Julia stopped. She couldn't bring herself to say the word.

"That's what they're investigating, Julia," Fran said somberly.

"So then, do you think that they think—"

Fran interrupted. "Julia, I don't know *what* they think."

"This is unbelievable," Julia said.

"It's past two o'clock," Fran said, taking Julia's arm. "We should go in."

* * *

Everyone said it was a lovely service. Despite her small stature, the Unitarian minister was a powerful public speaker with a resonant voice. Before the funeral she had met with the family and members of the philosophy department, so the eulogy was filled with personal anecdotes, both funny and poignant. Tyler was revealed as a stimulating teacher, a dedicated scholar, a loving husband and father, a fine athlete, and "the best of a new generation of poets."

The family, such as it was, sat in front. There was only one of Tyler's distant cousins, but Julia's parents were there and her sister, Margaret. Julia, flanked by her two daughters, sat up straight, dry-eyed, her face impassive. She was certainly holding up well, people must have said, noble and brave, like a young Jackie Kennedy. Fran, off to the side, surveyed the room, looking behind her for Lynette Rae Macalvie. She did not see her among those in the back, though it was hard to differentiate in that sea of blond heads.

The minister was telling a heartwarming story about the time Tyler had coached ten-year-old Caty's softball team, bringing them from behind to capture the city championship; how he had brought out the best in each little girl on the team. A number of the college girls were weeping copiously, and even some of the boys brushed away a tear or two.

In the far back, leaning against the wall, a tall, strong-jawed man had just popped a fresh stick of gum into his mouth. Slowly he moved his head, scanning the crowd. When he caught Fran Meltzer's eye he gave a nod of recognition and perhaps the slightest, briefest smile.

14

Fran was glad that Julia had at least the good sense to have Tyler's body cremated, so there wasn't that hideous drive to the cemetery; more talk about what a wonderful person Tyler was, struck down in his prime; and college girls crying so that mascara ran in black streams down their cheeks. Fran remembered her parents being buried out on the Island in a double plot, the two coffins going down side by side into the ground with a thud. There was some Chinese proverb she remembered then: that you are never truly a grown-up until you have lost both your parents. She watched that first clump of earth drop on the coffins and squeezed her sister's hand; middle-aged orphans, the two of them. How could it be, both of her parents gone, so fast and final like that? For months afterward, she started to reach for the phone to call them.

Now, driving downtown with Julia's sister, Margaret, to pick up a tray of pastry before going back to the house, Fran felt an equal sense of bewilderment. Tyler's life over in a flash and Julia—the Julia she had known and laughed with and loved these many years—suspected of his murder. Julia *killing* Tyler? Well, it was just too unbelievable. Ridiculous.

Where had she, Fran, been at eleven-thirty when Tyler's body had been found in the gym? Frank Rhodes had asked her that morning. She had been home, she told him, painting a chest of drawers; two coats of enamel and still tacky to the touch on the day of Tyler's funeral. She had not told Detective Rhodes that she had called Julia that morning, had left a message on the machine.

"The service was good, I think," Margaret said, looking out the car window. "Not religious. Tyler would have wanted that." Fran agreed, looking over at Julia's sister in profile. She had met Margaret one Christmas vacation years before. Except for the red hair, which Margaret kept straight and cropped with an even row of bangs across her forehead, Fran doubted that she could have picked her out of a lineup as Julia's sister. "It's going to be so awfully hard on the girls," Margaret went on. Fran said something about the natural resilience of children, something she wasn't sure she altogether believed.

Fran parked at a meter and walked with Margaret to Peterson's Bakery on Fifth Street. Margaret was about as tall as Julia but thicker in the middle, solid rather than willowy, so Fran did have that same Mutt-and-Jeff feeling she sometimes got while walking along with Julia. They stopped in front of a store called The Country Hearth to admire a quilt. "It's a beauty," Margaret said with enthusiasm. Fran agreed, although she did not much like quilts; it was depressing to think of one woman spending so much time on all that tedious stitching.

They were quiet in the bakery and during the walk back to the car, Fran feeling that under the circumstances, quiet was not a bad way to be. It was slightly overcast out, cooler than it had been the past couple of days. Margaret was wearing a long-sleeved green plaid dress with a Peter Pan collar and one of those golden circle pins that Fran used to wear in high school.

The dress along with the haircut made her look somewhat like an overgrown Catholic schoolgirl.

"I wish I could stay a while with Julia, but I have to get back for my son's graduation," Margaret said as they drove down the Boulevard to Julia's house. Julia lived in a more suburban section of town, one where everyone had lawn care service and basketball hoops above their garages. Then: "Something's the matter with my sister," Margaret said simply.

"Well, of course—" Fran began before she was interrupted.

"No, it was from before. I sensed something was wrong before Tyler died. I spoke to her on the phone a few times. And I could tell. With Julia I could always tell."

"Julia and Tyler were having some problems," Fran admitted, not thinking she should lie to Julia's sister.

"Another woman?" Margaret added quickly.

Fran was so shocked that she almost ran into the car in front of her. "Yes," she said, looking at the road but feeling Margaret's eyes on her.

"I thought so," Margaret said. She sighed but did not say anything else. Fran waited, then was relieved when Margaret did not ask for more.

The living room was already crowded with people. Julia was sitting on a chair, surrounded by members of the English department, who were standing or kneeling around her. There was a hushed din, like that in a conference room following a particularly solemn lecture.

Maria and Drusilla stood at the dining room table pouring coffee while Jean was cutting a bundt cake. Shoshanna directed Harvey down to the garage for more chairs. Margaret took the extra pastries into the kitchen, where Alice Blevins, her face puffy with tears, suddenly appeared and silently began arranging platters.

"Hi, baby," Fran called to Caty, who was standing off in a

corner of the kitchen, her face an unhappy scowl. "June Bear," said Fran, walking over for a hug. Born in June—in a week she would be fifteen—June Bear was Caty's name of familial affection.

"I hate them," Caty whispered fiercely into Fran's hair.

"Who?"

"Everyone. They're all in there," she said, pointing to the living room, "talking and eating." The noise from the other room was subdued, but there was a hum of conversation. "Introducing themselves, like it's a *party*. And my father's dead!" Caty burst out crying.

"Come." Fran led Caty down the stairs into the honey-colored family room, a recently converted basement. Bookshelves in beige laminate lined the walls, in the center of which was a thirteen-inch color television, a subject of controversy a year ago, Fran remembered. Thirteen inches. Tyler, reiterating the evils of MTV to the girls, would not get a larger set. Fran had been over when Tyler was arguing with them about it. The programs they watched destroyed their minds, he said. Caty argued that her *eyes* did not have to be destroyed as well by watching such a tiny screen.

The converted basement was a huge open space that could have used at least a nineteen-inch set. Against the wall, over by the washing machine, was a Ping-Pong table. Along the other wall was an Abdominizer, a blue plastic rocker that was supposed to help in doing situps. Less strain on the back, the ads promised. Julia bought the Abdominizer after seeing it advertised on her thirteen-inch television. Next to the Abdominizer were some weights attached to pulleys, a couple of barbells, and a larger set of free weights. On the wall was a chart recording each of Julia's fitness routines. Julia worked out almost as compulsively as Tyler.

Some years ago, Julia had convinced Fran to join a women's health club when they had a bring-a-friend, two-for-one special. Two hundred and fifty dollars for the whole year, Julia said, was quite a bargain. The Femme Fitness Center had computerized weight machines personally programmed for each client. Tinny computer voices— "You can do it, Fran"—accompanied each workout. Fran hated the machines, but not as much as she hated the aerobics instructors: neon-clad girls relentlessly jumping, kicking, screaming directions and encouragement. Perhaps she had gone to the Femme Fitness Center ten times the entire year. This averaged out to some fairly expensive saunas.

"Sweetheart," Fran said to Caty, calm now in her arms. She had always felt something special with Julia's younger daughter. There was a passion in her that reminded Fran of herself as a girl. "Grown-ups do that. Everyone feels sad about your dad. They talk about ordinary things, but there's a comfort in just being together."

"I can't believe it. I can't believe I'll never see him again. Never, ever." Caty threw herself over on the couch and started to sob.

Fran looked uneasily at the set of weights on the other side of the room. She thought of the heavy metal bar coming down on Tyler, crushing the throat, the bob of adam's apple, the indentation of soft flesh above the collar bone; blocking off all air going in, coming out, in, out, in, out; the simplest, most involuntary movement stopped with such a careless, swift, and silent brutality.

15

Frank Rhodes sat at his desk, thinking. It was his theory after almost twenty-five years in law enforcement that if a woman hurt a man, she probably had a good reason. If she killed him, Frank figured, she probably had an even better one.

For twenty-five years he had witnessed the intimacies of other people's lives, the violent consequences of their reckless entanglements and thoughtless choices. It was harder for him to make sense of it all without Carol to help sort things out. She had been a good listener. Better than that—a *hard* listener. She had listened hard to what Frank had to say, and acted as if nothing was more important than to sit and listen with her careful, sympathetic ear. She had opinions, of course. More of them, Frank observed, as she got older.

Now, in the time following his wife's death, Frank often worked something out in his head, played Carol's part, thinking of what she would say. "Probably an accident," he would tell her, though he could not get out of his mind the memory of G.P. lying on that bench, the weights balancing precariously above his white neck.

He had talked with Julia Markem in her kitchen the night before her husband's funeral. Julia had been composed. *Serene,* he might have said when describing her to Carol. No, he didn't think she was in shock, exactly. There was something about the woman that he liked, he had to admit—a kind of earnestness and a desire to please.

Julia had insisted on making fresh coffee, asked if he had eaten dinner yet. There was so much food in the house, she said. People kept bringing over casseroles. He had watched as she measured the coffee, then set out chocolate chip cookies on a china plate. She was wearing white shorts and a pink T-shirt, her red hair pulled away from her face with barrettes, no makeup. Frank noticed as she reached up to take a coffee mug down from the shelf that she had very nice legs, long, elegant white legs with slender ankles. She was barefooted. He looked away.

The case was strange. He did not imagine Julia Markem as the kind of woman to let herself get out of control and make a scene, let alone kill a husband. Even a husband who behaved badly. On the west side of town near the railroad there were women who could give an unfaithful husband what for. And there were the country women living with men who still farmed little left-over plots of family land or who worked as tenants for some of the big companies—those women could be tough. Once he had been called out in the country to a house where the woman had knocked her husband down and stuck a pitchfork into his ass.

Now as he sat alone in his office, Frank tried to sort out everything that Julia had told him the night before, his meeting with Charlotte Pintel, what G.P. had said.

Frank got up and poured himself another cup of coffee. The mug had been given to him by his daughter, Leenie. It said something about women holding up half the sky. "So the husband wanted to go to counseling, but he didn't want to give up the girlfriend," he said to himself. Julia had told him this the night before in her pretty white kitchen, newly remodeled with oak floors and white, white cabinets and a high-tech stove with so many dials and buttons that it looked like the inside of a spaceship. Frank had been apologetic about asking so many questions to someone who had so recently suffered a loss, but Julia seemed willing to talk, relieved even.

Frank set the yellow pad in front of him and wrote some key words as thoughts streamed through and he tried to organize everything into a story that made sense. It was almost as if it were before dinner and he and Carol were sitting on the living room couch (her feet tucked under her, her look expectant), talking about their day, drinking a beer.

The other woman's name is Lynette, Frank continued in a running interior dialogue. She is a student of the professor's, quite a bit younger (some slight show of scorn would register on Carol's face at this point). The professor tells his wife he won't stop seeing Lynette. He says he doesn't know how he feels. He says he loves the girl but remains in the house with his wife for several weeks (Carol would lift an eyebrow). They have said nothing to the children. The husband says he is confused. He asks his wife to go together with him for marital counseling. She says she'll think about it, but instead she goes to the apartment of the other woman and confronts her. (Why do you think she would do that? Carol might ask at hearing this part.) The girl has believed that she and Tyler really love each other and they're going to get married and live happily ever after. But the wife goes to meet the girl and lets her know in no uncertain terms that that's not the way it is at all. That Tyler has another agenda; he wants to see if he can still save his marriage, can work it all out with therapy.

Frank finished in quick summary: Then Lynette disappears, calls in the next morning at work that she's taking a couple of days off, family emergency; and that same day Tyler Markem is found dead in the gym and everybody says what a tragic accident and what a loss, such a talented teacher. And nobody knows—except this best friend, Fran Meltzer—about the affair (plus the therapist, of course, whom Frank had not yet called, who probably won't talk, confidentiality and all).

"The girlfriend seems a prime suspect," Carol might say. "Convenient for her to leave town just like that."

"What about the wife?" Frank would say. "What if she has a really whopping life insurance policy?"

"How whopping?" Carol would want to know.

Frank chewed thoughtfully on the eraser, his brows knit. On the yellow pad were the names: Julia Markem, Lynette Macalvie, George Lawson, Francine Meltzer, Brian Potts, Lyle Dixon, Alice Blevins. Of course, not all of them were suspects. Some were the *possible* suspects for what was the *probable* accident: one embittered, angry wife; one angry girlfriend, mysteriously unaccounted for; one alcoholic teacher in danger of losing his job. Frank glanced over each name, underlining some with a pencil.

George Lawson was the third name. That morning, Charlotte Pintel had told Frank that George Lawson was possibly the last person to see Tyler alive. From the office window, she had seen them walking together to the gym about twenty minutes before eleven the day Tyler Markem was found dead. She said that Tyler had recently taken George under his wing, developing a physical fitness program for him that included walking around the track, some situps, and light lifting. He had been worried about George the whole spring semester, Tyler told Charlotte. George was so upset about the committee's upcoming review that he was tense all the time and needed some physical outlet, Tyler had said.

Frank had spoken briefly to George Lawson after the funeral. George said that he did, indeed, walk to the gym the morning of Tyler's accident, but after changing in the locker room, he started to feel sick and exhausted. He hadn't been sleeping much, he told Frank, and instead of working out, he had decided to leave. He went home, took a couple of aspirins, and was back in bed by eleven-thirty. Saying this, George was shaky, mottle-faced; the smell of old booze seeped through his pores, lay under the minted smell of his breath.

"It actually wasn't because of Tyler that George would lose his job. It's because of the alcoholism. The committee was going to make the decision the next week," Charlotte Pintel had told Frank.

"And Tyler Markem was on that committee, right?" Frank said.

"Well, yes, but if anything, Tyler was George's support. Tyler was George Lawson's *friend,*" Charlotte admitted grudgingly. She didn't seem to want to say anything good about Tyler Markem.

"Still, Tyler Markem was the one who had taught George Lawson's poetry class when he was incapacitated? Isn't that right?" Frank pressed. "Could George have been threatened by that, the possibility that Tyler wanted to take away the poetry class?" Julia had mentioned the situation the night before. It was the first thing she had told Frank after he asked her if Tyler had any enemies that she knew of. Then, as soon as she said it, she took it back. Frank wondered: would someone actually kill a person because of wanting to teach his poetry class? It seemed too absurd a motive. Then again, maybe poetry was more important to a college professor.

Of course, there were the students. Frank hefted the bulk of Tyler's file. There was also the possibility of an angry student, someone who got a bad grade and wanted to get back; a student who was so angry or humiliated or both that he became crazed enough to kill. There was just such a case a while back in the Mid-west, right at the University of Iowa—a student with a gun who killed half the physics faculty.

Frank calculated how every single semester, a professor had brand-new classes. It would be twenty or so students if the class was a seminar, sixty or more for a big lecture. Three or four classes a semester. And for those professors who taught summer school in addition? That could be *hundreds* of students every year. Frank paused to ponder that for a moment and opened a fresh stick of gum. There weren't that many jobs where someone got to meet—and judge—hundreds of new people every single year. Most people were stuck day in and day out with the same old people in their office, the same old work crew. But as a teacher, you would meet hundreds of new people every year! That was a lot of possibility for running into someone who would like to kill you.

Brian Potts. He was the student Leenie mentioned. Charlotte Pintel knew the story, too. Tyler Markem threw a chair at Potts in front of the whole class. There were some witnesses who said that Potts was angry, threatened to punch Markem's face in afterward. Potts was in Grandview this summer, bartending in town at The Hull, that sports bar on the north side of town. Frank made a note to take a ride out to The Hull after his meeting with Fran Meltzer.

Lyle Dixon was the one who had found the body. He was just a scared kid who could hardly speak when he found G.P. in the office. Lyle Dixon had been helpful and cooperative talking with Frank in the office. No, he didn't see anyone else in the weight room when he walked in and saw Tyler; he didn't even see anyone at all in the gym. Yes, he had tried to get the weights off Tyler's neck before he called for help. Lyle's voice broke saying this, Frank recalled, and the boy kept staring down at his sneakers.

Frank and Jonny Verlaine had interviewed Lyle only briefly at the scene. Lyle lived in a small town about an hour west of Grandview and had already gone home for the summer. Frank wrote Lyle Dixon's home phone number in the margin of the yellow pad.

Alice Blevins was mentioned by both Charlotte and Julia. Not only had she been close with Tyler Markem, but she also knew all the politics and behind-the-scenes dealings of the college. "The president's right-hand gal," Charlotte had called her.

Frank rubbed his eyes, looking at the report that had just come back from the lab. There had been prints all over the barbell, not only Tyler's but all the others: Lyle Dixon, from when he found the body; then G.P. came in and lifted the barbell off; one of the ambulance workers had also touched the bar. Plus there were others, mostly indistinguishable prints, probably from guys who had used the bar earlier that day. Nothing to go on at all.

Frank sat at the desk, absentmindedly scribbling over the names, connecting them all with spirals and waves of doodles. A wave of lethargy overtook him. He looked at his watch: six-thirteen. Fran Meltzer was late.

16

Fran drove down Main Street, up Crescent, and back down Sixth three times before she finally figured out where the Grandview Police Station was. She had passed the station hundreds of times since she had moved to this city, yet she realized now, already fifteen minutes late for her meeting with Frank Rhodes, that although she could visualize the building—the dark red brick, the gleaming brass posts along the entrance, the police cars lined up outside, ready to go—she actually had no idea what street the police station was on. Fifth Street? Sixth? Walnut?

And what was she going to say to the police? Fantasy flashes of herself in court, defending Julia. Could Julia have *possibly* killed Tyler? If Julia went to jail, Fran would have to take Caty and Beth. They'd want to stay in Grandview and be with their friends. If they went to Maine they'd end up with Julia's family wearing green plaid jumpers and going ice fishing.

Heading north on Sixth Street for the third time, she saw a police car turn west onto Walnut and followed it. By the time she parked across the street from the station and ran up the stairs to the second floor where Frank Rhodes had his office, it was nearly six-thirty. "I'm sorry," she said as she burst in, panting.

Frank Rhodes, sitting across a desk and reading a file, looked up. "That's all right," he said calmly. "I wasn't going any-where." He had a mellow Midwestern demeanor that, instead of having a settling effect, made Fran slightly nervous. That, and the fact he was a cop. There was something about men in uniform she recognized, something alien and sinister. Although he wasn't in uniform now. Fran noticed that he had even changed from the suit he had worn to the funeral. He was wearing a white shirt, open at the neck, his sleeves rolled up to the elbows. He had lean, muscled forearms covered with dark hair. Appealing. Still, he *was* a cop.

"Coffee?" On a plastic table over to the side of the room were a coffee maker, dirty spoons, and the smeary remains of jelly doughnuts. There was no one else in the front office, though next door were the sound of male voices and the hum of a copy machine. "We'll be more comfortable in here," Frank said, ushering her into another room off to the side.

Surprisingly, it was a lovely room. There was an oak desk, an Oriental rug, family pictures arranged in clusters along the tops of the bookcases. It was a welcoming space, neat, peaceful. Fran glanced quickly at the photographs. The most prominent was a color glossy of a baby with a gummy smile and a pink bow atop a hairless head. "My granddaughter," Frank said, catching Fran's gaze. "She has teeth now. Though not much more hair."

"Granddaughter?" Fran said, lifting her eyebrows. She had thought he was about her age, a little older maybe. She wanted to look at the pictures again, to see his wife, but she did not. For a brief moment she had a pang of jealousy for the woman this soft-spoken man with the muscled forearms came home to, for the family so proudly displayed.

"The morning Tyler was found—well, the afternoon, really,

it was almost noon when the boy found him—do you remember what you were doing, Ms. Meltzer?" Frank put the coffee in front of her on the edge of his desk. She asked for cream.

"Yes. I was home. I was painting a chest of drawers I had bought the week before at a garage sale," Fran said, stirring in the white powder he gave her, trying not to get it all over his desk. Usually, especially when there were no classes, she could hardly remember what she did from one day to the next. But she remembered the chest, unfinished still, sitting on one corner of her dining room. After Julia called, Fran, paint smeared along each arm, had left for the hospital in a rush.

"Were you alone?" Frank Rhodes asked.

"Yes." Fran waited a moment but Rhodes did not go on. "I'm not a suspect, am I?" she asked casually.

Frank smiled. "No," he said. "You're not a suspect."

"Because I could be, you know. I don't really have an alibi as to where I was." Fran looked him in the eye. "Same as Julia," she added.

"Do you want to be included as a suspect, Ms. Meltzer?" Frank asked.

"No," Fran said. "I don't think so."

"And then Julia Markem called you to say that her husband was taken to the hospital," Frank went on. "About what time was that, would you say?"

"I'm not exactly sure. I know it was after twelve."

"When Julia called to tell you that Tyler was at the hospital— was that the first conversation you had with her that day?"

"Yes," Fran answered again. She did not reveal that she had tried Julia only the hour before and had gotten her answering machine. Well, he hadn't asked, had he?

Frank Rhodes shifted in his chair and rubbed his eyes. He looked tired. It was almost seven o'clock. Fran wondered if there was a specific time that he left the office every day or if, when something special—like this—came up, he just worked around the clock as policemen always seemed to do in the movies. In the movies policemen were always on stakeouts, hours on end, sitting in cars with the windows rolled up and eating fast food.

"I'd like to talk to you about Julia Markem and what you know about the Markems' relationship," Frank said. His eyes were a dark, rich brown, but there was, Fran thought, a sadness to them.

Fran began at what she thought was the beginning, describing a twenty-year marriage that by most standards was a successful one. Working together at the same college, two wonderful children, the house with its new kitchen. She told Frank how she and Julia had become close friends over the years. Yes, she said, she probably knew Julia and Tyler better than anyone else in town.

"You would say that you were their best friend, then?" Frank asked.

"Julia's, yes," Fran said firmly. "You understand that I never did like Tyler."

"A number of people didn't, it seems," Frank said.

"He was very arrogant. A difficult man." Fran caught herself. What was the point? Tyler was dead. Did she really want to make a case for someone's killing him?

Frank Rhodes unwrapped a fresh stick of gum, flattening the wrapper with his finger. "Was there abuse in their marriage? Any violence that you know of?" He moved the pack across the desk to Fran.

"No," Fran said quickly. She declined the gum. "No, there was no abuse." She thought: unless you counted acting like an asshole as abuse; unless you counted fucking undergraduates while your wife kept dinner warm for you. "No abuse that I know of," she added.

"And you say that you thought the Markems were happy together," Frank said.

So what's happy, Fran wanted to say, thinking of her mother, Sylvia Meltzer in all her splendor, a woman who suffered long with a man who worked too hard, snored too loud, and saw the world through the gloomy, narrow lens of a Depression survivor. "Well, if anyone could have been married to Tyler, it would be my friend Julia. She was very . . . I don't know . . . *accommodating.*" Fran went on, describing Julia as someone who liked to please, a good mother, a loyal friend.

"And yet, her husband had this affair," Frank interjected.

"Some men do."

"Men in happy marriages?"

"Maybe." She took a sip of coffee. It had an aftertaste of scorched dishwater. "Look, Detective Rhodes. Tyler had this affair and others as well. I don't know all the details. And I'm not a psychologist. But it seems to me that the problems Tyler had with his own ego and sexual identity might have very little to do with Julia," Fran said flatly.

"Did you know the girl Tyler was seeing? This Lynette Macalvie?"

"I had her in a class," Fran responded.

"And?"

"She got a B-minus," Fran said.

"Anything else?"

"She is remarkable only for being unremarkable. She's the kind of student I could never remember from one semester to the next," Fran said tartly.

"What kind of student is that?" Frank asked.

"Cheerful. Uncomplicated. Blond." Fran crossed her legs and leaned toward him. "I'd like to ask, if you don't mind, what's happening with finding Lynette Macalvie? Don't you think it would be a good idea to talk with her?"

"Another officer has been working on that. We've called her parents' home. They don't know where she is. The Holiday Inn where she works says she called in on Sunday evening and told them she wasn't coming in for the next couple of days. The manager didn't know anything else. No one there knew she was involved with Markem. She's due back at work tomorrow for the three to eleven shift. We'll go over and see her then. Thing is, she might not even know that Markem's dead."

"Well, she'd know he was dead if she killed him," Fran said.

"Yeah, she'd know then," Frank admitted, looking as if he were stifling a smile. "Let me ask you something else. Something I'm kind of curious about."

"Shoot."

"Okay. There was Lynette, but there were also other women besides her. Julia told me about that last night. The secretary in the philosophy department wasn't surprised, either." Frank folded his hands on the desk and paused, looking at her for a few moments. "Now you knew this information as, well, correct?"

Fran nodded, her heart quickening. "Well, it wasn't something I knew from before," she explained. "Right after Tyler told Julia, Julia told me," Fran said. "She drove over to my house that very afternoon. We're best friends," she added.

Frank looked puzzled. "Now help me out here, Ms. Meltzer. When Julia found out about Lynette, Tyler told her about other women as well. Why do you suppose a man would tell a woman that? That there were other women, too." Frank shrugged, shaking his head. "I mean, what's the point if your wife doesn't already know about other women? Seems like just adding fuel to the fire."

Fran didn't know if the detective was baiting her or actually wanted her interpretation. She thought a moment, treating the question with some seriousness. "I don't know why a husband would do this to his wife. Maybe to hurt her. To have some power over her. Maybe to come clean because he feels guilty, and telling a wife that there were other women as well somehow justifies his belief that he was unhappy all along. That this affair wasn't just one middle-aged crazy. He was looking for something and then, beyond his control, he happened to fall into love." As soon as she said it, Fran thought that the explanation sounded pretty good.

"And Julia told you. She confessed to you her suspicions now about other women."

"Well, she didn't know any longer what was true and what wasn't. There was this visiting professor once from Chile whom Julia suspected. And there seemed to be women on some trips that he took. There's this woman that he's friends with, Alice Blevins, who works for the president of the college. Though if you knew Alice, that's kind of hard to believe. Still, she and Tyler have always had tickets to the chamber music concerts together. Julia's pretty tone deaf, not into music the way Tyler is." Fran paused. "Was."

"But Julia believed he had an affair with Ms. Blevins?" Frank asked.

"I don't really think so," Fran said. "She just mentioned it. Because after Julia found out about Lynette Macalvie and Tyler told her that there had been many other women too, well, she began to get suspicious of everyone. She began to get a little paranoid." Immediately, Fran wanted to take back the last few words. The description of Julia as paranoid would not make a good defense—unless, of course, Julia ended up pleading insanity. Fran recalled her conversation with Julia. *Alice Blevins,* she had exclaimed: *Julia, you have to be crazy!*

"And of course there were the students," Frank said.

"Of course."

Frank looked down at the name on his yellow pad, then looked back up at Fran. "So Julia shared with you these suspicions," Frank said. "She was upset and sought your counsel to help her figure out what was going on, correct?"

"Julia and I are best friends," Fran said emphatically, aware as she said it that the term sounded vaguely childish. It was like saying "forty-two and a half" when someone asked how old you were. Fran added, "Julia tells me everything."

"Did you know then," Frank asked, sort of offhandedly, "about the insurance policy?"

Fran felt the back of her neck begin to tingle. "What do you mean?"

"The life insurance policy that Tyler Markem had."

"Oh, the one with the school? You mean the insurance policy we have with the college?" It was a good life insurance policy. Two and a half times your salary given as a lump sum. Extra taken out every month from your paycheck and matched by the school. Fran had figured out that she was worth about a hundred and fifty thousand. Her sister, Roz, was the beneficiary. Not that Roz needed it. Roz was married to the leading breast man at Long Island Jewish Hospital. Roz bought three-hundred-dollar Ferragamo shoes. Dozens of them. It was Roz who commented that what was found in Imelda Marcos's closet some years ago did not seem excessive to her.

"Tyler Markem had the college insurance policy, yes." Frank Rhodes paused, looking at her face. "But there was an additional policy."

"An additional policy?" Fran asked, confused. Well, that could be. Julia told her everything, but it wasn't as if either of them were really interested in the specifics of the other's financial portfolio. "I guess I didn't know about that," Fran said, shrugging as if this revelation were no big deal.

"It's a generous policy," Frank told her. "It was taken out years ago by Tyler's mother. Her estate keeps up the payments."

"How generous?" Fran wanted to know.

"Three hundred and fifty thousand dollars generous," Frank said.

"Oh," Fran said. She tried not to appear surprised. She gazed over at the photographs on the bookcase and caught a glimpse of a posed studio photo with an autumnal background. There were four children of various teen ages; a man and woman stood behind them. Fran recognized the man as Frank with more hair, though still thinning.

"Julia never mentioned any life insurance policy that Tyler's mother had taken out for him?" Frank asked.

Thoughtful, Fran bit her lip and tried to remember. "I don't *believe* so . . ." she said with some hesitation. "I don't think Julia ever mentioned that."

"That, along with the policy from the college . . . you know it would make your friend one rich widow," Frank said, leaning back in his chair.

Fran looked him square in the eye and sat up straighter herself. "Listen, Detective. There's no way that Julia Markem killed her husband," she said firmly. "I'd bet my own life on that."

Twenty minutes after Frank thanked Fran Meltzer for coming down to the station, they ran into each other in the Taco Time restaurant on Walnut Street. He was embarrassed to see her but didn't exactly know why. Maybe because he found her attractive and he was trying to maintain a professional distance. This was not usually a problem for him at work. The few women they had on the Grandview Police Force and in the surrounding areas were young enough to be his daughters; he never saw them in any other than a paternal light. Then there was the office secretary, poor Doris Duncan, a single mother just a few years younger than him whose life was characterized by the constant turmoil of her children.

Occasionally there were flirtations with some of the female lawyers, flirtations Frank never initiated but went along with just to show that he wasn't such a goody-goody as they might think. Most of the women lawyers he met were married. They liked him because he was easygoing and respectful, and they enjoyed teasing him.

Once last winter, as they were walking out of the courtroom after a particularly harrowing domestic abuse trial, a public defender by the name of Kathy Klingerman asked Frank for a lift home when her car wouldn't start in the below-zero weather. She was very animated in the car. "Why don't you just keep going," Kathy said to Frank as they headed south down the highway. "Let's end up someplace warm, like Mexico, and share a bottle of tequila on the beach." Then she stretched back on the seat, and her heavy winter coat fell open to reveal a voluptuous chest that Frank had not noticed under her conservative suit jacket.

Frank laughed to show he knew she was just joking around, but then wondered, after stopping at her house and seeing her trudge up the snowy driveway, if indeed she was.

"Well, Detective Rhodes! Long time no see," Fran said when Frank walked by her table at Taco Time. "Another one of Grandview's fine dining experiences?"

Fran mentioned something about the bean burritos and how she suddenly had this craving. Frank felt that she, too, was embarrassed at seeing him there. There were a few student types scattered about the other tables and some unhappy-looking families. No one was sitting alone.

"Care to join me?" She looked up expectantly.

"Oh, you're almost finished," Frank said, seeing the empty wrappers on her tray. "I don't want to disturb you."

"I was just going to get some coffee," Fran said, blotting her lips with a napkin.

"I'll get you some," Frank said, moving to the counter. He ordered a bean burrito and started to ask for the open-faced tostada with everything on it, then envisioned himself eating messily while Fran drank her coffee and watched him. "Two burritos, please." He picked cream and sugar for the coffee in case she wanted some and walked back to the booth where she was sitting, chin in hand, looking out over the parking lot.

There were questions he had not asked yet. Her view of George Lawson, for example. When Frank spoke with him,

George had implied a long-time friendship with her, even alluding (maybe Frank was imagining it) that at one time, there had been something more than just a friendship.

"I thought you might want cream," Frank said, sitting opposite her. He set out the little packages beside her cup. "I've noticed that people from the East Coast like their coffee light."

"Well, maybe you should be a detective," Fran said wryly, stirring the coffee in slow, seductive circles. She looked on as he started his burrito. "The first couple of bites are heaven. Then you're sorry you got involved."

Frank was very hungry, but he ate slowly, careful not to drip taco sauce down the front of his shirt. "I don't like to cook for myself," he told her. "I know I don't eat right most of the time."

They sat in the lit window of Taco Time for almost two hours, talking about the case, although the tone had changed. She seemed less guarded, more relaxed; and he wasn't so much investigating as listening to Fran share stories and observations. She was a smart woman. No doubt about that. And even if she did not like Tyler Markem and was best friends with his wife, Fran Meltzer's opinions did not seem to him to be clouded by bad judgment or bias the way most people's might be.

Eventually, they started talking about other things. He told her about living in Grandview all of his life and how his father had been born on a farm only three miles out of town and had started Rhodes Shoes right before Frank was born and still went in every day to the store.

"Rhodes Shoes? That's your family's store? I just bought a new pair of sandals there," Fran said. "That sweet old man is your father?"

Frank nodded. "Did you buy Birkenstocks?"

"Uh-huh."

"That's what all the college people buy. They look like shoe boxes to me."

Fran laughed. That's what her sister, Roz, had said when

Fran wore them last summer on a trip home. "Is your wife's family from here, too?" Fran asked.

Frank told her about Carol, how they had gone to high school together; he told her about the accident but he didn't go into details. He told her about his kids and how he worried about Leenie, about how awful it was for him when his oldest boy, Bobby, got in trouble with the law. First OMVUI, then passing bad checks. He told her how he had quit drinking himself two years ago. Then smoking. After the meal, gum wrappers formed a little pile in front of him on the table.

Fran had a second cup of coffee and then a third, listening to him all the while, asking questions, offering up stories about her own life. They laughed so hard about something that the couple in the booth behind them turned their heads to look. By ten o'clock, they were the only people in the restaurant. The girl behind the counter came out and washed down the tables with a rag smelling of bleach and gym socks. Frank looked at his watch and said he'd better be on his way. He was going to ride over to The Hull and speak with that student, Brian Potts. Fran said she too had to get going. It was late. They went outside together. Frank walked her to her car, waited for her to start it up, and watched as she pulled away.

17

Two women left the bar, laughing and holding on to each other, one of them bumping up against Frank when he held open the door. "Excuse me, darling," she said, laughing again.

Frank was last in The Hull eight months before, when Bobby had thrown a going-away party for Mark, who was about to leave for Germany. The group had included Frank and Grandpa Rhodes and some of Mark's old high school buddies and a couple of guys that Bobby hung out with from the construction crew before he lost his job after the cutbacks. Everybody got rip-roaring drunk except for Frank, who drank 7UP with lime, and Grandpa Rhodes, who had one beer and promptly fell asleep at the table.

That was the night that Bobby wrecked his car by driving through the living room window of a house owned by Archie Cook, mayor of the city of Grandview. It was a Pella picture window, newly installed. Bobby said the large expanse of dark-ened glass made him think that the mayor's house was an exit road off the highway. Archie Cook, although safe with his wife in a bedroom toward the back of the house, was not amused.

Frank was not amused either. It was Bobby's second drunken driving offense, and the story made the front page of the *Grandview Tribune*. Although Frank had done his share of driving under the influence when he was younger, nothing he had ever done had shamed the family. Bobby spent two weeks in jail. He got no special treatment because he was Frank Rhodes's kid. When he came out, Bobby seemed as irresponsible and adolescent as ever.

Tonight at The Hull was Ladies Night. Free drinks for the ladies until ten o'clock. When Frank came he saw them lined up against the bar: women in too-tight jeans with too much to drink looking like made-up chickens for the plucking.

By now the men had drifted in: working guys with lined, outdoor faces under their caps; old high school athletes; a few still in suits—probably salesmen staying at the Holiday Inn across the way.

Frank saw him, Brian Potts, standing behind the bar, a big kid, probably close to six feet three, with a neck like an ox and brown hair cut short, shorn on the sides to show scalp. Potts was wearing a bartender's striped apron and a white T-shirt with the sleeves rolled up. His biceps looked like rounded chunks of rock.

Brian Potts was busy, pouring out beer on tap and sliding the mugs down the wooden bar with a practiced finesse. Frank stood in the doorway, watching for a while before he made his way over to the bar.

There wasn't a stool, so he hunkered down on the end next to a middle-aged woman in white pants and a low-cut yellow blouse. She was smoking one of those long brown cigarettes, and after she exhaled, she gave Frank a tired smile. "Crowded tonight," she said with the flat voice of a woman disappointed in life.

Frank said that it was and ordered a diet Pepsi.

"Coke okay?" Brian Potts asked. He wiped the bottom of the glass before setting it down on the bar. Frank paid for the drink and took a couple of sips before reaching into his wallet to take out the ID and badge. "I'd like to talk to you," Frank said when Brian Potts came back with the change.

It was just the same as everyone had seen a hundred times in the movies, yet people were always surprised, flustered. Brian Potts's jaw dropped practically to his chin. "You're a cop?" he asked. The woman with the yellow blouse sat back on her stool to get a better look at Frank.

Brian called a girl who was waiting tables to fill in behind the bar and took Frank through a door marked Private next to the men's bathroom. Inside was a desk, a couple of folding chairs, and a brown tweed couch with some of the stuffing showing through the springs. Frank sat on one of the chairs and Brian on the other, tensely at attention, his bulk overlapping the seat.

When Frank started to talk about the death of Tyler Markem, Brian exhaled noisily and seemed to relax. "Oh, man," he said, shaking his head. "I thought you were going to get us again for serving underage. My boss said one more time and *I go,* since I'm the night manager. I don't think that's fair, do you?"

Frank said that he did not.

"I mean, if we're real busy, and one of the girls serves a kid in the back, how'm I supposed to check everything out?" Brian breathed another sigh of relief. "Oh, man. I thought my ass was grass this time. I really need this job. I got car payments and insurance coming up you wouldn't believe."

Frank asked Brian Potts where he was the Monday morning that Tyler Markem's body was found in the gym.

"Where was I?" Brian asked.

Frank nodded, waiting.

Brian scratched his chin. "In the morning?"

"Before noon."

"Hey, man, you mean is this like a murder? I read about it in the paper. They called it an accident." Potts paused and his flat, dull eyes became suddenly animated. "Wasn't it?" Frank replied that's what they were investigating.

"Wow!" The boy looked astonished. "That's really something. To think somebody could have killed Dr. Markem." He let out a low whistle. "How about that, huh? Weird thing is, I had just seen the guy. I mean I hadn't seen Professor Markem since I took his class, and then there he was on Saturday night at the bar. Then he was talking to this woman at a table."

"What did she look like?"

"Redheaded. Kind of pretty. I looked over once and it seemed like they were arguing. I thought it must be his wife. The way she looked at him, I thought she was his wife."

"When Markem was at the bar, did you talk to him at all?"

Potts shook his head. "Nah. It was Saturday and we were pretty busy. I kinda said like 'How's it going?' but to tell you the truth I don't even think he recognized me. Teachers. As soon as you're out of their class, they don't remember you. And I never see him on campus. I'm a business major. Accounting. So I don't get into the English and philosophy building much. I met my requirements junior year, the year I had Professor Markem. I don't need too much of that humanities crap for my major."

Frank again asked Brian Potts where he was on that morning.

"Me?" Brian asked, pointing to himself as if there were a lineup from which he was being singled out.

Frank nodded.

"How come anyone's asking *me?*" The boy seemed truly perplexed.

"There are a lot of people we're asking," Frank told him.

Brian stuck his tongue out in concentration and rolled his eyes toward the back of his head. "Let's see now. Monday. Monday." He blinked earnestly a few times. "Well, Monday morning I was with Louise. Louise Ericson. She's my girlfriend. I didn't work Sunday night and we were together at her house watching movies. She rented *Terminator II.*"

"And Monday?"

"Well, I slept over that night and Monday morning we were still sleeping, I guess. Or . . . you know. Maybe fooling around a little. I didn't have to be at work until two that day. And Louise, she's just finished school for the summer. She's going home to Chicago in a couple of days to look for a job. There's nothing here in Grandview. That's why I sure didn't want to lose this job here. Pretty easy work and good money. And I get free dinners in the restaurant." Brian smiled sweetly.

"And this Louise Ericson will corroborate your story?"

"Well, sure. She's my girlfriend."

"All right," Frank said, writing her name on a pad. "What's your girlfriend's address and phone?"

"Well, the phone might be disconnected. Like I said, she's moving back to Chicago on Saturday. Her address is 727 Clark Street." Brian put his hands on his massive thighs and moved closer to Frank. "Hey, can I ask you? What's this all about anyways? Except for the other night, I haven't even seen Professor Markem since last year. Why are you coming to me?" The boy's eyes narrowed and Frank detected a small spark of something he couldn't quite determine, something that said— despite Brian Potts's apparently amiable nature— "Don't mess with me!"

"Have you ever run into Tyler Markem in the gym?" Frank asked.

"I never go to the gym at school," Brian said scornfully. "They don't have enough equipment for me. I'm in the weight club at Mann's Fitness Center." He sat up straighter now, puffing himself up. "I'm into some pretty rigorous competitions."

"You had Dr. Markem for a teacher last year—you were in his Introduction to Philosophy class—and there was some altercation?"

"Altercation?"

"An argument. A fight you had with Professor Markem in

front of the class. He threw a chair at you," Frank reminded him.

"Oh yeah, *that.*" Brian Potts started to smile. Then he began to chuckle, shaking his head back and forth. Soon he was slapping his knee, guffawing in full-blown laughter. "You think I killed somebody 'cause of *that?* You think I killed Professor Markem 'cause he got pissed, told me where to get off?"

Frank took out a fresh piece of gum, looked hard at the boy. "There were witnesses from the class that day," Frank said, remembering what Leenie's friend had reported. "Witnesses who said that you were very angry at Markem—"

"Well, sure, when a guy throws a chair at you, for Christ's sake," Brian interrupted. "When a guy throws a chair at you, yeah, you're bound to get a little upset, you know?"

"You were heard to threaten him," Frank said, knowing he was treading lightly now in the murky waters of hearsay and innuendo.

"Naw!" Brian flicked a beefy hand at Frank, dismissing the very notion. "Soon as I calmed down myself and left the class, I knew he had a point. I mean, I can be a pretty rough guy, And I had my feet up on the desk and was reading the paper after class had started and the professor, well he got pretty pissed and told me to take my feet off the desk and put away the newspaper. I didn't like the way he told me. Made me feel like I was back in grade school or something. Set off something in me. I don't know, maybe it was just a bad day. Anyway, I just looked up at him, and met his gaze, you know, and purposely didn't move a muscle. I was *going* to move, put the paper away and everything, but I was going to do it in my own sweet time, just to show him that I wasn't going to be bossed around by some candy-ass professor." Brian paused, swallowing. His Adam's apple was unusually thick. "So then, the next thing I know," Brian went on, "this chair comes flying at me from across the room. The metal chair by his desk? I reach up quick-like and break the momentum. I mean, that chair would have sailed past me and nearly could have killed somebody, I swear to God. I thought Markem was really crazy!"

"Were you very angry at Markem at this point? Did you threaten him?" Frank asked.

"I don't know," Potts answered. "I don't remember what happened right after. I left the class. I do know that I went to see Markem the next day. I apologized to him. I told him I acted real badly in his class. I said I was sorry." He paused in reflection. "And you know what?"

"What?"

"Professor Markem apologized back to me. He said he was sorry, too, sorry that he lost his temper. He said he shouldn't have ever thrown a chair. We shook hands on it. We said 'no hard feelings' and shook hands. I remember 'cause the guy had quite a grip. A real bone-crusher, you know? I thought just maybe he was trying to show me something even then after I had apologized."

"Does anyone else know about this?" Frank asked.

"About him throwing the chair?"

"No, about you both apologizing to each other in his office." Brian sucked his lower lip. "Jeez, I don't know."

"Would you have told Louise about the incident?"

"I wasn't going with her then," Brian said, his brows knitting together.

"Anyone else?"

"Was I going with anyone else?"

"Okay, were you going with anyone else?"

"Hmmm. Let me see." Brian made little popping noises with his mouth. "Yeah, then, a year ago last spring, then I was going with Nicole Stephens. I was dating her just a couple of months. I don't know if I told her anything." He shrugged. "Even if I did, she probably wouldn't remember anything. Nicole's a space cadet. That girl couldn't remember her own phone number."

"And you haven't seen Professor Markem since?" Frank asked.

"Well, I finished that philosophy course with him. I went back and finished the course."

"You remember what grade you got?"

"Yeah, I did all right. C-plus, I think."

"You've not seen Professor Markem this year at all?"

Brian shook his head. "Maybe just walking by on campus. Not any particular place that I can recall."

Frank nodded. He got up to go and thanked Brian for his time. "Is there anything else you think could help us? Anything you know about Markem that you think might be useful?"

Brian Potts held open the door. Standing next to Frank, Potts wasn't quite as tall as he appeared. It was the bulk that made him appear looming. Brian shook his head. "I don't know what to tell you. I really don't know anything about this. What I know I read in the paper like everyone else. I thought what happened was an accident. At the gym where I lift there was a guy there one time whose arms locked when he was pressing. Someone came right over to help, but the bar came down in the guy's face. Knocked out some teeth. I remember him spitting blood all over the floor. Blood with teeth in it."

"What happened to Professor Markem very well could have been accidental," Frank said.

"Oh, yeah," Brian agreed heartily. "I mean, I can't believe that anyone would *want* to kill Professor Markem. Not him!"

"Why do you say that?" Frank wanted to know.

"Hey man, Professor Markem wasn't like your average tight-ass college professor. He was a *great* teacher. Really funny. Entertaining. Man, nobody slept through *his* lectures. I mean, that's one of the reasons when after we had that—what'd you call it, that altercation—that's one of the reasons that I went to Markem and apologized."

"What's that?"

"Because I didn't want to drop that class. No way I wanted to drop that class."

"You really liked him as a teacher, then?"

"Man, you kidding?" Brian Potts shook his head, and Frank now saw in his face the sorrow and the loss as he said the words: "Hey, Professor Markem was the *coolest,* man. He was the best teacher I ever had!"

18

After leaving Taco Time, Fran did not go home right away but
took a ride to the Ledges, a wilderness area at the edge of town,
preserved only recently from encroaching suburbia because
Stanley Detnor, a professor at Stimpson, had, one morning with
his Methods of Archeology class, discovered an Indian burial
mound in a place where developers had hoped to build a subdivi-
sion. Dr. Detnor's discovery caused great consternation at
Grandview, further dividing the townspeople against the college. Many of the Stimpson faculty were outraged that the
real estate developers would try to push through legislation to
redefine and rezone what was, after all, an archeological trea-
sure. Debate followed at the heated city council meetings. Tyler
had spoken eloquently of the need to preserve and honor the
past and of the ethical concerns of destroying part of the heritage
of native peoples. Fran, even knowing the political incorrectness
of the view, sided with the developers. Why deny people hous-
ing because of some old bones?

Now, however, driving around the winding country roads,
Fran was glad that the Ledges remained untouched. It was a

beautiful summer night, still and clear and fresh—the stars bright as aluminum foil, the intermittent sparkle of lightning bugs along the road turning the countryside into a fairyland. It was the kind of night one would take a lover out for a drive in a convertible and park someplace with the top down. Fran didn't have either a lover or a convertible, but the inclination was there nonetheless.

Over the burritos, Frank Rhodes had told her that he was widowed, and although she professed sympathy, the information about his single status made her heart skip a beat. Then she thought of that joke—the one about the woman who meets a man in a bar, a man who has recently been let out of jail for killing his wife and children—"Oh, so you're single?"

She did not share the joke with Frank Rhodes. Instead, she showed concern and made eye contact longer than was necessary. "It must be difficult to be alone after such a long marriage," she said gently. She told Frank about Damian (whom she was married to only a fourth of the time that Frank had been married to Carol) and said that even though she and Damian had been separated and living apart when he died, she had never completely gotten over the loss.

Recently—she did not share this information with Frank Rhodes, either—she had begun to think for the first time about being alone, about spending the rest of her life alone. She had been a long time now without a man. The last had been Bill Chandler. Fran had been with him the summer before at his cabin on Woman Lake in northern Minnesota. He had given up a magazine writing job in the Twin Cities to live at the cabin full-time. He was writing a novel with an "apocalyptic twist," a book, he told Fran, that "the world might not be ready for."

Bill Chandler grew or hunted his own food and built all the furniture in the cabin. For dinner he made wild mushroom casserole and mooseburgers and fresh tomato and basil salad; he and Fran sat at a table built from the trunk of a Douglas fir and slept on a mattress stuffed with hay. There was good sex, but in between there was too much drinking. Although he made dandelion and rhubarb wines, Bill somehow managed to actually buy expensive scotch. There was also self-absorption and dark talk about the state of the world.

And there was the outhouse, a stinking hole in the ground behind the cabin complete with black-bellied spiders and snakes. The last few days of the visit, Fran admitted that she had had enough; she told Bill she was not really an outhouse and moosemeat kind of gal, and what would he think if they spent the weekend in a hotel in St. Paul before she flew back to Grandview? The treat was on her.

Bill Chandler was insulted. It wasn't the money, he insisted. It was just that he couldn't go back to that kind of life. A life with processed and plastic everything and the bombarding of his senses with noise and pollution and the grotesque moral decay of the material world. "How about for a weekend?" Fran asked.

That was the last time she saw Bill Chandler, even though he wrote and even called on occasion (collect, from a pay phone in town), and wanted her to come back again. Once, drunk, he called late at night to tell her how lonely he was and asked her to take a leave of absence from teaching and come live with him there in the cabin in the north woods. Then Fran told him in no uncertain terms that if she never saw an outhouse again, it would be too soon. And, she told him, she found the sound of the loons on the lake frankly annoying.

One of Fran's rules, as a grown-up, was not to date a man whose car was in worse shape than hers. Bill Chandler had no car at all. That had to have been a sign.

Now it was almost a year since she had been with a man. One year without a man's arms around her, without the scent of a man's body on one side of the bed in the morning. It had been too long. But instead of observing her sexual urges diminishing or drying up from lack of use as one might expect,

Fran more often felt herself turned on without due cause, wet and wanting, at peculiar times like during chamber music concerts or while trying on clothes in the mall or—most inappropriate of all—at Stimpson faculty meetings.

There George Lawson sat across from her in sodden grumpiness, and Harvey Boxtel with his sweet Pillsbury Doughboy hands scraped out his pipe and sighed, and pedantic Sam Hollyhock scratched his bald dome and looked bored; there was also Milton Harkness, with his 1970s muttonchop sideburns and foul breath that always smelled like sardines and shit; and old Dr. Waller (eighty if he was a day, though retirement was supposed to be mandatory at Stimpson at age seventy-two) droning on and on and on about the decline in the quality of freshman writing; and Julia, efficiently taking notes; and Diane Lubacher, a new, young, earnest American Lit scholar who had the thin, wispy hair of a newborn and a little, itty-bitty girl-voice that drove Fran crazy; and Dr. Loren Best, a Mormon with a half-dozen kids, always on leave and schlepping his entire brood around the country. Aside from Julia, whom she loved, it was a motley crew.

And what about tonight? It wasn't exactly as if dinner had been a music and candlelight affair. She and Frank Rhodes were, after all, sitting in a turquoise-and-orange booth eating with plastic utensils in a Taco Time in Grandview, Illinois, and discussing a murder.

So why, when they got up to leave and Frank lightly touched the small of her back as he guided them down a narrow aisle, did Fran feel the beginnings of a moan rising in her throat? Why, as she and Frank walked out to their respective cars and he stood for a moment, his hand on the hood of her car, saying he would get in touch (he meant professionally, of course) did she actually sense her insides quicken with anticipation?

Now, driving out of the Ledges, Fran rolled down her window, breathing in the night air, tapping her fingernails along the steering wheel. She was listening to 102, KCBI, the oldies station, where the disc jockeys had the same adolescent humor of the boys she went to high school with. The DJ, introducing a Marvin Gaye song, tried to sound Black: "An oldie but goodie, a blast from the past, put the needle to the tracks, separate the soul from the wax; if you miss my mess, man, you're at the wrong address; you got a hole in your soul!" Then came Aretha, pulsing her way into the night: "R-e-s-p-e-c-t, find out what it means to me."

Fran sang along, driving up the street to her house, then sitting in the garage with the volume turned up to finish listening to The Supremes sing "You Can't Hurry Love."

The kitchen had the burned, stale smell of overheated coffee. "Shit," Fran said aloud, going over to turn off the Melitta Aroma-Time, a gift from Roz in New York. The coffee maker came with a real gold filter that should never have to be replaced "in your life-time," Roz told Fran. Roz was rich and she was also generous. Most of Fran's expensive kitchen equipment, as well as much of her clothing and jewelry, had been gifts or hand-me-downs from Roz.

Fran looked at the light on the answering machine, which was blinking three times, went over and pressed "playback," then went to a kitchen drawer to look for chocolate. She found a quarter of a Nestlé's Crunch bar buried among the spatulas.

The first message was from Roz. Even long distance, her sister's voice had the threat of imminent presence, as if she could just show up in the doorway at any moment. "Franny, where are you?" Roz said in a semiaccusatory sort of way. "It's seven o'clock here. Six o'clock your time," she added, as if Fran wouldn't know. "I'm just calling to find out how the funeral went. Are you *all right*? Call me. I love you."

The second message was from George Lawson, who sounded as if he had spent the last hours being beaten by terrorists. "This is George," he said in a broken croak of a voice. "Can you call me back tonight? I need to talk to you."

The third message was from Julia. "It's me, Fran," she said

crisply. "Call me as soon as you get in. I have something to tell you."

Fran went to the refrigerator to get herself a glass of wine, unbuttoning the blue jumpsuit as she went, taking off the belt, a bracelet, her earrings, kicking off her shoes, throwing down her purse, leaving a trail of herself as she went down the hall to the bedroom. Sitting on the edge of her bed, the wineglass held between her knees, the blue silk jumpsuit in a shimmery mass at her feet, Fran knew two things were about to happen.

One was that she was going to get involved in this investigation—she was going to be an active participant, not someone to be called in for questioning as merely a bystander or prospective witness.

The other thing she knew—the knowledge of it fluttered inside her at that moment, like a tiny bird pressing itself against a glass window—was that she was about to embark upon another journey, going to that place she'd been before and missed now with a longing that was almost palpable. There were the physical signs: the shivery feeling as if a string from somewhere low in her belly were being pulled up toward her breasts; the melting sensation she had behind her knees; the way her skin felt soft and yielding to the touch. It wasn't sex exactly. Well, it was. But it wasn't *only* sex; it was something else as well: that feeling right before she let herself be led—without reason or forethought or deliberation—to a place at the edge so that someone else becomes the single most important, consuming presence. Then there was the letting go, floating a little, silly, obsessed, embarrassed by the vivid fantasies always in the forefront of her consciousness while she went about the most ordinary chores.

It was hot in the bedroom, which had been closed up all day, the sun baking the western side of the house so that the heat made the room smell of old wood and plaster. Fran pulled back the curtains and opened a window facing the empty backyard. A full moon was set so low in the sky, sitting directly atop a neighboring garage, that it looked as though it could roll like a beach ball down the slope of the roof and bounce away. Silver light danced along the telephone wires and illuminated the shrubs and bushes along the back with a greenish glow. Fran sighed, walked naked across to her bed, lay down under her navy blue satin comforter, and picked up the phone.

"Why didn't you tell me before?" Fran asked, when she heard Julia's hello.

"Franny? Wait a minute." Julia excused herself and told someone that garbage bags were under the sink. "I'll take the phone to my room," she said to the same audience. Fran imagined Julia walking with the portable phone up the stairs into the apricot-and-gray bedroom with the four-poster bed she had shared with Tyler. "Hello?" Julia said again.

"I was just down at the police department. Answering questions. Julia, why didn't you *tell* me?"

"All right. Tell you what?"

"About the insurance policy," Fran said. "The one that Tyler's mother had taken out."

"Oh, that," Julia said. She sounded tired, distracted. "Oh, Fran, that's not really important."

"Detective Rhodes seems to think it is. Julia, the police think that Tyler's death may not be accidental. You knew he had a girlfriend and a 350,000-dollar insurance policy. Sweetie, that makes you a prime suspect."

"Do you think that?" Julia asked, her voice suddenly cool.

"Of course not!!" Fran said emphatically. "But while *I* don't," she added, "someone else might."

"This is ridiculous!" Julia sounded angry. "The whole thing is ridiculous! What happened in that gym was an accident. I can't believe that anyone would actually want to *kill* Tyler." There was a long pause. "Franny, what do you think?"

"I don't know," Fran said. "I honestly don't know. It's just when I was talking to this detective, there seemed to be so many questions."

"Fran, why are the police telling *you* this?" Julia wanted to know. "Isn't my insurance policy classified information or something?"

"We got close. I managed to get some things out of him."

"That tall guy with the sweet smile? Rhodes?"

"He does have a sweet smile, doesn't he?"

"Fran, what's going on here?" Julia sounded alarmed.

"Wait a minute. That's my question. So how come you never told me about the insurance policy? Julia, that's a lot of money."

"I don't know. It wasn't as if I were keeping it a secret or anything. Tyler's mother took out an insurance policy after Beth was born. Her brother sold insurance at the time, and she bought the policy from him. I know, it was excessive. But it wasn't something I ever thought about." Julia added, "Until now."

"And then there's the fact that you knew about Lynette. And the way she suddenly disappeared the day Tyler was found. I mean, the cops have a right to be suspicious, Julia." There was such a dead silence that Fran thought for a moment she had been disconnected. "Julia? Are you there?"

"She's back," Julia said finally. "That's what I was calling you about."

"Lynette's back in town? How do you know?"

"She called me. About an hour ago. She asked to see me. I'm going over to her apartment at eleven-thirty. Everyone here will be sleeping by then. Their plane is tomorrow at eight." Julia's voice dropped to a whisper. "I can't wait for them to go. God, I know it's an awful thing to say, my parents and Margaret have all been so terrific, but it's such a strain to have them here. I feel like they know that I'm lying to them."

"You're not lying to them. You're just not telling them everything."

"It's a kind of lie," Julia said. "With the kids it's easier. Saving them from having a tarnished image of their father . . .

at least, I seem to have a mission for doing that. Of course, with this investigation everything could very well blow up on us and they'd know."

"Sweetie, do you want me to go with you?" Fran asked.

"To the airport?"

"Well, that, too, if you want. I meant tonight, to Lynette's," Fran replied.

"No, I don't think so."

"How about calling the police? Telling them she's back?"

"I wanted to hear what she had to say first. If the police come and start questioning her right away, maybe she wouldn't be so anxious to talk to me."

"She seemed anxious?" Fran asked.

"Yes, she really did. Of course, she was terribly upset."

"I'm going with you. You're not going to that apartment by yourself in the middle of the night. She could be the killer. Finish you off just like she did Tyler."

"You've been watching too much television," Julia said.

"I hardly watch television. Since the end of 'ThirtySomething' . . ." Fran trailed off wistfully. "Listen, I'm coming with you. Pick me up in half an hour. I'll be waiting."

Without getting out of bed, Fran called her sister. They talked for about ten minutes, Fran giving the details of the funeral in a clinical way. "You sound tired," Roz said. Fran used that as an excuse to end the conversation, promising to call again on the weekend.

George Lawson didn't answer, although Fran let the phone ring only four times. Well, she *had* tried to call him back. She'd had to get out of bed to find the phone book to look up his number. George was not on her automatic dial. Her parents still were, and she did not know how to take them off.

It was Tyler who had first set the phone system up for her a few years ago. All he had taught her how to do was change the message on the answering machine, something she did with regularity. She remembered Tyler laying out the directions on her kitchen table. Even though there was often tension between them, he seemed to enjoy doing things like that for her and was generous when Julia offered him up to change the furnace filters or go on Fran's roof to check a leak.

Once he came over armed with a hard hat and a tennis racket to remove a bat that had gotten into the house through an opening in the fireplace. Fran recalled huddling with Julia in the kitchen until Tyler called an all-clear, bringing in the dead bat on the flat of the racket. Even stone dead the animal had a sinister quality that made Fran shiver afterward. Tyler had a beer, and he joked around, saying, oh sure, what kind of feminists were they, anyway? A real woman would have bitten the head off that bat. But he had been good natured, pleased with his own success, and Fran was grateful.

Suddenly, looking at all the numbers on the automatic dial (including a pizza place whose number had changed and should also be taken off), Fran felt a sudden sorrow. Tears welled up in her eyes, and she let them come, crying at the same time she pictured in her mind's eye Tyler sitting at that kitchen table, healthy and alive. He was reading aloud the directions for setting up the automatic dial, though she was not even listening. He had been earnest, sitting there in her kitchen, trying his best to make something work for her.

It was not the first time she had cried since learning of Tyler's death, but it was the first time she had found herself actually missing him, mourning him. "I'm sorry," she said, under her breath, to nobody in particular.

19

Fran was already waiting at the front step when Julia's car pulled into the driveway. "How are you doing, sweetie?" Fran asked, opening the car door. Then she saw that Julia was smoking a cigarette.

"I know." Julia's voice was tight. "Don't say anything." She opened the window and started batting the air around. "When everything settles down, I'll stop."

"That's all right. I wasn't going to say anything," Fran lied.

"It's just been so tense in the house. Dealing with everyone's feelings, all those emotions. Being with the children. Caty came in and slept with me last night. She put her face into the pillow and said she wanted to smell Daddy."

Fran let out a small coo of sympathy. "Poor baby."

"Only thing is, Tyler hasn't been in that bed for weeks. Everything's been washed." Julia turned and blew a puff of smoke out the window. "And then my parents . . . oh God, Franny, they mean well but they're so difficult to be with. My father keeps talking about the weather. My mother doesn't want to leave me alone. She planned to have my father go back with

Margaret and she was going to stay another week. Finally, I told her I just *wanted* to be alone. I know I hurt her feelings."

"What about your sister?" Fran wanted to know.

"I think Margaret knows something. I mean, apart from Tyler being dead and the police asking questions and all. I've told everyone that it's just a routine investigation, that the police always do this when a body is found without any witnesses. There's no way my family thinks this was anything but an accident."

Fran confessed. "I told Margaret about Lynette."

"You did?"

"Not her name or anything, not about who she is. Just that there was another woman. She seemed to know anyway. I'm sorry that I didn't tell you. It was after the funeral, when Margaret and I went to the bakery, and I didn't get a chance to see you alone."

"It doesn't matter, I guess." Julia sighed. "Who knows what's going to come out of this investigation anyway?"

"Margaret didn't say anything to you? I didn't give her any details at all. She guessed. She asked if there was another woman and I told her yes. That's all I said. Didn't she ask you about that?" Fran asked, surprised.

"She probably thought that when I was ready, I'd tell her," Julia said.

Fran thought how amazing it was to be able to be so controlled, to respect another person's privacy so completely: to be a gentile. She imagined how Roz, equipped with such a bit of knowledge, would go about relentlessly extracting the rest of the story. As if she knew what Fran was thinking, Julia added: "We're New Englanders. We don't talk unless it's necessary, and we're not big on sharing what's in our hearts." Just for effect, Julia put the broad "a" on "talk" and "hearts." "Here we are," Julia added as she pulled up in front of the Greenbriar apartments.

"Park the *car,"* Fran imitated in her best New England accent. She looked around. "Hmm. Bit of a slum your husband's girlfriend lives in," Fran said, curling her lip. There was trash all around, remnants of student leave-behinds as they packed to go home for the summer. In front of the apartment a stained mattress and the broken pieces of a bookcase lay propped up against bags and boxes of junk. "Well, I suppose this was better than fucking her in a dormitory," Fran said, stepping around a pile of yellowed newspaper.

"Why should I say you're with me?" Julia asked, ringing the bell for 1-F.

"I'll tell her I reevaluated her grade from last semester. I'll tell her I've decided to give her an 'A.'"

"Oh, Fran!" Julia exclaimed as the door opened. Then: "You remember Professor Meltzer," Julia said simply to Lynette Macalvie, standing there in the doorway.

Lynette's eyes were a bright, washed-out blue, and the skin around them was puffy and pink. "Please come in," she said, poised as if she had invited them over for tea. Fran and Julia followed her around a suitcase and a roll of blankets and pillows in the middle of the hall. "Sorry about that," Lynette said over her shoulder. "I just got in and called work before I even unpacked. Claire, one of the girls I work with, told me." Her voice broke off in a strangled sob.

She was blonder than Fran recalled. Also chubbier, though it could have been the clothing. Lynette was wearing blue spandex biking shorts and what looked to be the top of a floral swimsuit. Her white arms and broad back had a substantial fleshiness that Fran would not have noticed on a quiet student, sitting in the back of a class more suitably dressed. There was nothing cheap or even sexy about Lynette. She was blond and fair skinned and slightly chubby, and looked as wholesome as a farm-fresh egg.

"I can't stop crying," Lynette confessed, sitting herself down on the wicker sofa. She pulled a box of tissues over from the coffee table and delicately blew her nose, while Julia and Fran stood in the middle of the room, watching her cry.

"You just found out about Tyler?" Fran said with disbelief. "You didn't know?"

Lynette nodded and blew.

"What exactly *do* you know?" Julia said coolly.

It took a couple of minutes for Lynette to catch her breath. Wheezy snuffles filled the room as Fran and Julia waited expectantly. "That he's gone," Lynette said softly, weeping into her hands.

"And what else?" Julia asked calmly.

Lynette gulped a few times and looked back and forth from Fran to Julia. "How could this be? This is a nightmare. I went away to think about what was going on, to think about what happened." She looked plaintively at Julia, as if for support. "After you came over Sunday morning, I didn't know what to do. I just wanted to run away and have some time by myself to think."

"What else do you know except that Tyler is dead?" Julia persisted. Unbidden, she and Fran sat on opposite sides of Lynette: Julia on one end of the sofa, Fran in a wicker chair under a hanging plant whose spidery leaves touched the top of her head when she sat all the way back.

Lynette took another deep breath. "Well, I know it happened when he was lifting weights." She turned to Fran. "He kept himself in such wonderful shape." Fran nodded knowingly. "And I found out that the police have been searching all over to find me," Lynette went on. "I know the police are looking into this as a murder because Tyler was found all alone. Claire told me they've been to the Holiday Inn three times already looking for me. They've called my parents and have them *very* upset. Was this necessary? I mean, what do my *parents* have to do with this?"

"What do *you* have to do with it?" Julia pressed on. "Where were you for the past four days?"

"I *loved* Tyler!" Lynette said fiercely. "I could never, ever hurt him!"

"Well, I think, Lynette, that the police really are pretty interested in where you were for the past four days," Fran added gently, feeling as if she and Julia were in a good-cop, bad-cop routine.

"Where were you?" Julia repeated, her arms crossed over her chest.

Lynette's voice was girlishly whiny. "An old boyfriend of mine, his family has a trailer near Lake Westin. They used it mainly for hunting. But last year his father had a stroke. They've been trying to sell it, and I knew no one would be there now."

"Wasn't the trailer locked? How did you get in?" Julia asked.

"Jason used to take me there," Lynette answered. "I knew where the key was." Fran and Julia sat on either side of Lynette, waiting; Fran stared down at Lynette's bare feet. Lynette's toenails were painted a bright, bubble-gum pink. They were thick, plump toes attached to the solid, wide feet of a peasant girl. As if feeling Fran's gaze, the toes began to wiggle, hiding themselves in the shag carpet. "It's under the bottom step," Lynette added. "There's a magnet attached to the wood under the step. The key is there."

"When did you leave?" Julia wanted to know. "It's about an hour's drive to Lake Westin, isn't it?"

"An hour and ten minutes," Lynette said. "I left Monday morning. Before eleven o'clock."

"Did you get gas here in town before you left?" Fran asked, looking up from the toes. She glanced at Julia and thought, for the moment, that they were pretty terrific together, she and Julia. Lynette answered all their questions, compliant as a schoolgirl—which, in fact, she was.

Lynette told them that the tank was full before she left, that she got to the trailer and slept, since she hadn't had a wink the night before after Julia had left. About three in the afternoon, she had gone into the town of Westin and bought some groceries, paying with a check.

"But not until three," Fran noted. "I mean, you don't really have any alibi for where you were at eleven-thirty, the time Tyler was . . ." Fran paused dramatically. "The time Tyler had the accident," she said.

"I had just gotten to the trailer. I was cleaning it out and opening up the windows. There were mouse droppings all over the kitchen." Lynette shuddered. "I had brought my own blankets and pillows, and I set them up in the back bedroom and took a nap after I cleaned up." Suddenly Lynette looked sharply at Fran, then at Julia, then back at Fran. She pulled herself up straight, planting her pink, thick feet in front of her with resolution. "I didn't kill Tyler," she said firmly. "I couldn't kill anyone, least of all someone I truly loved. I didn't kill Tyler," she repeated.

"Lynette," Fran said gently. "Why did you call Julia tonight and ask her to come here to see you?"

There was a long silence. Lynette's jaw was still firm, but her eyes filled again with tears. "I'm so sorry," she said, turning to Julia on the couch. "I'm so, so sorry." Lynette began to weep, leaning toward Julia as if waiting for comfort. Instinctively, Fran sat back, feeling the scratchy fronds of the fern right above her head. "We've lost him," Lynette said plaintively to Julia. "I just needed to share that with you, I guess. I'm sorry."

Lynette cried and cried; Julia sat stiffly beside her. What Lynette was sorry about, Fran wasn't exactly sure. Sorry for having the affair? For hurting Julia and her family? For killing Tyler? Finally Fran cleared her throat to get Lynette's attention. "What are you apologizing for?" Fran wanted to know.

Lynette looked up, her face swollen and soaked with tears. "Apologizing?" The word hung in the air like a balloon. Lynette blinked a few times and looked at Fran, puzzled.

"Well, you said you were sorry," Fran noted.

"Oh," Lynette answered, her mouth forming a little pink *O* itself. "I meant that I was sorry for Tyler. That he was dead." Lynette turned to Julia. "I can't believe it, is all. Can you? I can't believe that we'll never, ever see him again." The tears began again in earnest. "And I missed the funeral. I left him and missed the funeral and didn't even know what was happening." Voicing this, Lynette started to cry louder, her fleshy white shoulders heaving with each sob. She made a fist and punched a pillow beside her on the couch.

"Let's go." Julia rose, two red dots of anger across each cheek. She signaled Fran with a nod of her head.

"You can't possibly believe anyone would want to kill Tyler?" Lynette said, still crying on the couch. "I mean, I know I'm supposed to go to the police, but I just don't know what to tell them."

"Tell them the truth," Fran said, hearing her own voice sharp and precise. Just the facts, ma'am. Tell them the truth.

"The truth is," Lynette said, holding herself tight, her chin thrust out—in only seconds she seemed to go from sloppy blithering to haughty defiance— "that Tyler and I loved each other. I know we hurt you," she said, acknowledging Julia towering above her. "But we really did love each other. And I came to believe that what you told me on Sunday night, about Tyler wanting to go to counseling with you and not seeing me again . . . I came to the realization that what you said simply was not true. That you were just telling me that in order to hurt me and drive me away." Lynette stood up then, next to Julia. She was a good three inches shorter than Julia, but she had about twenty pounds on her and an upper torso that looked broad and strong. In an actual fight, Fran would have to put her money on Lynette. "I don't believe that Tyler would leave me. He *loved* me. He wanted to *marry* me!" Lynette faced Julia, shoulders squared.

"Perhaps," Julia said coolly, turning on her heel. She wended her way past the pile in the middle of the living room. "Fran?"

She nodded over to Fran, who was still plugged into her chair under the plant.

"What should I tell the police?" Lynette said plaintively.

"Tell them what you just told us," Julia said. "Tell them that Tyler loved you and was going to marry you."

"My parents are going to find out," Lynette said miserably.

"I'm sure they already know," Julia said. "The police have called them a number of times trying to find you. They're probably worried." Julia actually sounded maternal. "You should call them tonight."

"I will," Lynette said, wiping her eyes with the back of her hand, looking sleepy and innocent. "Julia?" she asked, walking them to the door. Fran and Julia paused at the same time, practically bumping into each other. "What about George Lawson?"

"George Lawson?" Fran repeated, recalling his voice on her answering machine sounding about a hundred years old, beaten and scared and sad. "What about George Lawson?"

"Should I tell the police about that girl and the sexual harassment incident? Tyler was the only one who knew." There was the slightest hint of a smile on her face. "He told you, didn't he?" Lynette added to Julia. There was something else in Lynette's face, Fran saw: defiance, perhaps, but also a look that suggested something small and smug and—Julia had been right in her description—something almost schoolteacherish. ("There now, class, we don't know as much as we thought now, do we?")

Julia remained impassive. "Tell them whatever you want," she said, turning her back and walking out the door.

"Did you know anything about this?" Fran asked as she followed Julia out to the car. Julia was silent, walking quickly, and Fran had to take three steps for Julia's every one. "Damn it, Julia," Fran said as soon as they were inside the car. "Do you know what that business was about George?"

"I suppose we'll find out soon enough," Julia said calmly, reaching for the pack of Marlboros on the dash. The light from the match made her red hair glow like flame.

20

Frank came in early the next morning to spend some time reading Tyler Markem's students' evaluations. They were interesting. Most of the students thought highly of him, that was for sure. They said things like: "Best teacher I ever had," "Dr. Markem is a brilliant lecturer," "Challenging, dynamic teacher." Students wrote about how Dr. Markem made them "really think," how he taught them to look at the world differently.

There were also students—a minority, but a significant number nonetheless—who apparently despised Tyler. These students wrote about Tyler's arrogance, his bad temper, his egotism, his ability to intimidate and humiliate; a few mentioned what they saw as "a cruel streak." The criticisms were repeated, and the feelings that came through on these evaluations revealed more, it seemed to Frank, than simple dissatisfaction. There was an undercurrent of real hostility and personal affront.

Frank put the student evaluations in separate piles. Raves were on one side of the desk: over fifty students who wrote, "Best teacher I ever had at Stimpson."

There were eighteen negative evaluations over the last few years. Counting summer school, that averaged out to two each semester. Two students every semester who thought that Tyler Markem was not only a bad teacher but a bad person as well. But did any one of them think it strongly enough that they would try to kill him?

Around nine o'clock Doris Duncan stuck her head in the door and told Frank that she had to leave for a few minutes. "I'm just running across the street to Bowers," she said. "Andy forgot his lunch money again."

Frank got up to get a cup of coffee. He unwrapped a couple of fresh pieces of Big Red, then went over to the window and watched Doris walk across the street in the bright sun. He had never looked at Doris from this perspective before. She was wearing sunglasses and a short blue dress with puffed sleeves. A jauntiness to her walk made her seem optimistic.

Across from the police department was one of Grandview's schools: Lucinda Bowers Elementary. An oil painting of Principal Lucinda Bowers, gray-haired, severe, and benign all at the same time, hung in the entrance. The school, over fifty years old, had a new addition put on in the early sixties. Bowers Elementary was where Frank and his brother and sister had gone to school, swinging their metal lunch boxes, walking from the big white house downtown on Sixth Street where they lived. Memaw and Pepaw, his mother's parents, had lived with them, as had his mother's younger, slightly retarded brother, Freddy.

Growing up with Uncle Freddy in the house was like having another brother to play with, only another brother who would never be mean or beat you up. It wasn't until Frank was in his teens that he began to see that Freddy, over forty by then and still enamored of the tin soldiers that he and Frank used to play with, was impaired in any way and therefore deficient.

At Frank's wedding to Carol, Freddy, all dressed up in an ill-fitting black suit, his hair slicked back with Brylcreem, took Frank aside; then Freddy stuffed a wad of bills into Frank's hand—*ones* from his paper route—and slapped Frank on the back in a manly way. "She's pretty," Freddy said simply. "You're lucky." (For years after, watching her face as she lay next to him in bed, he recalled his uncle's words: She's pretty. You're lucky.)

There was a flurry of births and deaths in the Rhodes family in the mid to late sixties. First Pepaw died of heart failure, and then Bobby and Patricia were born, and then there was Memaw's death from some kind of female cancer that nobody ever talked about, and then Mark was born. And then that fall, Uncle Freddy, coming home from the Safeway with a sack full of groceries, walked straight into a school bus that was turning out of Bowers Elementary onto Walnut Street. It was the driveway that faced the police station, right where Frank Rhodes was looking now.

Frank went back to the evaluations, rereading the ones he thought could give him a sign. One, written in a cramped script, denounced the atheism that was rampant on the Stimpson campus, "especially in someone like Professor Markem." Frank wondered at that. Especially in Tyler Markem, or someone *like* him?

After a while, he went to the front office to get a doughnut. His favorites were the creamy lemon, the filling thick and tart and glutenous on the tongue. In the box next to the coffee machine he found nothing left but sugar doughnuts and plain.

Doris Duncan had returned and was concentrating on writing something, deep in thought, rubbing her chin. On a napkin on her desk lay an untouched jelly doughnut.

Just then Jonny Verlaine came in, looking flushed and excited. "How's it going?" Frank asked.

"Hey, boss, got a minute? I need to tell you something."

Frank took Jonny's elbow and led him back into his office. Verlaine's smooth, unlined face was covered by a sheen of perspiration. "Hot out, isn't it?" Frank asked.

"The air doesn't work in the car," Jonny said, taking out a white handkerchief and mopping his face.

"What's up?" Frank wanted to know. "You find Lynette Macalvie?"

"No. We're just waiting on her coming back to work later this afternoon. That's what the manager said. But you know you asked me to run a sheet on that kid? The skinny kid who found Markem in the gym?"

"Lyle Dixon," Frank said.

"Yeah, well, this is kind of interesting. I mean, he was clean, no record or anything, but you know what I found out?"

Frank shook his head.

"Well, another thing I did was, I got some of the kid's records from the college and all. I got his transcript."

"Okay," Frank said, waiting.

"And guess what? Right there on the transcript for last year it lists a philosophy course that Dixon took last year: Introduction to Philosophical Concepts, it was called. A year ago. Last spring."

"And . . . ?" Frank knew what Jonny Verlaine was about to say.

"And the teacher of that particular philosophy course for that particular semester was none other than Tyler Markem. This kid, Lyle Dixon, had Markem for a professor the year before! How about that?"

Jonny looked so excited that Frank felt the air around them stirring. "How about that is right," Frank said, his heart quickening. He tried to recall that first interview with Lyle Dixon in G.P.'s office and what had been said. Sure the kid was shook. He was scared. Frank had asked Lyle if he knew Tyler Markem. What had the kid responded? Frank couldn't exactly remember. It was more that the kid knew *of* Tyler Markem. Well, of course, everyone did. It was a small school. But he hadn't been any more forthcoming than that. Certainly, Lyle Dixon had not indicated that Tyler had been his teacher.

"That kid never came off like he knew the guy, did he,

Frank?'' Jonny Verlaine folded his hands across his broad chest and leaned against the wall. He looked handsome and groomed in his uniform, like a pinup for a police recruitment poster. ''I mean, the kid was upset, sure, but it wasn't upset like he really knew the guy personally or anything, remember? It was just because he found the body.''

''Well, that's upsetting enough for most people,'' Frank said. ''To find a body.''

''Yeah, but why wouldn't the kid say, 'Hey, that's my teacher.' Why wouldn't he tell us that he knew Markem?''

''We didn't really ask him,'' Frank responded.

Jonny Verlaine shook his head. ''Come on. Even if we didn't ask. Most people would volunteer that information.''

''I know,'' Frank said. ''You're right.''

''Dixon lives in Manning. I spoke to his mother. He's got a job this summer at a fertilizer plant. Thought you might want to take a little ride out there with me this morning.''

Frank looked at his watch. Possibly they could go to Manning and question the kid and get back in time for him to see Lynette Macalvie. ''Okay,'' Frank said, grabbing his sports jacket off the back of the chair. ''Let's go.'' Walking down the hall out to the car, Frank mused almost to himself: ''You know, I wonder . . .''

''What's that, sir?''

''What he got.''

''Pardon?''

''The kid. Lyle Dixon. What grade did he get in Markem's class?''

Jonny Verlaine smiled. ''He got a C. It was the only one. Everything else was A's and B's.''

''Thanks,'' Frank said, walking out the door. Outside, the air was already thick with the heat of the day. Across the street, a few children were on the school playground. Frank stopped for a minute, watching two boys in contest on the swings, each going so high that it seemed as if the swing could circle the bar. There were always stories of kids who had gone so high that they circled the bar. Had anyone, ever, really?

The boys on the swings slowed and jumped, racing each other across the playground to the ball field, where some other boys waited with bats and balls. Frank got into the car, rolled down the windows, and he and Jonny Verlaine headed out of town.

21

During the drive, Jonny Verlaine's allergies acted up and he sneezed about a dozen times in a row. Jonny said he had been seeing a new allergist. "Not a real doctor," he told Frank. "Some homeoquack from Peoria."

"A what?" Frank asked.

"Well, he isn't exactly a traditional doctor. He does homeopathic medicine," Jonny said. "My sister swears by him."

"Doesn't sound like he's doing you much good," Frank noted as Jonny continued to sneeze.

"He's giving me something that will make me sicker at first," Jonny said between sneezes. "Herbs and shit. You're supposed to get sicker before you get better."

"Great. And you pay for this?"

"It's some kind of theory: 'The Crisis of Healing.' First you get sicker while all the toxins start clearing out of your body. Then you stabilize. It's kind of like when you quit drinking. How sick you feel for a while."

"Uh-huh." Frank dug into his jacket pocket for another piece of gum. "What else do we know about this kid?" Frank asked as he drove. His own drinking had never been a secret, but he still didn't like to talk about the topic. ˙

Jonny Verlaine blew his nose and opened up the folder. "Nothing much. 'Lyle Dixon, Rural Route 3, Manning, Illinois,' " he read aloud and then looked up. "No record. Not so much as a speeding ticket. Lived in the dorm by himself and worked in food service fifteen hours a week. Also had a Sunday paper route downtown. Going to be a senior this fall. Good student. All B's and A's, except for that C he got in philosophy."

They drove along in silence until they came to the Manning exit. They passed a turkey farm, and Frank switched the air conditioner from "fresh" to "recycle." "So what do you think?" Jonny asked.

"What do I think about what?" Frank asked.

"Philosophy. You think philosophy is so hard? You know, difficult to understand and all?"

"I don't know. I don't even know what philosophy is," Frank confessed. Along the road beyond the fence were vast numbers of turkeys. Some were housed in tiers of metal cages, but many bobbed and pecked along free in a field.

"Philosophy has to do with the meaning of life. What life is all about and shit like that. You know: like someone's philosophy of life. You got one?" Jonny asked.

"A philosophy of life?"

"Yeah."

Frank thought a minute. He did, actually. After Carol's death and his spending so much time alone, he had taken stock, thought often and deeply about life—his own and life in general. "No," Frank answered softly. "I don't think so."

"I do," Jonny Verlaine said, smiling. He turned to Frank and started a recitation: "Don't lie about anything big; don't forget your mother's birthday; rotate your tires; don't eat yellow snow . . . I don't know. What do you think it is they really learn in a philosophy class?" Jonny asked.

"Beats me," Frank said.

A truck pulled out from the farm piled two stories high with caged birds; turkey feathers floated in the air in front of the windshield like snow flurries.

Lyle Dixon was a small, homespun-looking boy who wore round, wire-rimmed glasses and appeared younger than his twenty-one years. He was brought into a back office and deposited by a foreman who left him with the instructions to remember to punch out if he was going to leave the premises. Lyle stood in the doorway, looking to Frank to be invited to sit.

"Please sit," Frank offered, pointing to a straight-back chair. The room had the ambience of a principal's office, and Lyle sat at the edge of the chair, looking uncomfortable and frightened. Delicate and pale, dressed in blue work pants and a blue summer work shirt whose short sleeves came too far down his thin arms, Lyle looked as if he had spent a good deal of his boyhood indoors, reading science fiction or working on model planes. What had this kid been doing in a gym was the first question that came to Frank's mind, seeing the boy now before him. He remembered asking that very question, in fact, the morning Tyler was found, but the answer hadn't appeared in the deposition. Now the question took on more significance. What was Lyle Dixon doing in the weight room of the gym? The kid looked as if he couldn't life a paperweight up off a desk. "Lyle," Frank said tenderly, because tender was the way he felt looking at the sad, pale boy whose shirt said LYLE in a fancy script across the pocket. "What were you doing in the gym on the morning you found Tyler Markem?"

"I told you that already," Lyle replied. "When you interviewed me right after." His voice had a thin, reedy quality, and his eyes looked back and forth between Frank and Jonny Verlaine. "You were both there," he added, puzzled.

"I know," Frank said. "We'd like you to tell us again."

The boy drew a breath and looked around the room before

he began. The front of the office had three panels of textured glass, and through it the workers on the floor made wavy and distorted motions. Basically, Lyle repeated to the officers what he told them before. He had been in the gym cleaning out his locker at the end of the semester. He had neglected to do that the last day of class because he had to go directly to his job at food service and he didn't want to carry everything with him. "There's no place to put anything away where I work, and I didn't want my stuff to get ripped off," he said.

Frank asked, "You were taking a class?"

"Spring semester. I was taking a fencing class," Lyle replied.

"Well, okay. But the locker room is off to the side. Why'd you go into the weight room?"

The boy shrugged. "I don't know. I just stopped in on the way out of the gym."

"To do what?" Frank asked.

"I don't know. I just stopped by," Lyle said again, chewing on his bottom lip.

"Did you hear anything? Any noises?" Frank recalled asking the question before, during the first interview.

"No. I didn't hear anything."

"Were you going to lift some weights then, Lyle?" Frank asked. The boy shook his head and looked down at his lap, flicking a thumbnail. "You don't *have* to go through the weight room to get out of the gym, do you, son?" Frank asked. Lyle shook his head; he continued working on his thumbnail, moving to the area around the cuticle, which was red and raw. "Was there someone there in the weight room that you were looking for?" Frank continued. "A friend you thought would be there?" The boy shook his head once more. "Lyle, look up at me, please," Frank said. He requested that sometimes of his own children, especially Bobby, with all the trouble he was always in. Look up at me. Look up and tell me the trouble that you are in now. Lyle raised his head, blinking behind his thick glasses. "Lyle," Frank said gently. "You can tell me, son."

Lyle turned toward the glass partitions and then spoke so softly that Frank had to bend over toward him to hear. "I just go in to the weight room sometimes," Lyle said wistfully. "I just go in to look."

Frank caught a breath, and even Jonny Verlaine's wheezing stopped for a moment or two. "You go to look?" Frank asked. When Lyle did not respond, Frank said, "I see." An awkward silence followed, broken only by Lyle Dixon's incipient sobs. He was holding everything in—his mouth clamped shut, his thin arms hugged around each other—and the cries began as a series of whimpers. "Lyle?" Frank said; he reached out a hand to touch the boy's shoulder, then pulled back.

"I didn't do anything," Lyle said. Tears pooled up behind his glasses, which magnified them into a shimmery wetness along his long lashes. "I didn't do anything, I swear. I just found him there. He was just *there,* lying there on the bench with the bar straight across his neck, and he was totally *still.*"

Jonny Verlaine coughed a few times as if to introduce himself. "Did you know it was Professor Markem right then? Did you know who it was when you first saw him?"

Lyle looked only at Frank when he answered. "Yes," Lyle whispered. Then: "I went over just to make sure."

"Lyle," Frank began cautiously. "I need to ask you something." Pausing, he cleared his throat and took out a fresh piece of gum.

"Yes, sir." Lyle removed his glasses, quickly wiping his eyes with the backs of his hands.

"Lyle, why didn't you tell us the first time that you knew Tyler Markem? That, in fact, he had been one of your professors the year before," Frank said.

Lyle shrugged his narrow shoulders. This time he looked back and forth from Frank to Jonny Verlaine. "I dunno. I was upset, I guess. I didn't say I *didn't* know who he was, did I?"

"Well, it's kind of peculiar," continued Frank. "Because both Officer Verlaine and myself were under the distinct impression that you knew who Professor Markem was, you knew his name, but there was no indication whatever that Markem had been your teacher. I mean, why wouldn't you tell us that?'' Lyle, looking miserable, shook his head. ''Is there something that you're hiding, son?'' Frank asked. This time he did reach out to touch Lyle, placing a hand on one of the boy's bony shoulders. ''It's better to tell the truth now. To give us as much help as you possibly can.''

Lyle spoke in a short, halting cadence: ''I had him as a teacher. A year ago. I don't think he liked me much. The papers I wrote for him. He never thought the thesis was clear. Sometimes I'd go to his office. To talk to him . . .'' Lyle trailed off and went back to his thumbnail. ''I couldn't stop thinking about him after the course was over.''

''What were you thinking about?'' Frank asked.

Lyle shifted uncomfortably in his chair. He cleared his throat. ''Sometimes I'd just think about being in his class again, talking to him, explaining my point and all. I'd picture myself saying all the right things and then he'd be really impressed with me. He'd think I was smart.''

''You were attracted to Professor Markem?'' Frank asked. Lyle nodded. ''Physically attracted?''

''Yes,'' Lyle answered, his voice barely audible. ''Physically and mentally, I think. Professor Markem was a brilliant man.''

Frank leaned in closer to the boy. ''And did Professor Markem know of the feelings you had for him?''

Lyle looked up, surprised. ''No. No, of course not.''

''And so we can presume,'' Frank went on, ''that these feelings were not overtly demonstrated and so in no way reciprocated by Professor Markem.''

''Oh no! Not at all!'' Lyle was emphatic. It was he, Lyle, who was attracted. ''It was more a crush than anything else,'' he said, shrugging, his face reddening. And it had been his secret. He had told no one about it. No one.

"Do your friends know, Lyle? Or your parents . . ." Frank hesitated. "About your life, you know, that . . ."

"That I'm gay." Lyle finished the sentence and faced Frank, looking him squarely eye to eye. He sat up taller then. "My father's dead," he said in a clipped way. "Probably just as well. He would never understand. Yes, my mother knows. But it's only recently. And she's still processing."

"Processing," Frank repeated.

"She's still working it over in her mind. She knows, but I don't think she's totally accepted the fact."

"What about at school?" Frank asked.

"I've only told a few people this past spring. There's a support group on campus. And I've been to counseling at school. Both have helped me a lot." Lyle looked imploringly at both the officers. "Listen. *I am* gay. And I go to the weight room sometimes just to look. It's like looking at girls on the beach for a straight guy, you know what I mean?" Lyle looked over at Jonny Verlaine, who sat stonefaced and silent. "I just pass through and look sometimes, that's all. And I did have a thing for Professor Markem. It's true. My fencing class last semester ended at eleven, right around the time he'd start his workout. I figured out that he was there almost every day at that time. He'd say hello to me sometimes. To tell you the truth I don't think he even remembered my name or what grade he gave me.

"I went in that morning. The morning that I found him. The building was empty. I didn't think anyone would be there, and I was leaving for home the next day. I don't know why I even went in. I wasn't even thinking of Professor Markem then. I just walked by the weight room, just because it was there, you know? Then, when I first saw him there, I didn't think he was dead or anything. He looked so peaceful and still, as if he were resting between repetitions. His hands were still on the bar. Of course, I should have told you that I knew him. I don't know why I didn't. It's not as if I lied exactly, but I didn't think you would understand. . . . Not telling you was wrong. It was because I was attracted to Professor Markem and"—Lyle looked so steadily into Frank's eyes that it was Frank who finally turned away to break the connection of his gaze—"I suppose I was ashamed."

"So what do you think? You believe him?" Jonny Verlaine asked when they were about a mile past the turkey farm. It was after one o'clock and Frank was hungry. He was thinking about one of those skillet dinners at the pancake house along the highway. Two eggs over easy so they run into the hash browns. Or the Denver skillet with chopped peppers and onions and maybe a side of biscuits and gravy. No smoking for over a year and he had put on just about ten pounds. Not too bad.

Carol had always resented the way he could eat so much and never gain any weight at all. She used to threaten: "If you think I'm going to stick around growing pear-shaped watching you eat double cheese baconburgers, you got another think coming." After the children were gone, every diet she went on, he went on as well—for the dinners at least. Weight Watchers. The Pritikin Plan. Once they ate two weeks' worth of hard-boiled eggs and tomatoes on the Women's Ski Team Diet. Frank didn't mind. For lunch he had his fast food and doughnuts in the office. Carol lost and put back on the same twenty pounds through the years, though Frank could hardly tell the difference. She was curvy in the right places and substantial where a woman should be, he thought.

Like Lyle Dixon, Frank had a secret, too. It was that Carol Anne Jenson Rhodes was the only woman he had ever made love to. When you started so young and you were faithful, that was the way it worked out. And God, they were both young. Not even seventeen.

Then they had sex in cars, on blankets in the park, sneaking into the basement when her parents were away. Afterwards, he used to call her when he got home, his voice filled with the ache caused by their parting. He would have to speak softly because there was only one phone in his house, and it was located in the uncarpeted hall where words could echo up the steps to his parents' bedroom. "I miss you," he would tell her before they would say good night.

When they finally married, sharing a small apartment downtown while Frank studied for the police exam and worked in his father's shoe store, he thought that the best thing about marriage was the afterward of sex in their own bed; of falling asleep with his wife's head on his chest, or cupped against him; or being able to reach over at any time during the night to her warmth; or even just being able to listen to her breathing in the night.

Jonny Verlaine's breathing was ragged and he reached for tissues on the dash. "So what do you think?" he asked again.

"I believe him," Frank said. "He was scared. And I think he felt guilty." Jonny was silent. "What about you?"

"Well, let me run this one by you," Jonny said. "Suppose the professor and this kid were all alone in the gym. It's the end of school and no one is around. And the kid is just looking at this good-looking guy, half naked, who's lifting these weights. So maybe the kid kind of loses himself a little, gets really bold, you know, makes a pass."

"Yeah," Frank said, signaling Jonny to go on.

"Okay. So here's this gay kid, and he's real shy and withdrawn, but suddenly he gets up the courage to make a pass. Maybe he says something or touches Markem, pinches his ass, I don't know. How do fags pick up each other, anyway? Okay. So Markem, he's not like that—which we know. So he rejects the kid's advances. Markem gets real mad or puts him down. Or worse, he *laughs* at the kid. Yeah, that would really be awful. To approach a guy and have him laugh at you." Jonny was really going; Frank had never heard him talk so much.

"So then Markem turns his back, lays down on the bench and begins to lift, and the kid is overcome. He just loses it, you know. Just goes over to Markem, who's pressing, panting away, and the kid goes over and slams the bar down on the guy's neck."

"Then he'd stick around to report it?" Frank asked.

"Well, it's not like it was premeditated or anything. He didn't mean to kill Markem."

"I don't know," Frank said, rubbing his chin. "Unless we got a confession out of him, there's not much there to prove anything."

They drove down a winding county road. Farmland stretched for miles on both sides. There was a sign for a bump in the road, but no bump followed.

"Still, there's something about the kid that gives me the willies," Jonny said.

"That's because you got nervous when he looked you over."

"I didn't get nervous," Jonny protested.

"Guys in uniform," Frank said, laughing. "Everybody's hot for a guy in uniform."

"Very funny," Jonny said, brushing imaginary lint off his shirt.

"Did I ever tell you about the time when I was on night shift, I don't know, maybe fifteen years ago, and this woman would always call about a break-in, always about three in the morning? I'd get there and she'd come to the door in these outfits. See-through negligees and baby dolls. And first I thought, well, it was the middle of the night and maybe someone was there. She just woke up and she was scared. She called about a half dozen times one year. Then the outfits got more extreme. There was something she wore once, a corset with her breasts pushed up." Telling this now, the memory of the woman's breasts rimmed with black lace, Frank felt a tinge of excitement.

"So did you boff her?" Jonny wanted to know.

"Naw." Frank shook his head.

"Why not?"

" 'Cause she was crazy. And a crazy woman is always trouble. And anyway," Frank added, "I think it was the uniform. Once I showed up with another guy—fat, old Mel Harolson? He was in uniform and I wasn't and guess what? She came on to *him*."

"Man," said Jonny Verlaine, wiping his nose. "Crazy or not, I would have boffed her."

22

Fran had not slept well. At two and three in the morning there had been noises everywhere: settling walls made her jump, and approaching cars seemed to slow ominously just as they drove by the house; her neighbor's dog, by day a playful beagle pup, made intermittent howls of anguish that cut off in a sudden silence. At five-thirty, just as a blue dawn was peeping in from the edges of the curtains, she fell into a fitful sleep, dreaming she was out in a fishing boat with George Lawson, who was waving fish around by the tails and threatening to capsize the boat. "Do you think I don't have it in me?" he yelled into the ocean spray, a drunken Ahab. "Do you think I don't have it in me?" Half-alive fish flopped around by his feet, and waves flooded the rocking boat. Fran awoke, open-mouthed against a damp shoulder, tasting salt.

By nine-thirty she was showered, her legs shaved, hair coiffed; two new coats of polish—Poppy Passion—were applied to both finger and toenails, and enough bronzing gel rubbed onto her cheeks to baste a Thanksgiving turkey. She chose her outfit with equally careful scrutiny, emptying half of one closet and two drawers onto a pile on the bed. She tried on a purple floral sundress (too garden-party) and cutoffs with a white T-shirt (too coed) and a black Lycra halter (too sleazy) and khaki shorts with a striped polo (too L.L. Bean) and a gauzy cotton Indian print skirt (too ethnic) and finally settled on a short red T-shirt dress, which was casual but not careless and sexy but not obvious and frankly looked fabulous with Poppy Passion nails and all that bronzing gel.

A little after ten she called the Grandview Police Station and was told by someone who sounded peevish that Detective Rhodes was out of town and would be gone until later that afternoon. Fran left her name and a message for him to return her call. She poured herself another cup of coffee, feeling somehow as if she had been stood up by a date.

Restless, she tried George Lawson at ten-thirty, again ten minutes later and again ten minutes after that, letting the phone ring this time, hoping to wake him out of his usual morning stupor. He didn't answer. She tried him at the office, but the secretary, Martha, a sweet-natured woman habituated to covering for George, said he had not been to the office at all since "the accident." Furthermore, Martha was upset because George had not yet gotten his grades in from the end of the semester. "They were due the day before yesterday in the registrar's office," Martha told Fran. "I called them and said with the accident and all how mixed up everything was, but they said the grades have to be sent out to the students this afternoon—no matter what." She repeated the final three words as probably they had been emphasized to her. "George was supposed to bring his grades to the registrar himself this morning. He was supposed to hand-deliver them by eight o'clock. They called twice already this morning and said they haven't gotten them. I haven't a clue where George is, do you?"

Fran could picture Martha, puffed up and fretful, a worried mother hen at her desk. "I don't know," Fran told her. "He called me last night. There was a message on my machine when

I got home, but I wasn't able to reach him." Saying this, Fran felt guilty, remembering George's sorrowful voice on the machine and her return call of four obligatory rings.

"Well, if you find out where he is, will you tell him that they're waiting on his grades in the administration building? He better get them in pronto," Martha said. "The dean is already angry enough at poor George."

"Sure," Fran told her. *Poor George* was how Martha looked at it. Coming from an alcoholic family herself, Martha had a soft spot in her heart for substance abusers. It was her theory that the administrators at Stimpson were just itching to get rid of George because as older faculty, he simply cost them too much money. Easier to fire him and get some new blood for half the salary.

"I think I'll take a drive by George's house and stop over later at the office," Fran said casually.

"Oh, would you, dear? That's so thoughtful of you." Martha was only about ten years older than Fran, but she had a maternal attitude toward the younger faculty. Fran didn't mind, especially since her own mother was gone; Fran often found Martha a comfort. "To tell you the truth, I *have* been just a little worried," Martha confessed. "Though he's probably just, you know, sleeping in and has unplugged the phone. He's been so distraught recently."

More likely passed out cold and wouldn't hear a phone if it were ringing in his ear, Fran thought. She wondered if Martha knew anything about a sexual harassment complaint. Probably Martha would take George's side. Martha was like that: a team player, herself honest but blindly loyal. Fran could picture Martha, one of the faithful, testifying with heartfelt enthusiasm about the impeccable character of Clarence Thomas. "Martha," Fran said, turning off her coffee maker with one perfectly manicured Poppy Passion finger, "you don't have to worry. George will be all right. I'll come by later."

"Oh, thank you, dear," Martha said, sounding mollified. "I'd hate for George to get in more hot water than he's already in."

Hot water. He's immersed in it, Fran thought, hanging up the phone. Up to his stupid, scrawny neck. She thought of George in hot water, sitting up to his neck in a boiling cauldron while hungry administrators surrounded the fire, sharpening their knives and licking their chops.

George lived in one of Grandview's more expensive, more gracious neighborhoods. The houses on his street backed up to Stepping-Stone Park, so named because someone in designing the park had arranged flat flagstone paths connecting the hiking trails to the playground and the picnic areas. Beyond the fence surrounding the tennis courts there were stepping-stone paths to the water fountain and to the park toilets, and stepping-stone paths led to the baseball field, down to the brook, and out of the woods to the parking lot. Seen from the air, Fran imagined, the park looked like a children's board game.

George's house was on a choice piece of property, the last house on a cul-de-sac with the edge of the park as a backyard. Fran had been inside George's house probably half a dozen times in the fourteen years she had been at Stimpson: once for an eerie dinner party when she had first come to town (she recalled only that the dining room was very dark, and Mrs. Lawson stayed in the kitchen, sitting on a stool by the stove, smoking cigarettes and tying knots in string); then a few other occasions, for faculty parties and receptions.

There was one other time that Fran was not fond of remembering, a weekend (the "lost weekend," as she referred to it when talking with Julia) many years ago, before she met Damian and after the mysterious Mrs. Lawson had disappeared. George had invited Fran for a special dinner, a tête-à-tête it turned out to be, the two of them in front of the fireplace with boiled lobster and Caesar salad and chocolate truffles and vodka gimlets as strong as antifreeze.

He was not someone she would choose, but years ago George, viewed from a certain perspective, could have been almost dapper, remote with a debauched and slightly dangerous edge. She was working very hard, trying to get enough articles published to get tenure, and didn't have much of a social life. Why did she do it? she asked herself later. Maybe it was just a bad week, but she was very lonely and she got very drunk and so she slept with him, knowing as every second passed that she was making a mistake. The next morning she came down the stairs, sickened to see the lobster carcasses, like giant red roaches, eviscerated on the kitchen counter.

Regrets, she had a few, so the song went. Definitely one of Fran Meltzer's regrets would be that drunken evening spent in George Lawson's unwashed bed (even the aromas of lobster and aftershave did not mask the odor of stale sweat on the sheets) and the time following, when she had to fend him off from a pursuit so relentless that it subsided only with the announcement of her impending marriage to Damian.

Now, coming up the narrow driveway, Fran realized that indeed it had been years since she had been to George Lawson's home. She turned off the ignition and sat for a few moments, looking at the house, appalled. It was more than neglected. Paint was chipped around every window, the front of the storm door had a broken panel, and torn plastic insulation flapped uselessly along the shell of a screened-in porch. "What a dump!" Fran said aloud, imitating Elizabeth Taylor in *Who's Afraid of Virginia Woolf,* who was imitating another actress from another movie.

Then she noticed the morning newspaper sitting on the top step.

Slowly Fran got out of the car and looked around. The dead-end street on this bright summer morning was quiet; behind the house were the woods. Lovely, dark and deep, Fran thought, peering into the cool depths of dense pine and oak, and despite the fact that she was standing in the sunny driveway, gooseflesh rose along her arms.

The next house closest to George's was a low-to-the-earth contemporary, windowless on the street side so that from this view, the house looked like a bunker along a road in some war-torn, inhospitable territory. "Okay. Here we go. Let's see what's going on," she finally said aloud.

Standing on tiptoe, she peered into George's garage; his car, a white Ford Taurus, new last year, was sitting inside. She walked up the front steps and paused, lifting the lid on the brass mailbox next to the door. No mail. She rang twice, listening for footsteps, then knocked, leaning over the steps to peer into the front window, where heavy drapes had been drawn. She could see nothing at all. She knocked again and waited. Hesitantly, she tried the door and, although in a town such as Grandview it was not the least bit unusual for people to leave their houses unlocked, her heart did skip a beat when the knob turned easily in her hand. She looked again over her shoulder. No one was on the street.

Pushing the door open, she remained outside on the steps, bending at the waist into the darkened hallway. "George? Yoo-hoo, George, are you home?" she called out, attempting to sound casual and neighborly. "George?" The house smelled closed up and sour, like a place where an old person had been sick. She took a breath and ventured inside. "Anybody home?" The hallway was slightly grand, with a high ceiling, a crystal chandelier, and a winding wooden staircase with a carved oak bannister. She noticed that all the pictures on the wall along the stair were crooked. "George?" she called again, more half-heartedly this time. The living room, strewn with papers and books and empty glasses, was off to one side of the hall, the library on the other. In the library, Fran could only glimpse a similarly littered table and the backs of two wingback chairs in oxblood leather.

Gingerly she tiptoed down the hall toward the kitchen and pushed open a swinging door. ''George?'' she called out. Her own voice startled her so that she jumped back, nearly tripping over a white cat that had begun to rub up against her bare legs with a petulant, insistent mewing. ''Go away,'' Fran hissed. ''Go away. Scram!''

Fran, who did not particularly like animals, loathed cats. They gave her the creeps. And this particular cat—a decidedly unhealthy-looking white Angora with red eyes and a bald patch along one hindquarter—under these particular circumstances, really gave her the creeps. ''Go away!'' Fran yelled, stamping her foot, though the cat continued to mew pitifully, now moving to circle an empty dish on a kitchen floor so filthy and scarred that it looked as if workmen with muddied boots had been moving furniture all morning.

''Oh, my God,'' Fran said, her gaze moving along the kitchen counter. The cats (another equally hideous longhair emerged from a corner) had apparently knocked over a half-full carton of milk, which had spilled into an open silverware drawer, covering spoons and forks in a white puddle a couple of inches deep. Food in various stages of mold and decay lay out along the counters, hardened into sculpture on the plates. All around the kitchen were bottles: Jim Beam, Jamison's Irish Whiskey, J & B. On the kitchen table next to a plate of congealed macaroni and cheese were empty beer cans, balanced in a pyramid like those the college boys displayed in their dormitory windows. A litterbox filled to overflowing with cat turds so dried out that they looked like tiny logs of petrified wood was peculiarly placed in front of a door leading out to the backyard. Fran supposed either that George did not use this door or that he was trying to trap a burglar coming through the back entrance.

Disgusted now, more than afraid, she closed the door to the

kitchen and yelled, "George. George Lawson!" as loud as she could, the words fairly echoing in the hall.

About five minutes later she found him, facedown on the upstairs bathroom floor, wearing only the bottoms of green pajamas and one slip-on moccasin. She had screamed when she saw him, though thankfully she was not alone at the time. Repulsed by the cats and the condition of the kitchen (true, she let her own dishes go, but this was ridiculous), she still did not quite have the moxie to walk up the stairs to investigate further by herself and so had left to go next door to the bunker house, where she rang the bell and was greeted by a perfectly normal looking woman with a cute, chubby baby in her arms.

Sighing in relief, Fran introduced herself, explained the situation, and asked the woman to accompany her next door.

"Shouldn't we call the police?" the woman asked, a syrupy drawl in her voice.

"I'll feel silly," Fran told her, "because I'm sure everything's all right." There was a pause. "Probably," she added.

"We just moved here," the woman from the bunker house confessed, "and Ah don't even know who lives next door."

Just as well, Fran thought, leading the way into George's smelly house.

"We came here from Texas," the woman continued, walking alongside Fran. The way she said *here* made the word into two syllables. The baby's eyes were wide with excitement at being in a strange place. "My husband was with a company down in Houston, but they laid off hundreds of people and my husband just sent out resumes all over the country; he wanted to come back to the Midwest, anyway, where he's from; we almost went to Des Moines, and he had an offer also in Bloomington, Indiana, but it would have been a huge pay cut . . ." Walking up the stairs, Fran had an urge to straighten the pictures along the wall. "There were some possibilities in Chicago, but we just didn't want to do such a big city again and then the research park at the college here offered him—" Seeing a man's body, white and still, on the floor of the bathroom interrupted the woman's description of her husband's career options. Fran screamed, and the woman jumped back, hugging her baby against her breast. "Oh, Lord in Heaven!" the woman exclaimed.

In a flash, Fran later didn't even remember how, she was handed the baby and stood calling 911 from the phone in George's bedroom while the woman dragged George out to a flattened position and proceeded to administer what Fran believed to be CPR.

"The address, please," a man's voice said on the other end, sounding mechanical. "It's Parkway. The last house on the dead end next to Stepping-Stone Park," Fran explained, her head spinning. The baby took the phone wire in his mouth and began to gum it.

"104 Park Way," the woman yelled from the bathroom between breaths. Hearing his mother's voice, the baby furrowed his brow in a worried way and began to whimper.

"104 Park Way," repeated Fran.

"Is he breathing?" the man on the phone wanted to know.

"Is he breathing?" Fran yelled toward the bathroom.

"Not yet. But there's a pulse," the woman yelled back.

"Not yet, but there's a pulse," Fran repeated, beginning to feel important.

The man on the phone said an ambulance would be there within minutes and to please send someone outside to wait in the street and direct the medics into the house. Fran hung up the phone. "Come, let's go see Mommy save George's life," she said as they walked by the bathroom. "Look! There's your mommy." Fran bounced the baby up and down on her hip as they stood in the bathroom doorway, and he began to chuckle.

"Da da da da dada da," said the baby, cheerfully watching his mother bending over George Lawson's half-naked body, her dress pulled up past her thighs so that she could straddle him. Her hands worked expertly on his pale chest; her mouth pressed against his. "Come on," the woman whispered in George's ear when she stopped for breath herself. "Come on. Come on. Come on." George lay under her, pale and passive, his brown hair swirled into a moist mat along the top of his head. The woman's lips, her splayed legs, her hands, enveloped him, so that instead of breathing life into George, she seemed to be sucking him into her.

Fran and the baby stood watching them for a few seconds; the baby made saliva bubbles with a delicate popping sound. Dizzy, Fran leaned against the wall and held the baby close; he smelled fresh, like talc and ripe melon. "I have to go downstairs to wait for the ambulance," she told the woman, who looked up, her lips puffy and red.

"Can you get me a towel?" the woman asked. "There's some emesis here." She had turned George's head sideways, so his mouth was parallel with his shoulder.

Fran took a towel off a rack by the shower and handed it over, seeing by the pool alongside George's head what *emesis* meant. The woman draped the towel over George's shoulder, turned his head, opened his jaw with her hand, and began breathing into him again. It was a small-minded thought, perhaps, selfish and mean-spirited but, seeing George at that moment, wet with saliva and vomit, Fran was indeed grateful that she had never taken it upon herself to learn CPR.

Outside, she stood with the sweet-smelling baby in her arms and waited for the ambulance.

23

The Holiday Inn on Highway 34 was only a year old, built to accommodate visiting businesses to the research park, which was itself new, built to accommodate those who would offer money to Stimpson College in exchange for expertise in the form of scientific study, consultation, and research. At the college, computer scientists were now creating programs for software packagers, and sociologists were doing demographics for advertising companies, and biochemists were getting hundred-thousand-dollar grants from cosmetic firms.

It was a controversial arrangement, this wedding of academic brain with financial brawn. The city council of Grandview had unanimously endorsed the research park, anticipating the growth both of new businesses and already existing service industries. Then the council had hurriedly floated bond issues for accessing the land that the research park would be built on. Now there were billboards—"Grandview Welcomes Your Business"—out by Highway 34, and new motels.

Some members of the Stimpson faculty (the humanities types who did their research in libraries rather than laboratories) thought that the waters of academic research should be pure, untainted by the murky desires of the marketplace. This faculty saw the very existence of the research park as a threat to the tenets of academic freedom. And Tyler Markem had been one of those most outspoken against the creation of the research park.

Now, riding with Jonny Verlaine toward the Holiday Inn, where Lynette Macalvie would be working behind the reception desk, Frank could remember seeing Professor Markem's picture on the front page of the Grandview newspaper: Tyler Markem, delivering fervent addresses to the faculty council about the ideals of academic freedom and the nature of scholarly pursuit.

Frank's own view was short-range and personal. At the time the concept of a research park was first discussed, his son Bobby had lost a job in construction and, after a rocky year on his own, boozing too much and doing drugs, had come home to live with Frank. The building of the park meant hundreds of new construction jobs in Grandview and Bobby's making enough money again to get a place of his own. Frank had been for it a hundred percent.

''If you could come up with someone who could verify your whereabouts, that would be helpful,'' Jonny Verlaine said. Lynette Rae Macalvie was trying to recall if anyone had witnessed her arrival at Lake Westin the Monday morning that Tyler Markem's body was found in the Stimpson gym.

She sat with Jonny Verlaine and Frank Rhodes in a conference room on the first floor of the Grandview Holiday Inn. At two o'clock on this afternoon in June the motel was not busy. Checkout time was noon, and it was still too early for new arrivals. The maids, mostly girls from the college themselves, were busy cleaning out the rooms. Lynette had brought the two police officers to the freshly sanitized conference room; vacuum tracks ran the length of the rose-colored carpet, and new plastic-wrapped glasses sat on the table next to the ice bucket.

"I shouldn't have left town," Lynette began. "But I was so upset. Before I saw Tyler . . . he's so persuasive and when he talks sometimes, well, I guess I just wanted to think some things through by myself, you know?"

Jonny nodded.

"And the other thing, I guess I should tell you, I mean I didn't think that much about it until now, until I found out you're doing this investigation and everything. Well, I got this real peculiar message on my answering machine."

"When was this?" Frank asked.

"Well, this was just that Sunday before I left. The night before Tyler's, you know, accident. It was after his wife had left my apartment. I was packing and I had gone downstairs to take the garbage out, and when I came back, my machine was blinking, you know? And I was glad. I mean, of course I thought it was Tyler and I was glad that I had missed the call because I knew he would talk me out of getting away by myself and I just didn't want to talk to him yet. So I listened to the message." Lynette took a gulp of air. Spots of color appeared along her neck. "And it was this voice, I think it said, 'What are you doing . . . leave him alone, bitch.' The *bitch* was very clear. I'm not so sure about the rest. But it was scary." Lynette hugged herself and shivered.

"Was it a man's or woman's voice?" Jonny asked.

"Well, I don't know. It was a strange voice. Sort of like the voice in *The Exorcist,* you know?"

"We'll have someone stop by later to pick up the tape," Frank told her.

"The tape?" Lynette's face fell.

"You have the tape?" Frank said.

"Well, I mean, I have the tape, but I erased the message. I listened to it twice and it kind of gave me the willies, you know what I mean?"

Frank sighed. He got up from his chair and went over to the window, looking through the curtains at a parking lot. "All right, tell us about driving to the lake." He came back and sat down across from Lynette at the conference table.

"Well, I drove straight through. I didn't stop in town for supplies on the way in," Lynette was saying. It was Frank's opinion that the young woman seemed remarkably unruffled considering the circumstances, articulating clearly and meeting their eyes. She was pleasant enough looking—blond, wide-eyed, a bit pudding-faced—not anyone who would be considered the object of a man's obsession; certainly not anyone who would be considered a likely subject for a murder investigation.

Frank had some sympathy for Lynette's parents. He had been careful in the recent phone calls not to alarm Mrs. Macalvie; he told her that Lynette was merely needed to answer some questions. But when her daughter could not be found, Mrs. Macalvie went into a tailspin, calling the police in three states and trying to put out a missing persons bulletin—even though Frank had informed her that it was not standard procedure to issue a missing persons on a subject over eighteen years of age who, even with whereabouts unknown, had left voluntarily and called in at work.

"Was there anyone at all who could have seen you at Lake Westin?" Jonny Verlaine asked. "Anyone who could identify you?" He was leaning forward in his chair, a hand on each muscled thigh. He was just a couple of years older than Lynette, and they looked almost like brother and sister, both fair-skinned and snub-nosed. Jonny was more reticent with Lynette, gentler, than he had been just a few hours before in the interview with Lyle Dixon.

Jonny was a good cop. He was learning the ropes, taking on a bit more responsibility now. He was young, but he wasn't like some of the other young cops, hot-headed and wild, close to the edge of the law themselves. These days, the boys in town who became police officers were the same boys Frank used to arrest on OMVI's while they scooped the loop on Saturday nights. Jonny wasn't like that. Frank trusted Jonny.

Lynette shook her head. "I don't think so. I mean, I just drove right through the town to the trailer. I didn't stop."

"Did you stop for gas along the way?" Frank asked.

"No," Lynette said. "The tank was already full." Lynette looked puzzled. "You know, that's just what Professor Meltzer asked me last night when I got in. I told her I had a full tank before I left."

Frank sat up straight in his seat, bumping his knee on the table in front of him. "Fran Meltzer?"

"She teaches at the college. She's Julia's friend." Lynette paused, blinked her blue eyes right at Jonny and added: "Julia, Tyler's wife."

"Why did you see Ms. Meltzer? This was when, exactly?" Frank wanted to know.

"Last night," said Lynette. "She and Julia both came over to my apartment pretty late. Around eleven. A little while after I got back from Lake Westin."

"Why is that?" Frank asked.

"Why they came over?"

"Yes."

"Well, I had called Julia when I got home." Lynette sat up and perched forward, as if to better explain her position. "Maybe it doesn't make any sense to you. But there's something very lonely about having a secret relationship. You can't share things with other people. And then when I found out he was gone . . . well, I needed to speak with her." Lynette paused. Her voice caught suddenly, her blue eyes pooling with tears. "I guess I needed to be with someone who felt the same as I did about losing Tyler."

Jonny got up from his chair, went to the bathroom, and came out with a handful of tissues. "And she brought her friend with her. I don't know why," Lynette went on, blowing her nose. "I was in Professor Meltzer's literature class the fall semester."

"Small world," Jonny said, catching Frank's eye.

"Well, it is a small college," Lynette said earnestly.

"I'll drop you off to do some of the paperwork," Frank told Jonny as they drove out of the Holiday Inn parking lot. "Then I'm going over to the college to see a couple of people."

"What about that old drunk—what's his name—the poet?"

"George Lawson. Yeah. If he's around. He didn't answer at home; the secretary said he didn't come in yet to the office either. I'll stop by and see. Also there's someone else, that Blevins woman. Her name has come up a couple of times."

"She a teacher, too?"

"No, she works for the college president. She writes grants. She's supposed to know a lot of the who's who kind of stuff on campus. Apparently she and Markem were pretty close."

Jonny's eyebrows shot up. "How close? Boy, this guy Markem got around."

"Not like that. They were friends. Went out for lunch sometimes. That's what Fran Meltzer told me."

Jonny's eyebrows lifted again at the mention of Fran Meltzer's name, but he didn't say anything else and was quiet in the car all the way to the station.

"Anyway, I called this Alice Blevins this morning, too, but *her* secretary said she was in the library doing research." Frank looked at his watch. "She's supposed to be back by now."

"You know what it is with all these damn college types?" Jonny said as they pulled up in front of the brick building. He cocked his ear for a moment. "The car sound funny to you?"

Frank listened. The car always sounded funny. The Grandview Police department had been on an austerity budget for the last few years now. No raises. No new equipment. And they had to drive junkers with the air conditioner always breaking down. The only money coming out of the public coffers these days went into the research park. Frank raced the motor and listened again. "I don't hear anything," he said finally. "Anyway, what is it about the damned college types?" Frank wanted to know.

"They're never around," Jonny said. "They don't seem to have *real* jobs like other people."

"Teaching is a real job," Frank noted.

Jonny Verlaine snickered. "Yeah, they teach a class here and there, every Monday or Wednesday, but then they're off in the library doing research or home taking naps or going to the gym or some goddamned thing.

"Look, suppose this wasn't an accident," Jonny went on. "I mean, suppose this guy Markem was actually *killed* in a public place at eleven-thirty in the morning. Eleven-thirty on a goddamned Monday morning and not a single one of them has an alibi worth a shit. The only ones who were actually at work at that college are the secretaries!"

24

One of the things Frank liked best about living in a small city like Grandview was that everything was convenient. From one end of town to the other was a distance of maybe five miles at most. In less than fifteen minutes after leaving the Holiday Inn, Frank had parked the car and was walking across the green grass of the quad over to The Knoll, where the president of Stimpson College had his administrative offices.

Frank knew the president, Chalmer Von Eaton, a distinguished silver-haired man in his late sixties with the gravelly voice and liquid charm of an old-time southern orator. He and Frank had been in touch over the years on certain matters of campus security. Then last year there was what the Grandview paper called "rioting," during the spring celebration of Dandelion Days, a two-day student affair with festivals and floats and inordinate amounts of beer.

Frank thought the disturbance was more street party than riot, though a plate glass window had been shattered in Campustown and a group of boys had carried a Volkswagen bug and set it on top of the steps of the administration building.

President Von Eaton vowed to ban Dandelion Days unless the students got the rowdyism under control, though his threat was yet to be tested. This May, it had rained on Dandelion Days and the parties had to be indoors.

The offices at The Knoll were all skillfully decorated with Persian rugs and brass door knockers and marble fireplaces with busts of dead Greek guys on the mantel. Frank announced himself to a woman whose desk was situated in what seemed to be a rotunda with a view to six different offices along the periphery of the room. All the offices had open doors and huge windows so there was a lot of light, and the buzz of voices and ringing phones gave the place a lively atmosphere. President Von Eaton's office was up a winding stair behind a stained-glass window.

"Can I help you?" the woman at the desk said, looking up over a pair of half-glasses.

"I'd like to see Alice Blevins, please," Frank told her.

The woman pointed toward the office at the rear of the rotunda. "Her door is always open," she said.

Frank's shoes echoed down the hall, but Alice Blevins did not greet him as he stood in her doorway. He stood for a moment watching as she faced the amber screen of a computer, her fingers busy at the keys. "Excuse me, Ms. Blevins?"

"Yes?" The woman turned. Frank recalled how Fran Meltzer had described Alice Blevins—"plain as a potato"—and thought how that description fit the woman before him. Alice Blevins had small eyes, graying hair, and slightly lumpy features. Frank cleared his throat, entered, explained his mission before he was offered a seat. At the mention of Tyler Markem's name, Alice Blevins's lumpy features began to soften. "I'm sorry," she said quickly, reaching for a tissue on her desk. "Tyler was my dear, good friend." She offered Frank a chair. "Please sit." Frank pulled a barrel-backed chair closer to the desk. "It's hard for me to get used to the idea that he's gone." Daintily, she blew her nose and sniffed.

"I'd just like to ask you a couple of questions," Frank said quietly. "Do you mind if we close the door?"

"Oh." Alice Blevins smiled, getting up to comply. "We're all one big family here in the president's office. I even forget that some people have private conversations." She walked across the room, her heels silent on the plush patterned rug. "You know, it's the architecture."

"Excuse me?" Frank said.

"The architecture. How everything revolves around a central point, the president's office looking over all the offices here on this floor. The architecture encourages this communal feeling. That's why we're all like family here, and everyone always keeps the doors open." She came back and sat down next to Frank, now wheeling her chair closer to his, practically sliding into him. "Now," she said. "Isn't this cozy?" She had the slightly formal manner and posture of the nuns Frank used to see when he and Carol would go for parent conferences at St. Cecilia's, Grandview's only private school, where Bobby went for one year when he was having reading difficulties.

"How long had you known Professor Markem?" Frank asked, taking out a small notebook, using it like a barrier between them. There was something about the woman, an intensity, that made him a little uncomfortable. He found himself holding the notebook up, tilting back in the chair.

"Well, known him, I'd known Tyler since he came to this college, what is it, oh, years ago. Twelve? Thirteen? I met him the first time at a poetry reading he gave to the college," she said, smiling sadly.

"And his wife?"

"Well, yes. Of course I've known Julia, too."

"You see them socially?"

"Not exactly." She pursed her lips. "I was close with Tyler. He was my friend."

"You and Julia didn't get along?" Frank asked.

"It wasn't that," Alice Blevins said. "It's just Tyler and I

were on some college committees together and then we served
about six years ago on the Board of Quartets—we started the
chamber music series here at the college. We have a very
fine program. Have you ever attended, Mr. Rhodes?'' Frank
confessed that he had not. ''Well, Tyler and I actually started
the series together. We worked on the grants together.'' She
leaned back in her seat, her hands folded across her chest.
''Tyler and I were both passionate about chamber music. Passionate!''

''And you attended these programs with Markem?''

''Of course!''

''His wife. Did she go?''

Alice shook her head. ''In the beginning, a few times perhaps,
but Julia wasn't really interested in music.''

''You saw Professor Markem at other times? I mean socially,
apart from the concerts?'' Frank asked.

''Well, we had coffee together. And lunch, sometimes. We
were friends. I was going through a difficult time. My daughter
was living in Atlanta and she was in one of those religious
sects, you know, and writing that she didn't want anything
more to do with me. Tyler was wonderful to talk to. He helped
me to deal with that.''

''Were you and Tyler . . . ever . . .'' Frank paused. ''This is
difficult to ask. I don't mean to offend you, Ms. Blevins. But
were you and Professor Markem ever anything more than
friends?''

Alice Blevins sat straight in her chair, looking even more
nunlike, and sucked in her cheeks. ''Just what are you suggesting, Detective Rhodes?''

''Did you ever have an affair with Tyler Markem?'' Frank
inquired evenly.

She looked so long and so intensely at Frank that he finally
dropped his eyes onto the notebook in his lap.

''Certainly *not,*'' she proclaimed. A grandfather clock in the corner of the office ticked loudly while Frank waited. Alice Blevins did not elaborate.

Frank went on, as if reading something listed on a questionnaire. "And did Professor Markem ever talk to you about women he was seeing? Women other than his wife?"

"Certainly not!" Alice repeated.

Frank kept on. "But you were friends. Professor Markem must have talked to you about his marriage."

"The truth is, I talked more personally with him than he did with me," Alice said. "He was a very wise, compassionate man. He helped me a great deal. He mentioned his wife sometimes, but it was in a very peripheral way. He talked about places they had been, movies they had seen. That sort of thing. And he never spoke badly about her that I can recall. Ever!"

"So you had no knowledge of any infidelity on the part of Tyler Markem?"

"No, sir. None at all—"

"And as far as you knew, the Markems had a normal, happy marriage?"

"I didn't know normal marriage *were* happy, Mr. Rhodes," Alice said tartly. She brushed her thick bangs flat to her head with the palm of one hand.

"You did not have any knowledge that Tyler Markem was cheating on his wife?" Frank continued.

"The Tyler Markem I knew was not a cheat. He was an ethical, principled person," Alice said, her small eyes darkening to pin-points of anger. "But in fact, I did not know all that much about his private life."

"Just one more question, Ms. Blevins. Last Monday morning, when Markem's body was found. Where were you between eleven and eleven-thirty that morning?"

Alice Blevins smiled tightly. "I was right here at my desk. I've been working all week writing a new grant which would coordinate visiting scientists to teach at the college and work at the research park. I'm sure my secretary will be able to verify my presence here." She got up, went over to the wooden door, opening it. "I always leave my door open. We're all one family here," she said stiffly.

"I appreciate your help, Ms. Blevins," Frank said, rising.

"No problem." Alice Blevins extended a firm hand.

He took a last quick look around. The expensive mahogany desk. The brass vases holding eucalyptus. An antique settee off in the corner. On the paneled walls were prints of Stimpson College from an earlier time, one showing a horse-drawn carriage parked in front of the administration building they were now in. Two large windows took up almost the entire northeast walls behind the desk. From one, Frank could see the quad, the rows of maple and pine along the bike path, the massive oaks on the green expanse of lawn. Through the other window, Frank could see the entrance to the Sage Memorial Gym.

25

"George told the doctor that it was accidental," Fran said into a pay phone in the lobby of Sanford Greeley Hospital. "We could barely understand him because he kept falling asleep, even after they pumped him out. He said he took sleeping pills and then woke up and didn't remember and apparently took some more." Fran paused. "And I'll bet he washed them down with a couple of shots of Jamison's." She paused again, breathing heavily. "Wait a minute. God, I'm still hyperventilating." She panted into the phone. "Julia, it was so horrible finding him there on the floor like that."

Only a few hours before, she had watched as the medics strapped George to the gurney, then had followed the ambulance to the emergency entrance of Sanford Greeley Hospital. It was the second time in one week that she had run, breathless, through those same doors. The same emergency room nurse, the blonde with the oversized glasses, raised her eyebrows in recognition. "I'm with him," Fran said, awkward, as she followed a prone George to one of the cubicles. He was conscious by that time, though his skin matched the blue-gray walls of the room.

"So he's going to be fine?" Julia asked.

"Sweetie, 'fine' is a relative term. Being a fifty-year-old unemployed alcoholic without any friends or family is 'fine' only if your standards are low."

"He's not unemployed," Julia protested.

"Yet."

"Fran, what else do you know? Did you find out something about that sexual harassment charge?"

"Martha's here with me. I've been getting an earful."

"Tell me."

Fran sighed heavily. "Oh, sweetie, I don't want to do this over the phone. I'll come by later. You'll be home?"

"Shouldn't you stay with George?" Julia asked.

"No, Martha's here. He's going to be sleeping anyway. He must have taken enough stuff to knock out an entire seminar."

"Oh, God, Franny. That's awful."

"He was so lucky. The medics said, if that woman didn't know CPR, George would have died for sure. You know the house next door? The one without any windows? The couple just moved here from Texas. And she used to be an emergency room nurse, can you imagine? The way she took over, I thought I was with Florence Nightingale."

Julia confirmed Fran's view: "He was really lucky."

Just then, Fran saw a tall man in a white shirt, sleeves rolled to the elbows, stooping to speak to the woman at the information desk. He nodded, thanking her, and started to walk down the hall. He was chewing gum. "I'll talk to you later, okay?" Fran said into the phone.

"Are you coming over now?" Julia asked.

Fran took a few steps out, pulling the phone wire as far as it would go. A man and a woman, each holding a small child, walked in front of her. "Detective Rhodes?" she called out around them. "Frank?"

"Fran?" Julia was still on the line. "Is that cop there with you?"

"Uh-huh." Fran wet her lips, smiling as Frank came up beside her. "I'll call you when I get home," she said, hanging up the phone.

"How you doing?" Frank stuck out his hand and she shook it, feeling the gesture both formal and intimate at the same time.

"Are you here to see George Lawson?" Fran asked.

"I got the call that he was here. I was supposed to go over this morning to see him, but then I had something to do out of town."

"And then you went to see Lynette Macalvie," Fran said. Standing next to him, she had the sense of his being too tall, like her first husband, Paul Kravitz, the jazz pianist, who, with his height and silent brooding, always made her feel as if she were a cute, frisky little puppy, nipping around his long legs, trying to get some attention.

"And then I went to see Lynette," Frank said, beginning a smile. "Good detective work, Professor." Then, as if he, too, felt too tall, he leaned with an elbow against the wall, a posture that shortened him by several inches.

"George is on the third floor, west wing," she said. She walked with him back down the hall to the elevator. When it came, Frank went in first, pressing the Hold button to let the others enter. An older man with a cane came in, followed by an exotic, cocoa-and-cream-colored woman with skin stretched tight across her cheekbones. She was trying to maneuver a cart containing dozens of rattling test tubes filled with blood.

When the elevator doors had closed Frank turned to Fran. "Maybe after this visit, we could go back to the station again. There are some student evaluations I'd like you to look at."

"You want me to see them?" Fran questioned.

"Well, as a teacher, maybe there's something you can tell me about certain ones, something that we wouldn't see. You know what I mean?"

"Sure," Fran said, not sure at all.

The others got out on the second floor. "I went through them pretty carefully," Frank told her. "Professor Markem had some students who seemed to be furious with him. I'd like you to read them yourself."

Fran agreed, though as far as she knew, the only thing that had made the Stimpson College students really furious in the past several years was the raising of the drinking age to twenty-one. "So you know about what I do?" Fran asked. The elevator doors opened on the third floor. They walked down a hall filled with artwork, framed and ready for sale. Most of the pictures were watercolors of splashy sunrises and fields of blowing wildflowers.

"What you do?" Frank asked.

"You know about my interest in graphology?"

"Pardon?"

"Handwriting analysis. I thought that's what you were talking about, why you wanted me to read the evaluations." Fran told him about her expertise. "I mean, it's not a real degree or anything," she explained. "Strictly amateur status. But I did take this course. And I've read a lot about it."

"That's fascinating," Frank said as they stopped in front of a room across from the nurse's station. George was sleeping peacefully, his mouth open, snoring away like an old uncle who had fallen asleep in his chair. Sitting next to him, knitting a baby sweater of pale blues and yellows and pinks, was Martha, who looked up with a surprised smile. "Oh, I thought you were going home, dear," she said to Fran. "Did you forget something?"

*   *   *

It was late afternoon when Frank took Fran back to the station and tried to sail her past Doris Duncan, who was typing up something with one hand while feeling the back of her head with the other. Recently Doris had done something different to her hair. Her former style (Frank could not recall it exactly, would not have been able to pick it out of a lineup) had unobtrusively framed her face. But this! Doris's hair was now tightly curled into something almost pubic and cut so short that the shape of her head and profile stuck out in bas-relief.

"Here are your calls," Doris said to Frank. She had stopped typing to offer him a slip of paper but kept feeling her hair with her other hand.

Frank ushered Fran into his office, pulled out a chair, and offered coffee. He brought her a cup with added cream and put it down on a napkin on top of the desk, feeling her watch him as he moved about the room.

"I didn't know that you did handwriting analysis," Frank said, going over to a file cabinet and taking out the stacks of evaluations that Charlotte Pintel had given him. He sat down at the desk in front of Fran, rearranging the piles that he had read through the night before.

"Write something for me," Fran told him.

"Me?"

"Yeah, write something for me: your name, where you live. Write me a few sentences describing the weather."

Frank laughed. "Okay." He reached into his shirt pocket and uncapped a fine-line, felt-tip pen. "Any pen will do?"

"That's perfect."

"Okay. Here goes." He wound up slightly before setting pen to paper, exaggerating the movement as Norton used to do on "The Honeymooners."

"Just write quickly in your usual handwriting."

"I don't know," Frank said. "What if some deep, dark secret about my character is suddenly revealed?"

"I won't tell anyone," Fran said. "Write."

Frank wrote: "My name is Franklin James Rhodes. I live at 944 Meadow Glen Road in Grandview, Illinois. The weather outside today is hot and sunny with high humidity. I am a detective with the Grandview Police Department." He passed the paper across the desk to Fran.

She rested her elbow on the edge of the desk, chin in hand. "Hmmmm," she said, studying the paper. "Let's see now." Frank straightened up in his chair, waiting. "All right," she began. "The first thing I see is a reflective character. You think things through carefully, balance all the equations before coming to any decision." Fran looked up. "That would be understandable, of course, for someone involved in your line of work." She went back to the paper. "All right. See the way your *gs* go straight down to a line, no fancy loops?" Frank nodded. "That shows determination," Fran went on. "A constant nature and dependability. On the negative side that might mean a certain conservatism."

"Is conservatism negative?" Frank wanted to know.

"Well, it could be. You know, someone who doesn't much like change, doesn't travel well, has certain routines that he doesn't like to deviate from, that sort of thing."

"An old fuddy-duddy," Frank said. He was thinking of the books, all lined up next to the chair for his nightly reading.

"Exactly!" Fran said, laughing.

"What else?"

"Well, along with the conservatism, I think, is a general reticence. You're not very outgoing. Not the guy at the party to put the lamp shade on his head." Fran went on, "See how your script tilts like that to the left? But you're also loyal. Faithful to your word and what you believe. To other people, too. You can be counted on."

"I think I can," Frank said modestly.

"Oh, this is another side of you." Fran leaned over to examine the paper more closely. "Everyone has contradictions in their personalities," she told him. "This"—she pointed out certain letters where the loops crossed over—"means that you have a passionate nature. It could be hidden, not exhibited very much. Your quiet, conservative demeanor might mask it from others. But this"—Fran underlined some of Frank's y's—"does reveal quite an intense passion. And a strong physical drive. You like sex," Fran said matter-of-factly.

Frank felt the tips of his ears begin to redden. "Who doesn't?" he said with a short laugh.

"Plenty of people don't," Fran said seriously. "You look at handwriting a lot and see that there are some people who are either repressed or have very weak erotic components."

"Anything else?" Frank looked down at the paper as if he could figure it out for himself.

"How long have you been a cop?" Fran wanted to know.

"Almost twenty-five years," Frank told her.

"And you were married only one time for about that long?" Fran asked.

"That's correct."

"See?" Fran smiled, pleased with herself. "See how your life pretty much reflects what your handwriting reveals about you?"

"Oh, I don't know," Frank said, leaning back in his chair, stretching his long legs out toward Fran.

"You don't know what?" Fran asked, her face falling, so in that split second Frank felt bad that he was teasing. In spite of her quick-witted ways, there was really something very earnest about her.

"I don't know," he repeated, smiling to show he was only joking around. "Someday the spirit's going to move me. Someday I might just dance around with the lamp shade on my head."

They had been working together over the evaluations for a couple of hours. Fran read and reread the eighteen negative ones. It was true the students who wrote those evaluations felt very strongly about Tyler Markem. Many felt they had been wronged by him. Students wrote that Professor Markem was an unfair grader. That he played favorites. "But these are common student complaints," Fran noted. "All teachers get some evaluations like these."

There was nothing in the handwriting of even the most angry, dissatisfied student to reveal any real, deep-rooted hostility or instability. "There's just no pathology in evidence here," Fran said. "The handwriting of a sick or disintegrated personality is often extremely hard to read," she explained. "It's muddied with blobs of ink that close up the letters."

"That makes sense," Frank said.

"Of course," she went on, "we're going on the assumption that someone who kills another person is a sick or disintegrated personality. But in this case, we could have a completely normal person as the killer. Someone who is not a killer type, per se, who, in fact, would never, ever kill again. Killing for this person would be a one-time thing. An aberration." Fran finished off the coffee that was in her cup. "It's just that in this one instance, well, let's just say that the person really got pissed off," she said.

Frank nodded. He was impressed with her analysis and felt at that moment a certain admiration, the same kind of pride he would feel when a rookie cop made some astute connections. "That's good," he said.

"There's something else, too, I should tell you," Fran began. But just at that moment, the door opened and Doris Duncan popped her close-cropped head into Frank's office. "I'm going," she said, slamming the door with a thud. Frank felt himself tighten.

"Your secretary," Fran said. "You don't really care for her much, do you?"

Frank pulled back. "Doris is all right," he said guardedly. The truth was that he often found Doris intolerable. What was the best thing that he could say about her? That she had never committed a felony. That had been a private running joke with Carol, that Doris had never committed a felony. He didn't know why, but after Carol's death, he had become increasingly short-tempered with Doris, the humor gone from him concerning her indolence and dullness. Sometimes he was annoyed, just at the very fact of her being. Perhaps that was it: her very being. Her very being alive when Carol was not.

"I didn't hire her, but she's been with the department a long time," Frank told Fran, trying to maintain some semblance of the loyalty ascribed by his handwriting. "Why do you say that I don't like her?"

"Because it's true," Fran said, crossing her legs. Her dress, bright red against her tanned skin, rode up her thigh. She was dark-skinned, like that pretty woman in the elevator. Fran's eyes were big and dark, too, so dark that her pupils could not be distinguished. In the movies, Frank had always been attracted to exotic-looking women. As a boy he had had his very earliest erections seeing Sophia Loren walking wet out of the ocean and Gina Lollobrigida flying through the air in *Trapeze*. "And it's a shame," Fran went on. Frank noticed her hands crossed demurely in her lap, her nails also bright red and wickedly pointed. Lately he was looking at women all the time, especially the parts of them all the time.

"A shame about what?" Frank asked, finding his voice.

"Well, it's a shame, because a good secretary could be an invaluable source of information." Fran smiled seductively. At least Frank thought it was a seductive smile.

"What kind of information?"

"I had a long talk with Martha—she's the English department secretary—when we were sitting in the hospital watching George sleep. Maybe there are other things you need to know," Fran said.

Frank felt a gnawing in his stomach and looked at his watch. "Listen, it's getting late," he told Fran. "Are you hungry?"

She told him that she was.

"How about going out somewhere for dinner? We could talk about this some more," Frank said, slightly surprised at his boldness.

"All right," she said. "Sure."

He rose, gathering the evaluations and putting them back into the file cabinet; he took the coffee cups out to the sink next to the main office, came back in and checked the lights. "Where would you like to go?" he asked.

Fran walked out of the room a few steps ahead of him. "Not Taco Time," she said over her shoulder.

26

Even before they were seated, Fran wondered whether or not she would let him pay for dinner. It was not clear even that he would offer, not clear *what* the arrangement was. This wasn't a date, though walking in together—he held the door—there was a certain awkwardness. It was Friday night and they were out to dinner in Grandview's best Chinese restaurant. Grandview's *better* Chinese restaurant, really, since there were only two; she wouldn't count Wong's, the take-out place in Campustown.

The hostess at Yen Sun walked them past the silk butterflies in gilt cages and the waterfall with green foam lily pads; the lights, emanating from paper lanterns with a pinkish glow, were dim enough to please even Blanche Dubois. Fran asked the hostess, a Chinese woman with black-and-white-streaked hair pulled into a tight chignon, if there was a quiet table in the back room. "Sorry," said the woman, "all filled tonight." She led them instead to a table in the darkest, farthest corner of the main room, smiling as she instructed them to enjoy their dinner.

A waiter came to take their drink order. He didn't ask if they preferred separate checks.

But this was not a date. Perhaps something like a business dinner. Frank Rhodes wanted to continue the discussion. And hadn't he said that her help in explaining the student evaluations and analyzing the handwriting was valuable to the investigation?

Fran ordered a vodka martini with a twist and asked Frank if he'd like to split a carafe of sake with the meal. "No," Frank said, staring down at the menu. "But you go ahead."

The waiter waited, pen poised. "No, thank you," Fran said demurely. "The martini will be fine."

"And you, sir?" the waiter asked.

Frank ordered a diet Coke, then looked at her. "Sorry, I don't drink."

"Oh, sure," Fran said quickly. "Nothing to be sorry about."

"I miss it," Frank said, meeting her level gaze. "That's something they don't always tell you when you're going through the program. How damn much you're going to miss it. Especially at certain times." He was saying this as if she already knew, and in a way, she supposed she did.

"I wouldn't have ordered a drink," she told him. "Does it bother you?"

"Oh, not at all." Frank moved his hand across the table, almost, but not quite, reaching her arm. Instead he stopped somewhere to the left of her teacup. "Sometimes I think I like just being in the company of someone enjoying a drink."

"A vicarious pleasure," Fran said.

"Right. Vicarious. That's exactly the word." He nodded and went back to the menu.

"What sounds good to you?"

"You know, I hardly ever eat Chinese food," Frank confessed. "One time I had sweet and sour pork. I liked that."

"Should I order for us?" She added, so as not to appear aggressive, "I've come here a lot, so I know what's good."

"Go ahead." Frank closed his menu, folding his hands in front of him on the table. They were nice man-hands, slightly veined, with square nails and some dark hair along the knuckles.

"Okay. Let's see. Do you like eggplant? Scallops?"

"I don't know," Frank said. "I don't think I've ever had either."

"The garlic eggplant is one of my favorites," Fran said.

"I'd like to try it then," Frank told her.

"How about soup?"

"Sure. Soup sounds good." Frank smiled agreeably.

When the waiter returned with their drinks, Fran ordered garlic eggplant, scallops in a black bean sauce, and spinach-bean curd soup. At the last item, Frank's eyebrows raised. "It's really wonderful," Fran assured him as the waiter made a little bow and hurried back to the kitchen. "Listen, if you don't like what I ordered, the whole meal is on me. How's that for a deal?"

"No," Frank said simply.

"No?" Fran smiled and took a sip of her martini.

"Because," Frank said, "I asked you out."

"Hey, Fran!" Harvey Boxtel walked up to the table, flanked by his family. "We just finished," Harvey said, pointing to the back room, separated from the main dining space by a bamboo partition. "Great meal!" Harvey sucked contently on a toothpick, suppressing a belch, holding one hand against his stomach. "I ate too much."

Harvey had one of those bodies peculiar to academics: narrow-shouldered, high-bellied, his pants belted somewhere under his armpits. "They make moo shu vegetables, no pork, if you ask them," he said to Fran. Shoshanna stood next to Harvey, now fixing a look of dark severity on Frank Rhodes. Their two daughters stood on Harvey's other side. Fran began to introduce them all. She mentioned each name, hesitating before the introduction of the Kovner-Boxtel girls. Ada and Allison. But who was whom? Less than two years apart, the girls, now into adolescence, each with glasses and braces and scattered pimples, were remarkably similar. "Ada and Allison," Fran said as if they were more or less a unit. "Detective Rhodes," she said, by way of introducing Frank.

"You are with the Grandview Police Department?" Shoshanna inquired fiercely. She was dressed in a green velour sweat outfit and carried a black leather shoulder bag. Fran had a sudden flash of Shoshanna in an Israeli army uniform, a gun slung over her formidable chest. Frank told her that, yes, he was. "I see," Shoshanna said, turning abruptly toward Fran. "And how is George doing? You've been with him this afternoon, yes?"

"I felt so bad," Harvey began, apologetic because he had just found out that afternoon, he said. Sam Hollyhock had told him when he went in to pick up the mail. In fact, he was now going home to call Martha for an update on George's condition.

"George is okay. They pumped him out pretty thoroughly," Fran said. She stopped herself from going on, since it seemed inappropriate to be talking about George Lawson's getting the contents of his stomach cleaned out when Harvey was standing there all puffed up with moo shu vegetables and she and Frank were anticipating a tableful of food.

"It's terrible, isn't it?" Harvey clucked. Then leaning closer to Fran, he said, "Honestly. Do you think this was an accident? Or do you think he was actually trying . . ." Harvey stopped, glancing over at his daughters. Both Ada and Allison looked bored and sullen. "Daddy, could we go to the car?" one of them said.

"It's locked," Shoshanna told them. "Go sit over there." She pointed to a red vinyl bench by the fountain. Although the suggestion sounded like an order coming from Shoshanna, the girls didn't move. One sighed audibly.

"I don't know, Harvey," Fran said. "He's been very depressed, so it wouldn't surprise me."

"Nothing would surprise me lately," Harvey said, looking over at Frank. Regardless of his assertion that nothing would surprise him, there was a look of wonder on Harvey's smooth white face.

The waiter appeared with a steaming tureen of soup, stopping in front of Harvey and his family, who were blocking access to the table. "We should go," Harvey acknowledged. "Can I call you later, Fran?" he asked.

"Sure. Call me."

"See ya," either Ada or Allison called over her shoulder.

Frank said he liked the soup, although he added about a half dozen shakes of soy sauce and left most of the tofu in the bottom of his bowl. "Tell me what you were going to tell me at the station," he said. "It's something about George Lawson and Tyler Markem, isn't it?"

Fran finished the last of the martini; the warmth of the drink and the soup and the dim lighting made her feel soft and acquiescent; she could tell this man anything. "All right," she said, sighing. "Here goes."

Martha, the department secretary, was the first person Fran had called after she got to the hospital that morning. "George doesn't have any family. He's divorced and both his parents are gone," Fran told Frank.

"No children?"

"No," Fran said. "No family at all." She thought for one moment how that would be her description, as well: divorced; both parents dead; no children. Then her sister, Roz, looming large and loud, drove the lonely image from her head. It made Fran uncomfortable to identify with George in any way. "No real friends, either, I guess," Fran added quickly. Of course she, Fran, had Julia. And her Friday club, all of whom would rally around her bedside if she happened to take an overdose of anything. "But Martha is a very nice person, who's always kind of been there for George," Fran went on. "I know Martha's been having him for Thanksgiving with her family for the past several years. And Martha's the one who's been checking him in and out of rehab. Anyway . . ." Fran took a deep breath.

Frank waited. "Anyway . . ." he added.

"Well, Martha told me this pretty upsetting thing this morning while we were waiting together in the hospital. She hadn't told anyone else, and she thought that Tyler was the only other person, besides the girl herself, of course, who knew. That made Martha a little edgy, I guess. That's why she told me. Although Lynette apparently also knew. She mentioned it to Julia and me when we saw her last night. I just thought there was something going on, some kind of competition with Julia. You know, that she knew something that Julia didn't. It was as if Lynette's knowing proved that she was closer to Tyler, do you know what I mean?" Fran felt herself getting all worked up again. Martha had volunteered only the basic story—she was not a gossip—but Fran had pressed for details. They had been sitting in the waiting room, waiting to be allowed in to see George. By the time Martha finished the story and the nurse came in to announce that George would live, Fran felt like killing him.

"Would you care to share this information with me?" Frank said, offering her the last of the soup. "I'm not sure I'm following this."

"There's this student, Tricia Early. I had her last year in my comedy course—"

"Comedy?" Frank asked.

"Well, we don't do stand-up routines or anything like that. We read books, social satire, comic novels: it's a real course." Frank nodded. "Anyway, I remember Tricia because of her name: 'Early.' And she always came in late. She had a dance class right before and had to change, so she was always late to class."

"Yes," Frank said.

"So it *was* kind of funny, you know. 'Early' and she always came in late, don't you think?"

"It's funny," Frank said. "Go on."

Fran took a breath, feeling anxious. For some reason, she was uncomfortable saying it all—maybe because she had once slept with George and a part of her felt forever marked by the act. Though God knew that during the history of her single life, there were other regrets. A small number of other one-night stands as well. Still, none had the capacity to shame her as the time with George. Sitting now in front of Frank, she suddenly felt the tawdriness of George, and involuntarily she gave a little shudder.

The waiter came with the food, standing by them, silent as a shadow as he took their soup bowls; delicately he set down thick white plates and a bowl of mounded rice, and uncovered the steaming silver tureens. "Let's eat first," Frank suggested, as if sensing her discomfort. "Enjoy the meal. There's time to do the business later."

"Yes," Fran said gratefully. She watched him spear a scallop, hesitating before bringing it to his mouth. "Enjoy the meal."

He really was a very open man, this she had known from their long encounter in Taco Time. He was open, especially, she thought, with all those qualifiers: for a midwesterner, for a gentile, for a cop. Not that she had ever known a cop. No, that was not true. One of Damian's uncles had been a police officer in Chicago, though he was retired by the time Fran had met him at the engagement party. Damian's family were a rowdy bunch, their stories long-winded from drink and enthusiasm. Fran could hardly remember the policeman uncle, recalling only his stolid presence in front of some sports event on TV.

Tonight she talked with Frank laughingly about the hazards of dating, especially of getting set up by friends. Fran revealed how Shoshanna Kovner-Boxtel had once set her up with a teacher in Shoshanna's elementary school, a nice man, though clearly gay, who cut all his food into tiny bite-sized pieces on the plate and excused himself after the meal to "go potty."

Frank told her how he went out once with a friend's divorced neighbor who, following the date, began to send over casseroles with unusual notes attached. "I mean, the first one, with the tuna-noodle casserole, I didn't think anything of it: 'If you like this, there's more where it came from.' So, I thought, sure, more tuna-noodle casserole."

"But?"

"But a couple of casseroles later, she got really . . . I don't know, kind of strange."

"How strange?" Fran wanted to know.

"Oh, I don't remember."

"I don't believe you for a second. You do, too," Fran said. Frank laughed and poured them each the last of the tea.

"Tell me," Fran urged.

Frank signaled the waiter for another pot. "I'll tell you later. First you have to tell me about George Lawson and Tracy Early."

"Tricia," Fran said. "If you're going to be a good cop, you have to pay attention to these things," she added.

"I am a good cop," Frank said seriously. "Tell me."

Fran took a breath and it came out all in a quick blurt, not at all the roundabout, explaining way that Martha had slowly revealed in the hospital waiting room. "He exposed himself," Fran said clearly. "The student, Tricia Early, came in to talk to him about taking his poetry seminar in the fall and George was sitting behind his desk and when she got up to leave, George also got up and his fly was undone and he was exposing himself to her."

Frank stirred sugar into his tea. "Oh, boy," he said and took a sip, the dainty cup disappearing into his hand.

"And then this girl ran out into the hall and into Tyler Markem, who had been her philosophy teacher, and she must have been crying or looking distraught because she ended up in Tyler's office telling him what happened, and Tyler told her that George was under a great deal of stress lately and in therapy and must have been very drunk, and somehow Tyler convinced this kid that what George did was really an accident, that he wasn't flashing her at all but was so out of it that he must have forgotten to zip up and was she sure that he was really so fully exposed, because probably George had no idea what he was doing."

"So he convinced the girl not to report the incident," Frank surmised.

"Correct."

"When was this exactly?"

"Martha thinks the incident occurred just a few days before Tyler's death. Tyler and George were spending a lot of time together then."

Frank took the swizzle stick from Fran's martini and put in into his mouth like a cigarette. "So why do you think Markem stopped the girl from reporting this?" he asked Fran.

"It's hard to figure why he did that. Maybe he just didn't want George to lose his job. Maybe he believed it himself—that George was just a little sloppy putting himself away."

"Men don't get that sloppy putting themselves away," Frank said. "If she saw him and he was exposed—"

"Well, from what Martha told me, now it's not even clear that she saw him. Or how much of him she saw," Fran said. Having seen George herself that one time, she could understand repressing the event. Fran had an urge to call Tricia Early and share her distaste. "Better forget that one, honey," Fran would tell her.

"You know, Tyler had this quality," Fran went on. "He could really go out of his way for you. Sometimes I felt guilty because I didn't trust his sincerity. I always felt he didn't do anything for someone else out of a generous spirit. I think he liked having people indebted to him."

"Well, Lawson would surely be indebted to Tyler for saving his ass on this one," Frank said.

They stayed at the restaurant through pot after pot of tea, until the place emptied out and the waiters brought out the carpet sweepers and set all the other tables, talking to each other in hushed Chinese. Finally, Frank got up and stretched; Fran noticed that he left a very big tip.

"Oh, you never told me," Fran said as Frank was driving her home. Her own car was still in George Lawson's driveway. She thought briefly of asking Frank to take her there but decided she would get it tomorrow.

"Never told you what?"

"About the casserole lady. What was in her last note?"

"I really don't remember," Frank said.

"I really don't believe you."

"I can't."

Fran insisted. "You promised."

"Ah, give me a break. I really don't remember."

"You do. What was it?"

"Scalloped potatoes and ham. My favorite," Frank said.

"The note. What'd she write?" Fran was firm.

"The note said: 'I would like you to eat me,'" Frank said, not taking his eyes from the road.

They sat for a while in the car in front of her house and talked about interviewing George Lawson when he was well enough to speak. And perhaps finding Tricia Early. "This could get pretty ugly if it gets out," Frank said, shifting to look at Fran. "I remember all those letters in the *Grandview Tribune* after all that business about the research park." Frank's hand rested casually along the back of the seat; the motor was still running. "There's a lot of people in this town who don't like the college professors very much. Who think they're a lot of perverts and pinkos anyway."

It was dark in the driveway and not a light was on in the house. "You should have a timer," Frank told her. "You shouldn't come home to a dark house like this."

"I guess you're right," Fran said.

"They're easy to set up. Leenie did it herself in her New York apartment."

"I don't do mechanical or manual," Fran said. "I don't even pump my own gas."

"I thought you were one of those women . . ." Frank paused, searching for the right word. He knew "women's libber" was not the phrase.

"A feminist?" Fran offered.

"Yes," Frank said, as if the word had simply eluded him.

"Well, I am," Fran said.

"Well, then you should know how to pump your own gas and put in an electrical timer for your own protection," Frank told her.

"There are certain things I do not *choose* to do," Fran said somewhat haughtily.

"Now *I* don't believe *you*," Frank said, teasing, his voice soft with affection.

He moved nearer to her on the seat and she leaned toward him. She heard his breath catch before he kissed her, which he did, once, gently, briefly, before pulling away and then kissing her a second time. He stopped again, and when she didn't say anything the kissing began again in earnest. He was a naturally gifted kisser, a man who liked kissing, she could tell.

He stopped after a while and just looked at her. "Well," she said finally.

"I'd like to call you," he said. He got out of the car and walked her to the door.

It would be different, she thought, flinging off her shoes in the living room. Not only the difference in their backgrounds and educations, and who they were. But different because he was a widower. She had never been with someone who had lost a partner, and she was glad that Frank Rhodes was widowed, although she felt slightly guilty because Carol, from all the things he had said about her, seemed like such a nice person. But there was something to be said about widowed as opposed to divorced. Widowed, which seemed to indicate a seal of approval of sorts, a union that had been successful up until the very end. (Well, not so for Julia and Tyler, perhaps.)

It really wasn't so much she was glad that Frank Rhodes was widowed, but glad that he had never been divorced. There was something stable and dignified in his widowhood. It seemed to Fran that as she grew older, she had less and less patience for divorced men, less tolerance for the recycled problems of other women's sad baggage. Though she supposed there were men who could say the same about her.

She would have invited Frank in, but the house was a mess. All the clothes she had tried on that morning were strewn around the bedroom (not that Frank Rhodes would see the bedroom; still, she did think of it), and there were glasses and papers and a couple more pairs of shoes littering the living room. A flash again of a comparison with George Lawson's sloppy single state. Well, at least there was no food dried into clay in the kitchen. And no cat shit.

She checked her messages: two from Julia, one from faithful Roz, one from Maria to say that Friday club would be at her house the next week. She took a seltzer from the refrigerator and called Julia. It was past eleven. "It's me," she said, taking a swig from the bottle. Moving back and forth from the tawdry to the sublime, she told Julia all about George's exposing himself and her kissing Detective Frank Rhodes in the driveway of her house. "I cannot believe it! Oh my God! Oh my God!" Julia kept repeating over and over again, sounding like one of Stimpson's sorority girls.

"Did you hear anything else about George?" Fran asked.

"What else is there?"

"I mean, how he's doing. Have you called the hospital?"

"I spoke to Martha a couple of hours ago. He seems to be all right. His color and everything is better. Martha said that he's totally incommunicative, won't even talk to her, just looks away. She's worried about his emotional state. As soon as he's well enough, they're going to put him upstairs in the psychiatric unit."

"Did your family all get off okay?" Fran asked.

"My mother asked again if I wanted her to stay. Right in the airport. She was practically pushy."

"*Asking* if you want her to stay is not pushy," Fran explained.

"Oh dear, Franny, what a day!"

"How are the girls doing?"

"They're very sad. Tonight they're sleeping together in Beth's room. Last night, both of them came into my bed in the middle of the night and we all cuddled together. Caty was sobbing in her sleep." Julia paused. "You know what's strange?"

"What, sweetie?"

"I'm so angry at Tyler."

Fran heard a muffled cry on the other end of the phone. "Julia?" She waited.

"I'm so angry," Julia repeated. Then: "But I still miss him, you know?"

A part of her was relieved that the condition of the house dictated that she could not invite Frank in. She needed time to think. Anyone looking at the situation with a clear head would know that having an affair with the chief detective on a murder case when your best friend is one of the prime suspects, was probably not a good idea. Though Frank Rhodes didn't think that Julia was capable of such a crime. He said so over dinner. "I've been around enough," he had said. "And you sort of get a sixth sense about some things."

Fran agreed readily. Of course, Julia was incapable of killing anyone, she said. Although she did not tell him of Julia's peculiar behavior at the funeral. That and the unanswered phone the morning of the accident, when Julia had insisted she was home all morning. Fran's own sixth sense seemed particularly dulled.

But she knew she shouldn't have an affair with Frank Rhodes. Not yet, anyway. It wasn't right. What if she herself turned out to be a suspect? And why not, actually? She was at home, painting a chest of drawers when Tyler died. Home alone. Not exactly an airtight alibi. If she were to have an affair with Frank Rhodes, wouldn't there be some conflict of interest here? She was ruminating about this, brushing her teeth, when the phone rang.

"I just called to say good night," said a deep masculine voice. Fran looked down at her bare feet and watched her toes curl up like little shrimp. "Well, good night," she answered softly.

"It's not too late, I hope. I was trying for a while and the line was busy."

"I was talking to Julia," Fran said. He did not ask about what.

"I had a real nice time tonight," he said.

"Listen, Frank . . ." she began.

"I'm listening."

"I was thinking tonight. About us. You know, about having a relationship. And you working on the case and everything and Julia being my best friend and, I don't know. It might get kind of complicated, don't you think? If we start something between us now. What do you think?" Stopping, she felt her heart pumping in her chest. Silence.

"I think it's already too late," Frank said finally. "We *did* start something."

"Oh," Fran said.

"But if you don't want to—"

"Oh, I didn't say that," she protested. "I mean, I would like to see you again. For us to go out. But I think we should wait . . ." She went on and on, explaining; as usual, explaining too much, so by the end of her speech she was not sure what he would be thinking. There was no response on the other end. "Frank?" she said. "Are you there?"

"Well, I think you may be right," he said finally.

Fran's heart dropped, disappointed. What did she want, after all? That he would be so smitten that he would be unable to resist, imploring: No, no, I *must* have you, no matter the consequences?

"Of course, afterwards . . ." Fran continued lamely.

"Afterwards?"

"You know, when the case is closed," she said. She thought that eventually Tyler's death *would* be declared an accident—and wondered how soon that could be. "After the case is finished, I would like to see you, Frank," she said, lowering her voice toward a seductive tone.

"Well, it'll be just business for a while, then," Frank said, sounding suddenly distant. "But I expect to need your help wrapping up a few other things. I'm tied up all day tomorrow, but I'll be in touch."

"Sure." For a brief moment, she envisioned Frank Rhodes literally tied up, bound with ropes and blindfolds and gagged by whoever had killed Tyler Markem. It was a sudden reality that she might be falling for someone who actually lived a dangerous life. Over dinner, he had told her of a drug bust out in the country, where in an empty trailer he and Jonny Verlaine had found automatic weapons, loaded and poised to shoot from every window.

There was a long pause through which she felt his silent attention. "It's late," he said finally. "Were you in bed?"

"Yes," she said huskily, though she was sitting on a kitchen stool, still holding her toothbrush, a smear of Colgate across the front of her red dress.

"Good night, then," Frank said. "Sleep tight."

She sat for a while with the phone in her hand. "Good night, Frank," she repeated, after he had already hung up.

Revenge: July

27

It was hot: midwestern-July-bake-in-the-sun hot. The sun reflected off the brick buildings, and even the leaves on the trees seemed wilted from the scorching heat.

With all the students gone, the Stimpson campus had a lonesome, deserted quality, like an empty stadium after the big game. In high school, that had been one of Frank's favorite places to go to think—the Grandview Giants stadium, late at night when the hoopla had died down. The old high school was just at the edge of town then, in a field surrounded by farmland; the stadium was up on a hill behind the school, looking down on both the town and the college. At night, from the top of the bleachers, Frank liked to watch the lights of both making friendly flickers in the dark.

Frank had been a Grandview Giant himself, had worn the purple-and-white uniform for basketball and baseball at Grandview High. He was tall enough and adequate in basketball. But in baseball he shone. Baseball suited his deliberate, contemplative nature; he loved the thoughtful rhythms of the game and the way individual accomplishment evolved into team patterns.

Now he walked from his car toward Grayson Hall, feeling the heat pulsing, shimmering off the pavement. Inside, the building was refreshingly cool and dark, but upstairs, in the philosophy office, it was as cold as a meat locker. Charlotte Pintel, dressed in a beige raincoat buttoned up to her neck, cradled a phone between her ear and shoulder as she typed on the keyboard of a computer. She held up a finger when she saw Frank in the doorway and then returned to typing without missing a beat. "Yes, it's cold in here," she was saying to someone on the other end of the phone. "I'd call sixty-two degrees cold, wouldn't you? It's summer, you know, and I'm sitting here in this office in a lined trench coat." To Frank she said: "We can't regulate the temperature in our own offices." Back into the phone she replied: "Yes, I would like you to send someone up from the physical plant. This is the third time this week that I've had to call for him to come and adjust the damned thermostat." She turned back to Frank with a sudden smile. "Hey there," she said. "How you doing, Detective?"

Charlotte had become, in the past few weeks, a regular participant in the investigation. An investigation that, to Frank's mind, was winding undramatically to a close. Cause of death: accident.

Everyone was turning up with alibis.

Lynette Macalvie had suddenly remembered that heading out of town for Lake Westin, waiting for a stoplight before turning east off Highway 34, she had waved to Rob Burnette, a young man who had been in a biology class with her that semester. When Frank called him, Rob Burnette indeed remembered waving back to Lynette, indicating also that the interchange, which took place about ten miles outside the Grandview city limits, occurred right before he was supposed to be at work at the Standard station on Highway 34 at eleven o'clock that morning.

Just about the same time that Tyler Markem would have been going to his workout in the gym.

It was Victoria's Secret that was Julia's alibi. When the package came, delivered to her door: item #549933 from the Victoria's Secret summer catalog—boxer shorts and pajama shirt, 100% cotton, cornflower blue, size medium, $29.95— Julia suddenly remembered. Of course she *was* home, she told Frank again. She had called the toll-free number right before the hospital called to tell her of Tyler's accident.

Frank checked with Midwestern Bell. It wasn't *exactly* right before. A phone call from Grandview had come in at ten forty-five that morning. Figuring it out, he supposed that yes, it was possible that a woman could purchase a pair of pajamas from a mail order catalog, drive three miles across town to the Stimpson campus, go to the gym undetected, drop a three-hundred-pound barbell across her husband's neck, and drive the three miles home again to be there in time to receive a call from the hospital. But it hardly seemed likely.

And George Lawson, recovered from his suicide attempt, had checked himself into an alcoholic rehab program near his sister in Des Moines. While no one actually saw George leaving the gym that morning, George's demeanor suggested only a sad, troubled man who deeply missed the only friend he had. "This is it," he told Frank before he left. "Tyler was the only one who really cared about me. And I've made a promise to his memory to straighten out this time. For good."

Even the business with the student, Tricia Early, seemed to lead nowhere. No, she said, from her parents' home in suburban Chicago, she was not thinking of pressing charges against Professor Lawson. Dr. Markem had convinced her that what happened was just an accident. And she felt so terrible about the death of Tyler Markem, "a wonderful human being." She was not returning to Stimpson anyway. She was moving to Colorado with her boyfriend.

"Dead ends," Frank had said to Fran just yesterday on the phone. "I'm thinking about closing out the case." Although they had seen each other just one other time—ostensibly to rework a list of Tyler Markem's associates and acquaintances—Frank had called her almost every night, usually late, just to talk. It was not exactly a relationship, though she must have heard the longing in his voice.

Charlotte opened a drawer and took out an envelope, handed it to Frank. "I opened it only because I thought it was business," she explained. "It's from a philosophical conference he was supposed to attend in the fall."

The outside of the envelope indeed looked as if the contents would relate to professional matters. "Professor Tyler Markem" was neatly typed on an address label. "Philosophy Department, University of Iowa," was the return address.

Frank sat in a chair in front of Charlotte's desk and opened the letter. It was a form letter; there was information about the annual midwestern Philosophical Society Conference—registration fees, times, places to stay. On the bottom of the sheet, however, was a handwritten line: "Same time this year?" It was unsigned except for a crimson-colored lip imprint in the shape of a kiss.

"Any idea who this is?" Frank asked Charlotte.

Charlotte shrugged, looking casual, though her eyes were glassy with excitement.

"I'll take this back with me," Frank said, putting the envelope in his jacket pocket. "Thanks."

"Uh, I need to ask you something. There's someone coming this weekend. The teacher to take Professor Markem's place?"

"Yes?"

"Well, summer school is going to start after the holiday. Will you be needing to get into Professor Markem's office again?" Charlotte asked.

"I don't think so," Frank told her. There were mostly books left. They had taken anything that might be seen as evidence. He got up to leave.

"Well, should we put an end to this crime scene business, then? Take the tape and the signs off the door so the new teacher can get in?" Charlotte seemed a little sad. As if this were the end of something.

That afternoon Frank was driving to Aurora for a July Fourth celebration with his daughter Patricia and her family. In the car he had an overnight bag and a present: a boxed set of perfume and body lotion from JCPenney. The Fourth of July was also Patricia's birthday. Until she was ten years old, Patricia had thought that the fireworks marking the holiday were meant especially for her.

He stopped back at the station to deposit the envelope Charlotte Pintel had just given him in a box with some of the other items found in Tyler Markem's office. Now Frank took out the envelope, bringing it to his face and sniffing for fragrance. Carefully he put it in a plastic shield to protect the imprint. It would be easy enough to find the woman with the crimson lips. In his mind he pictured a similarly married woman professor, disappointed to learn that her lover's death prevented this year's romantic interlude.

There was something shocking about that crimson lipstick kiss on university stationery. He smiled, thinking of sharing this information with Fran Meltzer; picked up the phone and dialed her number. "Would you like to do a little more handwriting analysis? I need your expertise," he said. Same time this year, the note said. Though one written line would most likely not be able to give sufficient information.

"Of course," she said, sounding surprised. "Sure."

"I'm going out of town tonight. To my daughter's in Aurora. Can I call you when I get back tomorrow night?"

"Sure," Fran said again. "You want to tell me what's up?"

What he almost told her was that he just wanted to see her again. That for the past few days, he found himself thinking about her all the time. "Nothing much," he said. "Just some notes here that I'd like you to take a look at."

"All right, then," Fran said.

"Are you going to watch the fireworks tonight?" Frank asked. Every Fourth the Grandview Jaycees sponsored fireworks in the park, and the whole town turned out.

"I don't think so," Fran said.

"Well, if you're out tonight, be sure to lock up. Holidays are favorite times for break-ins."

"I'll be sure to lock up, Detective," Fran said. "Yes, sir!" This had become something of a theme with them—what he took to be her general disregard for personal safety.

"Always. Not only on holidays, though," he said.

"At night, I lock the doors," Fran told him. "But if I'm home in the middle of the day and I run in and out all the time. . . . I'm in Grandview, Illinois, for pete's sake. Not New York."

Frank reminded her that he was investigating a murder in Grandview, Illinois.

"Hey, have a great time with your family," Fran told him before they hung up.

He wondered; if she wasn't going to the fireworks—where was she going?

At Julia's that night, Fran was pouring two glasses of wine, about to bring one to her friend, who lay stretched out on the living room couch. "Just a half glass," Julia called. "I don't think with these muscle relaxers I should be drinking wine."

Fran spread cream cheese on pieces of dark rye, then added anchovy, red pepper, and fresh cilantro before she quartered each slice of bread and arranged it all on a white platter. The phone rang, and Julia picked up the portable receiver beside her on the coffee table. Fran heard Julia say that she was feeling a little better. No, she wasn't in much pain at all today, but the doctor had said that she needed bed rest for at least the next few days. Julia said something else that Fran didn't hear because a round of firecrackers went off in a neighboring yard. Fran cut up a Granny Smith apple and arranged the slices around the platter.

She entered the room with everything on a tray and saw Julia, pensive, the phone resting on her chest. "Who was that?" Fran asked lightly. At least, she tried to sound light rather than inquisitory, which is what she felt. She sensed that she should be looking for something—what, she didn't know—then she felt guilty that she was looking at all.

"Oh dear," Julia said, biting her lip. Julia never said "Oh shit!" when something happened. Certainly not "Oh fuck!" as Fran was wont to do. Sometimes Fran wondered how she could really be best friends with someone who said "Oh dear" all the time.

"Is it your back?" Fran came forward slowly, putting the tray down on the coffee table. The day before, Julia had strained her back bending over in the garden to pull out a weed.

"That was Charlotte Pintel," Julia said, looking stricken; Julia's skin had a chalky tone that made her freckles stand out. "The police have opened up Tyler's office. The new person in philosophy is coming this weekend from Ohio to look for an apartment, and he wants to be able to use the office." The new person, a graduate student from Ohio State, was someone Sam Hollyhock had hired over the phone for a one-year appointment to teach Tyler's courses. Julia looked up expectantly at Fran.

"So?" Fran asked.

"Well, all that's really left are Tyler's books. I took everything else out. The police went through all the stuff, too. Charlotte knows I'm laid up, so she's going to go in tomorrow to pack up the books and bring them all over here."

"That's all right, isn't it?" Fran said tentatively.

"No," Julia said, reaching over for the wineglass, her long fingers slowly stretching around the stem.

"No?"

"Franny, you have to do me a favor. A big favor." Julia, wincing, managed to move herself up a little on the couch and face her friend.

"Anything," Fran said, trying to sound as if she meant it. Well, she did mean it. Julia was her best friend. Julia would do anything for her. It was only right that Fran would do the same.

"I need you to go to Tyler's office tonight. You don't have to pack anything. Charlotte can do that tomorrow. Just give a quick look through. Just see if there's anything there that shouldn't be."

Fran was confused. "Julia, don't you think the police would have taken anything they thought was suspicious?" Fran wished she had talked longer to Frank before he left, grilled him a little about what else he had. "I really don't understand."

"It's because of the girls," Julia said. "I have to protect them." Julia's chin stuck out with determination. "I don't want anyone else to know about Tyler's affair. And if Charlotte Pintel knows, she'll tell Martha and the whole English department will know and Harvey will tell Shoshanna and I can just see his daughters listening . . ." Julia ran the likely channels how the news would be picked up by Beth and Caty, who "don't need to know something they can never ask their father about."

"But everything that could be incriminating is gone from the desk," Fran told her. "All those things from Lynette we saw. There are only books left." Fran, who wasn't used to not catching on, was not catching on. "Julia, what are you thinking of?"

"Tyler *always* stuck things in books: messages, or notes to himself, or letters. One time the library called because he actually left a check he had written in a book. After the police lifted the ban, I was going to go clear everything out myself, but now, of course . . ." Julia reached gingerly and took a canape. "There just might be something in a book."

"Something like what?"

"Like I don't know what. Like another disgusting moon-spoon-June love poem stuck away in a book. Like another one of those adorable cards or something."

"Well, if Charlotte is just going to box the books and bring them over, she won't find anything."

"Fran, Charlotte is so nosy. And don't think that woman wouldn't love to get some dirt on Tyler."

"So you want me to go over to Grayson Hall *now* and flip through all of Tyler's books?" Fran asked, incredulous.

"I said it was a big favor, didn't I? Fran, if you won't do it, I understand," Julia said, her mouth tightening. "I have a key this time. We don't have to break in."

"I didn't say I wouldn't do it," Fran said. "I just don't think it's really necessary, is all."

"It is," Julia insisted.

Fran sighed and made a sandwich of two of the canapes together; the salty anchovy was delicious in the soft, bland cheese. "It'll be dark soon," Fran said, looking out the window.

"I'd go with you if I could, Franny," Julia said tenderly.

28

From the window of Tyler's office in Grayson Hall, Fran could see the fireworks. She turned on the desk lamp rather than the fluorescent overhead. Aside from the exit signs and the stairways, it was probably the only light on in the entire building.

She started with the books on the highest shelf, moving a chair over so she could reach, taking out a few at a time, splitting them and fanning through the pages as she held the book aloft. Out fell some handwritten notes; an occasional bookmark floated down to the floor, cut-out articles, shopping lists. After completing the top shelf, she got off the chair and examined each piece. Tyler's handwriting was large, flamboyant, straight up and down with firmly crossed *t*'s: the definitive script of an energetic, arrogant man.

The entire west wall of the office was lined with books, hundreds and hundreds of them. She sighed, moving on to the second tier. Outside she saw against the night sky bursts of color and drops of bright, white light falling like beads from a string of pearls. It was so quiet in the building when the fireworks stopped that she could hear her own breathing. The light of the exit sign right outside the office cast an eerie red glow on the opaque glass of the door. Fran stopped and listened. The building seemed to pulse from the silence. "Shit," she said, under her breath. "Shit, shit, shit." The *s*'s hissed softly in the silence.

Fran did not think of herself as a brave person. She was assertive, yes. And gutsy. But then, gutsy only in personal encounters with salespeople or hostile students. In matters of physical danger, she was a chickenshit. Give her an icy highway, a plane (she always felt flying constituted a physical danger), an unsavory person in a suspicious circumstances—and suddenly she was unable to think or act with any clarity at all. Once, playing hide-and-go-seek at ten years old with her friends, she found herself immobilized with the fear of discovery; unable to run home-free; humiliated to find she had peed in her pants when she was suddenly tagged.

She wanted to call Frank. Probably he would not have come here with her tonight even if he were not out of town. Though what she was doing here now couldn't be against the law. The police had already been here, after all. And Julia had given Fran the key, so it was not as if she was breaking in. But it was creepy here like this in the massive, dark building, explosions shattering the hot air outside as if in some war-torn city where rockets illumined the night as a matter of course.

She found nothing in the books on the second shelf except more notes, philosophical ruminations, a few index cards, a coupon for Folgers coffee. On the third shelf there was a slip of yellow paper with a phone number on it, a local Grandview number she did not recognize. No name. Fran pocketed the paper and put the book back. On the shelf next to the desk was a gold letter opener with Tyler's initials engraved in a florid script and a lumpy hand-thrown clay mug with DADDY in blue letters that had dripped down to the base of the cup.

Seeing these very personal effects gave Fran a sudden sorrow.

She also felt like an intruder, more now than when she and Julia had entered Tyler's office without his permission while he was still alive.

It was almost eleven by the time she got to the last shelf, and her eyes hurt from working in the weak light. She paused a moment, listening again at the door, thinking she heard the *whoosh* of air as the door to the stairway was opened. She stopped and held her breath, waiting, her ears pricked for the sound of footsteps. Outside, the fireworks had ended in a grand finale, a *rat-tat-tat* of sound lasting almost a full minute. Now, through the opaque glass, the hall seemed tomblike, bathed in the bloodred aura of the exit sign. She stood, stiff and still until her knees, locked in place, began to ache. "Do it," Fran said, mouthing the actual words rather than saying them aloud and walking on tiptoe over to the last shelf. "Finish up."

It was there, in the most obvious place, the last shelf closest to Tyler's desk, that she found it. The book, *The Critique of Pure Reason* by Immanuel Kant, was close enough to have been taken down by anyone sitting at the desk without even rising from the chair.

Inside the book, somewhere near the end, bending the spine at an odd angle, was a fat yellow campus mail envelope with Tyler's name on the outside, a typed label whose return address was the administration building. The envelope had once been sealed shut but was now bound only by the string that makes a figure eight in closure. Fran held the envelope for a few moments. It seemed heavy in her hand. Finally she took the string in two fingers and began to unwind.

Inside the envelope were pictures. Colored Polaroid pictures, each of the same woman, each in the same setting—on a bed. Fran held the pictures under the light and felt a flush rise along the back of her neck.

There were five in all. Two were of the woman in black bikini panties, a black garter belt with fishnet stockings, and a half-bra, also black, that pushed up her breasts so they looked like two mounds of vanilla ice cream sitting in a dish. The woman was reclining at an uncomfortable angle on a bed made up with a purple-and-pink floral comforter. There were large piles of books on the wooden headboard behind her and two stacks of books on the night table next to the bed. She was a pale-skinned, large-hipped woman in her late forties; quite ordinary looking with a wide nose and grayish-brown hair, blunt cut with bangs across her forehead. She did not look sexy. She looked, rather, like someone's high school algebra teacher who, on a dare to show that she was really a sport, took off her clothes and put on some audacious costume.

In the other pictures the woman was naked, large and very white, except for the dark triangle of pubic hair that revealed itself in two photographs between her modestly crossed legs. She seemed choreographed, one hand cupping a breast, offering up a plump brown nipple from between two splayed fingers; in the next picture one hand was lost somewhere between her legs so that it appeared as if she did not have a hand at all but only a stump of a wrist. In the last picture, her legs were awkwardly splayed, as if she were anticipating a gynecological examination; she managed a smile, broadmouthed yet tentative; the expression reminded Fran of the forced grimaces in the school photographs of her niece and nephew that Roz sent at the beginning of every school year.

Fran stared and stared, shaking her head. "There she is," Fran said, in the softest possible whisper. "Alice Blevins in all her splendor!"

29

The phone was ringing when she walked through the unlocked
back door, and she stood, heart pounding, in the kitchen, listening to her own welcoming voice as the machine picked up:
"Whatever I'm doing I'd rather be talking to you!" She waited
for the final beep before the message. "Fran, just wanted to
know how everything went. Are you there? Pick up." There
was a pause. "Oh, all right. Call me as soon as you get in."
Fran held her breath until she heard Julia's reluctant good-
bye. The machine clicked off. She stood there for another few
seconds, the envelope clutched to her chest. It seemed unnatural,
not answering the phone—Fran, a woman who since puberty
had bounded up steps, leapt from bed, raced wet from the
shower toward a ringing phone. But now, something held her
back. She wanted to talk to Frank. And right now she wished
more than anything that she knew his daughter's married name
so she could call him in Aurora.

Fran put the envelope with the pictures in a kitchen drawer,
covering it with a blue dish towel. She bit her lip, looked around
the kitchen, took the envelope out of the drawer. She got out

a roll of aluminum foil, tore off a fair-sized sheet, and carefully wrapped the envelope, pressing flat along the sides until the package looked like a slim chicken filet. Opening the freezer, she deposited it behind a stack of Healthy Choice Herbed Chicken dinners. Then she took out a pint of Ben and Jerry's Rainforest Crunch ice cream and began to eat some out of the container while she sat at the kitchen counter and ruminated on the sudden turn of events: Alice Blevins. Dirty pictures of Alice Blevins. This was more shocking to her than the news that Tyler had been cheating on Julia. More shocking, even, than his death.

She had known Alice for almost ten years, though—naked photos aside—she had not really known her well at all. Had not *wanted* to know Alice Blevins well at all. Which was a shame because really, there was not an abundance of bright single women at the college. She and Alice could have been friends. *Could* have been, if Alice were not so distinctly humorless, so grimly dedicated to the cause of Stimpson College in all its purple-and-gold glory.

Everyone knew how invaluable Alice was to Stimpson, how she worked tirelessly to promote the college any way she could; how President Von Eaton frequently referred to Alice as "my right-hand gal," an embarrassment that no one seemed able to call him on.

Alice Blevins had been divorced a long time. Her ex-husband, Pierre Blevins, a sculptor in the Stimpson art department, had had, in fact, an affair with one of *his* students, had gone to Florence with her for the Art Abroad program and never returned.

Fran recalled from her Friday club the story that the week after Pierre left for Italy, Alice opened up his studio and had a garage sale, selling every one of Pierre's sculptures for less than a dollar. Drusilla, in fact, had a Pierre Blevins bust of a sad-eyed Madonna on her mantel.

There was only a dollop or so left of the Rainforest Crunch, but with a steely measure of self-control, Fran put the container back in the freezer, pausing before closing the door. A freezer probably wasn't the best place to store photographs. Especially Polaroid ones. The cold might mix the chemicals some way and ruin the image. Fran pictured the naked Alice, blue-skinned, blurring around the edges in the freezer. It was money people usually hid in freezers. Cool cash that wouldn't get burned in a house fire.

Quickly Fran looked about the kitchen. An empty barley or rice canister. The bottom of the recycling bin. Inside a pot on that high shelf above the sink. The counters were so cluttered that she could easily just leave the pictures out behind some dishes or old newspapers. Tomorrow morning, for sure, she was going to get this place in order. Right now, she just didn't have the energy.

She took the package out of the freezer and walked around the room, the foil cold in her hand. What was so important about hiding these pictures after all? Why did she feel she *had* to?

In the living room, she carefully drew the curtains, checked the doors, and sat down on the couch, taking off the foil and rolling it into a ball. She wound the string around to reopen the envelope and took out the pictures, noticing this time the volumes of books surrounding the figure on the bed. Books and books. That, too, was a surprise: Alice was a reader (from general conversation, Fran believed that most administrative types were not). She straightened out her arm, holding the pictures back to try to make out some of the titles, recognizing only that the books were all hardbacks, which seemed to denote a certain seriousness.

She looked at the main focus of the pictures again. It was the split beaver shot (she knew the term from Paul Kravitz, her first husband, who enjoyed pornography) that really made her jaw drop. There it was: a slash of a vagina, clear, shiny red, like the pulpy inside of an overripe persimmon. What was in Alice Blevins's head to send Tyler something like this? Who *took* these pictures? And had Alice actually sent the pictures through campus mail?

Fran got up and headed for the bedroom, easing her way past the ironing board set up in the hall. Tomorrow she would put everything away. There was still a pile of clothes to be ironed in the basket; the pressed clothes were hung on the steel rod across the door to her bedroom. When she bought the house, that room had belonged to a teenage boy whose height and weight were charted on the wall and who must have spent hours doing chin-ups in the doorway. Fran never took down the bar, finding it useful for hanging clothes.

She looked around the room, absentmindedly kicking a pile of dirty laundry out of the way. Lifting one side of the mattress, she slid the pictures underneath and stood back, biting her lip. Under the mattress. A cliché, really. She removed the envelope and went to her closet, looking through the piles of sweaters and T-shirts on the shelves.

She jumped when the phone rang this time and picked it up before the second ring. "Franny?" Julia's voice had a worried edge. "Where were you?"

"I just walked in the door," Fran lied, her heart sinking. She had never lied to Julia before and was not exactly clear why she was doing it now.

"Well?"

"Yes, well it just took a real long time to go through all those books," Fran told her.

"And?"

"Well, there's nothing really."

"You didn't find anything?" Julia sounded disappointed. "You looked through all the books?"

"Oh, there is something." Fran reached into her pocket for the yellow slip of paper. "There's just a slip of paper with a telephone number on it. There's no name or anything." Fran felt grateful that there was something to report.

"That's it, huh?"

"Yes." Fran looked at the paper in her hand, but Julia did not ask to hear the number. "How are you feeling?" Fran finally asked.

"I don't know. I'm just not moving. If I don't move, it doesn't hurt. Tomorrow, if I can get up, I'll go to the doctor's."

"I'll drive you," Fran offered.

"That's okay. Franny, you're not getting any work done because of me. Beth can take me. She loves any opportunity she can to drive."

"Julia, what if something happens and your back is out . . ." Fran began. Beth, newly licensed at sixteen and already the recipient of two violations, did not inspire confidence. "I want to take you."

"No, really," Julia said.

"What time should I pick you up?"

"You need to get some work done. You've been in this thing with me for the past two months. You must be way behind."

Fran, who in April was way behind on a new book contract, didn't admit to anything. "I insist on taking you to the doctor tomorrow."

"You are so pigheaded, Franny." Julia sighed. "And such a good friend. How about if I call you and see how my back feels in the morning?"

"Okay, let me know," Fran said, relenting in the fleeting hope, insubstantial as a shadow, that Julia's back would suddenly be better and she would not need to go to the doctor at all. There were suspicions Fran found difficult to admit even to herself. But she felt—what was it, exactly—*set up* somehow, unable to tell Julia about the pictures because a part of her believed that Julia already *knew* about the pictures.

"You know what else? Something strange happened after you left," Julia said.

"What?"

"Well, I got this call. It was like heavy breathing, some sounds . . . only not really like an obscene phone caller."

"Julia, what do you mean?"

"I don't know. It just sounded *funny*. At first like a bad connection. Then like someone breathing out really loudly, like someone getting angry and trying to get control, you know?"

"Are the girls there?"

"They're upstairs watching a movie. I'm not afraid. It's just strange here now, being alone. You begin to think things."

"What are you thinking?" Fran asked.

"Well, it's creepy, that's all. One time, Tyler was out of town and this man called in the middle of the night and wanted to know if I was lonely and you know, that he had something for me. I hung up really fast, but to this day I don't know if it was just a fluke that an obscene phone caller got me when Tyler was gone or if it was someone who actually knew us."

"Probably just a student," Fran said. Then she laughed. Julia used to tell her that. How students would call, speaking to Caty and Beth, never leaving a message or a name. "Just a student," they'd say as if they were not entitled to any additional identity.

It was Fran who said good night first; they both said "I love you," the way true best friends sometimes do. Fran stared at the phone in its cradle, vaguely aware that a sad resonance seemed to hang in the silence.

She thought how conspiracy theories could eventually make anyone paranoid. Plots and twists kept replaying themselves in her head like late-night movies. Maybe she was being duped, set up, framed. Julia did seem to expect her to find something. Still, it was difficult to imagine Alice Blevins and Tyler in a sexual relationship. On the other hand, there was the evidence. Though perhaps those pictures were not meant for Tyler at all.

She looked at the pictures a third time before putting them in a shoe box in the back of the closet. Alice Blevins's hair was a strange color. Not quite gray, but a sort-of faded, dusty brown. Her pubic hair, however, was shockingly black against the white skin of her belly and thighs.

Fran concentrated on the face in each photo and held her hand to cover the naked body, looking only at Alice Blevins's pale, nondescript face. There was something in the dark eyes, a look difficult to describe. Something hard and determined and defiant. This is me, Alice seemed to be saying: plain as a potato, thick-middled, dusty-haired. This is who I am. And this is what I'd do for love.

30

"See, Dad. She wants to share her cereal with you!" Frank looked at his granddaughter, who was smiling coyly, her chubby hand clutching a spoon that she offered to him. "Mmmmm," he said, leaning toward her, pretending to eat some of the baby food, which looked like wallpaper paste.

In his daughter Patricia's home in Aurora, Frank sat eating breakfast with her and baby Suzanne. His son-in-law, Randy, had just left for work, leaving in his wake the smell of aftershave and the buzz of the electric garage door. Frank's shoulder still tingled from the slaps of Randy's affectionate good-bye. Randy sold computer equipment on commission, and he was always pounding someone on the back in a hearty way or saying "Hi there!" even if he had just come in from another room.

"Do you want more coffee, Daddy?" Patricia asked. She held the pot aloft, a look of pleasant anticipation on her face. She wore a robe and big floppy slippers. Frank was reminded of how she had looked in the photographs of the children, eager on Christmas morning. Carol had made albums full of those pictures: the boys, their cowlicks matted from sleep; Patricia and Leenie, overstuffed in quilted robes.

Frank held out his cup. "I'm going to go home after breakfast," he told her.

"Daddy, no!" Patricia's lower lip drooped; frowning, she sat down next to him in a heavy huff. "I thought we'd take Suzanne to the park and then meet Randy downtown for lunch."

Frank took a sip of coffee. "Can't, Patty. I have this case, you know. I made an appointment to interview someone." It was not exactly the truth, but he was planning to call Fran when he got back, maybe stop by her house with the letter from the lipstick lady. Then he was thinking of closing the case up for good. What would further searching uncover except more extramarital affairs? Really, it wasn't any of his business.

"You didn't tell me."

"I forgot."

"Well, you could still leave after lunch, then," Patricia said, sulky.

"I'd like to," Frank told her, suspecting she knew that he did not.

What was it about coming to his oldest child's home that always made Frank immediately want to leave? He did not enjoy making Patricia feel bad. But for every invitation he accepted to spend the night, he turned one down. Said he was busy, an emergency had come up. Growing up as a cop's kid in a small city, Patricia knew that was sometimes true. But not always.

Last night. He had wanted to leave last night after the dinner of hamburgers from the grill and potato salad and his favorite, homemade blueberry pie; after he had watched Patricia open her gifts, his seeming meager and inappropriate. Carol would have bought Patricia something she really wanted. Carol would have known what to buy.

But he went instead with Randy and Patricia and the baby to a park to watch the fireworks, and sitting there, amid all the young families and lovers on blankets and couples who had brought their lawn chairs and thermoses of iced tea, Frank felt old and awkward and very much alone.

Later, stretched out on the open-up couch in Patricia's living room, Frank looked at the ceiling and thought of kissing Fran Meltzer, recalling how responsive she was, kissing him back, making soft, purring noises in her throat. She had put one hand on the back of his neck; the other gently rested on his thigh. Now, thinking about kissing her like that in the darkness of the car made his whole body ache with longing.

Fran was right, of course. It was—well, unprofessional to have an affair with someone involved in a case he was working on. *Affair.* Hearing her use that word took him aback. It seemed sexy. He had never thought of himself as someone who would be having affairs.

"Just through lunch, Daddy. You never have any fun. You're always working," Patricia said. Then she cocked her head, listening for a moment, as if suddenly picking up some special radar. She stared him full in the face. "Are you seeing someone, Daddy?" she asked slowly.

"Who?"

"A woman. Have you been going out with anyone?"

"Why do you ask?" Frank turned his attention to a piece of toast, buttering it industriously.

"I don't know. You're acting funny. Distracted. And remember, I was talking to you a while ago. About Randy's sister-in-law's aunt who just got divorced?"

Frank said that he did not.

"You know, the woman owns that little gift shop, Peggy's, right downtown?"

"She's Peggy?"

"Yes."

"No."

"No, what?"

"No," Frank said, "I haven't gone out with her." He had

taken the woman's number from Patricia, left it written on a piece of paper, soon misplaced. Then one day he had been walking downtown, passed the gift shop and caught a glimpse of a woman talking to a customer. He thought for a moment that, no, that could not be *the* Peggy; she was too old. Her head, bent in tying a ribbon on a box, was gray, the arm winding the ribbon around, thick and loose-skinned.

He went into the store, picking out some wrapping paper and a stuffed panda for Suzanne. The woman had a pleasant apple-cheeked face and a smile that showed too much gum. He realized that she was probably about his age, not really old, then. Middle-aged. Though *he,* in fact, was probably not middle-aged, if middle-aged meant he was indeed in the *middle* of his life. After all, he was not planning to live almost to one hundred.

"Someone else, then?" Patricia insisted.

"Patty!"

"What?"

"Leave me alone," he said firmly.

"Well, Daddy, how does it feel? You sure used to grill me when I was going out." Patricia went to the sink, ran a washrag under the tap and efficiently wiped her baby's face.

"I'm not going out," Frank told her.

"Hmmph," Patricia said, untangling the baby from the mess of spoon and bib and the straps of her high chair. "We're going up to get dressed. Can you wait at least until I'm out of the shower before you leave?"

Frank said that he would. "Bye-bye," Suzanne called, waving over her mother's shoulder.

31

It was already late morning when Fran awoke with a start, sweat-drenched from sleeping with the blanket up all the way over her head. She had been dreaming of Julia in a big office, surrounded by telephones. Small lights were flashing, calls were coming in, going out. Julia sat in a big leather chair, a phone on each ear, like a business mogul making deals. In the dream, Fran stood in the doorway, watching. It was only when Julia caught her eye that Fran knew: it was Julia working it all out, making the connections, setting it up; it was Julia sitting behind the desk and orchestrating Tyler's death.

The bedroom was hot. Without getting up, Fran reached over to the wall and felt the vent, leaving her hand dangling down until the blood rushed to her fingers. Damn. No air. A fuse must have blown. She knew what to do. Tyler had shown her— had shown her at least three or four times, in fact. Go down to the basement and turn the circuit breaker back on. It was simple. Why could she never remember what to do? All the switches in the basement were clearly marked: kitchen range and lights, back bedroom, bath, etc. Still, the idea of even touching something electrical was frightening. What was in her head to think she could own a house? When something went the least bit awry—when the garbage disposal backed up or there was a leak in the roof, or like now, when the air conditioner conked out—her initial response was to think of moving.

She had bought the house because Julia and Tyler had urged her to. "You're a tenured professor; someone in your position should not rent," Tyler had said. Her position. Tyler always talked about the work they did in the loftiest professorial terms.

But he did know how to restart a circuit. And he was there when she had bats in the attic.

She threw back the covers and stayed in bed another twenty minutes. It had been a fitful night, listening to the odd creaking sounds of her old house. She was up half the night, her body tense as a rail, and she fell into a deep sleep only after dawn.

She was tormented by suspicion.

Julia. Elegant Julia, lying on her couch, enjoying the food Fran had prepared, so grateful that she was there; Julia, saying how guilty she felt because Fran was giving up her holiday to be there.

It was peculiar. "What holiday?" Fran had said. It wasn't as if the Fourth of July was anything special. It was, she felt, a particularly goyish holiday, right up there with Christmas Eve and Easter Sunday. And it wasn't as if she had any better place to be.

Then, afterwards, Julia's request to complete the search of Tyler's office. And it had to be then. That very night. Right after Julia had been saying how very guilty she was feeling about Fran giving up her holiday and all.

It was almost—*almost*—as if Julia had planned it. Had known those pictures were going to be there, had known there was going to be *something* in Tyler's office and had set Fran up to find it.

Supposing Julia had known about the pictures all along? Had come across them weeks ago, but never told anyone. Never told Tyler that she knew. As far as Tyler was concerned, he and Julia were still going for counseling. At least *thinking* about going. Suppose Julia had found those pictures first. And seeing them had pushed her over the edge. But why on earth would Julia want Fran to see the pictures?

Fran's mind was still spinning as she put on a robe and went down the creaky basement steps to flip the circuit breaker, stopping in the middle of the stair to listen. The basement was old, dark and dank and filled with cobwebs. She noticed that in the far corner of the basement a casement window was cracked and made a mental note to call someone to have it fixed. She looked over her shoulder at the top of the stair. Maybe the air conditioner would turn back on by itself. "Stop it!" she said aloud, bounding down the last steps and going toward the utility box. She was a scaredy cat. Had always been. Alone in the house, she never rented a movie like *Jagged Edge* or *Basic Instinct* or any of those psychological thrillers where you never knew who was normal or who was devious and sick. She couldn't even watch "Mystery" on Public Television. As soon as the violins foretold suspense, her palms got sweaty.

She opened the metal box, flipped the top switch, and heard the fan go on. "Okay. Okay," she said, going back up the stairs to make coffee. It was after eleven. She dialed Julia's number, clearing her throat so she would sound chipper when she made the offer again to take Julia to the doctor. "Hullo?" Someone, not Julia, answered after the sixth or seventh ring.

"Caty? Beth?" Fran asked. "Did I wake you? Is Mom around? How come she doesn't have her machine on?"

Silence. Then, "Oh, hi, Aunt Franny," the voice said, warming, though none of the questions were addressed. "How are you?" It was Caty, who yawned noisily into the phone. "I don't know if she's here. I just got up."

"Could you look, hon?"

"Sure." More yawns. Then a noise like the phone banging against a wall. "Sorry, I dropped you," Caty said, giggling.

Fran heard footsteps padding slowly away. The coffee made its last few drips into the pot and she poured herself a cup, leaned against the kitchen counter to drink it, waiting.

"She's not here," Caty said a few minutes later. "Can I take a message?"

"Did your sister drive Mom to the doctor?" Fran asked.

"Doctor?" Caty's voice rose, registering concern.

"You know, for her back?"

"I don't know. Was she going to the doctor?" Caty said, confused.

"Honey, is Beth there?" Fran asked.

"I think she's still sleeping. You want me to wake her?"

"No," Fran said quickly. "You don't have to do that. I just wondered if Mom wanted me to take her to the doctor. That's all."

"Well, maybe she's feeling better and went to the office or something," Caty suggested.

"Sure, probably," Fran said, feeling her palms begin to sweat, though the air was now blowing in cool from the vent above her head.

"I'll tell her you called, Aunt Franny." Caty yawned again, hanging up the phone before Fran even began to say good-bye.

32

Intermittently through her adult life, but always when she was about to embark upon a new love affair, Fran began an exercise program. She thought it diverted some of that manic energy and brought her hormones under control. Now at forty-two, she also felt in need of some major tightening. Naked in front of the bedroom mirror, she grabbed a roll of extra flesh around her stomach, then turned to look at the backs of her thighs. Sighing, she leaned back against the bedpost in the same seductive pose that she had perfected at fourteen years old in the pink-and-white ruffled bedroom of her Long Island home.

Her breasts were good. Better than good. Full and nicely shaped with pretty brown nipples that still pointed straight out. This, the lack of sag and relative perk of nipple, she attributed to her never having nursed a baby. Though given a choice, she would have preferred breasts like an old bellows and a child.

Sometimes, in dark, self-pitying moods, she counted the miscarriages and figured out what could have been. A child of eleven. Of ten. Another almost eight. In fantasy, she brought them to life, never as a brood but one at a time. Standing in the door of her closet, a dark, ringleted little girl in bangles and beads playing dress-up, walking awkwardly in high heels. A boy with Damian's muckle-mouth and soulful eyes, coming to her for a good-night kiss. Reading with him, cozy under the couch's afghan.

Now she put on black biking shorts that stopped the circulation in her thighs and an old, paper-thin T-shirt of Damian's that she could not bring herself to use as a rag. She closed the blinds in the living room before popping the Cosmopolitan Cross Impact Aerobics tape into the VCR. "Let's go, girls," she said to the screen, whose image projected twenty-year-olds, all dewy and impossibly cheerful. "You're doing a great job," the leader, Kathy, said after the first routine. The other aereobizers smiled encouragingly. "Feel that body! Move that body!" Kathy made ladylike grunts during the leg lifts. She was a voluptuous blonde, porcelain-skinned, a Wisconsin milkmaid. Her cleavage shimmered with healthy sweat.

"Go fuck yourself, Kathy," Fran called back, huffing to keep up. As soon as Fran had mastered one step, Kathy was off doing jumping jacks or grapevine or clapping above her head, so Fran remained always a beat or so off, clumsily trying to catch up.

The phone rang just as Kathy was shouting: "Step-kick-step-kick, turn it around, shimmy, kick, kick!" The last routine before the cool-down. The cool-down, with a lot of well-deserved stretching, was the only part that Fran actually liked. She jogged into the kitchen, listening to the machine pick it up: a loud click signified a hangup. Running back into the living room, Fran raised her arms overhead, feeling a pulse in her fingertips. Head rolls and calf stretches followed. "Make this part of your routine every day," Kathy was saying as Fran pressed Rewind and headed for the shower.

She made the water very hot, standing under it a long time, feeling the heat against the tense muscles in the back of her neck, letting the water pound against her face and breasts. The water pressure in her house was strong. Tyler had offered to put in a water-saver shower head as he had done in his own home, but Fran declined. Her hair was so thick, she told him, she would never get it properly rinsed. Somehow he had taken offense. Julia's hair was thick, too, he had countered, and the water-saver head worked perfectly well for her. Fran remembered having this conversation on the patio of the Markem's house. It was during the summer, a few years before. Shoshanna and Harvey were there. Also Sam Hollyhock and his first wife, Helen, who had felt Fran's hair, remarking on its luxuriant thickness.

She was standing naked, drying her luxuriant, thick hair with a towel when she heard the front door open and close. There was no mistaking it was the front door because of the particular squeak of the old screen and the *thump-click* of the heavy interior door. Unlocked. Despite the fact that last night the house was sealed tight, this morning, after getting the paper from the front porch, she had neglected to lock the door again. She had a sudden flash of Frank Rhodes *tsk*ing with disapproval.

Wrapping the towel tightly around her, she stood, ear pressed to the bathroom door, her jaw dropping when she heard footsteps down the hall. Light, almost delicate footsteps along the wood floor. Fran caught her breath. The footsteps stopped. Or at least she could not hear them anymore. Likely that the person who entered was now treading softly on the Oriental rug in the living room. Trembling, Fran stood against the towel rack and bit off a thumbnail.

The bathroom door itself was not locked. The lock, old and ill-fitting, demanded that the door be aligned in a precise way, too late to accomplish now without considerable noise. Fran held her breath, then let it out slowly in an aerobically correct way. She heard cabinets and drawers open and close, getting louder as someone progressed through the kitchen, moving along the wall of cabinets next to the table. She pictured the person in the kitchen. Not a real person but a bent black shape, rummaging through the messy kitchen drawers, angry in the search.

Fran wished she had some clothes on. She also wished she had taken the cordless phone into the bathroom as she sometimes did. As she surely would have done had she thought that Frank was in town and was perhaps going to call.

Trapped. If she opened the bathroom door and made a run for it, straight away and down the hall toward the front door, she could probably make it. She had the element of surprise. The person in the kitchen surely thought no one was home, given that the car was hidden in the garage.

She could run quickly out the front door into the street in a towel, screaming her head off, heading for any neighbor's door. But what if no one was at home? Or what if the person in the kitchen had a gun: one straight shot as Fran ran down the hall into the small of her back. A burst of red blood against the white terrycloth towel. Even if she lived, it would be wheelchair time for sure.

Or a knife. In the kitchen, right next to the revolving spice rack, was a present from Roz, one of those magnetic knife holders with four expensive knifes, hand-forged high-carbon steel, made in Germany, guaranteed to slice the thin skin of a tomato, sharp enough to cut easily through the thickest chop. Fran pictured someone in the kitchen, clutching one of those knives; the thought of the sharp stainless blade cutting through her own soft flesh made her so dizzy that she sank to her knees right there on the bathroom floor.

After a few minutes she heard the footsteps move from the kitchen, along the hall again, past the bathroom toward the bedroom. More drawers. Then the shifting of hangers in her bedroom closet.

It would be easier now to make a run. The bedroom door did not directly face the bathroom, and if she was very quiet opening the door, she could be tiptoeing out of the house before the intruder realized what was happening.

She was mulling this whole thing over, about to get to her feet, when the bathroom door slowly opened and there, looming before her in nylons and comfortable shoes, her weaponless hands flying to her chest as she saw Fran crouching in a towel on the bathroom floor, was none other than Alice Blevins.

Both of them screamed.

Alice was the first to speak. "You weren't home. I called just a while ago. Then I knocked and knocked. No one answered." Alice stood in the doorway, her hands now clenched at her sides. Her tone seemed wrong. Accusatory, angry.

"I was in the shower. I didn't hear you," Fran said, her voice breaking. Shakily she rose from the floor, wrapping the towel more tightly around her, tucking the end into the cleft of her breasts. She stared goggle-eyed at Alice, imagining Alice's breasts through the navy-and-beige print blouse she wore, the dark thatch of hair beneath the plain denim skirt.

"I believe you have something that belongs to me," Alice said. When she spoke her nostrils flared angrily. Her lips, pressed tight together, were the color of stone.

"What do you mean?" Fran wiped her forehead with the back of her hand to keep water from running into her eyes.

"I want them back," Alice said grimly, looking more determined than even Shoshanna Kovner-Boxtel on her most severe day. Alice took a step, a very slight step into the bathroom. "Don't lie to me," she added. "I know you have the pictures."

"All right," Fran said, nodding. "All right." Something in Alice's manner suggested she was not about to hear any excuses. Timidly, Fran raised a hand. "I'd like to get my robe first, if you don't mind."

Alice walked with Fran back to the bedroom, watching in the doorway as Fran searched through a pile on the floor beside the unmade bed. She picked up the purple caftan, keeping the towel around her while she put the caftan over her head, then reached underneath to pull the towel off when she was properly covered. Fran recognized the irony in the effort of this modesty, considering Alice's exposure. Fran wrapped the towel around her wet hair, then straightened up, feeling a bit more settled. "What's going on, Alice?" Fran asked gently. Alice was clench-jawed and breathing audibly.

"I followed you up to Tyler's office last night," Alice replied. The faintest suggestion of a smile began in the corner of her mouth. It was strange. The smile, mocking and inappropriate, reminded Fran of Tyler. How he sometimes had that arrogant, smug smirk. Alice brought her hand to her own pale throat. She was wearing a single strand of pearls. "You got there just a minute or so before me. I was waiting. I knew the police had lifted the seal, and it was the first chance I had to go up. No one would be there on the holiday. And I knew Julia hadn't known about the photographs. She would have given them to that detective, and he would have come to talk to me about them before," Alice continued. "So I was going to the office myself last night when I saw your car, and I just parked in the lot across the street and watched you go up. I was there, right outside his office door, when you found the pictures. I knew when you saw them. I heard the gasp."

Fran moved some magazines and seated herself on the bed. "So you and Tyler were having an affair," she said simply. From where she sat there were two Alices before her: one, dark and foreboding in the doorway, the other reflected in the mirror above her dresser. Fran watched as both Alices clenched and unclenched the fists they brought to their chests. Fran could still not quite get over this. First there was the idea of being followed. Then the sense of intrusion as Alice appeared so boldly and unapologetically in Fran's home. But more than that was the realization: Tyler having an affair with Alice Blevins. Tyler and Alice Blevins. Fran tried to look at Alice anew, but all she saw before her was a middle-aged woman with a bad haircut and small eyes the color of raisins.

"It wasn't like that," Alice said. "It wasn't an *affair,* something cheap or tawdry. Tyler loved me. We loved each other.

Julia never understood him. Never was giving enough to him. He wouldn't leave her, though. Family, the children, really, were everything to him. Oh, the children. He was a wonderful father to those girls. He'd never leave while they were still home. I knew that. That was our understanding. But what we had together . . . what we had . . ." Alice's voice trailed off into the anguish of having to explain the ineffable.

"Alice," Fran began, before realizing how she, too, was at a loss for words. Alice was holding herself, rubbing a hand sensuously along her shoulder, her arm, as if in memory of Tyler's touch.

"We were together for over two years," Alice continued. "No, it wasn't only erotic. We were really soulmates. Secret soulmates, Tyler and I. You see, I was the inspiration for so much of the new poetry he was writing lately. Poetry he couldn't even show to anyone because it was so intensely personal . . ." Alice went on, a torrent of repressed passion. Who, after all, had she had to share her obsession with for these two years? "A love like ours, driven underground because of duty and obligation, I can only tell you, Frances, it reaches an intensity of mythological proportion!"

Oh boy, Fran thought. "Francine," she said.

Alice cleared her throat and looked abashed. "I'd like those pictures," she said in a sudden, sharp staccato.

"I'll get them for you," Fran said. She went to the closet and reached up to the top shelf, taking down a shoebox that contained the white sequined pumps she had worn to marry Damian so many years ago. She opened the box and took out the envelope, pausing for a moment. "Wait a minute," she began. It wasn't exactly as if Alice had a right to the pictures, after all. They were Tyler's property and so, by right, should be Julia's now.

But Alice came up quickly and snatched the envelope out of Fran's hand. "All right, then," Fran said, sitting back down on the bed. Fascinated, she watched as Alice unwound the string and took out the pictures. She leafed through them slowly, stopping at each as a special memento of a treasured time: staring for a long time at one picture, smiling; her mouth almost puckering into a kiss at another. Alice let loose a groan as she came to the last picture, swallowing hard. "He knew he couldn't have me for himself all the time," Alice said, looking up, tears in her eyes. "But he wanted me with him, to be able to see me like this, stripped and open to him; baring my soul, making myself vulnerable, for his eyes only, he told me. He wrote a series of poems about these pictures, did you know that? No, of course not, how could you? One poem was called 'Double Exposure.' It was published last year in *Poetry Magazine.*"

Fran straightened up on the bed. "Last year?" she asked, puzzled. "You sent these pictures to Tyler last year?"

"I didn't *send* them to him," Alice said. "Tyler took these pictures of me." She stared at the last photo, touching it fondly, rubbing small circles with a fingertip. "He wanted to have me opened to him forever."

Alice stared at the picture again, her face beginning to soften with desire. "Opened to him. He would have me with him always. After he died, I wanted to put this picture in with him, in the coffin, to be buried with him. But *she* had him cremated," Alice said scornfully. "His beautiful, beautiful body burned to ashes. That's how much *she* appreciated him." Alice turned to the picture and began to moan. "It was a matter of trust, don't you see? Of pledging myself to him to let him have me this way. Oh, oh, Tyler!"

Fran opened her mouth to respond, then shook her head. Alice had closed her eyes, sighing painfully, her head flopped back in a swoon.

"Of trust?" Fran said finally, finding her voice. "You talk of Tyler Markem and *trust* in the same breath? You've got to be kidding!"

Interrupted in her reverie, Alice blinked and raised her head, looking as if she were surprised to find someone else there in the room with her. "Don't say that!" she said, her eyes shining with tears. "Tyler and I loved each other. What we had was beautiful and sacred. Someone like you couldn't understand. No one could understand."

Fran felt her face getting hot, anger rising in her chest. "Alice, what's the matter with you? Tyler *used* you. He screwed you and took some dirty pictures, that's all." Seeing Alice before her, a quivering, soppy lump, made Fran even angrier. She felt angrier than she had been at Julia for letting Tyler stay in the house while he was still seeing Lynette. Angrier than she had ever been at Tyler himself. "He *used* you," Fran continued, her voice rising. "The way he used Julia, and that dumb-bunny student Lynette Macalvie, and God knows how many other women who were taken in by his charm and his talk of truth and beauty and sacred love and art and inspiration and all the other bullshit about how woefully unhappy he was with a wife who didn't understand him, which is, God help us, the oldest cliché in the book. Give me a break, will you? Why are women still buying this shit!" Fran was practically shouting now at Alice, who stood hunched over in the doorway, still staring at the pictures of her naked, glorious self. "Those are dirty pictures, Alice. Dirty pictures are what you're so heartbroken over. Sleazy pornography. Just something Tyler used to jack off with and maybe laugh about. He *used* you, Alice. He was a user. Tyler Markem was a bastard, do you understand that? An arrogant, self-aggrandizing, lying, cheating bastard!"

Suddenly there was a wail, something between a howl of indignation and a war whoop. Bent down, her shoulders drawn up for the attack, Alice lunged across the room at Fran, butting with the top of her head and her drawn fists so that on impact, Fran toppled off the bed, somersaulting onto the floor on the other side.

When Fran looked up, the wind so knocked out of her that she could hardly breathe, Alice was standing over her. "Don't you *ever* talk like that about Tyler again," Alice said, her voice tight. Fists clenched, Alice looked gigantic to Fran, looming over her like that. Alice's muscled forearms looked strong enough to lift even the heaviest weight, and her raisin-colored eyes were absolutely murderous with rage.

33

"Did you . . .?" Fran began, her voice breaking. "Tyler . . ." Unable to fill in the complicated reality, she attempted to sit up. Her head was throbbing; raising a hand to her forehead, she felt a bump already beginning to rise.

Alice's mouth worked crazily, like a marionette's whose strings were being haphazardly yanked. She seemed to be crying, but her lips opened and closed in anguished silence.

"Alice?" Fran asked. Through the thin material of the caftan, the bedroom wall felt cool against her back. "Are you all right?" Although the blinds were shut, Alice appeared to be gazing out the window, her lips continuing to form silent words. "Alice, I think I need to put some ice on this," Fran said, feeling her forehead. "It's going to be a bad bump." She started to rise from her place on the floor, careful not to make unnecessary movement, then began to edge her way along the side of the room toward the door.

"Where are you going?" Alice asked, slowly turning; her face had the vacant gaze of someone in shock.

''I need some ice,'' Fran said, lifting her hair so Alice could see the bump.

''You're bleeding,'' Alice said dully.

''I am?'' Fran walked over to the mirror above the dresser. A thin line, about two inches long, ran diagonally across her forehead toward her left eyebrow. ''It's only a scratch,'' Fran said, reaching for a tissue on the dresser. ''I must have cut myself on the edge of the bedboard.'' The bump, however, was already puffing out a sizable dome in the middle of her forehead. ''I need ice,'' Fran repeated, making a polite little curtsy before moving backward to the bedroom door.

''I left my purse in the kitchen,'' Alice said, following Fran out.

It was more a surprise than anything else. The gun, ominously black and shiny, looked strange in Alice's hand. Placing the straps of her straw summer purse in the crook of her arm, as if she were about to go shopping, she opened the clasp of the purse and slipped the pictures inside.

''Oh!'' said Fran, jumping back when she saw the gun. The barrel (was it even called a barrel, or was that just for rifles?) was pointed directly at the bump on her head.

''Put the ice back,'' Alice instructed. Obediently, Fran slid the tray back into the freezer and shut the door. ''Now walk over to the table and sit down,'' Alice said. ''And no sudden moves.''

Fran did as she was told, making her way slowly across the kitchen floor as if she were treading water. ''I have to think,'' Alice said, sitting next to her.

The air conditioner kicked on. Fran felt cool air blowing from a vent on the wall next to her chair. Alice worked her bottom lip, looking past Fran out the opened window. Fran followed her stare. The yard needed mowing.

''No one would ever think it was me, would they?'' Alice asked, rubbing her thumb nervously along the handle of the gun. "Hard-working, dependable old Alice." She let out a short, bitter laugh. "Alice Blevins, the president's right-hand gal!"

Not so little, Fran thought, recalling the pictures.

"You're surprised, aren't you?" Alice wanted to know.

"I sure am," Fran agreed. Although she was watching Alice with wary concentration, Fran was not afraid. She had been afraid in Grayson Hall the night before while searching Tyler's office. And later when she came home, listening for sounds in the night. Terrified only twenty minutes ago, huddled in a towel behind the bathroom door. But here, sitting with Alice Blevins at the kitchen table, Fran really wasn't afraid. Even with a gun just a pass-the-salt length away.

"Of course Julia would be the prime suspect," Alice said, almost to herself. "But she couldn't do it. She has no guts. No passion."

Guilt passed over Fran like a hot flash. How could she have ever thought Julia a murderer?

Alice hunched forward, looking down at the table, her tiny eyes barely visible under her thick gray-brown bangs. Fran wondered for a moment what Alice would look like with her hair blown back away from her face, lightly feathered on the top and perhaps colored a warm brown with some highlighting. Feeling her own hair air-drying into unmanageability, she longed to scrunch along the back of her head with her hand. But she would not lift up her arm. No sudden moves.

"It was an accident," Alice said, looking up. "I just went that morning to talk with him. To help him see what a mistake he was making, getting involved with that girl. A *student,*" she said bitterly. "You know, my husband, well, my ex . . . oh, it doesn't matter." Alice thrust out her chin. "Anyway, it's not *right,* I don't think." Sitting next to her at the table, Fran was close enough to see the makeup covering the dark circles under Alice's eyes, and the two hairs growing on one side of her jaw.

"How did you find out about Lynette?" Fran wanted to know.

Alice sighed. Her left hand, ringless, the nails bitten to the quick, lay flat on the table. On her wrist she wore a man's watch with a thick leather band. "I had been feeling a kind of distance from him all spring. I knew he was busy writing, so I didn't want to bother him. To be demanding in any way. He hated that, especially when Julia pressed him with domestic obligations. She always seemed to do that, you know. Just when he was in inspiration."

Fran recalled the times when Tyler's "inspiration" had coincided remarkably with Beth and Caty's childhood illness or teacher's conferences. "Did you ask him if he was seeing someone else?" Fran asked. To be cheating on one's wife was one thing. To be cheating on one's mistress certainly took a special kind of chutzpah.

Alice shook her head. "I didn't want Tyler to think that I didn't trust him." She leaned across the table and looked hard into Fran's face. "Yes. Trust. I trusted him. Trusted that he loved me. Because we had something few people ever, *ever* experience in a lifetime!"

"So he finally told you," Fran said. "He told you about her."

Alice sat back in protest. "No. He couldn't. He would never want to hurt me." She looked down at the gun in her right hand as if surprised that it was still there. "But I saw them together," she went on, "in one of those little coffee rooms in the student union. I just saw them sitting together at a table there when I was going by. Tyler and this very blond, silly-looking girl. And I knew at once. When you have the kind of relationship that Tyler and I had, you know these things."

"He saw you?" Fran asked.

"I don't think so. No, I don't think he did. But I couldn't reach him later that afternoon. Or the next day. It was the end of the semester, and no one was keeping regular office hours. And I was never allowed to call him at home."

"So you went to see him in the gym?" A part of Fran was amazed at how agreeably Alice was answering her questions.

"Well, I didn't think he'd be alone," Alice said. "I mean, I thought there'd be other people around in the weight room. I just wanted to talk with him, that's all. I just went over there to see if we could set up a time to talk, that's all. To go out someplace after work. I certainly didn't expect to have any altercation right there in the gym."

And you certainly didn't expect to kill him, Fran thought.

"It started out just like any ordinary day," Alice added. She glanced down at her watch. "Just this time, too. Almost eleven-thirty. I was sitting at my desk, looking out the window, waiting for him to come by, just like always." Now she looked out Fran's window, almost wistful with recall.

"Like always?"

"Well, I used to watch him go by every day around eleven on his way to the gym." Alice smiled sadly, brushing crumbs with the side of her hand, smoothing them into a neat pile near the edge of the table. "He would walk out of Grayson Hall and go by my window every day. Sometimes I'd be at the computer and feel him coming toward me. You know, I could feel this pull that would make me look up, out the window. It was as if a magnetic field was drawing me to connect with something outside the window. And then I'd look out and see him walking."

"Did he know?" Fran asked. "Did he know you were watching him every day when he went to the gym?"

Alice shook her head. "I didn't want to tell him. Then he would have waved or something. Recognized that I was there. I just wanted to see him coming to me like that. Not self-conscious or anything. Just *there*. I liked to watch him walk."

"That morning, he was with George, though," Fran said.

Alice nodded. "George looked very bad. Small and shriveled, like an old man. Of course, everyone appeared small next to Tyler."

"So why did you go to the gym? I mean, if you wanted to talk with Tyler and he was with George."

"Well, almost as soon as they went inside, I saw George leave the building. Then he walked back across to the parking lot next to Grayson Hall. I didn't know why. But I presumed he was getting his car and leaving. So I just got up from my desk and left to go over myself."

"What happened?" Fran asked gently.

"Tyler was there, in his shorts, without a shirt on, already into his routine. When I came in, he was doing situps. Not really situps. Crunches. You know those kind of situps where your legs are in the air?"

"I know what crunches are," Fran said.

"Tyler did three sets of forty, every other day. He was in the third set when I came in. So I just said hi, and stood in the doorway and waited for him to finish. He said hi back, but he didn't seem happy to see me. When he finished the set, I told him that I needed to talk." Alice's voice broke with emotion.

"What did he do?" Fran asked.

"Well, he didn't *do* anything. He didn't even acknowledge that I was there. He started on one of those machines. One where you have to straddle it and lift the weights with your legs?"

Not the execution site, Fran thought. "Uh-huh."

"There was no one in the weight room. No one at all, not even anyone in the main part of the gym playing basketball. Everything was totally silent. I said, 'Tyler, I want to talk to you about what you're doing,' and he still didn't answer me. Then I said, 'I know you're having a relationship with a student.'"

"That caught his attention, I'll bet."

"No!" Alice cried. "He stopped for a minute and looked at me with this look of . . . oh God, it was a terrible look. Like he really hated me. Then he went right back to doing those exercises. Kept on, grunting, making those sounds that they, you know, that they make working out. I stood in front of him and said his name again. He continued to do the leg lifts and didn't answer me. I thought I was dreaming. Or that I was invisible or something.''

''Was he looking at you?''

''No, he just kept on with those leg lifts. I don't know. He must have done thirty or forty of those and then started in again. Finally, I touched his shoulder.'' Alice paused for breath. ''That's when he hit me.''

''He *hit* you!'' Fran leaned closer to Alice, her arms crossed in front of her on the table. Except for the gun between them, it was as if they were having the most intimate of chats.

''It was probably more a push, like 'get away from me,' than an actual hit. He kind of smacked me in the middle of my chest. But hard. I started to cry. He didn't even seem to care. He just got up and went to the free weights, began adjusting the bar, unscrewing the end and adding more weights. He was sitting on that bench adding more weights, and he started telling me these things. He was very, *very* cold.''

''What things?''

''It was like: 'Don't tell me what to do. You're not my goddamned mother. You're not even my wife.' And he was cruel. His voice had this awful hardness. He kept saying, 'I don't owe you anything.' I couldn't believe how mean he was. It didn't seem like Tyler at all. He said: 'I love Lynette. I'm leaving Julia at the end of the summer to go live with her.'''

Fran blinked in confusion. Leave Julia? As definite as all that? She tried to get the time frame on what Alice had just said. That meant that the day Tyler died, he was planning to leave Julia? But hadn't Julia said how he was talking about going into therapy with her this summer: therapy for both of them to try to save the marriage?

''He lied to me all along,'' Alice continued. ''He told me he would never leave Julia. Never. He loved me, but he would never leave his family. I understood that. I accepted the limitations of the relationship. I know he loved me, but he made it clear that he would *never* leave Julia. *Never* leave Julia," Alice repeated.

The ringing phone startled them both. "Don't answer it," Alice said, holding up the gun. They both sat, staring at the phone. The answering machine picked up on the fourth ring.

Julia's voice was apologetic. "Sorry, Franny, you must have been worried. Beth took me to the doctor early this morning. We were both gone when you talked to Caty. She's not all that with it in the morning, is she? Anyway, it's nothing serious, the doctor said. Just a muscle spasm. Tension, he thought. So what do I have to be tense about? Ha-ha. Where are you, anyway? Caty said you just called a little while ago. Listen, call me." There was a brief pause. "Love you," Julia added.

Fran looked at Alice when the message clicked off. Her mouth was set tight again, her eyes were burning. "Alice?" Fran said softly.

"Love you. Love *you,*" Alice mimicked. "So what do *I* have to be tense about. Ha ha ha ha ha ha." Alice's laugh grew more derisive. "He wouldn't leave her. His *wife.* His precious family and his lovely *wife!* Do *you* know how many Saturday nights I've spent alone while *she* was with him at dinner parties and movies, because they were a *couple,* a married *couple* and he said to me, 'Alice, I want to let you know right from the start, I want to be completely honest with you and let you know.' Oh, how could I not know? He laid it out clear, as if it were a business contract: 'I want you. I love you. But I'll never leave her. And if that's too difficult for you, Alice, I'll understand.'" Now Alice sounded like Tyler. That unctuous professorial voice he used when he was explaining something that he thought should be painfully obvious to anyone who had a lick of sense. Alice even had Tyler's body language, the stiff posture, the self-assured thrust of chin. She was a terrific mimic. Fran had never seen this theatrical side of Alice.

"Did you ever do any community theater?" Fran asked.

"You're very good." She knew it was a mistake as soon as she said it.

"You," Alice spat. "Always making a joke. You and your smug little friend, Julia. Oh, you'll have a good laugh together at this one, won't you?" Alice got up from her chair and pointed the gun at Fran's head. "You and Julia having this little laugh. Poor Alice Blevins, Von Eaton's right-hand gal. Well, this joke's not going to be on *me!*" Alice got up from the table and started waving the gun around; she was only a few feet away, and for a split second, Fran imagined herself hitting Alice's arm, knocking the gun to the floor.

"Easy, Alice," Fran said softly, barely moving her lips. "Don't do anything you'll regret, now."

"You think I'd regret killing you?" Alice sneered. "Tyler is gone. Nothing can bring him back. Do you really think I care about anything else? About you or Julia or all those bitches at Friday club or this third-rate college with all these pampered, over-permed girls?" Alice pressed the gun to Fran's temple.

"Please," Fran said, closing her eyes. She waited for the click she thought one was supposed to hear before a gun was fired. Saliva filled her mouth.

"Get up, bitch," Alice said, yanking Fran's arm. "We're going for a ride."

34

"The Ledges is beautiful this time of year," Alice said vaguely as Fran rose from the table.

Fran pictured herself, forced at gunpoint to drive past happy picnicking families to the remote area surrounded by the Ledges' bluffs; parking the car and schlepping with Alice through the secluded wooded trails to the Indian burial ground; and there, in the wild, among unidentifiable flora and fauna, shot at close range to be left in a crumbled heap, her Jewish blood slowly seeping into the Native American sacred mound.

And how long would it be before someone finally found the body? She had a flash of herself as animals nibbled and gnawed at her flesh, leaving what was left to decompose in the July heat. It was not the parting script she had envisioned.

Frank Rhodes would have to call her sister with the news. Well, first perhaps the news would be only that Fran was missing. No evidence of foul play, he'd say. No signs of forced entrance. "What?" Roz would say. "What are you talking about!" she'd yell into the phone, aggression, the first line of defense before grief.

As the older sister, Roz was devoted and, since the death of their parents, so fiercely attached that she called almost every other day. Fran did not tell her sister everything, given Roz's proclivity to worry a migraine into a tumor and to check references for any man Fran had lunch with. "A cop?" Roz had said about Frank Rhodes. "Do you know the statistics of domestic violence in the homes of law officers? They're this close to the edge, Franny," Roz had said. "Just this close to the edge."

Because they were having the conversation on the phone, Fran had only to imagine how close to the edge Frank Rhodes must be.

Now Fran regretted not calling her sister that morning to tell her about the pictures. Or last night, telling Julia. Why had she not told Julia? It would serve Fran right, then; turning into compost in the wilderness because she had not had sufficient trust in her best friend; because she kept things from a loving sister who was her best ally.

"Move it," Alice said, thrusting the gun into Fran's ribs like someone in a gangster film. "We'll take your car," she instructed, pushing Fran toward the garage. "You drive."

"Okay," Fran said, making her away around the dozens of bags filled with the plastic she had been planning to take to the recycling center. "Easy." She opened the door and got in. "The button is on your side," she said, noting the automatic opener control that rested atop the visor in front of Alice. Because the device had a loose clip and sometimes fell off when she was driving, Fran had moved it over to the passenger side. Usually when she drove with someone, she put it in the glove compartment.

Fran started the car, but Alice made no move to open the garage door. For a few moments, Fran thought that was Alice's plan. Both of them dying from the carbon monoxide fumes, their bodies found slumped over together in the front seat. (And the pictures of naked Alice right there in her purse. What would anybody make of this? The *Grandview Tribune* writing another article about the radical feminists at the college: "Lesbian Lovers Suicide Pact!")

Finally, Alice's hand reached up and pressed the button. "Just pull out and head north to the Ledges," she said, looking straight at Fran as they drove away. "And no funny business."

Alice's eyes were angry and strange, like the small, glassy eyes of expensive stuffed animals. When Fran was a little girl she had a tiger with those eyes, and she always made Roz turn his face to the wall before they went to bed.

They passed a baseball field on the next street and, at a red light, Alice turned to look at a game in progress. A boy hit a line drive, clean and hard; a cheer went up from the stands as he raced around the bases. "Do you like baseball?" Fran asked, wanting to make some connection and to show she was not afraid. She felt whisked away, taken against her will, like at Jones Beach, when a wave used to wash over her and tumble her down. Go with the flow, her father used to say, those summers at the shore. Don't fight it.

Alice shrugged. On the sidewalk in front of the fence were children on tricycles. Two ponytailed girls were doing cartwheels on a lawn.

Fran took a long look at the town those last few blocks, staring out the car window like a prisoner peeking out from behind bars at the free world moving about in its random, careless way, where everything denied seems suddenly significant, bittersweet and poignant. The sun spread layers of light across the roofs of houses, filtering through the leaves of maple and oak, full and bursting in the first throes of summer.

A station wagon filled with teenage girls pulled up next to Fran at the last light at the edge of town. She turned toward them and began to blink frantically with her eyes: three short blinks in repeated patterns in what she hoped would be recognized as a call for help—SOS, SOS!

The fluffy blonde in the passenger's seat covered her mouth with her hand and began to giggle. When the light turned green, the car turned the corner and drove out of sight.

"Turn right. Now!" barked Alice, as if sensing something was going on. She butted the tip of the gun into Fran's side. "Right again. Here!" The sign to the Ledges was gone, stolen probably by some Grandview High Giant who had it in his bedroom. "I think this is the way," Alice added as they approached a gravel road.

They drove over an old wooden bridge and then passed a farm. In the distance, Fran could see the farmer riding a green-and-yellow tractor out in the field; he looked so far away, so small, as if he were one of those children's toys her niece and nephew used to play with: the little wooden peg of a farmer who fit into the hole of his little wooden tractor. Fran thought that soon she was going to be murdered, and everyone else would be going on with the most ordinary tasks: the farmer riding up and down the rows on his farm; Beth Markem turning fish fillets at McDonald's; Frank Rhodes wadding up a fresh stick of gum to put in his mouth.

"Listen," Fran said suddenly to Alice. "Why don't we not do this."

Alice didn't respond but sat staring out the window, craning her neck, as if searching for important landmarks.

"Alice, listen to me," Fran went on. "We could just tell the police the truth. That it was an accident. You were angry, sure, who wouldn't be? But you leaned over to talk with Tyler and the weights, well, they just fell on him. You got scared and ran. Really, you could get off." Hearing this version of the story articulated didn't sound half-bad. Fran began to believe it herself. With a random jury there were sure to be women whose husbands screwed around, whose boyfriends had cheated on them; it was more than likely. He lied to me, Alice would say, sitting tearful and proper on the stand. She would wear her navy blue polyester suit and sensible shoes. He said he loved me, Alice would say. The Betrayed Mistress Defense. It could fly. "Alice," Fran said again, "I really think a jury would be hard put to convict you."

Alice lunged toward Fran, suddenly screaming, her face a mottled red. "Listen, you cunt, I don't give a flying fuck what you think!" A fine line of spittle sprayed across Fran's cheek.

In reaction to either the spitting or hearing the word *cunt* so viciously expressed by someone wearing pearls, suddenly Fran felt impelled into action. She slammed her foot on the brake, causing the automatic garage control to fly off the visor and smack Alice full in the face.

Quickly Fran released her safety belt, flung open the door, and jumped from the car, landing painfully on one knee; she pulled her other leg away in time, missing the back wheel of the car by just inches. The car continued along the rocky road, bucking and finally stalling before it rolled slowly into a ditch.

"Hey," Alice yelled from the car. "Hey, get me out!" Fran could hear Alice but not see her, because the passenger's side was slanted down into a ditch engulfed with weeds. Shakily Fran rose to her feet, and when she looked across the field, she saw the farmer, or just the top of his cap, beyond a slope. He was perhaps only a quarter of a mile away.

Fran could hear Alice cursing from the car. "Fuck! Shit! Bitch!" Shocked, Fran glanced back again and saw that Alice, looking wild, had scrambled across the seat to the driver's side and had managed to get the door open. Now she was clawing her way through the tall weeds, trying to make her way out of the ditch.

Fran began to run. She ran down through a ditch on the other side of the road and up toward the field to the farmer, who had turned sideways now, riding off to the horizon. On the farmer's ears were black headphones. It didn't matter. She didn't have the strength to really scream. All her energy was put into running. She raised one hand up to wave, but the farmer sat up on his tractor, oblivious.

A purple ankle-length caftan, with yards of billowing fabric, was not the perfect outfit to run away from someone who was trying to kill you, Fran realized, bunching the material in a ball above her waist. She ran. Go, go, go, she said, cheering herself on.

Although a part of her braced for the sound of a shot, she did not look back. She ran, the loamy soil filling her sandals. She was afraid that she would twist an ankle in the furrows of the field, but still she ran as fast as she ever had in her life. Go, go, go, she repeated, running so fast, as if in a dream where soon she would be taking off and flying above the ground. She ran, feeling as though her pounding chest would burst against the effort—this after a half hour of high-intensity aerobics—and ran and ran until finally, she reached the tractor just as the farmer started to turn his head, slow and smooth.

She saw his lips form words, "What the—" as she opened her mouth and a scream emerged, though muffled by the noise of the machine. The farmer came to life, pulling off his earphones and jumping down to her from the tractor. Where she pointed down the road, they could see her brown Honda Accord, tipped over like a dead cow in the ditch.

Alice Blevins was nowhere to be seen.

35

Although she knew Frank was in Aurora, Fran was still disappointed that it was Jonny Verlaine who showed up at the old farmhouse to drive her home. As if he sensed this, Jonny told her Frank had already been called and was on his way.

The farmer and his wife stood out in front of the porch waving good-bye, looking, with their serious, plain faces and work clothes, like a chubbier version of the couple in the Grant Wood painting. "Good-bye," Fran called to them. The farmer's name was Elroy S. Petersen; at least that was the name painted on the metal mailbox beside the road. Although he had saved Fran's life, he had not formally introduced himself. Mrs. Petersen had wrapped up a loaf of fresh-baked cranberry bread and put it in the car. Fran supposed she would see them again at the trial.

She would be forever grateful that Elroy S. was armed. That the shotgun he had in the house was loaded and ready to go. Mrs. Petersen had been taking cranberry bread out of the oven when her husband burst through the back kitchen door, half dragging Fran into the house. "Call 911," he instructed his wife, depositing Fran in a kitchen chair. He got the gun, then took the phone himself, explaining the situation with equanimity as the gun rested against the kitchen table. Elroy took off his cap and scratched his scalp, springing to life a head of iron gray hair. "Got a kidnapping here. Woman with a gun, a little off the deep end, I suspect." He gave precise directions to the farm. A mile on the Kelly blacktop. Southeast this. Three-quarter-mile that.

Right before the police came, Fran and the Petersens looked out the living room window to see Alice Blevins walking up the gravel road. She had her straw purse over her arm and with her other hand was shielding her eyes from the sun. "That her?" Elroy asked, looking to Fran, then back to Alice again. He seemed disappointed.

"Yes," whispered Fran. Of the two, Fran in a purple caftan with gold lamé braid, her uncombed black hair wild about her head, and Alice in her beige plaid blouse and denim skirt— well, it was clear who seemed the more suspicious character. "She must have the gun in her purse," Fran added.

"Oh my," said Mrs. Petersen, standing behind her husband.

Alice stopped in the driveway, planted her feet, and looked square at the farmhouse. Surely, even with the sun, she could see the three of them through the sheers that covered the living room window.

Mr. Petersen went to the front door, shotgun under his arm. "Now you just hold it right there, Miss," he called through the screen. Alice didn't seem to see him but just turned and continued walking. The police found her only a few hundred yards up the road when they drove by.

Through all the questioning, Alice Blevins remained mute, her mouth moving in that strange puppet way that Fran had witnessed in her bedroom that morning. Eventually Alice climbed gracefully into the back of the police car, to be taken to the the psychiatric unit of Sanford Greeley Hospital.

Jonny Verlaine stayed behind to take Fran home. He started sneezing as soon as they got into his car. "Something in the damned country air," he said.

When they drove past Fran's car, still in the ditch, she began to cry. "Hey, we got a tow," Jonny told her. "And they'll bring your car back to you this afternoon. You can come down to the station when you feel better." He offered her the box of tissues he had on the dash.

Fran thought of Alice Blevins's eyes. Of the strong, determined hands that forced the weights across Tyler Markem's neck. "She was going to kill me," Fran said, feeling still the jab of the gun against her ribs. "She killed Tyler and she was going to kill me, too."

The first thing Frank Rhodes did when he saw Fran was walk across her living room to the couch where she lay and take her in his arms. This was right in front of Jonny Verlaine, who had answered the door. "Oh, you really got a good one here," Frank said, pulling away, holding her face in his hands. The bruise was turning a sickly yellow-purple, and the bulge of her forehead made her eyes appear small.

"I'm all right," she said, smiling bravely to show that she was.

"I'm going to go now, Chief," Jonny said. "I'll write this all up at the station. The perp has been admitted to the psych unit. We can go see her anytime." Frank waved Jonny away, thanked him, said he'd be by soon. "It'll take me a while to write this all up, Chief. So you just take your time," Jonny told him.

"You got any booze?" Frank asked after Jonny closed the door. Fran's eyes got wide—as wide as they could for being all puffy. "For *you,* silly, not for me," Frank added. "A shot of whiskey to help you relax, I'm saying."

"I'm pretty relaxed," Fran told him. As she said this she closed her eyes for a moment; there on the couch, she felt like an odalisque in her purple caftan.

Frank took her hand, kissed the palm, a gesture which made her feel faint. Then gently, ever so gently, he kissed her on the lips. Pulling away, he said, "We can do this now, don't you think? Julia isn't a suspect anymore."

"No," Fran said. Quickly adding: "I mean, no, Julia's not a suspect."

He looked good. He must have got some sun yesterday because his arms were smooth and tan. He was wearing one of those washed-out J. Crew shirts, forest green, which clung to his flat stomach, opened a few buttons to reveal a substantial amount of dark chest hair. "I like that shirt," Fran told him.

"Leenie sent it to me," he said. "Both my girls keep ordering me things from catalogs. Now I'm on all the lists. I get a lot of mail." Tenderly, he stroked the side of her face, brushing back her hair.

Fran smiled again, but she felt her eyes fill up with tears. "I'm so glad you're here," she whispered.

"When Jonny called me I was at Patricia's, but I was just leaving. I must have driven down here ninety miles an hour." He bent his head toward her, kissed her along the side of her face, across her brow; her hair, a tangle of black, shiny curls, smelled fresh as flowers.

"What happened to Tyler wasn't any accident," Fran said weakly.

"No."

"And it wasn't Julia," Fran said, beginning to sniffle.

"Of course it wasn't Julia," Frank said. He pulled the hair off her forehead, kissed her at a spot right next to the bump. "You were so brave," he told her.

"So, if I hadn't found those pictures. I mean, if Julia hadn't cared about protecting Tyler's precious reputation, wanting Beth and Caty still to think he was super Dad . . . well, Alice would have gotten the pictures back herself. And then, who would have ever known?"

"Julia was right to try and protect her girls. Children should be able to think the best about their parents. He was part of them," Frank said, sitting back. "If you think your father is no good, then you have to think that a part of you is no good, too."

"How'd you get so smart, Detective?" Fran leaned languidly against the pillow, looking teasing and seductive.

"Hey, I once took a psychology class at the community college," Frank told her. He added: "And it didn't mess me up all that much."

He got up to make her a whiskey and water; she called instructions about where the glasses were. When he came back and sat beside her, he moved a book over to put her glass down on it, then kissed her once more. "I'm glad this case is pretty much over now," he said.

"What will happen to Alice?" Fran wanted to know, taking a sip of her drink.

Frank looked pensive. "Well, she probably had a better chance before she came after you with a gun. I mean, if it were just Tyler she did in and in her mental condition . . . well, she probably could have gotten a light sentence because of diminished capacity. Now? Hard to tell. Depends on the lawyer, I guess."

"Sure, the lawyers in this town," Fran said scornfully. Though the divorce from Damian should have been a simple, no-fault division of property settlement, her lawyer had spent hours filling out forms in triplicate and calling Fran to verify the minutest detail.

"I don't know. Jim White is pretty good. So's that guy Timmons. He's a real bulldog. Thing is," Frank added, "a woman like that *is* dangerous. You want her put away for a real long time."

"I was never all that scared," Fran said. "Except maybe when I was running away; then I got really scared."

They sat for a while on the couch, until the sun slanted in the windows on the west wall. "I should go back," Frank said. "I want to go with Jonny to the hospital." He cleared his throat. "I'd like to come back later. To see you tonight." He looked at her face for a long time and saw someone who was wise and funny and true of heart. He got up to go, pausing in the doorway, and turned back to look at her again.

"Frank?" she said. "What is it?"

"You know, it's really funny," he said. "You think you have a life. I mean, you have the life you know, with all the people who were always a part of it and everything just plays out one day at a time with no surprises. It wasn't very long ago at all that I had this other life. All filled with kids and coming home to eat and then rushing out again to drive them here and there; and going somewhere to watch Patricia in a dance recital or the boys in a basketball game. And the house was filled up with kid things, the phone ringing. Always so busy, I never had time to think, but it just felt right that this was my life, you know. It was mine. And then it was over, just like that, it seemed." Frank snapped his fingers. It was a loud, assertive snap. "And now . . ." He paused, shrugged his shoulders.

"And now?" Fran repeated.

"And now, I think I'm going to have a whole new life," he said, walking out the door.

Later, in the heat of the afternoon, Fran was sitting on her front porch swing, reading the mail, when Julia emerged slowly from her car, walking stiffly like a dignitary leading a parade; in one hand she held a crook-handled cane, which clumped across the pavement. "Oh, look at you," Julia cried when she got close enough to see Fran's swollen face. Then, "Careful. Better not hug me," when Fran rose to greet her. Julia raised an arm in warning.

"Look at *you,*" Fran said, tears filling her eyes again. Julia was wearing a white cotton sun dress embroidered with daisies, a gift to Fran from Roz. It was too Sunnybrook Farm, Fran said when she gave the dress away, though on Julia it was just right. Now, wearing no makeup, her red hair pulled away from her face with two white barrettes, Julia looked so sweet.

Fran's throat choked tight with emotion. An hour before, she had cried watching from the window as Frank Rhodes folded a stick of gum into his mouth before he got into his car. Then she cried reading a letter from her niece, Jessica, at summer camp, describing her crush on a waterfront counselor. Now, the sight of Julia, fresh and innocent, walking bravely toward her, made Fran begin to sob in earnest. Everything seemed so sad, so sweet, so filled with the possibility for heartbreak.

Maybe almost getting shot to death by Alice Blevins had resulted in something akin to PMS. "Should you have driven?" she asked Julia. "What about your back?"

"I'm all right," Julia said. "I tried not to shift. I managed to come all the way over here in second gear." Julia smiled, a pleasant, slightly gummy smile. She had great teeth without ever having had orthodontia. Fran remembered Tyler's saying this with some affection one time at a party, encouraging Julia to show her smile. "Frank Rhodes called and left a message when I was at the doctor's," Julia continued. "He said you probably needed to talk to me right away. Franny, are you all right? What in the world happened?"

"Hey, remember that Polaroid camera you gave Tyler . . ." Fran asked, then waved her hand. "I'm sorry. Wait a minute. Let's go inside."

They went into the house, Fran's head throbbing so that she headed straight toward the couch; Julia, placing her weight carefully with each step, chose a straight-backed chair by the fireplace, where she sat slowly and leaned her cane against an end table.

"So?" Julia said expectantly, her mouth half open, ready with questions but waiting. From the west window, a bright light washed the room, catching the glint of Julia's gold earrings, making her red hair shimmer. She sat tentatively, her slender hands resting quietly in the folds of her dress.

Fran adjusted herself on the couch. She was still in her purple caftan; underneath, her knees were raw where pebbles from the road had cut into her skin; her bare feet were still dirty from the farmer's field. Suddenly she felt a burden lift off her, a burden she hadn't noticed the weight of until now, seeing Julia sitting composed and calm: Julia in her white dress.

They looked at each other across the room, their eyes locking; each for a few moments held the other's gaze. Then they both smiled: veterans of their forty-second year. Friends.

"So," Fran said, taking a breath to begin.